STEPHAN TALTY

BLACK IRISH

headline

Published by arrangement with The Random House Publishing Group,
a division of Random House Inc.

First published in Great Britain in 2013
by HEADLINE PUBLISHING GROUP

1

Cataloguing in Publication Data is available from the British Library

ISBN 978 1 4722 0013 6 (Hardback)
ISBN 978 1 4722 0014 3 (Trade paperback)

Typeset in Adobe Garamond by Palimpsest Book Production Limited,
Falkirk, Stirlingshire

Printed and bound in Great Britain by
Clays Ltd, St Ives plc

Headline's policy is to use papers that are natural, renewable and
recyclable products and made from wood grown in sustainable
forests. The logging a
to conform to the enviro

HEADL

An

BLACK IRISH

For Edouarine Vilceus

Acknowledgments

Thanks to Linda Marrow for welcoming Absalom Kearney into the world, and Scott Waxman, for getting her there. To Asher, Delphine, and Mariekarl. And to the young men and women of Abbott Road, 1978–82.

Jimmy Ryan awoke into a feeling of space, blindfolded. He wasn't in the car trunk anymore, at least, and for that he gave a rushed, silent thanks to God. He'd hated tight spaces ever since he could remember. When he was young, his sadistic fuck of an older brother would tackle him to the ground and clamp a hand over his mouth, coiling around him like a python, whispering in his ear, 'You're trapped in a pipe, Jimmy boy, and you're going to die. You're trapped in a pipe . . .'

He breathed out to keep the panic down. He rolled his shoulders forward. His hands were tied behind him to the back of the chair he was sitting on. The coarse grain of the rope rubbed painfully against his wrists; it was thick, fraying. His legs were so tight against the chair legs it felt like his veins were iron filaments that had broken off and bit into his skin when he moved.

He heard traffic, faintly off to his left. He counted off the seconds. By the count of ten, three cars had passed. Had to be Seneca, busiest street in the County. But where on Seneca?

He sniffed the air. The smell was familiar. A memory flickered and then died before he could grasp it. It was an old and bitter smell, something from his boyhood.

He was losing feeling in his toes. He wriggled them furiously.

The last thing he remembered, he'd been checking gas meters, heading to the back of 98 Seneca, the Radio Shack with an apartment out back. There'd been a dog there last time, a half-deranged pit bull whose whole body trembled whenever he came by, with rabies or hate or whatever the fuck. That morning he'd put his steel-toed Wolverine boots on special, to kick its teeth straight out its asshole. He'd been walking down the driveway, snow flurries drifting down from a gray sky . . .

I

Something moved now. Off to his left.

He listened, but the sound died away. The feeling of complete exposure ran over his skin like acid.

He had to piss. Jesus Christ, he was going to piss his pants.

He became aware of the sound of his own breathing. It came back to him a half second later, different somehow. His head lifted up. It was a big space he was in. A warehouse? He tried to think if there was one on Seneca, but the map of the County had fled from his mind. Or was he upstairs in a large attic? That made more sense. Lots of big houses on Seneca.

He felt something approaching from his left, moving slowly.

He tried to speak. 'I . . . I . . .'

It came close to him. He drew back and turned his head away, the chair creaking with the stress.

The thing stood there, blocking out the sound of traffic, then moved on. Jimmy's heart bloomed painfully in his chest, shooting darts of adrenaline all over his body. Slowly, he turned his head to the right, trying to follow the moving shape.

He wanted to talk slow, to remain in control.

'What . . . what . . . do . . . you . . . want?'

His own voice floated off into the emptiness.

No answer.

The thing moved around in front of him. He could feel its physical mass. It was as if some ancient animal sense had woken along the nerves of his skin to compensate for the loss of sight.

He couldn't keep it up. He had to know. The words spilled out over chattering teeth. 'Tell me what the fuck you want, you cocksucker, or I swear to God . . .'

The thing moved again, slowly, to his left now. For a moment he thought, It's not human, it's something else, some fucking demon.

A footstep. And the sound of breathing.

It was human.

Jimmy let out a shaky breath. Then he considered some of the things he'd done in his life and thought this was maybe worse. He desperately tried to think of one good thing he'd done, just one thing.

'Listen for a minute. I have two boys waiting for me at home. Their names are Brendan and Sean.'

The ssssnick of a knife being whipped out of its scabbard.

'Listen to me!' he screamed. 'They'll be terrified right now – shit, and my wife too – just let me call them and tell them I'm all right . . .'

A blade pinched the skin over his jugular. He felt the blood bunch behind the point of the steel.

He nodded, his eyes clenching shut and water leaking out under the right lid. The ragged breathing was closer.

After a few seconds, the blade withdrew.

He lowered his head. He was going to piss his pants and he didn't give a fuck.

Silence. Then a gurgling sound.

Jimmy thought at first that a drainpipe had opened up, some runoff from rain. But it was January, the ground frozen hard as granite.

It was the thing making the noise.

He listened, quiet. They weren't real words, or were they? Another language? It sounded like wet strangled sounds pushed into the air. Was it speaking through some kind of device, trying to disguise its voice?

'What? I can't tell what you're—'

It lurched forward, pushing air in front of it. Jimmy flinched back, jamming his chin down into his chest, but the blow never came.

'Who are you?' His voice shook. He took a deep breath, then tried again.

The thing was coming close. His eyes teared up.

'Show me your face!' Jimmy shouted.

He heard movement and the knife cut the rope behind him. He realized his hands had been tied separately to the back of the chair. Now his right hand was free and throbbing. He brought it around and felt for the blindfold. But the knife jabbed into the flesh and he dropped his hand with a curse.

A grunt and the floor shook. The thing was kneeling in front of him. He twitched back.

'You faggot, don't you . . .'

For a second he thought of reaching out and clawing its eyes out. I can

3

blind this son of a bitch. His nails bit against his palm as he felt their sharpness.

But then, a wave of depression. It would gut him for sure. He was helpless.

Suddenly, the blade pressed against his throat again, dimpling the flesh.

'Okay, okay!' he shouted. The knife withdrew. Jimmy knew what it wanted.

He took a deep breath and slowly reached out in front of him. When he touched something, he hissed and curled his lips. It was a face.

Jimmy's finger touched something on the forehead. He began to trace a shape.

'What the—?' he said softly. He found the end of the scar, then traced it back.

A hand grabbed his wrist roughly and he cried out. It began pulling his fingers down. The hand was rough-skinned and strong.

'What are you . . .'

He didn't want to do that. Not that.

A grunt.

'I don't care who you are. Don't you understand?'

His hand was wrenched downward and then released. Jimmy took a breath. His hand trembled as it brushed over a flaring nose. He felt the thing's breath on the hairs of his hand. He paused.

Jimmy cried out as it turned the knife. The long edge of the blade was against his skin.

'Okay,' he said. 'Okay.'

He let his fingertips move down. A top lip, the flesh slightly cooler here. Teeth.

'You sick goddamn animal. I won't do it. I won't.'

He jerked his hand back.

Stabbing pain from his stomach. Spiking up and up. He roared, 'Stop!' but the sound came back as babble.

He reached out again and touched the thing's forehead. The pain stopped as suddenly as it had begun.

Jimmy sat there, panting. Finally, his trembling hand moved downward.

Moaning now, he let his fingers flutter down over its forehead to the eyes. They were open. His fingertip grazed over the right eyeball. It didn't close.

He touched the lips. Turning his head away, he let his fingers crawl forward over the teeth. And with a flash, the picture of a young face came to him. He snatched his hand back; his chin sank onto his chest.

'Oh, God,' he whispered. 'I knew it. I knew you'd come back.'

The thing stood up and he felt it move behind him. With a jerk, his chair was tilted back and it began to drag him away.

The chair lurched and smashed against something. A leg splintered. Then again. Jimmy gathered all his reserves of strength and with a groan pulled against the rope around his left hand until he thought he'd dislocated his shoulder. It was too tight. He couldn't get loose.

The chair smashed down again. We're going down steps, Jimmy thought. We were in an attic, and now we're going down steps to the street. It's going to be all right. He's going to let me go.

Jimmy thought of his brother and wished he were here.

The sounds of the chair on the stairs filtered away and the church nave grew quiet again. The stained-glass window on the west wall showing the martyrdom of Saint Stephen by stoning grew dimmer; a cloud passing. The distant clatter of ice sliding off a roof came through the thick stone walls but barely registered in the chill air.

There was the muffled sound of a door slamming that seemed to emerge from beneath the cold flagstones. The sound carried across the empty pews and the baptismal font, long covered in dust, the silver circle around the drain rimmed with dirt.

And then the screaming began.

ONE

Detective Absalom Kearney took the exit for the Skyway and the Ford nosed upward, climbing with the gray asphalt. Lake Erie was frozen over and far below and to her right, and Buffalo's industrial waterfront to her left, as quiet and still as an oil painting. The factory smokestacks rode past, even with her windshield, but not a smudge of smoke drifted up from them. The waterfront was dead, slumbering for the past three decades. When Absalom used to ride along this part of the highway with her father twenty years before, she'd sometimes hear the smoke-stacks keen as the storm winds hit them.

She rolled down the window. The smokestacks were silent. The squall hadn't peaked yet.

The crest of the road was ahead, only slate-colored sky beyond. Three stories up, the Skyway was a ribbon of concrete spilled across the clouds. The elevated drive was Buffalo's only stab at Futurism. When the future had actually arrived, the city hadn't liked it much.

The wind shook the car with a guttering rattle. Abbie gripped the wheel harder.

She felt the fear grow inside her again, blooming like a growing rose in a sped-up film. She took the Skyway every time she had to go to South Buffalo instead of driving down the 90, where the highway hugged the earth all the way to the exit at Seneca Street, by the junk-yard that seemed to hold the same hundred wrecked cars she'd seen there as a child. Abbie told herself she took the road above the lake because she wanted to face the thing that terrified her. *Which was what, exactly?*

White tendrils of snow skimmed ahead of her Ford Crown Vic, pushed by the wind. The front edge of the storm was blowing in, the winds playing before the squall blew up into its full power, spinning a spider web of frozen lace. Her eyes followed them as the road rose. Endlessly intricate patterns, hypnotic to watch them form and break, form and break.

There were no cars up ahead, not a single red brake light in the tall, rippling curtains of snow. The empty highway made her think that if she moved the wheel just two inches to the right she would put the car into the railing. A lull, the bang of ice, and then water. Lake Erie in January was a freezing tomb. Death in fifteen minutes. She'd looked it up, whether to calm herself or scare herself she had no idea.

She could almost hear the snow crystals scour the asphalt. They made a rough, hissing sound that grated on your eardrum. It was like the shushing of a dogsled heading into blankness, disappearing into the advancing storm . . .

She leaned and turned up the radio, which the last detective had tuned to a country station and which she hadn't bothered to change. She found the University of Buffalo station playing some obscure eighties synth music.

When she told her partner Z about how odd she felt driving Buffalo highways, he'd asked her why. She'd brushed it off then, but now she knew. *It's the emptiness. The enormous emptiness. Or the loneliness, that was it, the feeling of being alone in a place that should be filled with other people, cars full of families headed to the supermarket, to the restaurant on the lake, to the hockey game.* Buffalo had built miles of highways during the boom years, enough for a million people. The people that were going to come but didn't. *Why not? Where'd they disappear to? What happened to them?*

Now the gray roads splayed across the city, empty half the time. The local joke was the only way Buffalo would get a rush hour was if Toronto got hit by a nuclear bomb and panicked Canadians came pouring south. You could drive for twenty minutes at a time at three on a weekday afternoon and not see another car pass you. The highway system was a network of veins laid across a dead heart.

But she couldn't talk about those things, because eyes were already

8

on her. She'd only been in Buffalo PD for a year. At thirty-one, she was already on her second police job. If she messed this up like she did Miami . . .

The radio crackled. 'Detective Kearney, this is Dispatch. McDonough wants to know your ETA.'

A missing persons case in the County. Must be a family with some connection to the Department, because the missing guy had only been gone since Monday. Just two days. And the officer on scene had called in to check on Abbie's progress, making the family think their missing son or daughter was a priority. Usually, they would just ask the family if Danny or Maura preferred crystal meth or alcohol.

She kept her eyes on the yellow line as she reached to pick up the handset. The radio was mounted far enough away to give legroom for a bigger person – that is, one of the sprawling six-foot men that the Department seemed to breed, not the average-sized Abbie. Finally, she hooked the cord with a French-polished fingernail and brought the handset up.

'Kearney to Dispatch,' she said in a husky voice. 'Twenty minutes.'
'Ten-four.'

She descended down the back slope of the Skyway, the lake coming up on her right and then the raggedy little marina where her father had liked to fish in the spring. Next to it were the hulking grain elevators, massive concrete silos that, like all the old mills down along the waterfront, had been empty for decades. It used to be that ships filled with golden wheat from the West would come steaming into the harbor and unload their haul. The West grew it, and Buffalo milled it. Now the mills were bankrupt and kids with Irish pug noses and no concept of mortality fell to their deaths after breaking the silo locks and climbing up the inside on the rusty maintenance ladders. There wasn't that much else to do in the County on a Saturday night.

There'd been one just last week, a seventeen-year-old boy named Fenore who'd wanted to impress his porky girlfriend, who they found crying hysterically at the foot of the silo. Abbie had done one recovery and that was enough. The insides of the things smelled like rancid beer, and at the bottom, always the broken bodies.

Abbie had begun to think of them as sarcophagi, twenty-story vertical tombs facing out to the lake like some kind of postindustrial pyramids, the bones of the young inside. The whole city was entombed by the artifacts of its glory days.

She jumped off at Tifft Street, grinding the front wheels into a left turn, and shot off through the nature preserve.

Coming to South Buffalo was coming home, she guessed. But a little half-Irish girl from outside the neighborhood could never have been at home here, even if she'd been adopted and raised by a legendary Irish cop, the great and terrible John Kearney. Not a girl with an unknown father, who'd given her midnight-black hair, what they called Black Irish in the County. And if that wasn't enough, Harvard grads like Abbie were regarded as nothing less than two-headed aliens.

They called South Buffalo the Twenty-Seventh County, or the County for short, a patch of Ireland in the wilds of America. *Blacks need not apply; strangers, be on your way; and faggot, can you outrun a bullet?* Back in high school, her neighbors the Sheehans hadn't even let that poor redheaded kid John Connell come on their porch to pick up their daughter Moira for the freshman dance. Not because he was Italian or German or, God forbid, Puerto Rican, not because he was too poor or addicted to alcohol or sexually suspect or pockmarked by acne. No. It turned out his family was from *the wrong part of Ireland,* Abbie's friends patiently explained to her afterward. The Connells were from Mayo and the Sheehans were pure Kilkenny. 'D'ya get it now? He's the wrong county; the Sheehans won't have a Mayo boy on their doorstep.' Their faces shiny with concern, emphatic that she should understand the intricacies of Irish-American dating.

'Yep,' she'd told them. 'I get it now.'

Inside, she'd thought, *Looks like I can forget about getting a date in high school.* And she'd been right. Her raven-black hair, which was only accentuated by her pale skin and sky-blue eyes, her long-dead drug-addicted mother, and her unknown father had doomed her to a life as an outsider in the County, where ancestry was everything. She remembered the moment as the beginning of her disastrous romantic history, and probably her sharp tongue, too.

That had been in the nineties. Things were different now, people said. There were even a few blacks and Latinos sprinkled among the County's population, though you never seemed to see them walking the streets. Maybe they carpooled for safety and conversation.

But some part of the neighborhood never changed. The clannish logic. The hostility to outsiders. The secret, ancient warmth. The alcoholism.

As her partner, Z, said whenever someone from this part of the city did something completely inexplicable or self-destructive: 'WATC.'

'We are the County.'

No other explanation necessary. Or possible.

TWO

Abbie crossed South Park Avenue. When she got to McKinley at the corner of Bishop Timon High School, she turned the wheel right and two minutes later was standing in front of the house on Orchard Street. It was a two-story wood-frame house, with fresh light green paint on the front and and a newish Big Wheel in the front yard. She grabbed her notebook and went in.

The wooden front door was open. Abbie pulled open the screen door and saw to the right a bean pole of a cop with a large beak for a nose, standing with his hands behind his back as if he was guarding the tomb of the unknown soldier. Had to be McDonough. When he saw her, he nodded and tilted his head to the right. As Abbie stepped onto the tan shag carpet, she saw the arm of a couch, and then two legs in a pair of sweatpants, a Notre-Dame T-shirt, and then the rest of Patty Ryan. She was sitting mutely, tissue clutched in one upturned and closed hand that rested in the palm of the other. She looked up.

She'd been pretty, once. The face of the high school girl slowly being submerged in fat. She looked about thirty-eight, ten years younger than her husband.

'Mrs Ryan?'

Patty Ryan nodded, staring at her.

McDonough stepped into the silence. 'Patty's husband Jimmy hasn't been home for two days and hasn't called. His cell phone is going straight to voicemail. She says he—'

'He's dead,' Patty said. 'I know he is.'

'I hope that isn't true,' Abbie said, 'but we need to figure this out. Can I sit?'

You couldn't say 'may I' in the County or they'd look at you like you'd just arrived from Buckingham Palace. And spit in your eye.

Patty was about to say something, but she stopped. Her dark blue eyes bored into Abbie's. *She's probably never asked an outsider for help before,* Abbie thought. *Doesn't know how it's done.*

But need overruled everything else. Patty gestured robotically toward a corduroy-covered recliner. Abbie walked over, lifted a plastic truck from the seat, and sat down, placing the truck by her right foot.

'When was the last time you spoke to your husband?'

'Monday.' Patty stared straight ahead at a point over Abbie's right shoulder.

'On the phone?'

Patty looked at Abbie and nodded. Then her gaze returned to its spot.

'How did he—'

'Fine. He sounded fine.'

'Okay. Where was he calling from?'

'From his route. For National Grid. Checking gas meters.'

'Was he wearing his uniform?'

A quick nod. Her shoulders were hunched over her chest, and her arms were now wrapped around her body, her chin down. It was if she was coiled around something, trying to keep it from exploding into the room.

'I ironed it the night before. Jim liked to look good. He was a proud person.'

'Was there anything unusual about Jim that day?'

She shook her head.

'What about in the last few weeks?'

She muttered, 'No.'

Abbie nodded, then let silence flood into the room. The woman was on autopilot; Abbie had to shake her out of her waking coma.

Patty's eyes goggled at the wall, then she seemed to become aware of the silence. Her eyes shifted left and met Abbie's, who caught her gaze and leaned forward.

'Why do you believe your husband's dead?'

'A feeling. Felt it on Monday afternoon. It was . . .'

A tear appeared at the corner of Patty's right eye. It caught the lower eyelash and swung over, finally dropping onto the darkened skin around her eyes and starting down. There was something past caring in her look, like an animal tracked to its lair that is too exhausted to fight anymore.

'It was like Jim saying he was sorry.'

Abbie nodded slowly. 'Sorry for what?'

'For leaving me, for leaving the kids. For the two mortgages on this shitty house, maybe. For the Catholic school bills that I won't be able to pay anymore. For last Valentine's Day, when he got drunk and slammed me into the living room wall. Is that enough?'

'That's plenty. Was there anything else he could be sorry for? Something not to do with you and him?'

'What're you talkin' about?' Quick.

'Was there anyone who might have wanted to harm Jim? That bore a grudge?'

Patty was on it fast.

'"Bore a grudge"? What's that mean?'

'It means, was somebody ang—'

'You sound like someone from New York or somethin'.'

That wasn't an observation here. It was an accusation.

'Let's talk about Jim.'

'Where you from?' Her chin poked up and now her eyes were dry and hard.

'Does it matter?'

'To me it does.'

'Okay then,' Abbie said, closing her notebook and staring at Patty. 'I grew up five blocks from here.'

'That's imposs—'

Her face, curling into a snarl of disbelief, suddenly went slack.

'You're Absalom Kearney,' she said softly.

'That's right.'

Patty looked like she wanted to jump through her skin. She pointed at McDonough and turned her head, her eyes accusing.

'Why'd he say you were Detective Marcus?'

'That's my married name. I don't use it anymore.'

She glanced up at McDonough.

'And no one *else* is supposed to, either.'

McDonough looked away, his Adam's apple bobbing.

'You still married?' the woman said in a dead voice.

Abbie's bright blue eyes grew still. Then she shook her head no.

'And you came back here to take care o' your father?'

'Yes, I came back here to take care of my father.'

Only half a lie.

Patty regarded her, her eyes weighing what she'd just heard, growing softer.

'That's good. Maybe . . . maybe you'd understand.'

'Understand what exactly?'

Patty made a slow twirling motion with her right index finger.

'Around here.'

Patty's gaze fell to the carpet, a tan shag with lines of intersecting brown and black. Her eyes searched the patterns there. Then she got up.

'I never offered you anything.'

'That's okay. Really.'

The woman stood still, then turned.

'Just tell me what's bothering you. I want to find your husband.'

Instead of coming back to the couch, Patty shuffled to the fireplace. On the mantel the family photos, turned at different angles to the room.

Patty walked down the four feet of the wooden mantel, tapping on the white painted top absentmindedly. She paused by the first photo: her in a big white dress, thirty pounds lighter, beaming and holding the hand of a brown-haired man. Her finger touched the man's face and then glided down the glass. She took another two steps and got to the last photo. Abbie stood quickly, but Patty pulled the frame to her belly, blocking Abbie's view.

Patty stared at the wall above the mantel, hesitated, then glanced down at the photo before pressing it again to her body.

'Was your husband good to you, Detective Kearney?' she said, still turned away.

'Not really. He was good to himself, and then I got what was left over. How about Jimmy?'

'Jim wasn't no good either, tell you the truth. When we'd fight, he'd threaten to leave me, and I'd say to him, "You've been leaving ever since we were married."'

Patty turned, the picture held tight to her stomach, facing away from Abbie.

'You've been leaving me *ever since you got here*. Y'know?'

That almost-Canadian inflection in the phrase. *Y'know.*

'Yes, I know.'

'But now that he's gone, I want you to bring him back to me. Then . . .'

The hand holding the picture dropped to her side. Patty began to walk out of the room.

'Then I'll know what to do.'

Abbie watched her go.

McDonough turned and made the crazy sign by the side of his head.

THREE

Abbie walked outside and the cold air felt like it was cutting ice rings into her lungs. McDonough came up behind her.

'What a freak show. She's lost it.'

Abbie turned to look at him, her eyes burning. 'No, Officer, she hasn't lost it. And if you pull that hand-gesture stuff again, I'll see you do midnights on the East Side all winter. You up for that?'

'No.'

'Good.'

McDonough coughed.

'You really think he's dead?'

Abbie looked up and down the street of tiny cottages, rusting American cars, and small Toyota compacts.

She sighed. 'Yes.'

McDonough shook his head. 'I don't see it.'

Abbie's eyebrow arched. McDonough fidgeted and pulled his broad blue police hat tight over his flushed forehead.

'I'm one test away from getting my detective shield. And when I get it, I've put in my request to work with you, Detective Mar— um, Kearney. Tell you the truth, about half of my graduating class did.'

'Really? Why's that?'

McDonough shrugged. 'They say you're the best since your father retired, that maybe you're even better than him. And in the County, that's saying something. Your dad was the fucking gold—'

'McDonough?'

'Uh-huh?'

'Which photo did she choose?'

'Huh?'

'You say you want to be a detective, so I'm asking you, which photo did Patty Ryan take off the mantel when we were talking about her husband? You did notice she took one down, didn't you?'

'Um, sure.' He kicked the snow on the porch.

'Mm-hmm?'

'Was it the wedding photo?'

Abbie turned away. 'No, it wasn't. And that's what makes it interesting. Women *always* go for the wedding picture, because if you know anything about marriages, the wedding is almost always the high point for them. Men will almost always pick a photo from when they first met. Don't ask me why.'

'So you're saying she took a different one?'

'Yeah, that's what I'm telling you. Any guesses?'

McDonough looked vacantly at the street and shook his head. Abbie sighed.

'It was a five-by-eight of three men, man to the right with his back turned, the man to the left probably Jimmy Ryan, the other two unidentified, the middle one balding. Judging by the difference between Ryan's current photo and this one, it might have been ten or fifteen years ago. The three were standing on the lakeshore, probably facing the Canadian side, judging from the angle of the sun on the Peace Bridge to the right.'

Abbie slapped her notebook against her thigh.

'And, damn it, she walked away with it.'

'So why didn't you ask to see it?'

'Because she wouldn't have shown me. And she would have known that I know. And I don't want that yet.'

McDonough was staring at her with a dazed expression.

'Know *what*?! What is it that you know?'

Abbie sighed. Back in the County. The shadows, the undertones, the whatever you want to call it, were thicker here than in a Louisiana swamp. She felt it press down on her chest, the old familiar claustrophobia.

Why *had* she come back? On good days, it was to take care of her father, and to finally discover who she was, as corny as that sounded.

Because she hadn't found it anywhere else, not at Harvard, not in Miami.

And this was the last place left to look.

On bad days, it was because she felt at home in the city's windswept emptiness; its air of desolation suited her own.

She heard McDonough cough.

'If Jimmy Ryan is dead,' Abbie said, shaking off her reverie, 'then Patty has a good feeling why he's dead.'

'No shit! Is that what she meant when she said, "Then I'll know what to do"? Is she going to war or something?'

'Listen to what the woman said, McDonough. And how she said it. Did she seem angry?'

'No.'

'How would you characterize her demeanor?'

'More like, um, depressed.'

Abbie nodded. 'Very good. I think she's talking about burying Jimmy. Taking care of him one last time. It's as if she's already mourning him.'

McDonough smiled. 'Or killing the fuck who did it, more like it.'

Abbie felt the overwhelming urge to punch McDonough in the stomach. If there was one cop like him on the force, there were fifty. 'If you think she's a lunatic, a crazy woman you can laugh at and ignore, you're going to miss something. And if that happens, I'll make you sorry you ever put on the uniform. Is that understood?'

McDonough nodded.

'Good. I want you to start on your sweep. Get his picture out. The TV stations, the *Buffalo News*, the *South Buffalo Post*, websites, everything.'

McDonough scribbled in his notebook as Abbie headed to her car.

The County was divided into a long grid. There were four parallel main avenues that radiated out from downtown Buffalo, each with its own particular history. South Park was closest to Lake Erie, and it had been rough as long as people could remember. The legend was that there were more bars per square foot than anywhere else in the country except Reno, Nevada, but so many opened and closed every month that the number was in constant flux. South Park had biker bars, Irish bars, country and western bars, cop bars, old man bars, fireman bars, heavy metal bars, strip bars, steel plant bars (now welfare bars), bartender bars, hooker bars, and freak bars. A freak bar was a druggie bar.

Next came McKinley Avenue, broad and green. In its heyday it had been the best street in the County. Firemen with two jobs on the side dreamt of owning a house there, with its rich lawns, mowed by their owners – the County had never gotten rich enough to import immigrants to care for its hedges – sloping down to an elm-lined avenue. The major corners were anchored by huge, broad-shouldered homes built in the forties and fifties, and the two schools that parents worked two and three jobs to send their kids to. Bishop Timon for boys, Mount Mercy for girls (including Abbie, class of '98). The schools were still there, but the paint was peeling from the signs and drugs were slipping into the polished corridors.

Abbott Road was her old haunt, the working-class avenue where high school kids colonized every corner on weekend nights and raised hell. It had been Abbie's second home for her high school years.

Then came Seneca Street, which was descending into some kind of open-air prison. Cops didn't want to work Seneca anymore; too violent, too disturbing. Abbie tried not to think about it, honestly. It had once been a nice busy street, with hardworking families hoping to graduate to Abbott Road or move out to the suburbs. But now it was like a concrete patch of Appalachia. For all Abbie knew, they were having human cockfights behind the convenience stores.

Abbie worked out a grid in McDonough's squad car and four people began walking it – McDonough, Juskiewicz, Abbie, and her partner, Z, short for Zangara. Frank Zangara was a homegrown product, like 95 percent of the cops in Buffalo, but he was from the West Side, a black-haired Sicilian in the Department's sea of brown-haired Celts and redheads. They'd called him Animal until he reached sophomore year in high school and shot up to 250 pounds of muscle by working out in his basement gym while everyone else was running wild in the local parks, strapping cases of Strohs beer to their backs with belts and walking around like astronauts with their life-packs. After he'd gotten big, they'd still called him Animal, but with respect.

'This guy's probably in Vegas spending his 401k money,' Z said as they tramped through knee-high snow on South Park. There'd been a rash of those going around, husbands leaving wives or wives leaving husbands, without explanation or forwarding addresses.

'Not this time,' Abbie said. 'He's around.'

'Which intuition is it this time, women's or Ivy League's?'

'Cop's,' she said, cutting her eyes at him. 'Ever heard of it?'

Z laughed.

South Park was rutted with deep grooves in the ice, navigated by rusting cars. It seemed like the only new cars were the ones owned by city agencies, Health and Human Services or Sanitation. A new car on South Park looked like some kind of visitor from the future.

They split up and took opposite sides of the street. It had snowed that morning and many of the houses were draped by a blanket of white, like the felt sheet that wrapped the foot of a Christmas tree.

The houses looked drearily alike. Frozen in silence, their owners out working at Wal-Mart (where they'd be floor workers, not managers), at one of the few remaining auto parts plants out at the lake, in the firehouses, or in the bars. There were no bold colors splashed on the fronts. God forbid you should buy a whimsical mailbox, Abbie thought. The County tended to think alike.

She covered one block, then two. A slow mist of intense cold seemed to filter into her black riding boots, freezing the toes first. She'd chosen fashion over warmth, always a mistake in Buffalo. Abbie stamped them on the hard sidewalk and kept moving on.

Abbie glanced into a backyard, then another. She got to the end of the block and crossed over, kept walking, then stopped. Her eyes swiveled back slowly to the second driveway on the block and she turned and retraced her steps. There on the fresh snow were what looked like a series of black squirrel droppings.

'Hold on,' she called across to Z.

Abbie headed down the driveway. Suddenly, she shot the right flap of her down jacket back and unholstered her Glock.

Abbie saw Z start toward her from across the street, dodge a UPS truck, and then hurry to the sloping driveway.

'Blood trail,' she said as he hustled up.

The trail was ruby-red and fresh. It hadn't soaked down into the snow yet. The drops started two feet into the driveway off the street, just where two tire tracks ended at a narrowing of the fence.

He couldn't get the truck all the way back to the garage, Abbie thought. It was too wide across. Had to carry the body in from here.

The home had a sunken look, light blue with black trim and a swaybacked porch. She put her back to the opposite house and held the gun out in front of her, two-handed stance, as she sidestepped down the driveway. Z had his gun aimed at the house, alternating between the side door and the front entrance, which was reached past a chain link fence. The trail was leading toward the garage, a dilapidated shed of no discernible paint color with two broken windows looking mournfully out at the street.

Something snapped to her left. Abbie swiveled her gun to the sound, but it was shingles on the garage flapping up in the wind. She stepped carefully through the snow until she reached the single garage door. She pressed her back against it, turned and stood on her tiptoes to see through the filmy windows into the interior. But they were covered with old newspaper taped to the inside, and all she could glimpse through the holes was milky gloom.

Abbie looked down. The blood trail led straight under the garage door.

She pointed to Z, then to the handle of the door. Abbie pulled out her flashlight and held it up near her right shoulder, the gun leveled beneath it. She nodded to Z. He took a breath and reached for the handle. Z gripped it with his enormous right hand, turned to look at her and pulled. The door came shooting up with an ungodly shriek.

Eyes – red, green, and brown – glinted at Abbie from the darkness. She whipped the gunpoint from one to the next in quick succession. But the eyes didn't move. Lifeless, a constellation of dead things.

Abbie's shoes made a crinkling sound as she stepped onto a blue tarp, smeared and speckled with blood, that covered the floor. Another one hung from the wooden beams of the ceiling and shrouded the right corner of the garage. Carcasses were spread out on worktables, bones shining dimly in the murk. She caught her breath.

'Behind the tarp,' she said.

Z moved toward it, but stopped as his foot slid in something red and wet.

'Fuuu-uucck. What is this?'

'Animals,' she said, dropping her gun to her thigh, doing a quick inventory: deer, fox, bear. 'They're probab—'

Abbie felt the air shift and instantly began to pivot. The hanging tarp had snapped back and a man was charging at Z, a knife flashing in his hand.

'Z!'

Abbie snapped her boot out and kicked the man's knee as he went by. The knife swooped down and missed Z's arm by two inches as the man collapsed sideways and hit the tarp.

'Don't shoot!' she said, grabbing Z's arm.

'Who the fuck—'

Abbie took two steps toward the man – a burly six-footer with a bushy red beard, a ripped Carhartt jacket, and oil-stained jeans. He was clutching his left knee and his eyes glowed crazily in the gloom.

'Drop the knife,' Abbie said, her voice calm and her gun leveled at the man's forehead.

'Fuck you. Get the fuck out of my garage.'

'Buffalo Police,' Abbie said. 'I said drop . . . the . . . knife.'

'Police?' the man said. 'We ain't got any bitch detectives in the County.'

Abbie heard Z snort behind her.

'I'll introduce you to my fucking boot and—' he said.

Abbie made a small movement with her free hand. She took her case out and flipped it out. Her badge glinted in the weak light.

'So? The fuck you want with me?'

'Drop . . . the . . . knife, sir. I'm not going to tell you again.'

The knife – a ten-inch blade that looked like a prop from a gladiator movie – bounced off the tarp.

'Sit up.'

The man muttered and sat on his haunches, straining to sit up over his belly. He looked at Abbie with hatred.

'You live here?' Abbie said, the muscles in her shoulder finally relaxing.

'I think you broke my damn knee. Hell yes, I live here.'

Abbie studied him. He looked like some kind of mountain man, sawdust and small twigs in his hair, his eyes wild, goggling.

'What are you doing with all these carcasses?'

'It's called survival, bi—'

Abbie brought the gun barrel up and centered it between his eyes.

'It's called survival, lady.'

'Try "Detective,"' she said. 'Detective Kearney.'

The man made a 'psssh' sound and his pupils seemed to grow even smaller. Abbie wondered if he was on meth.

'Answer the question,' Abbie said.

'It's roadkill. Something gets hit on the highway, I got a trooper friend who calls me or maybe a trucker on his CB. I go and get it.'

'What's your name?'

'I don't have to give you that.'

It was the needless aggravation that wore you down in the County. People here – even the Poles and the few Lithuanians who'd wandered in – seemed to have an ancestral memory of being oppressed in a country they'd never been to, and they carried it with them always, like their mother had been truncheoned the day before.

'Actually, you do. Or you're taking a ride with us.'

'Fascism is coming. Sure as we're standing here.'

'Your name.'

'You'd just look me up in your computers anyway. Joseph Wardinski.'

'What do you do with the carcasses, Mr Wardinski?'

'I bring 'em back here, skin 'em, empty 'em out, and sell the meat. Or we freeze it.'

'And the heads?'

'Stuff 'em. It's called paxadermy.'

Z snorted but Abbie's expression didn't change.

'Somebody buys those?' she said.

'People up north. Farmers. Real Americans.'

The last was said with a narrowing of the eyes.

'You got a license for any of this?' Z said.

'License? This don't have nothing to do with the government.'

'This isn't the Yukon country, sir,' Abbie said. 'You need a license. Stand up.'

'The *Yu*-kong?' the man said as he struggled off the ground. 'The fuck's that?'

'This isn't the frontier is what I'm telling you.'

The man just stared at them, his mouth working silently.

'Listen, Mr Wardinski. Just take a deep breath and listen.'

Abbie holstered her gun.

'Some of this wild game carries disease. Trichinosis, other bad stuff. If you want to poison yourself, go right ahead, it's a free country last I heard. But you don't want to be feeding this stuff to your kid.'

'How'd you know I have a kid?'

'The Dora stickers on the third-floor window.'

The man said nothing.

Their radios blared in stereo. 'Detective Kearney, come in.'

'You're going to have the health inspector down here if you don't keep this place clean,' Abbie said. 'Check the meat before you use it. You know what to look for?'

The man looked down at his grease-black boots on the blue tarp.

Abbie motioned to Z and they started down the driveway. As they passed the man, he whispered something.

'What was that?' Abbie said, her voice dead quiet.

He stared at her, his eyes filled with a crazy urgency, and for a second she thought he would go for her gun.

'Detective Kearney, come in now, please,' McDonough bleated on the radio.

Z picked up his radio. 'This is Zangara, go ahead.'

'Nothing,' the mountain man said, turning away.

'We found him,' McDonough's voice was ragged. 'He's cut up ba—'

'Get off the radio,' Z barked, then dropped the radio to his side. 'Idiot.'

Abbie gave the mountain man one last look and then followed Z.

They hustled out toward Abbie's car. Abbie jumped in the driver's seat, turned the key, and revved the engine before swinging into a U-turn.

She headed over to Abbott Road, then made the right into Cazenovia Park. Black clouds were gathering above the park oaks.

'Z,' she said, turning to her partner.

'Yeah?'

'You see that guy?'

Z glanced at her. 'Yeah, I saw him.'

Abbie was quiet for a minute.

'Ever feel something's not really right in the city? That the clocks are . . . running backward?'

He made a face. 'No. I never think about that.'

'I do.'

'Whatever. Listen, Ab. Don't go spooky on me.'

'Going spooky' was Z's term for depression. They'd been through one major episode together. Her episode, of course. Zangara was a rock.

'It's this place,' Abbie said. She felt a wave of black-winged sadness come over her, thinking about the mountain man's daughter – the girl who loved Dora – eating roadkill and listening to her father rant against government mind control and the coming of the Last Days.

'You know what I say?' Z said.

'What?'

'Fuck this place.'

FOUR

McDonough had fumbled out an address on Seneca. Before they pulled up, Abbie knew it was St Teresa's, the church she'd gone to as a child. Now it was closed up, the parishioners having been shunted off to St John the Evangelist as the Catholic population died off or went astray. The faithful had protested for months, circling in the snow in front of the church with signs and rosaries in their hands. But the parish was too poor to afford so many churches, eventually the protesters' number had dwindled to nothing, and the church had been padlocked.

As they pulled up and walked to the arched entrance, there were a few people looking at them anxiously, milling around the church steps.

'Damn McDonough,' Z muttered. The County was well known for harboring police groupies. Half the people had relatives in the force and police scanners on their side tables or nightstands, running day and night, old men listening as they watched the light fade in their rocking chairs. Now the address was out, and probably the fact that they'd found a body.

'Who's in there?' a ragged voice called out as they hurried in. Abbie didn't turn her head.

They entered the gloom of the church. Light angled down from high windows, picking up dust motes. There was a scrum of people in the middle of the aisle. Abbie made out the slim form of McDonough, a fat bundled-up cop that must be Juskiewicz, and an old man in a blue jumpsuit. As they parted, Abbie got a glimpse at what they had been looking at – a thick pool of blood that had spattered the smooth flagstones, with a trail leading toward the back of the church.

The shocked looks on their faces begged Abbie to take the responsibility for what sat at their feet. She hurried ahead of Z.

'He's downstairs,' McDonough said.

Abbie nodded and the group moved off, with the thin cop in the lead.

'Who found him?' Abbie said.

'I did,' Juskiewicz said. His eyes seemed to apologize for the fact.

'Tell me about it.' They reached the stairs. Her flashlight picked out stone steps circling downward.

'I . . . I was doing this side of the street. I came to St Teresa's and looked for a place to get a peek inside. I started around to the east there and was looking in the window. I saw something on the ground, so I asked around until I found the caretaker.'

Abbie nodded. She knew the church by heart. She'd peeked in the same window years ago to find her father when he came to St Teresa's alone. She'd spot him, head bowed, four rows back, tilted over slightly because of the gun that must have poked into his right thigh as he kneeled.

They reached the basement floor. She'd only been down here twice, when she served as an altar girl. It was cold and it smelled like wax and clay.

Five feet away, Jimmy Ryan sat in a wooden chair, his face a smear of dried blood. His head wasn't human looking anymore; it looked like a black candle that had burned through the night, spattering wax downward. There was a yellow nylon rope clinched tightly around his neck extending down his back; it was looped around both his ankles and tied to the front chair legs, which were battered and scraped near the bottom.

Abbie began to move around the body. The men stepped back. She saw gouts of blood had fallen to the floor along with what looked like sheared-off sections of flesh, and she stepped carefully around them.

'He was stuffed in this little storage room over here. I don't know what—'

'It's called an undercroft,' Abbie said, walking closer to the body. 'They stored vestments and Bibles here.'

The undercroft looked like a brick-lined oven, at waist height, with a heavy wooden door, now hanging open. She shone her light inside and saw it was just barely big enough to fit a man inside. The floor of the space was smeared with dried blood.

'You dragged him out?'

'Had to,' Juskiewicz said. 'I couldn't tell if he was dead.'

'You could have felt his ankle, you idiot,' said Z, his face six inches from Jimmy Ryan's.

'Oh.'

McDonough pointed at Ryan's face. 'His eyelids—'

'Yeah?' barked Z, still angry about the radio.

'Well, they're gone.'

Abbie took her flashlight, crouched down level with Ryan's face. His blue irises, rimmed by broken blood vessels, were staring up.

'The killer started up in the nave,' she said. 'I wonder if Ryan was made to look at anything specific. A station of the cross, a saint.' Grotesque visions of Christ in agony, Saint Stephen the first martyr – the church had the whole set. And the ceiling beams of the church were painted in gold leaf with Latin script, she remembered, but if the killer was showing Ryan something, there was no way to tell now.

She pointed the beam of the flashlight at his mouth. Ryan's mouth was battered, the lips grooved with cuts and ripped at the corners. She shone the light inside.

'There's something in here,' she said. 'Hold on.'

Abbie reached into her pocket and pulled out a pen. She ducked down, shone the light in and, with the other hand, inserted the top of the pen inside Ryan's mouth, angling it up past the swollen, blackened flesh of his tongue. There was something between the flesh and the roof of the mouth. She tapped on it and it made a tiny clicking sound.

'I want to get this out,' she said to Z. 'Give me some light.' Z crouched beside her and shone the light past the hacked-up lips. The object was light brown and thin.

Gently, Abbie swept the pen tip across it and the object slid forward.

After two minutes of coaxing, it brushed against the inside of the dead man's cheek and hung halfway out.

'Is that a—'

Abbie withdrew the pen, laid it on the ground, then stood up and reached in her back pocket, where she kept a fresh pair of thin crime-scene surgical gloves, the talcum-free kind. She pulled one on her right hand, motioned to Z, then bent over and carefully reached with two fingers inside the corpse's mouth.

'Jesus fuckin' Christ,' McDonough said.

Z hissed at him.

She began to pull out the object. There was a gasp and the caretaker went running for the stairs. Abbie heard him begin to vomit before he hit the outside door.

Abbie showed Z the object. It was a toy monkey, a thin sliver of plastic with a painted face, black eyes, tan nose, red lips. The eyes were bulging and its little arms reached around and were clasped in front of its mouth.

'Speak no evil?' Z said.

'Maybe. Got an evidence bag?'

'Yeah.' He produced one out of his jacket pocket with a flourish, and Abbie laid it inside.

'McDonough,' she said. 'Go out front and make sure no one gets a look in here. Press especially. Juskiewicz, keep everyone away from the side windows. Grab the custodian and tell him no talking. To anyone.'

They nodded and hurried off.

Abbie began to shine her light around the little vestibule they stood in. Off to the right was the sacristy, where the priest could wash his hands, dress, and get ready for mass.

'Why a church?' Z said.

'And why leave the body down here?' All the gold, the statues, the holy things you associate with a church were upstairs. Down here was like a dungeon, bare as a graveyard.

'The church itself doesn't feel important to me,' she said. 'If you want to send a message, you take him to the altar. If the church is part of your agenda, you make it clear. You *use* something. He didn't do that.'

'But there are tons of abandoned buildings on Seneca these days. He chose this one.'

Abbie was trying to keep thoughts of Patty Ryan out of her mind. She had the time about right. Jimmy Ryan had been dead about two or three days.

'Nobody suspects a church,' she said, studying Ryan's left hand, tied behind the chair. The rope could be from his National Grid truck. She'd have to find it and check.

'People will search every frame house, every backyard shed before they come in here. They don't put the church together with murder and violence yet. These places are still sacred for them. So it gives the killer extra time.'

'Unless they were altar boys,' Z said. 'Right, Ab? Altar boys.'

Abbie shook her head. She was studying Ryan's thick brown hair. It was matted down in a ridge behind the ears, the hair packed down tight in a straight line.

'Look at this,' she said.

'What?'

Z came next to her, stooped to see her finger as it drew a line around the back of Ryan's head.

'Blindfold?' he said.

'Could be. But then the killer took it off. He made Ryan look at something. But what?'

Z stood. 'Fucked if I know.'

'Let's go upstairs. Call the techs and get them started down here.'

The nave was silent and dark.

'Got to knock on County doors,' Z said as they approached the front door. 'Get ready for stupid time.'

FIVE

Two hours later, the sunlight had turned the color of dirty pewter, as if iron filaments were hanging in the air, leftovers from the blast furnaces at Bethlehem Steel. Dusk was two hours away and the forecast called for continued snow squalls off the lake. Z was off talking to the neighbors, but Abbie wanted to find Ryan's trail before it was covered over.

The rope was standard work issue from National Grid. It was from the back of Ryan's truck, which they'd found parked three blocks away in front of a Dollar Store. Abbie had let Z process that scene, expecting little. The killer wouldn't have taken Ryan at the truck, but in one of the backyards of the County, scanning the windows that looked out on the yard to make sure there were no invalids, grannies, stay-at-home moms looking down on the scene.

But how did he get Ryan to the church?

Abbie pulled the zipper of her jacket up to her chin. Her lean body had never held heat well, and she could feel the temperature beginning to plummet.

She walked to the rear of St Teresa's. There was a parking lot here closed in from three sides. The rear service door had been forced open, the one that let out into the northeast corner of the parking lot. This is where the killer had brought Ryan in.

Buzzing fluorescent lights beamed down on eight inches of snow, crisscrossed by footpaths. The killer's footprints were here somewhere, but it was just as she'd feared. The County gossip machine, known as the newswire, had already revved up, and the lot was covered with footprints streaming in from every angle. Boots, shoes, sneakers, not to mention tire tracks. The people around here would lead their own investigation, probably better staffed and financed than her own. Some of the people looking into the death of Jimmy Ryan would probably be cops like her, but not working for the Department. Off the clock. County hours.

They protected their own here, and when one was culled from the pack, the killer was hunted down, dealt with, and then disappeared. The County was an organism that didn't push much into the outside world. It consumed everything it produced, good and bad. Its official motto was 'A Good Neighborhood to Grow Up In,' but it should have been 'Nothing Escapes Us.'

Abbie knew there were a hundred phone conversations going on in the phone lines that hung from the poles above her, not to mention the cell phone chatter bouncing off the local cell towers. She had to get to the witnesses before friends and relatives did, telling them to be smart and shut their goddamn mouths.

She followed the footsteps southwest across the parking lot, her eyes scanning left and right as she did. She came to the building that stood across from the church – the old rectory, which bordered Hayden Street.

The killer had either come this way or off of Seneca. Abbie guessed the former. Seneca, even though it looked like a second Depression had hid it, was still crawling with life during the day. Hayden, its dark canopy of trees blocking the light from above, was a much more inviting path. But how would he carry a man in broad daylight down a street filled with inquisitive eyes?

Impossible, she decided. Unless the killer had some kind of elaborate way to disguise him, Jimmy Ryan had been taken to the church in a car.

The sidewalk had been shoveled clear but she kept her eyes left, looking for footprints emerging from behind one of the frame houses that receded into the distance. The yards were of two varieties: either choked with snow-covered weeds, rusting bikes, even what looked like stalks of alfalfa pushing through the icy crust – or clean, bushes trimmed under the caking snow. People who'd given up or moved away, and the holdouts still grimly keeping their plots of land respectable.

'What're you doing here?'

Abbie turned. A dapper old man stood looking at her from under an Irish walking cap.

'Buffalo Police,' Abbie said, pulling her badge from her inside pocket. 'Do you live around here, Mr—?'

'Right across the street,' the man said, turning to point at a dark-green frame house with white trim. 'James O'Malley's my name.'

Everyone in the County was named James or John. She'd have to keep them all straight.

'Is this about Jimmy Ryan?' O'Malley said.

Abbie sighed. 'Yes, it is.'

'Well, I don't know anything about that.'

'I hadn't asked you if you did.'

He said nothing, only smiled.

'Were you in the neighborhood on Monday afternoon?'

'Where else would I go? Yes, I was here.'

'See anyone on the street? Strange cars in the church parking lot? Anyone you didn't recognize?'

The man eyed her from underneath his walking cap. 'Only the usual lot. The kids have no jobs these days, you know that.'

'Interesting. Which kids?'

'Oh, I don't know their names.'

'Mm-hmm. Anyone out of the ordinary, Mr O'Malley? Not from the neighborhood?'

'You mean the black men?' he said with a merry glint.

'Which black men?'

'The garbagemen! They come every Tuesday. County boys can't get those city jobs anymore, I guess. Terrible shame.'

'Plenty do. *You* know that. Anyone else?'

'No.'

'Uh-huh. And did you hear anything? Screams?'

'I'm hard of hearing, sorry.'

'You seem to be doing pretty well today.'

'It comes and it goes, miss.'

'Detective.'

He seemed amused by that.

'Let me ask you a question. What was the purpose of you coming out of your house for this little conversation?'

'We're friendly people around here. And what concerns the Ryans concerns us.'

She took out a card and offered it to the old man.

'That's good to know. Please let your neighbors know we need their help to catch the killer.'

The man only looked at the card fluttering slightly in the wind. 'God willing, he's burning in hellfire already.'

O'Malley tipped his hat and turned. Abbie watched him walk off, his shoe heels striking off the hard pavement like iron.

After stopping by headquarters downtown, Abbie parked in front of the Department of Health, ran in and spoke briefly with a bow-tied clerk at the information desk. A few minutes later, he emerged from the warren of cubicles and handed her two pamphlets. She thanked him and walked back to her car, tapping the pamphlets against her open palm and thinking about the wounds on Jimmy Ryan's face. She took the Skyway back to the County, white-knuckling it all the way, and parked in front of the house of the mountain man who cut up roadkill. She walked up onto the swaybacked wooden porch, noted the peeling of the paint on the house front, and lifted the thin metal lid of his mailbox. She placed the two brochures, 'Disease Precautions for Hunters' and 'Wild Game Hunting and Food Safety,' inside.

When she got back in the car, she started the engine, then looked up at the third-story window with the Dora stickers. The curtain didn't move.

What if he can't read? she thought. *What good will the pamphlets do then? What if he finds them and beats the little girl, because the pamphlets he can't read triggered a world of rage and shame inside?*

She thought back to Miami, and the memory caused her to twist uncomfortably in the car's worn vinyl seat. After six months there, she'd had a nice career with an upward trajectory, a condo overlooking the sparkling Atlantic, even an article in the *Herald* that called her a crusader for abused children. Six months after that, she'd woken up one morning in Liberty City crying her eyes out. She was fifty thousand dollars in debt because she bought things she didn't need and paid school tuition for the children of violent crime victims. In her spare time, she was stalking suspects in unsolved child abduction cases. She was lost.

Can't go down that road again, Abbie thought to herself now. She glanced again at the third-floor window. Then, with a sigh, she started the engine. Illiteracy was beyond her means at the moment.

The neighborhood seemed to ooze bad vibes. Where were the kids playing on the sidewalks? Where were the men shoveling snow or shouting to each other as they took down the Christmas lights from their front porches? There was a string of blue and white colored lights blinking in a picture window two doors down, but they didn't alleviate the gloom of the street. Two of the bulbs had burned out, and they were the wrong color anyway.

As much as she'd resented being an outsider here growing up, she'd always known that the Irish were as thick as thieves with each other – and she'd envied that. Now it seemed even that was gone.

A phrase she'd heard in the Cuban neighborhoods of Miami came back to her: 'Man,' they said there, 'is wolf to man.'

Abbie drove home and pulled in front of her apartment building on Elmwood Avenue, close to downtown and a good fifteen miles from the County border. Kids from the University of Buffalo were roaming the street in pleasantly wasted gangs, on their way to the bars on Chippewa Street. She pulled her coat around her as she searched for the key. When she was inside, she kept the lights low and walked softly across the bare wood floor.

She peeked in the second door.

'Hi, Dad,' she said.

Her father looked up from the leather recliner set next to his bed. Detective John Kearney had turned seventy-eight the year before, but his arms still looked like cords of cherrywood, red and thick, and his chest was broad. His eyes were sharp and the bluest blue she'd ever seen. It was his mind that was going.

'Is it you then?'

'Yes, it's me.'

He put down the book of crosswords he'd been doing. She sat next to his recliner, on the bed.

'Did you eat your dinner?' she asked.

'Some of it. I don't need much these days.'

He didn't look at her, his eyes pointed toward the corner. When he talked to her, it was always as if he was listening to another, more interesting conversation.

'I had the scanner on,' he said, his accent still bearing the traces of County Clare in Ireland. 'You found a body at St Teresa's?'

'Dad, please turn on the radio instead of that thing. It'll only send your blood pressure up.'

'What kind of animal would kill somebody in a church?' John Kearney demanded, the cords on his neck standing out.

She sighed. 'It might have been just an abandoned building to them. We don't know yet.'

'I know a construction worker who lives across the street.'

'Was his name James?' Abbie deadpanned.

Her father looked up sharply. 'And how did you know that?'

His eyes were oddly aflame. *What's he so worried about?* Abbie thought.

'Just a joke, Dad. Do you remember his last name?'

'James . . . James . . .' He searched the patterns in the crocheted blanket on his lap. 'He was from Connemara,' he said finally.

He's probably been dead thirty years, thought Abbie.

'Did the neighbors see anything?' her father mumbled.

'It's the County, Dad. Everyone was watching TV, curtains drawn. Blind, dumb, and deaf. You know that.'

''Tis a good place. I wish I was back there.'

Abbie stared at him, trying to control her breathing.

'I don't want to talk about that now. Are you going to sleep now? Why don't I help you into bed?'

Her father said nothing, just stared at the blanket.

If you wait up for me, why won't you talk to me? Why won't you ever talk to me about something important?

Abbie went into her bedroom, undressed slowly. She checked her shape in the mirror, turned to the side. She'd been losing weight lately, mostly because of working twelve-hour days. Her skin had gone beyond pale – which contrasted nicely with her dark hair – all the way to anemic looking. Her wide-set eyes, bright and intense, stared back at her. Her glossy black hair was pulled back in a ponytail; everything else took too much time. Her cheekbones were high – maybe there was some Native American blood in her family, on her father's side – her nose was pert, and there was a tiny shell-like scar above her left eye, the origin of which she'd never known.

Abbie turned in the mirror again, sighed – what good was it to lose a few pounds and look generally good if your skin looked like that? – and turned on the stereo. She kicked off her heels and it felt like her feet would bloom like balloons. Too many long days in a row. She lay down on the bed.

The disc player kicked into the CD she'd left in there the night before. Eighties music, preferably British and preferably sad, was all she seemed to be able to listen to lately. Yaz's 'Only You' came on, with its swirling, hypnotic video-game beat. The singer breathed out in a husky voice, 'Looking from the window above, it's like a story of love,' and Abbie closed her eyes. She hated when people said they didn't write songs like that anymore, but they didn't write songs like that anymore. The searing pain of the vocal was backed by a ridiculous synthesizer beat that seemed so innocent an eight-year-old could play it. The contrast pleased her somehow.

Abbie began to drift off. Suddenly, she heard a sound like someone being strangled. She snapped awake and raised herself up on her elbows. Her father cried out, then sighed. A minute later she heard the soft rattle of his snore. She went into his room, using the light from the hall to see. They'd moved everything from his home off Abbott and preserved it here. It was like having a museum exhibit – Irish widower cop, circa 1977 – in her spare bedroom. Commendations from the Department, his wife's laminated funeral card from Reddington Funeral Home pinned to the wall above his bed, a calendar from his old church in the County, and a stack of library books on the Korean War on the rickety bedside table. There were no pictures of Abbie, no pictures at all.

He'd forgotten to take off his watch. She reached down and pulled the old-fashioned expanding metal bracelet open, like an accordion, and slid it gently over his knobby wrist. She looked at the watch, saw that it had stopped running. Her lips pressed together for a second, and she wondered how long it had been sitting dead on her father's hand.

Abbie made a mental note to take the watch to the jewelry store for a new battery and laid it on his nightstand. Then she went back to her room, undressed, and got into bed.

The Alzheimer's is slowly getting worse, she thought as she lay under her white comforter. Not only that, he'd had two fainting spells in the last six months. The doctors hadn't been able to explain why, and that worried her. Now he'd forgotten to take off the watch. It used to be part of his nightly ritual to lay it on the nightstand along with his comb and his loose change.

She thought of the disease as a destroyer of memories, tunneling through her father's brain. She wondered which ones it would silently take tonight. Maybe the boyhood fall off a tall rock at Spanish Point on the Irish coast, the one that had resulted in a broken finger and left his own father furious. Or one of the clues that led him to catch the .22 Caliber Killer, Buffalo's only serial murderer and the case that had got him on the front page of the *Buffalo News*. Or the name of his dead brothers back in Clare.

Maybe the face of Abbie's mother, of whom no photographs existed.

SIX

In the morning, Abbie drove down Elmwood to police headquarters in her beloved green Saab. The building was a lovely old brick monstrosity from the 1940s that had been gutted inside to make way for modern offices. Homicide was on the third floor. She exited the elevator and saw that the 9 a.m. conference had already started.

Z nodded at her as she walked in. Perelli, her boss, looked up.

'Slept in, huh?'

'Yes, I did,' she said, but offered no explanation. Her father had been hacking up a lung in the night, and she'd run to the twenty-four-hour CVS for cough syrup. It was none of Perelli's business.

'I was telling the squad that the preliminary autopsy is out on Jimmy Ryan. There are some things you're going to want to see.'

O'Halloran, a broad-shouldered, bantam-sized detective with ginger hair and brooding blue eyes, passed her a pile of photos, eight-by-tens. They were blowups from the coroner's report. She stared at the first one. It showed Jimmy Ryan's face, cleaned of the caked and blackened blood. The sight was even more disturbing than she'd anticipated.

'Cause of death?'

'Strangulation. Looks like the killer used the nylon rope from the truck, looped it around his neck and legs, and let him strangle himself to death every time he kicked out. There's chafing on the neck that matches what you'd get with that type of motion.'

'What is that on his cheek?' she said.

'A number.'

The mark was crude, but it was clearly the number '1.'

'Was it postmortem?'

'No,' Perelli said, taking a sip of his coffee and grimacing. 'The killer did it when he was still alive.'

'Why would he do that? Just from a practical point of view, it would be much easier to make a clear mark if you waited until after death.'

'He wanted to inflict pain.'

'He did that in other ways,' Abbie said, paging slowly through the photographs. There was a circular cut underneath the belly button, and the coroner had made a notation in the margin of the photo. *Incision, multiple indiv. cuts within.*

'This cut is an inch and a half deep,' Abbie said. 'It looks like he was trying to carve a piece of flesh off him.'

'But he kept stopping,' said Perelli. 'Look at the hesitation marks inside the wound.'

Abbie brought the photo closer, and nodded.

'Extortion?' she said.

'Judging from early information that Zangara got from his bank, Jimmy Ryan didn't have shit to extort. Maybe the killer was trying to get something else?'

'Like what?' said Z.

'Information,' Abbie said.

'We have anything similar statewide? Something that tells us he's traveling and this could be his fourth victim?'

Alexander, the Department's lone black detective, shook his head before shifting his enormous bulk in his chair. 'Nothing. There was a prostitute in Syracuse two months ago with her right nipple cut off, but the detectives there like her live-in boyfriend for that one. They had a history of playing around with knives during sex and I guess it got out of control, he nicked her and she screamed, so he decided to go ahead and kill her.'

Perelli nodded and spun away from the table in his chair. A few seconds later, he came wallowing back and pointed at Alexander.

'Wait. You remember that thing three years ago, on the East Side?'

Alexander looked at Perelli blankly, then nodded. 'Oh, yeah. The old lady.'

Abbie looked at both of them. 'Wait, what was that?'

Alexander turned to her. 'It looked like a break-in robbery. A retiree living on her Social Security, black female, in one of the sketchier blocks off Delavan. The door was kicked in, some of her jewelry was gone. But then we looked at the body and it was obvious that the intruder had spent some time in the place. He'd left knife marks on her face.'

'What kind of marks?'

'He jabbed her in the cheek and forehead while she was laying in the bed, tied up.'

'Could be he was finding out where the jewelry was.'

'Could be,' Alexander said. 'But the good stuff was in the top drawer. That didn't take much looking.'

'He didn't take anything with him?'

'Besides the valuables? Nothing.'

Abbie nodded, then looked at Perelli. 'Feels different to me.'

Perelli sighed. 'Look at the file anyway. What else do we know about Ryan?'

After leaving the scene at St Teresa's, Abbie had gone to the Ryan home, interviewing the relatives who'd come by. A car had been idling out front as she pulled up, with two men inside. After she'd told Patty Ryan her husband was dead, two of her uncles had emerged from the car and come through the door to comfort the widow. Abbie wanted to ask them how they'd got the news before she delivered it. But she knew. The newswire.

'The wife was . . . unable to talk to me. After I gave her the news, she collapsed and had to be sedated.'

'Background?'

Abbie looked at her notes. 'Jimmy Ryan was forty-eight, grew up in the County, attended Bishop Timon, where he played JV football and got solid C's. He went to work for Mohawk Gas, which became National Grid. His brother told me there were no financial problems – no gambling, no drugs. I tend to believe him but I'll be checking the credit cards and the mortgage payments. The marriage was unhappy but not to the point of anyone leaving. We're going to be talking to his co-workers to see if they know anything, neighbors.'

'Zangara?'

'I spoke to his boss. Jimmy Ryan started in 1980 as a trainee, right out of high school. No major complaints but there never are right off. Respect for the dead and all that. I expect we find that Jimmy was just bumping along over there. Thirty-one years at the company and he was still walking through slush and dog shit to look at gas meters? Obviously he hadn't impressed National Grid too much.'

'So the question becomes, what was Jimmy Ryan talking about that caused him to get murdered?'

'Well, good thing it's the County,' O'Halloran said. 'They're probably lining up around the block to tell us.'

The detectives laughed, but Perelli glared at O'Halloran.

'I don't want to hear anything about how difficult working South Buffalo is, all right? It's like every other precinct. You have informants on the streets, you have skels in the bars who we give breaks to. Get them to talk to you. Work your sources. Do not let this County shit get in the way of carrying out your investigation.'

The detectives were looking down at their notebooks.

'Does everyone hear me loud and clear?'

They nodded.

'Okay, that's it.'

Abbie and Z walked back to their cubicles, glass-walled ones with black steel frames. Abbie sat down and began going through the crime scene photos more carefully.

'And these,' Z said, leaning over and dropping another sheaf of photos onto her desk.

Abbie picked up the new stack and paged through them slowly.

'He could tie a knot, couldn't he?'

The way the rope was tied was complex, looped three times, forming a collar above the knot.

Z nodded through the glass.

'I wonder if those are Navy ties,' she said.

Z shrugged. 'Dunno. I was Marines. They only taught us how to kill people.'

She went through the first batch a second time. *A murder victim is brought to a church,* she thought to herself, *tied up in a chair. The killer cuts off both his eyelids and carves the number '1' in his cheek. What did the '1' mean – that this was the first of many?*

The killing looked staged. Churches were very public places, deeply meaningful stages for the people who went there to worship. The potential for shock was high. But paging from photo to photo, Abbie didn't get the sense she was looking at a public announcement. More of a very intense private conversation. She looked at a color-saturated picture of Ryan's face shot from the left side, the pink flesh of the eyelids sheared away, the mouth battered and slightly open, his face tilted upward.

What are you seeing, Jimmy? What did he show you?

She felt like she could almost hear the killer's whisper. He wasn't taking things away from Jimmy. He didn't want anything. He was imparting something. He wanted Jimmy to know. To *learn.*

A one-way conversation. Be very quiet and listen to what I say. The cut full of hesitation marks, down near the belly button, told her that.

Maybe Ryan just wouldn't shut up, wouldn't listen to what the killer wanted so desperately for him to know.

'I'm going to his house,' she said after an hour.

Z, chewing on a cinnamon roll, waved.

It was a clear day, a blue sky arched over the lake. She jumped on the ramp to the Skyway.

After exiting at Tifft Street, she drove toward South Park, the road hemmed in on both sides by tall grass. She'd gone here with her dad on Saturday mornings. He would wake her up and say, 'Want to go chasing black rabbits?' and she would say yes because she knew how much he loved it, and because you didn't say no to her father. Never, ever. They would park their sky-blue Nova at the little turn-in where the workers had their hut and then set out on foot, along the trails made by people she never saw, her father and her always alone out there, he with his long stick for chasing off dogs and her with a doll for company. This was when she was eight or nine. The grass, as high

44

as a giant's head, would swallow them up and they'd be lost to the world for hours. The grass even blocked out the sight of the mills and the hulk of the Bethlehem Steel plants to the south. That's why her father had loved it, she thought. He could imagine he was back home in West Clare, climbing the hills near the farm, in the low rolling hills he'd described in such minute detail that she could have made her way from the tiny post office in Miltown Malbay to the bleak cross-roads of The Hand two miles away, though she'd never been to Ireland, not once.

They'd spot the white feet flashing in the grass as the rabbit turned to run and they'd give chase, her father's stick knocking against rocks and she struggling to follow the path of his muddy boots. They never actually caught a rabbit. Most times they would follow the serpentine trails until they emerged into a large clearing and found themselves at the edge of a huge pool of stagnant water. There were three or four of them in the Tifft Nature Preserve and they each had a different color, green or orange or yellow, as bright as antifreeze or Tang, glowing so intensely that they seemed lit from below. Curiously, there were never any mosquitoes flitting on the surface. And they would look at the Day-Glo surface of the pond, and Abbie would say, 'Why is the water that color, Daddy?' and her father would say nothing but stand there as the gusts of wind from the lake blew his thin wool pants tight around his tall legs. Then they'd walk back slowly to the Nova and go home.

Now she knew that the tiny lakes were acid runoff from Bethlehem Steel, left behind even after the steel work went to China and India and the plants locked their enormous gates for good. The company had donated the land for the nature preserve. The pools were now hidden by reeds that soughed in the wind whenever she stopped by to walk the paths.

In sixty seconds, Abbie was past the preserve. She drove to the Ryan house and parked out front. Someone had come by and shoveled the driveway, she saw. Patty Ryan would be the responsibility of the neighborhood now. In the County, if a loved one died of natural causes, you got hot food and sympathy. If they were murdered by persons unknown, you could expect months of complete attention. The kids would be invited over every afternoon to different houses. Meals would be prepared and dropped off around 4 p.m. (people in the County ate dinner early, still timed to the end of the shift at the steel plants). A friend would come by and hold your hand and when you came downstairs you'd find the air scented with Febreeze and the room cleaned down to the grouting. If you forgot to pay your bills, hands would sort through the mail and pay the overdue notices with checks from your checkbook, or from their own, without a second thought.

It was the other side of the County. Here, you were looked after. When you were weak or in pain, you could feel the pleasant crush of people who asked you no questions, who barely talked but who would stand outside your door day and night and guard your privacy, let you grieve and mend. It was invisible, unspoken, centuries deep.

Sometimes she missed it.

She rang the doorbell. Within ten seconds, the door was pulled open and an old woman with enormous round glasses was peering out at her.

'Who're you then?'

'Good morning, ma'am. Detective Kearney, Buffalo Police.'

The door opened wide and the woman reached for the handle of the screen door.

'Ah, come in. Come in.'

The screen door screeched as Abbie pulled it open and she followed the woman, dressed in faded jeans and a blue sweatshirt with an embroidered nativity scene on the front.

'I'm Jimmy's mother,' the woman said as they sat.

'Mrs Ryan,' Abbie said, startled. 'I'm very sorry for your loss.'

The woman ignored the words and tilted her head, her snow-white hair. She studied Abbie's face, inch by inch, unembarrassed. Her face looked weathered, but the expression was serene.

'You've grown so, Abbie.'

'Excuse me?'

Mrs Ryan smiled. 'I used to be the crossing guard at McKinley and Red Jacket Parkway. I watched you go to Mount Mercy every morning and come home every day at 3:45 sharp. You had a backpack, green and pink.'

The memory of the backpack – a beloved JanSport that she'd kept through high school and then lost somewhere – shot through Abbie like an icicle. She smiled.

'I remember you, too,' Abbie said. 'You had an orange slicker for rainy days. I always wondered why it wasn't yellow like everyone else's.'

'My husband worked for Harrison Radiator, he got it for me. It came from the plant. You're not going to charge me with stealing it, are you?'

Abbie studied the old woman's eyes, looming huge and cornflower blue behind her rimless glasses. Mrs Ryan looked back expectantly, as if they were going to talk about Abbie's classmates, what had become of Mary Beth Myers and that slut Kathleen Raftery, instead of her son, tied up and slaughtered in St Teresa's.

'I think the statute of limitations has passed. Mrs Ryan, is Patty here?'

'Upstairs sleeping. The doctor gave her something.'

Abbie nodded.

'Then can you and I talk about Jimmy?'

Something darkened in the woman's eyes, as if a few flecks of the blue iris had suddenly rotated and turned black.

'I suppose so. What do you want to know?'

Abbie shifted on the couch, pulled her white reporter's notebook out of her lapel pocket and found her pen. 'Did he have anyone who was angry with him?'

'Besides Patty? I suppose there were a few. See, Jimmy was my youngest, and the youngest is always the wildest. It was born in 'im. When he was fifteen, I'd hear a thump from his bedroom and know he'd fallen out of the top bunk he shared with his brother Michael. *Crash* in the middle of the night. Stone drunk from hanging out on the street corners. Abbott Road, I'm sure you spent a few nights there yourself.'

Abbie nodded, smiling ruefully. Abbott Road had been the meeting place for high schoolers up and down the County. You would meet your friends in front of Abbott Pizza, buy a slice and a Coke and then hang out on the corner for hours. The boys would have tallboy cans of beer in their pockets and would shyly offer you one like they were thin bars of gold.

'A few nights. Was Jimmy getting in trouble then?'

'When was Jimmy not in trouble in high school? He would come home with his clothes torn or I would find him in the bushes in front of the house in the morning. He was too ashamed to ring the bell when he was in that state. He would be cut up, horrible-like.'

Mrs Ryan turned to look at the fake fireplace, now switched off in the cold room.

'And—'

'Yes?'

Mrs Ryan's lips worked, but she said nothing.

'Mrs Ryan,' Abbie said quietly, 'everything you tell me can help me get to the person who did this.'

The woman looked stricken.

'Jimmy stole,' she whispered.

In the County, breaking someone's orbital socket in a brawl, blackout drinking, and crashing cars into storefronts were only signposts on the way to manhood. But stealing was a terrible thing.

'What did he steal?'

'Money out of my purse, to begin with.' She let out a breath and it was as if she'd shrunk inside her weathered skin. 'Then cars, money out of registers when the bartender wasn't looking, bottles of liquor from the corner liquor store, anything he could get his hands on.'

'Was he arrested?'

'A couple of times. We told him if it happened again, we'd leave him to rot in jail with the coloreds.'

Abbie frowned. 'What about drugs? Did Jimmy ever get involved with them?'

Mrs Ryan's cheerful mood seemed to be slowly disintegrating.

'Why would you ask me that?'

'I have to know what he was involved in. Who he associated with, who might want to harm him.'

Abbie stared at the old woman and it was Mrs Ryan who first looked away.

'I heard things, but I never saw him with drugs. Just the alcohol.'

'Where did he hang out at night?'

'Down on Chippewa, mostly. Then, later, the Gaelic Club.'

She knew it. It was a faux-grand building with two three-story-high Greek columns on the east end of Abbott Road. Irish immigrants had built the place, literally, with their own hands. Her father had been a member, and she'd swum in its pool. A memory of the locker room's smell came back to her: chlorine and decay.

'What they did with Jimmy was nothing but a miracle,' Mrs Ryan said proudly.

'He gave up stealing?'

Mrs Ryan's chin shot up as if she'd been slapped. 'You wouldn't have recognized him. Started going down to the Club, working the bingo nights. He'd put money in my purse for me to find when I was out shopping, 'stead of taking it. Never said a word, he'd just put twenty or thirty dollars in for me to have something extra.'

The corners of her eyes filled with tears. For the first time, Abbie felt she was watching a woman mourn. She reached out and touched Mrs Ryan's knee.

'That must have been lovely.'

'It filled my heart with joy. Only those who have kids know the worry of one going wrong. Have you any?'

Abbie shook her head.

'You ought to. Our young are all leaving us. I thought when we left Ireland and came to America we were done with all that. The Irish haven't any luck, Abbie, despite what you've heard. We came to Buffalo, thinking we'd be the first generation to watch our grandkids grow up, but now they're scattered to the four winds, just like our parents.'

'I know.'

'Which is why it's good you've come back.'

Abbie smiled despite herself. She knew there was no guile in the remark. Any son or daughter who came back to their parents was a hero in South Buffalo. If she'd been a black lesbian Communist sworn agent of the Devil, the simple fact that she'd returned and could be seen helping her father down the street would have outweighed all that. The County would have grudgingly welcomed her back. It had a value system all its own, and loyalty was near the top.

'What about Jimmy's old crowd, after he straightened out?'

'They tried to come around and entice him back, but he wasn't having any of it. And you can be sure' – Mrs Ryan leaned in, tilting her forehead down as if she were about to impart a secret – 'that if they darkened my stoop, I had something for them. Mr Ryan's old rabbit-hunting shotgun, brought straight from Connemara.'

Abbie let it pass.

'Did they make any threats to Jimmy? Sometimes when you break it off with people like that, they can have trouble accepting it.'

Mrs Ryan looked down, considering.

'There was one. A character named . . .'

She searched for the name, her blue eyes scanning the ceiling.

'Walters, or Williams. Yes, that was it, Williams.'

'Was he white or black?'

'Black.'

'Do you remember a first name?'

'It began with a "G." Gerald? Gerard?'

She looked at the corner of the room and her lips moved.

'No, Gerald.'

'And he threatened Jimmy?'

'It was all so long ago, Abbie.'

Nothing in the County was long ago. When no new blood flowed in, old animosities and feuds simmered for years, decades even.

'I'll look into it anyway.'

Mrs Ryan nodded.

Abbie let her eyes drift to the mantel. Mrs Ryan's gaze followed.

'There were some pictures of Jimmy there the other day.'

'Oh yes.' Mrs Ryan sprang up, agile despite her age. Abbie followed her to the mantel. There were six photos. The one that Patty Ryan had picked up yesterday hadn't been returned.

'There was another one here,' Abbie said.

'Really?'

'Jimmy with some friends. I thought it was a good likeness.'

Mrs Ryan began to look around the room in confusion. She went to the TV but on top there were only pictures of the children. Standing with her hands on her hips, she turned and surveyed the room.

Even she's not that good an actress, Abbie thought.

'I'll have to ask Patty,' the old woman said, two fingers to her lips pensively, the hand shaking slightly.

Abbie touched her on the elbow and Mrs Ryan turned.

'I think she has enough to deal with,' Abbie said quietly, inclining her head toward the stairs. 'If you could just look around quietly, that might be better.'

'Course you're right,' Mrs Ryan said, almost in a whisper.

SEVEN

As she drove rutted side streets to the Gaelic Club, Abbie's head throbbed. It was like black waves were washing at the base of the skull. Talking about the past always gave her a migraine-strength headache. She rubbed her neck as she navigated down Abbott Road. Then she called Z, still at the office, and told him to run the names Gerard and Gerald Williams.

As the cars wheels hummed on the road, she thought about Mrs Ryan. How could a mother be so calm after her son's death? She seemed more upset by the thought of him stealing a bottle of whiskey twenty years before than the fact that he'd been tied to a chair, tortured, mutilated, and then strangled to death. What did she have inside her to counterbalance that image? A thing that made sense of the death, that transformed it into something . . . what? Noble? Inevitable?

Her father had liked to talk about his work. Ireland and cops. When she was growing up in the house off Abbott, those were the only two things he'd talk to her about. They'd be sitting at the kitchen table, with her dead stepmother's yellow tablecloth on it and matching dish towels hung below the sink, and he'd say, 'When all's said and done, a cop's an intruder. He shines a light on all the things you're ashamed of in your life, and makes you face who you really are. God forbid you have to own up to it yourself.' The job had exhausted him. Forty years on the force and all he wanted was someone to come up to him and say, 'I killed the bitch because I'm a vindictive asshole – and, by the way, she wasn't cheating on me, I was cheating on her. With her little sister.' Or, 'The money's taped behind the toilet. I stole it because I'm lazy and I like nice things.' He swore that the first time a criminal made a full confession right off, he'd let them go with a hundred-dollar bill slipped into their palms. As a tip. It never happened.

She stopped at a 7-Eleven for a black coffee to clear her head. She kicked the hard slush from behind all four tires, thinking about the Gaelic Club as she walked around the car. It was the next obvious stop. The place was like the mother ship of the County. If you wanted to do anything in South Buffalo, if you wanted to get elected or laid or drunk or to show off your new car or to remember what it was like to be young, you went to the Gaelic Club. It was like walking into the lion's mouth.

Z called back. No black Gerald or Gerard Williams in the database. Only white guys. She told him to play around with the names.

Abbie angled her car against the Gaelic Club's warm red-brick exterior and walked to the front. The Club had been a monument to Irish power in the city when the bricklayers and carpenters and construction workers who flocked to an empty lot after work to build it had been young, their backs strong, their hair still chestnut brown or flaming red. They'd still been able, after a full day's work pouring concrete or laying brick, to come and do it again for a few hours while their families brought them ham sandwiches in cold wax paper and the officers of the Club ferried endless cups of beer. After it opened, the Club had been wall-to-wall with screaming kids running to the pool, the whole building resonating to the game of basketball in the gym, the sound of the ball like cannon shots, audible in every part of the building, while in the bar families ate their fish and chips and listened to the latest singer from Connemara or Dublin on the foot-high stage in the corner of the bar, directly to the right as you entered.

As Abbie walked into the small foyer, where old notices advertising folk singers or protest marches for the IRA were fluttering on a bulletin board, it was as if her mind was running on two parallel tracks. Now and 1989. In those days, she'd come to the Club on a Saturday afternoon to find her dad, the bar as loud as a carnival, packed with men and women in wool coats, the drapery of the brown and black and checked wool swaying like a theater curtain as people moved. That's all you saw, this curtain of coats, and at the center of it, always, his right foot in a black leather loafer perched on a three-rung barstool and a Seven-and-Seven in his hand, her father, holding court.

He would see her, order her a Shirley Temple, and the crowd would move back and allow her in. But her father would never take her up on his lap the way the other fathers did their daughters, or feed her the cherry from the Shirley Temple and stick the tiny pink paper umbrella in her hair after wiping it carefully with a napkin, the way that Mr O'Neill did with his girl Siobhan. And she would sit there waiting for his eyes to fall on hers, but after that first look, it was as if she'd become someone else's child. Another listener, another hanger-on.

She pushed open the glass door. There were three people in the bar: two of them as old as her father, sitting at a small table, and a young bartender. A down-market flat-screen TV was up on the wall, playing a game of Gaelic football – she recognized it at a glance – and the heavy brogues of the announcers called the action. As she walked in, the bartender froze and watched her approach.

'Hi, Billy,' she said.

Billy Carney smiled.

'No fucking *way*,' he said, placing his hands on the bar rail and leaning against it. 'Abbie Kearney.'

Billy had been the quarterback of the Timon varsity team in high school. She'd liked him. All the girls had liked him.

'You really are back.'

'I've been back for a year,' she said, climbing onto one of the rickety stools.

'Back in Buffalo, maybe. But not here.'

He pointed straight down at the wooden bar. Back in the County, he meant.

They shook hands and the touch started a third rail of memory. Weekend nights in Cazenovia Park. A shiver ran down her back.

'You always keep this place so cold?' she said to cover it up.

'If I didn't, the old ones would pass out,' he said, nodding to the two men whispering over amber-colored drinks. Both had heavy wool coats on, even in the bar, and one had some kind of blanket across his lap.

'And I'm always hot,' he added. 'Why pay the gas company?'

'You were always cheap.'

He laughed and the sound boomed in the near-empty room. Then he said, 'So, how are ya?'

'I'm a Buffalo cop. What else can I say? My dreams have finally come true.'

'And I'm a bartender. What a couple of County clichés we are. Only jobs left in this goddamn town. What're ya having? On the house.'

'A Diet Coke. Is this payback for junior prom?'

'What happened at junior prom?' Billy poured the drink, set it in front of her, picked up a pint glass from a dishwasher rack in front of him and began polishing it with a rag. His chin had slid back as if he were expecting a punch, the mouth grinning, the well-known dimples appearing under his cheeks. *God*, Abbie thought, *he's still a good-looking man*.

'You blew me off. Left me to go in the single girls' limo, with the ugly ones with braces and Anne Muidy. You remember, the really *fat* one?'

'I did that?'

'Yeah, you did that.'

'I have no recoll—'

'Shut up, Billy.'

He shook his head, laughing.

'I was an asshole. Sorry, Ab.'

'Not forgiven,' she said, and took a sip of the soda. No, pop. That's what they called it in Buffalo. Pop.

It felt good to be here, near him. She felt like a teenage girl again, but now she had leverage. She'd been places in the world and had a Glock on her hip. Things were a bit more even.

Abbie looked around. The walls seemed to vibrate with memories. The paintings of Irish martyrs, the scarves with DUBLIN and BELFAST scrawled across them tacked up to the wall, the smell of fresh sawdust and beer – they seemed to have some latent power that pulsed in the air.

'It's sad,' she said. 'This place always felt like it was the center of the world to me. We're going to the *Gaelic Club.* I was all excited. Can you imagine?'

Billy laughed.

'But it still has something about it, doesn't it?' she said.

Billy looked around the room, and it was as if his eyes were pinched against the sun. 'Because it's dying. Anything that's dying's beautiful for a while.'

'I was shocked when I came back,' she said. 'Remember the Last Chance Bar on Seneca Street?'

'Did I get thrown through the front window of that one?'

'If not, it would have been the only one on Seneca that you didn't.'

He laughed.

'I went by there yesterday. There's a hand-lettered sign in the window saying, "We sell rabbits and other snake food." *Snake* food.'

Billy nodded, the grin gone from his face. 'Yeah, I saw that.'

'Half the words misspelled.'

Billy grimaced. 'You know what a few of us are calling this place?'

'What?'

'We call it the Rez. Short for "reservation."'

Abbie studied him thoughtfully. 'I heard that from some skel on South Park. What's it mean?'

Billy looked at the two old men, then leaned in to her. 'The County is becoming one big Indian reservation, except with whites trapped inside this time. Businesses have pulled out, the government is MIA, they just left a bunch of poor people here, brought some liquor and junk food in and left us to . . . I don't know what.'

She felt a line of heat across her throat.

'You mean, like on the East Side? And every other ghetto in America?'

Billy didn't quite catch her tone.

'Yeah. You're right. Maybe we're getting a taste of what they did to blacks. Now they want to see if they can do the same to white people.'

From inside the County, Billy's theory made perfect sense. At the turn of the twentieth century, Buffalo had more millionaires per capita than any city in the entire world. It had mansions, it produced luxury cars like the Pierce Arrow, it had power and momentum, it was going to be the next New York City.

Now parts of it looked like some bombed-out alien planet.

Watching the place you loved go back to weeds and wasteland could wound you, Abbie thought. She didn't have the same problem. She'd never quite loved the County. She'd feared it.

'Well, the apocalypse aside, I'm here on business.'

Small nod from Billy.

'Jimmy Ryan,' she said. 'You knew him?'

'Everyone did. He was in and out of this place like he owned it.'

'What did he do here?'

Billy picked up a pint glass and began to polish it, watching the rag as it swooped around.

'The regular stuff. Came in and drank. Helped with the fund-raisers, brought some musicians in.'

'Billy?'

'Yeah?'

'Every time you polish a glass, you start lying to me. Have you realized that?'

'Do I?'

'Yes.'

'Lying? That's a strong word.'

She eyed him. Her ex-husband used to call it 'the look that can break rocks,' but she was unaware of its intensity.

'Jesus, Ab. I'm telling you what I know.'

'Correction. You're telling me *some* of what you know.'

Billy put down the glass. He glanced at the two old men, then searched under the bar. He came up with the TV remote control and thumbed the volume up. The sound of the announcer's voice filled the room.

'Come on, Clare,' Billy called as a man on the screen ran, tapping the hurling ball with the end of his stick. One of the old men looked up, then went back to his whispered conversation.

'Okay,' Billy said. 'Thirty years ago or so, Jimmy and a few other guys used to get together in the office and shut the door. They'd be in there for an hour or two. Everyone wondered what they were up to.'

'What did people think was going on back there?'

Billy looked at her, then down.

'If you pick up a glass and start to shine it,' Abbie said, 'I'm coming over this bar.'

'Maybe I'd like that.'

'No, you wouldn't. Trust me.'

'I don't know. They said Jimmy made a lot of trips after those meetings.'

'Trips where?'

Billy made the County face, a kind of inscrutable half grin, half grimace. It meant yes/no. East/west. It was all in how you read it.

'Don't,' she said. 'Don't you do that.'

He picked up a glass, began to shine it, just looking at her, his eyelids half closed.

'Like the man said, this is where I leave you,' he said. 'As bad as this job is, it's all I got.'

'Who were the other guys in these meetings?'

'One was an older guy named Marty. A lawyer. The other two I didn't know.'

'That's funny. Because you know everyone in the County.'

'Not these two. They came in the back way. You couldn't go near the office until they were finished.'

'What's Marty's last name?'

'Don't know.'

'Billy.'

'Swear.'

Abbie studied him. He looked back, his eyes wary but friendly, and he flashed his quarterback smile. It carried about half the impact it once did, but that was enough.

She breathed out, finished her Diet Coke, and picked up her notebook.

'That's what I hate about this place,' she said.

'What?'

'Even when people are telling you the truth, it *seems* like they're lying.'

Billy shrugged his shoulders, put the polished glass down.

'Bye, Billy.'

She hopped off the seat and began to walk toward the door, waving once over her shoulder.

'What're you doing on prom night?' he called after her.

'Sleeping with my gun,' she called back.

As she walked through the foyer, she glanced back and saw the old men had turned to stare at Billy.

As she got in the car, her cell phone vibrated in her lapel pocket. She pulled it out.

'Kearney.'

'It's Z. Don't worry, but your father reported a prowler. Units are heading over.'

A surge of fear rolled through her.

'How long ago?'

'Two minutes.'

She turned the key in the ignition and revved the engine, shot it into reverse.

'En route.'

'Gotcha.'

EIGHT

When she walked in the door, her father sat at the kitchen table with two young cops, one black, one white. The black cop half stood as she entered; the white turned his head and nodded.

'Detective Kearney, everything's fine,' said the black cop. She saw 'Jackson' written on his nameplate.

Out of breath, Abbie laid her keys on the table and looked at her father.

'Someone was jimmying with the door,' he said. 'My memory's slipping but my hearing's as sharp as a Kilkenny cat.'

Abbie nodded. Her racing heart began to beat slower. However painful the relationship with her father, the thought of losing him had brought on nothing less than terror.

'Did you find anything?' she asked Jackson.

'Well,' he said. 'One thing.'

The white cop stood up and turned toward her. She saw his nameplate: Bianchi.

'I found this hanging on the doorknob as we came up.'

In a plastic baggie he held up, Abbie saw a small child's toy. She took it in her hand and it sent arrows of fear through her.

A plastic monkey.

They hadn't announced that a toy had been found at the Ryan killing. Nobody knew. Nobody except the Homicide Division, the three cops on scene, and one caretaker.

She felt the men watching her.

'It's from a game called Evil,' Jackson said. 'I had one when I was a kid.'

She nodded. 'No note, no anything?'

'Nothing.'

'Neighbors?'

'Didn't hear a sound.'

She looked at her father. 'You all right, Dad?'

He was better than all right. He'd spruced himself up for the visitors. He was wearing a white dress shirt from the back of his closet, gray wool slacks, and the new cardigan she'd bought him for Christmas. He was wearing his black leather slippers.

'I'm fine, I'm fine. Now sit down again, lads, finish your coffee.'

The black cop, Jackson, smiled at her. 'Your dad was telling stories.'

'You don't say,' she said.

They took their seats again and Abbie nodded at them, then went down the hall to her bedroom. She unbuckled the Glock holster and put it on the second shelf in her closet, took off her shoes and sat on the bed. From the kitchen she could hear her father's fine tenor voice.

Abbie took the monkey and stared at it. Its left arm was straight down by its side, the other raised to its face. The right hand was covering the eyes. See No Evil.

Who sent this, she thought – *the killer or another cop? Is the County telling me to leave the investigation to them? If so, they can go to hell.* The very thought sent her blood boiling. *But if it's the killer . . .*

Her father's voice boomed from the kitchen. He was a great story-teller. It was the one thing that – though she wasn't his flesh and blood – she always wished he'd passed on to her, by osmosis.

'Now, there were two of us standing over the body,' she heard him say.

She listened for a moment. It was the First Ward story, or one of them. She recognized it from those nights in the Gaelic Club when she would stand by his side, not hoisted onto his lap but still claiming him by her nearness.

Abbie drifted back to the kitchen and leaned on the doorframe. *They'll think it's strange if I disappear after seeing the monkey,* she thought. *If it is a message, I can't let them see it hit home.*

Her father's face was lit from within, his cheeks flushed red.

'I said to my partner, Jameson, "Now, just what the hell caused you to fire your gun at this innocent man?"'

Her father saved the story – all of his stories – for company or for rare nights out. Not for her. For Detective John Kearney, charm was lost on family.

'Jameson is shaking like he's got a fever. He can barely speak at this point. First time he's shot his gun, y'see. His feckin' third day on the job! He's practically doing a tap dance around the guy, looking here and there, ducking his head down, looking for a weapon.'

Her father looked under the table, imitating Jameson's little dance, and the cops belly-laughed, the sound bouncing off the kitchen tiles.

'"He had a gun, he had a gun, a black revolver in his hand," Jameson keeps saying.'

Her father held up his right hand.

'Now, what did he really have there? A black spoon. He'd been stirring the spaghetti sauce on the stove. I went over and turned off the flame and I say to Jameson, "Jameson, you hairy Kilkenny beast of creation, can you not tell a spoon from a revolver? Have you never been inside a guinea's house? Have you no culture *at all*?"'

Sniggers from Jackson, who snuck a glance at his white partner. Of course. Bianchi. That was the reason her father was telling an Italian story.

'Now, I'd recognized the man as soon as we'd walked in the place. Jimmy Farelli, and he was with the Gallo gang, a hard man, you understand. The Gallos owned every bakery in the First Ward and were just beginning to get their oily fingers—'

He stopped.

'Excuse me, Officer Bianchi,' her father said, bowing in mock apology.

Bianchi waved his hand at her father. 'Don't even worry about it, Mr Kearney.'

Jackson, shaking with laughter, mouthed the words 'oily fingers' at his partner.

'Right,' said her father. 'Just beginning to get their garlic-smelling fingers' – Jackson squeezed his eyes shut – 'on the Irish unions, they were. But the point is Jameson had no idea he'd just killed a mob enforcer. The man was standing in his own kitchen, and there was no gun in sight. Jameson was still wet behind the ears and he'd just killed an honest, God-fearing man without a good reason. Even back then, that was frowned upon in the Buffalo Police Department.'

The old man caught her eye and smiled, some stray spark of his happiness flying across to her. Abbie gave him a half smile.

'So, we send out the call. Man shot at 34 Second Avenue. Now, every cop on the beat knows this is Jimmy Farelli's address, he's a known malefactor, the worst of the worst. So these beat cops come in one after the other, bend down to take a look at the body, then get up. Jameson is on his hands and knees, meanwhile, looking under the fridge, under the stove, crying, "The gun's got to be here somewhere!" No gun. Jameson's career is about to go the way of the Lindbergh baby.

'So, thirty minutes pass. The medical examiner comes in, examines the body, tells his assistants to carry it off. The man's still lying on the floor face-down. They roll him over.'

His father leaned forward toward Jackson.

'And what do you suppose they found underneath James Farelli on the night of June 16, 1974?'

The two cops looked at him like boys listening to a bedtime story.

'Four . . . black . . . pistols, lying on the linoleum floor,' her father said. He leaned back triumphantly, his head turning slightly to gaze at each cop in turn.

Their faces were puzzled.

'Four *guns*?' Jackson said. 'I thought you said—'

Her father smiled. 'He was unarmed when we walked in, sure. But every cop who entered that apartment had heard that there was no gun. So what do they do? Each one brought along their spare gun or some old piece of junk they had lying in the trunk of their squad car. They bent down for a look at the body and secretly stuck that pistol under the body. Without telling anyone else.'

The two cops stared in disbelief.

'That's imposs—' said Bianchi.

'No fear of a lie,' her father said, closing his eyes like he was a priest pronouncing on the truth of Christ's resurrection. 'There's a pistol under his right leg, an old revolver under his left, another one stuck under the man's belly, and a fourth one spilling out of his shirt. He looked like Pancho Villa. All that was missing was a bandolier and a sombrero.'

The cops looked at each other, then simultaneously broke into roars of laughter.

'Jameson nearly had a heart attack. Three hands reached out, grabbed a gun each, and the cops walked out the door. We left one pistol there, logged it as the guinea's personal firearm, and closed the case. Jameson was saved.'

The two cops shook their heads in wonder. Her father reached for his cup of tea – he'd never gotten the American addiction for coffee – and winked at Bianchi. Then he caught his daughter's eye.

'Look at her stare me down,' her father whispered to the two cops, pretending to wilt under her gaze. 'She doesn't approve, y'see.'

Abbie's eyelids lowered slightly as she regarded him.

'I didn't say a word, Dad,' she said, smiling.

Her father narrowed his eyes and held up a finger toward her. 'Every one of those cops went in there to save Jameson's ass. It has its own beauty.'

'If you say so. But Jameson was lucky he shot a mobster.'

He ignored her and turned to Bianchi.

'It'd never happen today,' he said.

'Probably not,' Bianchi said, gripping his gun belt and shaking his head.

'I wouldn't be so sure,' Abbie said.

'Mr Kearney, that's the single best cop story I've ever heard,' Jackson said. He nodded at Abbie, his eyes strange. *He's probably wondering what it was like to be raised by a legend,* Abbie thought.

'Come back tomorrow,' Abbie said. 'He's here all week.'

The cops stood up to leave.

'Thanks for checking this out,' she said as they shuffled past her out of the small kitchen.

'No problem,' said Jackson, stopping. 'Your father's a good guy.'

Abbie nodded and looked at her dad, finishing the last of his tea. 'He's something.'

They said their goodbyes and left. She listened to them clomp down the stairs. The front door clattered open and then banged shut.

'Dad,' she said, walking over to the kitchen table and sitting across from her father.

'Hmmm?' He was still in the glow of 1974.

'What did you hear?'

'Oh, a jiggling at the door.'

She laid the toy in the baggie on the table.

'Does this monkey mean anything to you?'

He didn't look down.

'A teenager playing a trick, Abbie. 'Tis all it is.' He tilted his cup and looked to see how much tea he had left.

'It was hung on our door.'

'Maybe a commentary on your gypsy background,' he said.

She smiled, but not her eyes. 'My neighbors are a bit more advanced than people in the County. What I need to know is if this was directed at me or at you.' Her eyes sought his, without success.

'I couldn't tell ya.'

'Take another look.'

She picked up the baggie with the monkey weighing down one corner.

Her father stared at the refrigerator.

'Over here,' she said, dangling the bag.

No response.

Suddenly, her fist smacked into the wooden table. Her father looked up, startled, as his teacup rang in its saucer.

'Damn it, Dad, it's *important*. The killer . . .'

His blue irises widened. 'Which killer, Detective Kearney?' he asked.

Abbie frowned. 'I meant whoever left this,' she said.

'No, you didn't,' he said slowly, and his eyes glimmered. 'Jimmy Ryan's killer is connected to this . . . this thing?'

'Why?' Abbie said, smiling. 'You've seen it before?'

He paused.

'Didn't I raise you never to answer a question with a question?'

'You raised me to always find the truth,' Abbie said, watching him closely. Finally, he turned away.

Abbie sighed. 'Okay. You want to talk about Jimmy Ryan? Tell me what you know about Jimmy Ryan.'

'It's getting late, Abbie. I'm tired.'

She went to say something but it caught in her throat.

'Dad, please.'

He coughed and crossed his legs.

'I'll ask around,' he said finally.

'Or you could give me the names and I could ask around. You're retired, remember?'

He took a sip of tea and looked at her out of the corner of his eyes. 'Maybe they should bring me back to catch this one.'

'You are something. It's under control, thanks.'

'Ah!' he said. John Kearney turned in the chair to face his daughter. 'Now, are you sure about that?'

Abbie stared at him, and for a moment her father was fully present, the eyes keen, the intelligence that had put a thousand men behind bars – and two in Forest Lawn Cemetery – lit up behind his eyes. Was he mocking her? Doubting her skills as a detective?

'I'm asking for your help, Dad.'

Her father frowned and looked away.

The kitchen went silent. She felt her heart slow. Abbie traced the ridges of his deeply lined face as he looked absently at the teacup, and suddenly she felt a sorrow so deep it was beyond tears. She remembered the times she'd woken as a child and found her father sitting at the foot of her bed, watching her in her darkened bedroom. It had happened a dozen or so times, always late at night. Once he sensed she was awake, he'd get up and leave silently. At first it had creeped her out, but then she'd begun to pretend she was still sleeping, so as to keep her father there.

If her father had just told her a story the way he had to those two cops, she'd be okay now, her depressions gone, her fears dispelled once and for all. She was convinced of that. *Wouldn't you do that for a random stranger, Dad, some wanderer you met in the Gaelic Club or on the streets of the County?*

And aren't we strangers?

NINE

Her cell phone ring had merged with her dream and gone off four times before she snapped out of sleep and grabbed it from her nightstand. Outside her window, it was just getting light.

'Hello?'

'You're never gonna believe who we found.'

It was Z.

'Who?'

'Gerald Williams. We got him.'

She sat up in bed, running a hand through her hair.

'Where?'

'Niagara Falls PD. He's in their open files. His real name is Gerald Williams Decatur. That's how we missed it at first.'

'Murdered?'

'And how. Three months ago.'

She paused. If it had been three days ago, she would have said that it was the same guy for certain. Three weeks even. But three months? Impossible to say.

'The same killer?' she said, lifting off the bed and walking to the bathroom.

'I don't know. I'm headed up to Niagara Falls to get the report. But whoever did old Gerald, they did him bad. Let's just say he didn't have an open casket.'

'Meet you downtown.'

She took a quick shower, dressed, made instant oatmeal for her father and left it in the microwave for him to heat up. She was out the door in fifteen minutes.

* * *

At HQ, she found Z in his cubicle, his feet up on the desk. A small black .22 with a brown grip was tucked into a leather ankle holster.

'You still carry that thing?' she said.

Z groaned as he reached over to pat the leather. 'The Slammer? Best friend a man could have.'

'Unless you're too fat to reach it in the clutch.'

She walked around his chair and stood behind him, leaning over. He had six of the crime scene photos spread across the top, and he was going over them between sips of coffee.

The Niagara Falls PD report was near his elbow. She took off her jacket, hung it on the coatrack, grabbed the file and dropped into her cubicle chair. She read through it quickly. Gerald Williams Decatur, forty-nine, last known address 121 Richmond Avenue, Buffalo. He'd been found at the Lucky Clover motel on Ontario Avenue on the Canadian side of the Falls. He'd paid thirty-two dollars for a basic room, which made the Clover a rock-bottom establishment. Since its heyday in the fifties, parts of Niagara Falls had sunk as low as Buffalo, its cheapest motels catering equally to bargain tourists and the drug dealers, transients, and other spillover from the normal world that piled up at border crossings like refuse at a sewer grating.

Gerald Decatur had been found sitting upright on one of the two single beds, propped against the wall. The nightstand that had stood between the beds had been moved and placed carefully near the bathroom door. The killer giving himself room to work, Kearney thought. Decatur was light-skinned, with a thin face covered with old acne scars and a scraggly goatee. He had a modified Afro cut short on the sides and had a cross earring hanging from his left ear. In the crime scene photos, his face had been crosshatched with deep cuts, pulpy red flesh squeezing up between the slashes. His green T-shirt was saturated with dark blood and his hazel eyes stared dully ahead, the eyelids still there. Two defensive wounds on the left hand: the killer had clearly immobilized Decatur rather quickly before going to work on his face. There was nothing cut into his body, no symbols or numbers or torture marks. Decatur had been killed by a single thrust of the blade to the heart, expertly placed and five and a half inches deep, according to the coroner.

The room had been paid for in cash. The worker at the front desk had seen no one enter or exit and barely remembered Decatur checking in. The rooms to either side had been unoccupied. A guest four doors down had called the front desk at 2 a.m. to say she'd been woken up by 'some animals throwing a party.' The front desk guy had done nothing about it, thirty-two dollars a night apparently not getting you much service in Niagara Falls. The cops had tracked down the guest and interviewed her, but she had little to add, saying only that she'd been woken up by what sounded like someone banging into a wall and a man screaming. But the noise had cut off mid-scream and never started up again.

Abbie hovered over Z again, peering at the photos. Their eyes moved over the images for three minutes before Abbie spoke.

'They know why he was there?'

'I spoke to the lead on it and Decatur got one suspicious call the day before he went up. All the other numbers on that day were family or friends, and all their alibis check out. This one was different. It came from a pay phone at the Buffalo Public Library. Call came in at 4:15 p.m. At 4:22 p.m., Decatur calls his brother and asks if he can borrow his car for Friday night. The night he was murdered.'

'So he gets a call, borrows a car, heads up to Niagara Falls but doesn't go to the casinos or the whorehouses. He gets a room in this little out-of-the-way motel and meets his killer. And no toy monkey found on the body or in the room?'

'Nothing.'

She nodded, her eyes tracing the cut marks on Decatur's face.

'What's it say to you?' Z said.

'Drug deal.'

Z nodded.

'Priors?' she said.

'A couple of street sales of weed and cocaine when he was in his late teens. Then he moved up to distribution. Caught with two kilos in 2004 and did five years downstate. He was caught violating once by his parole officer since getting out – associating with ex-cons. Was back in for six months starting last year. He's been out since early September. Which means he got his ass killed only a month or two after he left jail.'

Abbie studied the photos. She looked at the knife marks on Decatur's face, studying them almost as if they were paint strokes on a canvas.

'It's a different pattern. Whoever killed Jimmy Ryan was more controlled. Here the killer is just slashing and cutting.'

'You're right. If this *is* the same guy, you think Ryan was more personal?'

'Not sure. Maybe he learned he could do it and do it well. He could get Decatur tied up, torture him, play his games and get away. With Jimmy, he takes his time.'

'Could be.'

'Or not. We're missing something, Z.'

'Whoa, whoa, wait a minute. Missing something? We've been handed the whole storyline here.'

Kearney pulled her chair over, sat and stared at Z.

'How do you figure?'

'Way I see it, Jimmy Ryan wants back in the drug game and earn a few dollars. Calls up the only guy he knows from the old days, Gerald Williams Decatur, arranges for some kind of exchange. So Decatur goes to his source to get the goods. But maybe he forgets to pay, or it's a double cross from the get-go. The source follows Decatur to Niagara Falls, gets the merchandise back, tortures him to find out who was going to buy the stuff. Decatur gives up the name. Then the killer tracks down Jimmy Ryan, tortures him to find out where he's hiding the money, offs him and then, boom, he's in the wind.'

Kearney leaned back in her chair. 'Why does he carve a symbol into Ryan's forehead then? Look at these pics. The killer worked Decatur over for *hours*, I'll bet. You think a street guy like Decatur, an ex-con, is going to hold out for the sake of some white boy in the County he knew fifteen years ago? And Jimmy Ryan is going to give up his life for a few thousand bucks? If this was a small-time drug caper, they would have talked.'

'Okay, Okay,' Z said. 'Maybe you're right, Professor. Maybe both victims give up the goods early on. But think about it. What if the killer's a sadistic fuck who likes inflicting pain? Suddenly he finds himself in a room with a tied-up victim.'

'Early Christmas for a psycho.'

'Thank you. Boom, work turns into play. He starts jabbing them with the knife just for the fun of it. Ever thought of that?'

'Then why does he cut off Jimmy Ryan's eyelids?'

She tapped Z's desk once.

'I need to see the motel room.'

'The *room*? Jesus, Abbie, it's been cleaned up and rented out for months. There's nothing there.'

'I need to see it.'

'Why?'

'It's January. No one goes to the Falls in January, so just maybe the room hasn't been used too many times. In any case, I want to see it.'

'Please. Do we really want to do this? Get inside the mind of the killer and all that horseshit? I say we just be regular cops and I go home to my kids. You . . .'

Z shrugged his shoulders and swallowed his next words. Abbie leaned over and looked into his eyes.

'I have nothing to go home to, Z? Is that what you're saying? And that's why I get obsessed with these cases?'

'Now, Ab, I didn't say that . . .'

'Well, say it.'

He opened his mouth to continue, but Abbie held out her hand.

'This is what I'll do for you, Z. You find out who Decatur's source was before he got sent away. See if that person has an alibi for October 6. He didn't have much time to make new contacts after he got out of jail. And I'll go to Niagara Falls and pursue the real killer. Because this is *not* about drug mules.'

She slipped into the town of Niagara Falls and drove through the near-deserted streets. This place was suffering, too, just like Buffalo. But there was a different feel to the loneliness here. It had once been the honeymoon capital of the world, which meant the motel sheets, the curtains, the signs, and the souvenir ships – all were part of the memories of aging brides now living in Tokyo or Liverpool or Phoenix. All the thousands of cheap honeymoons that had taken place here seemed wounded by the current state of the city, Abbie thought, as if the decline in Niagara Falls might reach across the globe and poison the marriage of people who'd been happy here once.

You're really something else, Abbie. Stop dreaming about Japanese honeymooners and find your killer.

Before she'd left, she'd called ahead to Niagara Falls PD to clear the visit and had spoken with Detective Mills, the lead on the case.

'Anything new?' she'd asked him.

'Not really. We've been a little overwhelmed by the Outlaws thing.'

'Which Outlaws thing?'

'Are you kidding? Four months ago we had the beginning of a biker war. Six Outlaws were killed in their headquarters by someone with a machine gun – probably the Warlocks. Six dead in Niagara Falls is still news.'

'Right, I did hear about it. Did anyone hit back yet?'

'Nada. The whole county's on pins and needles. But somebody in an awful-smelling leather vest is going to die pretty soon now.'

Abbie laughed.

'So we've done the basic protocol with Gerald Decatur,' Mills went on, 'but not a hell of a lot more. If you guys can get the collar down there, I'll buy you a cold beer.'

Abbie had promised Mills she'd keep him up to date on her progress.

The Lucky Clover was a sixteen-unit motel on Ontario Avenue, a major thoroughfare that ran perpendicular to the Niagara River. The parking lot was slick with rain and she could see the plume of mist from the Falls off to the north as she pulled in. She got a plastic card key from a bored clerk who'd been off the night of the killing. Room 16. It was near the end of the row, a steel door with dents in it about waist high. It looked like it'd been kicked in a couple of times – the door cratered just below the doorknob – and then repainted in pale blue.

Abbie slid the key in the lock, waited for the light to turn green, and then opened the door. A musty smell rushed out.

The room was bare-bones: two twin beds, a squat twenty-inch TV, a small desk with a lamp on it and a wooden chair, a gray and pea-green weave on the carpet. The bathroom door was kitty-corner to where she was standing.

Abbie put down her Coach bag gingerly on the desk – she wondered if the maids even cleaned it, but it seemed like the safest bet – and went to the bathroom first. The glow of the light was greenish, the tub a dark blue, pitted here and there where the enamel had chipped. She pulled the top off the toilet tank and looked inside; it was a favorite hiding place for drug fiends, since no one wanted to open the thing. She ducked down to look behind the mirror. She checked the top of the light fixture. Nothing.

Abbie went into the bedroom and pulled the sheets back on each bed, bunching them at the foot, then studied the mattresses. The one farthest from the door was pitted with cigarette marks and small tears – impossible to tell when they were left there – but no blood. The one closest to the door had a huge liver-colored stain near the top, closest to the wall. Was it possible the motel owner had been too cheap to replace the mattress Decatur had been butchered on? She got a queasy feeling in the pit of her stomach. She pulled the sheets and the thin duvet covers back up.

Abbie moved the nightstand away from the wall and saw that the motel owner had bleached the carpet but hadn't even bothered to cut out the bloodstained section and replace it. Gerald Decatur's blood had mixed in with the green weave of the carpet until it appeared to be a large rust stain.

The double drawers of the nightstand were empty except for a Gideon Bible and a local guide, provided by the Chamber of Commerce. 'The Falls Is Back!' it read in big sea-green letters. There were quick stories with lots of exclamation points and pictures of the aquarium, yellow-raincoated tourists aboard the *Maid of the Mist* floating toward the Canadian Falls, and the 'Virtual Reality World at Ride Niagara.' Abbie flipped through the pages, read a line or two, and felt that she was now officially wasting her time.

She thought back on the crime photos. What possessed her to come up here? Her obsessiveness with cases was eating up her life again. Already she was down to four hours' sleep a night. For what? There was nothing to see here. Everything had been scoured, double-checked, sanitized. She sat on the bed and closed her eyes and she tried to block out the tinny music that drifted in from the souvenir shop around the corner. Suddenly, she got on her knees, ducked her head until it grazed the carpet, and shone her flashlight on the underside of the two beds.

Nothing.

If Gregory Decatur had been sitting propped up on the bed at the angle his neck had been in the photos, where would he have been looking? She sat on the bed, put her back to the wall, tilted her head slightly upward, and found she was staring at the last row of plaster ceiling tile, directly above the TV. Abbie got up, grabbed the back of the desk chair, pulled it next to the TV stand. She climbed on top of the chair, reached up with her hands and pushed the ceiling tile up. She brought her flashlight up and flicked it around. Dust, wires, and a scrunched-up Lays potato chip bag flashed in the bright beam. Nothing out of the ordinary.

Damn it, Absalom, go home.

She climbed down and sat on the wooden chair. Gregory Decatur was a random casualty in the drug war, a nobody killed in an out-of-the-way motel room where they didn't even burn the mattress after a customer was stabbed to death.

The killer wasn't your boy.

She was about to leave when she looked down at the wooden seat she was sitting on. With a sigh, she got up and flipped the chair over.

A leaping thrill of excitement ran through her. *Breathe in and out,* she said to herself. *Breathe, Abbie.*

Her heartbeat settled back down. She took a deep breath and knelt by the overturned chair, her knee brushing the pea-green carpet.

Taped on the underside of the chair was a brown plastic monkey.

She called Niagara Falls PD first, because it was still their case, although she was going to change that. Another voice picked up his phone.

'Homicide.'

'I'm looking for Detective Mills.'

'He's off shift.'

'This is Detective Kearney with Buffalo PD.'

'This is Magnuson. What can I do for you?'

'I was doing a check of the motel room where Gerald Decatur was found. I came across something Mills should know about.'

'I don't know anything about the case. You'll have to wait till Mills gets back.'

'Okay. When is that?'

'Monday.'

Abbie gaped.

'You mean to tell me that you want me to hold a critical piece of evidence on an active murder investigation because someone is barbecuing this weekend? Tell me I'm hearing things.'

'What I'm telling you is that this department is stretched so tight it's not even funny. If it's Mills's case, it's Mills's case.'

'What's his cell number?'

'Listen, Kearney. I don't take lectures from Buffalo bitches. I'll leave him a message. Now go fuck yourself.'

Abbie was shocked enough to be speechless for a second. There was a click and the call was cut off.

If they don't want the clue, I'll take it as a gift, she thought. She began to think over the appearance of the third monkey as she pulled her car onto the highway, heading south.

When she got back to the office, she found a manila envelope sitting on her desk. Z had left her the file with a Post-it stuck on it.

This was Decatur's source, the note read. Beside the handwriting was a poorly drawn frowny face.

She read through the file. The source was one Marcus Jones, a product of West Ferry Street. That put him two blocks away from Richmond Avenue, where Gerald Decatur had grown up. Both rough streets, both crawling with gangs and skels and the dealers who supplied them. The two had practically come up together, which on the East

Side of Buffalo meant a great deal. Jones had joined the BMF, or Black Mafia Family, gang in 1993 and had quickly become their main drug executive. The source of the supply seemed to be in Atlanta. The Major Crimes Unit had followed Jones down there twice in the mid-nineties, but both times he'd managed to slip away before he made the contact. A couple of days later, Jones was back in Buffalo and the price of cocaine had instantly gone down 15 percent.

When she got to the end of the file, she saw why Z had added the frowny face. Jones was incarcerated downstate on a drug distribution charge. He'd been convicted in 2009 and was doing ten years. Unless the prison had a very liberal prisoner release program, Jones couldn't have been the source of the call that brought Gerald Decatur to Niagara Falls and the dingy motel room.

So the murder wasn't based on old drug ties. And now the plastic monkey had made an appearance.

The motel case, Abbie thought, was a case of beginner's luck. Decatur had arrived unarmed at the crime scene and the assailant got the jump on him. As simple as that. The motel's surveillance camera had been broken that day, as Abbie had learned after going back to the office and questioning the clerk one more time. If it had been working, she'd be staring at a video image of the killer right now.

But Jimmy Ryan was different. The killer had abducted a fit man who could handle himself, got him into St Teresa's without anyone seeing, tied him up expertly and worked him over for hours. He'd left nothing behind he didn't want cops to find. He'd done intricate things with the knife, mutilated Ryan in very specific ways.

He hadn't been lucky with Ryan. He'd been proficient. And he'd carved the number '1' into his cheek.

Most killers who leave tokens at crime scenes have committed to their craft, Abbie thought. *There will be more toy monkeys*, she thought. *And more victims.*

TEN

Abbie drove down Elm Street in downtown Buffalo. She needed to fill out the story of Gerald Decatur, know what shape of puzzle piece he really was, before she could fit him into the overall picture. From the file, she knew Decatur had no living relatives in Buffalo. Either the streets, a family history of diabetes (mentioned in his jacket, from his hospital intake at the downstate prison), or emigration had taken them away. That left her only one choice.

She had to go see Reverend Zebediah.

Ever since coming back to Buffalo, Abbie had known she was going to have to make this visit sooner or later, even before the Jimmy Ryan case. The Reverend was too deep a part of her history here; out of respect, Abbie needed to see him. But she was afraid that it would all go wrong and that her warm memory of the Reverend would be replaced by a picture of a broken, cynical man. Buffalo tended to grind you down. Abbie was running out of good memories of the city, and she wanted to keep the Reverend safe.

She'd first met him during her junior year in high school. He'd been the resident minister at the City Mission, the homeless shelter downtown where her mother had ended her days, addicted to heroin and abandoned by Abbie's father, who had given his daughter her sky-blue eyes but didn't even leave her his name. Abbie had met the Reverend on one of her periodic quests to find her roots. He was the unofficial mayor of Buffalo's poor and mostly black East Side, and was in and out of the City Mission on a weekly basis. If someone needed a job, the Reverend knew a construction project that was looking for some minority workers to make its federal quota. If you needed a place to stay, he had a crumbling four-story former hotel on Hertel Avenue that he'd refurbished, if you could call mopping the floors, putting in some beds, and horse-trading for sheets and towels a refurbishment. If you needed spiritual guidance, he had the perfect line of Scripture to show you the way. If you needed a lawyer, he knew several who worked cheap and wouldn't take the DA's first plea bargain to lighten their workload. His clientele was multiracial and usually desperate.

The Reverend didn't drive around in a Cadillac, taking people's contributions and living high. He drove an old Oldsmobile Cutlass, worked nights, selling beer in the stands at Memorial Auditorium during hockey games. At the Aud, he was Zeb the Beer Guy, and sold more cups of Molson ale than anyone else there, his bald head shining with sweat by the end of the first period. With that money, and contributions, he kept a good part of the East Side afloat.

Abbie had started volunteering on weekends, part of the Reverend's free-floating mission. As a white girl, a *County* girl, working on the East Side, she was a curiosity. But people welcomed her in, and what she'd found there had astonished her. The County was a swamp of repressed emotions that erupted only during epic drinking binges. But in this part of town, single mothers had hugged Abbie when she went door to door on Thanksgiving with cans of cranberry sauce and yam, invited her to sit down and eat. Middle-aged homeless men in the bombed-out buildings on Delaware and Main had thanked her for the sandwiches prepared by the Reverend's minions in the hotel's basement. The men's fingers were often warped by arthritis or cold, and their eyes rheumy with alcohol, but they were grateful. They wept silently and called her 'daughter.' In the County, they talked of the East Side as if it was some kind of lawless wasteland, where family had broken down and people preyed on each other in packs. But she'd found people who could name their fourth cousins and who knew who those cousins were dating, where they worked, what their babies' names were.

On her after-school trips down the unfamiliar streets, she'd asked about her mother, over and over, never telling people she was Natasha Minton's daughter, but casually mentioning the name and waiting for the responses she'd dreamt of for years: 'Natasha? Sure, I knew her. Got family over on Delavan.' And then Abbie knocking on a strange door.

It had never happened. Natasha Minton had died at thirty-eight, leaving her two-year-old daughter nothing but a hazy memory of a woman in a yellow dress, holding her hand as they walked down Main Street. At the time of her death, Natasha was a recent transplant from the Midwest, by all accounts a secretive and mistrustful woman who barely made a mark on Buffalo. There were times Abbie hated her for it – *couldn't you have talked to someone,* she cursed silently, *had a single conversation about your past? Left me one pathetic little trail to follow? And who comes to Buffalo from the South anyway? How desperate to escape your past do you have to be to come* here?

The Reverend, she believed, had known about these whispered conversations. But he never asked about them, never spoke about her mother at all. She was sure he'd asked around, too, and his inquiries rippled far further than her own. If the Reverend didn't know you, you weren't worth knowing. But he'd never come to her pulling along a newly minted cousin, saying, 'This is someone you have to meet.' He'd done everything but that.

Now she was back to ask about Gerald Decatur.

She pulled the Crown Vic up to the converted hotel on Hertel, parked in front, and climbed the cement stairs covered with chipped green paint. The door was locked. The Reverend was probably on one of his many errands in the neighborhood, but he was never gone for long. She sat on the stoop to wait.

A little black girl with braided hair flying behind her came riding along on a bike, even though it was about two degrees above zero. She stopped to stare at Abbie.

'Hi there,' Abbie said.

'Hello,' the girl said in a somber voice.

'Do you happen to know when the Reverend will be back?'

The girl tilted her head. 'You talk funny.'

'Yeah, I get that a lot. What about the Reverend?'

'He's at the corner store gettin' some milk, but the mister there wanted to talk to him 'bout some problem with the power company.'

'Ah. Did he buy you that bike?'

'Yup.'

They spoke for a few more moments, and Abbie learned that the girl's name was Rashida Jackson and she was eight and smart as a thin whip. After Abbie had given her a card with her name on it – proof that she was a real live policewoman – Rashida bicycled off furiously to show it to her friends. Abbie watched her go, then turned to see the Reverend striding up the street, a plastic shopping bag in each hand. She rose.

His face, set hard as he approached, broke into a smile.

'Absalom Kearney, I'll be damned.'

He swept in for a hug, smelling of Old Spice. He stood back to look at her up and down, shaking his head.

'Grew up fine. I knew it, I always said so.'

'You always said I'd be knock-kneed and looking for a boyfriend till I was forty.'

'You got a boyfriend?'

'No.'

'Well, then.'

He unlocked the door and led her to the right to his office, which fronted his small and neat apartment. As she walked in, the smell of a fastidious bachelor – shoe polish, tobacco, and aftershave – brought her back twenty years.

'What about you, Reverend? No girlfriend, I see.'

'I'm married to the Lord's work, you know that,' he said. His smile grew until his white teeth parted to allow a peal of explosive laughter to fill the apartment. The Reverend looked good, Abbie decided. And she was relieved.

'Sit down, sit down.'

They sat and he slapped both hands against his muscular legs.

'It's good to see you, Absalom.'

'It's good to see you, too. I was afraid the city had worn you down.'

He shrugged. 'God never gives a man burdens he can't carry,' he said. 'But you've probably learned that yourself.'

'I'm still learning it, I guess.'

He smiled but there was concern in his eyes, a fatherly worry.

'You still searching, Absalom?'

'I think I'll always be searching, Reverend. For one thing or another.'

'You know what I mean.'

'I'm gainfully employed. I'm damned good at what I do. I'm kind to animals and small children. And I think you're gonna have to settle for that, Reverend.'

He laughed. 'No one can defeat a woman who is strong in faith, whatever faith that may be. Now, what did you come here to talk about?'

'Gerald Decatur.'

'Ah.'

He turned away sharply, as if she'd slapped him.

'We lost him.'

'I know. What can you tell me about him – towards the end, I mean.'

'They say he was back dealing drugs.' The ever-present 'they,' meaning the cops, the *Buffalo News,* the justice system.

'You don't buy it?'

The Reverend swung his muscled face back and forth slowly, his eyes never leaving her face.

'No, I don't buy it. He hadn't gone near the drug boys since he got out of prison. I'm telling you this from my heart. Six months before he was murdered, he was right here in this office and I had him going out to Dow Chemical up off the highway, for a job. He got that job and he was excited about it. Had a little apartment over on Genesee and a young girl he was getting serious about.'

The Reverend rubbed his knuckles in his other hand, massaging them as if he were wringing out a cloth.

'It perturbs me. After he died, I called out to Dow and spoke to his supervisor. Gerald hadn't missed a single day in weeks. The man had nothing but good things to say about him. He even asked me if I had another like him.'

Abbie frowned.

'That was a callous thing to say, considering.'

'I agree with you on that. Like I was sending them damn mules or something.'

'What's the girlfriend's name?'

'Monica. Monica Merriweather. Funny name. She's gone south now, like everybody else. Couldn't even go back to his apartment to clean out his things. I had to do that for her. I packed up what she wanted and sent it down to her in Texas, UPS. Got the address if you want it.'

She shook her head. 'Reverend, how can you be sure he wasn't back to dealing? Maybe he wanted to buy this Monica a nice birthday gift. Maybe he wanted to put a down payment on a car.'

'Because I know everyone he would have called to get the stuff, Absalom. And I asked them, believe me. They were as surprised as anyone else. *Somebody* would have known. And there wasn't a whisper.'

She nodded. 'Anything else I should know about him?'

'Nothing. He's forgotten already. Nobody gives a damn . . .'

He looked at her, his wide-set brown eyes considering.

'I care,' she said, and meant it.

'I'm going to choose to believe you. But you working for the police . . .'

He looked down at the scuffed hardwood floor, a patch of light glimmering on his bald pate, and shook his head slowly.

His eyes came back to hers. 'It gives me pause, Absalom.'

'For them or for me?'

'For you, child. But I'm happy to see you. You know what I mean. It's good to see you like this.'

He spread his hands out toward her, as if she were some kind of homecoming queen or the favorite candidate for mayor.

Abbie suddenly felt close to tears. She nodded and looked down quickly, pretending to study her notes. So many of the Reverend's 'projects' came back to him pregnant, addicted, or homeless. She guessed she qualified as a success story, and that's what the Reverend lived for: the rare girl or boy who returned employed and bright-eyed. She couldn't let him down.

I wish I could tell you how lost I feel, she thought. *I wish I could tell you I found my place in the world, but I can't.*

'It's good to see you again, Reverend.' They stood up and he gave her a hug that was fiercer than she anticipated.

'I'm proud of you, Absalom.'

Leaving, Abbie turned so that he wouldn't see her face.

When she got home, her father was in his room with his door closed. She did a load of whites in the washer and dryer in the basement laundry room, and tried to read a novel that the owner at the Talking Leaves bookstore down the street had recommended highly. But her mind kept drifting and, after she'd added the fabric softener, she put the book down and sat Indian-style on top of the dryer and let herself concentrate on the two thoughts that kept edging into her brain.

Gerald Decatur was not back into dealing drugs.

And: The Reverend was worried about her working for the Buffalo PD.

Two thoughts that troubled her equally.

ELEVEN

When the phone rang the next morning during breakfast, she snapped it up.

'It's Mills. Niagara Falls PD. You called?'

'I did. Can I tell you that your partner is an unprofessional asshole?'

'You could but I'd have to tell you that I already knew that. What'd he do?'

'Refused to put me in touch with you. Called me a Buffalo bitch, actually.'

Mills sighed on the other end of the line.

'I'll call him on it but don't expect an apology.'

'What I expect is basic professional competence.'

'Yeah, okay. What were you calling about?'

'I found something at the motel.'

'Yeah? What?'

'A plastic toy, a monkey. The same kind as one that was hung around my doorknob two days ago. And, between you and me, the same as was found in our Jimmy Ryan murder.'

She heard what sounded like the feet of a chair hit a hardwood floor.

'Say that again?'

'After I started investigating the Jimmy Ryan case, someone came by my apartment, tried the doorknob, then left a calling card. A brown plastic monkey. The same as was found forcibly inserted into Ryan's mouth. I found a near-identical one at the Lucky Clover.'

'*Where* at the Lucky Clover?'

'Taped to the underside of the chair.'

'The desk chair?'

'There was only one chair in the entire room, Mills.'

Silence.

'That's impossible.'

'Impossible? How can you say—'

'I checked the chair, Kearney. It was flipped over when I entered the hotel room. I remember staring directly at the bottom of the seat when I walked in.'

Abbie froze.

'I'm coming up there,' she said.

'Bring the monkey.'

When she got to Niagara Falls PD, Mills came out to meet her. He was slim, wearing a nicely cut blue suit, was a hair taller than her, with light brown hair, penetrating green eyes, and a nose that looked like it had been broken on several occasions. He wasn't exactly handsome, but he looked like someone you hoped pulled over when you were stuck on the side of the road with a flat tire. He stopped when he saw her.

'Kearney?'

'Yes?'

'I, uh . . .'

She lowered her head as he stuttered, his eyes growing wider.

'Not what you were expecting?'

'Buffalo cops named Kearney usually look like they're on their third heart bypass. Even the female ones.'

'Glad I could surprise you.'

He nodded, seemingly lost for words.

'Let's go,' he finally got out.

'Where to?'

'Tim Hortons.'

They got into Mills's Chevy Impala and drove for five minutes before pulling into the parking lot of the doughnut shop. Inside, Mills ordered coffee and a French cruller, Abbie just hot chocolate. The place was emptying out after the morning rush, and they grabbed a table by one of the plate glass windows that looked out on Ontario Avenue.

'Did you bring it?'

Abbie pulled the baggie out of her pocket and laid it on the table. Mills took a sip of his coffee, winced.

'Why do they keep coffee at two hundred degrees in this place?'

Abbie pushed the baggie closer to him. 'You're sure you couldn't have missed it?'

'No way. The underside of that chair is a light tan color, right?'

Abbie nodded.

'It would have stood out. I'd have been staring right at it.'

'Who else was in that room?'

'The tech, Johnson. He's been with us two years, solid record, no reason to suspect him but I'll see what I can find out. My partner—' He made a face. 'Who I read the riot act to about one hour ago.'

Abbie smiled.

'Least I could do,' Mills said. 'As far as the crime scene, that's about it. The motel owner came by but we kept him out of the room until we'd cleared the scene. He was too cheap to hire one of those crime scene cleanup outfits.'

Abbie blew thoughtfully on her hot chocolate.

'Could the killer really have come back to leave the toy? And why?'

'Who knows? But if I were you, I'd put an extra deadbolt on your door.'

She nodded. 'I did that this morning.' She'd gone to the local hardware store, bought a solid York that weighed about eight pounds and installed it herself.

Mills frowned and looked over her shoulder. 'Let's assume that Decatur was his first. He kills him, *doesn't* leave his signature, then moves on to Jimmy Ryan. Leaves the toy on the victim. Then he tracks you to your apartment, leaves a memento, then doubles back and places one at the Lucky Clover. It's bizarre.'

Abbie looked at him. 'He wants the cases connected.'

'Or he's focused in on you for some reason. He's leading you along.'

Their eyes met.

'What about checking cameras on the street outside where Ryan was found? Maybe he was lurking outside, saw you go in, got excited that such a—'

'A what?'

'A hot-looking detective had been assigned to his case.'

Mills smiled crookedly, a little abashed. Abbie gave him a dubious look. He was cute, but she had no time for a boyfriend at the moment.

'I checked the tapes. Nobody stood out. All locals. And besides, my name was on the newswire five minutes after I got there.'

'The newswire?'

'That's what we call the gossip mill in the County. It's world class.'

Mills shook his head. 'I hate those police geeks. If you want to talk to a cop, don't murder someone to get our attention, y'know?'

Abbie nodded. 'He may not have been watching me at the church. But we do know he was back in that motel room. He couldn't have been stupid enough to rent the room, but he got in there somehow. Video?'

Mills took a long pull on his coffee, then set it down. 'Let's go.'

Ten minutes later they were in the motel's back office.

The Lucky Clover owner had repaired the camera that looked down the long part of the L-shaped motel. Abbie told the desk clerk to start with Wednesday afternoon, after she'd been seen walking into St Teresa's. They ran the tape, the time signature in the corner flicking by so fast you could hardly read it.

Business at the Lucky Clover was clearly slow. The camera looked down a row of six doors, with a corner of the parking lot visible in the upper right of the picture and a portion of the side street next to the motel. Occasionally the lower half of a passing car flashed by, but there were no pedestrians walking this part of Niagara Falls. Number 16 was second from the end, but there were so few human figures in the videos that mostly what they watched was the light grow and fade until dark descended and the fluorescents in the canopy flickered on. It was like some kind of art film on desolation, Abbie thought.

They were on to Thursday night when Abbie saw it.

'Stop,' she said.

The clerk hit the mouse and the tape slowed.

'Go back.'

He rewound and a human figure flicked into the screen in backward motion, disappearing into number 16.

'Now run it.'

The clerk hit Play and the tape showed an empty row. Then a figure slid into the frame, hugging the wall of the motel. He had on jeans, white sneakers, and a green-and-black-checked jacket. He wore black gloves and on his face was a dark ski mask.

'Smart,' Mills said.

'He knew we'd be watching.'

The man turned to face the door on number 16 and squeezed up against it, like he was inserting a key.

'He's slipping a credit card or something into the door crack,' Mills said.

'How good are the locks in this hotel?' Abbie asked the clerk.

'Are you kidding me? The owner barely pays for soap, you think he's going to shell out for a good lock? A retard could get in there.'

Abbie marked the time he entered: 8:42 p.m. The door closed and the seconds swept by on the clock in the corner of the screen.

Two minutes thirteen seconds later he was out. He closed the door behind him, with his back to the camera.

'Not a big guy,' Mills said.

'I'd say about five foot nine. And he's right-handed.'

The killer stood in the flicker of the fluorescent lights, hands by his side, his back to the camera. Abbie brought her face closer to the screen.

'What's he doing?'

The suspect began to turn, almost robot-like, until he was facing toward the office and the camera mounted in the ceiling at the corner of the L.

'See how he's moving?' Mills said. 'He looks drugged. Downers?'

Suddenly, the killer lifted his head until he was staring straight into the camera. The steam from the killer's breath funneled out from the hole in the ski mask. The man stood there, arms straight down by his side. He seemed to be leaning toward the camera. Then he raised his right arm and gave a little wave.

Abbie stood up suddenly. A chill had run from her feet up through her spine like a stiletto of ice. She folded her arms over her chest to stop it before her body shook.

Something had spooked her, something almost familiar in the way the killer moved. *Do I know him? Was he at the Ryan scene or am I imagining things?*

When she looked away from the screen, she found Mills staring at her. 'Run it again,' he said to the clerk, never taking his eyes off Abbie.

They watched the tape three more times, always pausing on the killer staring at the camera, seemingly hypnotized.

'It's like he's trying to send you a message, like he knows you,' the clerk said, looking up at Abbie.

'Thanks for the analysis,' Abbie said.

Mills followed her out of the office.

'Where are you going now?' he asked her in the parking lot of Niagara PD, where her Saab sat waiting under a light coat of snow.

'Home.'

He nodded.

'You?'

'Couple of biker bars.'

'Oh, right, the Outlaws massacre.'

'No, I just like to hang out in biker bars. Care to join me?'

'Are you asking me out on a date, Detective Mills?'

'Call it anything you like. Just come have a beer with me.'

Abbie smiled. 'I'd only talk shop and bore you half to death.'

'It's you or my asshole partner. Have a heart, Kearney.'

'Another time. You have a good night, Detective.'

She got in the car, started it up, and began to pull out of the lot. Mills came walking toward the car. She lowered the passenger window and he leaned his arms on the sill.

'I know you know this already, but you don't want this guy taking a personal interest in you.'

'I'm a big girl, Mills. But thanks.'

He looked like he wanted to say more, but only nodded and stood up.

In the rearview, she saw him watching her until she turned a corner three blocks down.

The ride home took her along the Niagara River, high now as it surged toward the Falls, powering the lights of Buffalo from the enormous power stations built into the banks farther up. This was where the daredevils and the hapless boaters who went over the Falls in barrels would first become aware of the power of the Niagara, the jetting bursts of white water erupting across it the sign of granite boulders that dotted the riverbed like teeth. Now the water's surface was only a few feet from the level of the road, and the river threw lashes of spray across her windshield as it surged past.

The windshield wipers worked back and forth as she reviewed each piece of evidence, returning obsessively to a few relevant facts. The pieces didn't fit and Abbie knew it. Jimmy Ryan and Gerald Decatur, if they were setting up some kind of drug deal, were so far out of the majors that the deal couldn't have been worth more than a few thousand dollars. Neither had the contacts or the money to shift more product than that. And what kind of a drug connect works his victims over for what is walking-around money for even a medium-sized distributor? And then comes back to leave a souvenir to taunt the lead detective?

Abbie had the feeling that she hated most as an investigator: of walking along a path, feeling that she was getting closer to the truth but slowly realizing that her trail of small clues and inferences isn't leading her to the killer, but running parallel to his path. The gnawing sense that the killer wasn't walking ahead of her, running for his life, but was actually right beside her, just over her shoulder, watching, confident of outwitting her.

Maybe the County has intimidated me without knowing it, she thought. *Maybe I'm being too* nice. *I'm respecting the old neighborhood too much. I've been approaching this case like I owe the County something.*

'I don't owe it a goddamn thing,' she thought, then realized she'd muttered the words into the humming silence of the car.

Someone had carved up two human beings, and the source of that rage lay within the two-mile-square radius of the County. She was sure of it. But the residents had been strangely silent. Where were the phone calls demanding progress on the case? Patty Ryan refused to answer her calls. Where were the other cops hanging by her desk, asking for tidbits they could feed the grieving widow?

'Patty, they have someone they like. Just be patient.'

Or:

'Patty, I spoke to Kearney and this one is going to be solved. I can't say anything more, but trust me.'

No one had called, no one had come by. The County had buried Jimmy Ryan in some corner of its ancient memory, in an unmarked plot, or a plot known only to a select few, and Abbie didn't even know why.

And where did the Gaelic Club fit? The little murder wave could have its roots in the back-room stuff that Billy Carney had gotten a glimpse of. But they could have been cooking up anything: political deals, corrupt business schemes, new drug routes. Untangling the lines would be like cutting wires on a bomb. You never knew which one would blow the whole County wide open.

She checked the speedometer – 92 mph – and eased her foot off the pedal. The black, light-spangled arch of the Peace Bridge passed by on her right, the steel struts black against a gray-black sky. She pushed the button for the passenger window and let some of the water-choked air that swept across the river blow through the car. The spray – beaten to a near-mist by the rocks and the surge of the river – woke her up. Abbie breathed in a gulp of the cold northern air and then hit the button again. Soon she was sealed tight in the car as it headed south, listening to Depeche Mode sing about love and silence.

TWELVE

The next morning, as Abbie walked into Robbery-Homicide, Perelli looked at her from under his thick black eyebrows like she'd stolen his kids' lunch money.

'You have anything you want to tell me?' he said.

'I left you a report on the Decatur case. There's a connection.'

'Drugs?'

'We don't know yet. I'm not ready to call it a drug deal yet.'

'Well, get ready to call it something. It sounds like the killer is practically begging you to catch him. These guys in the County aren't international arms dealers with Lear jets and three passports. They have limited means, limited connections. They've barely been out of Buffalo their whole lives. The list of suspects has got to be a short one.'

Abbie took a deep breath, clenched her right hand and released it. 'I know that. When I have the guy, you'll be the first to know. Okay?'

He looked at her, his lips pursed. 'I'd better be.'

As she walked to her cubicle, she could feel Z examining her from behind.

'You look exhausted,' he said. 'Did you sleep?'

'I slept fine.'

'I hate it when you lie to me. Hurts my feelings.'

'Then don't ask stupid questions.'

'Listen, Linda wants you to come over for dinner. The kids miss you.'

Abbie felt herself soften a bit.

'How are they? Is Junior walking?'

'No, but he's eating. I think he's going to roll before he walks.'

'He is the cutest.'

'Come by and see. Tomorrow night. Pasta and Molson Golden ale.'

'Tell Linda thanks. But I just don't have time right now.'

She felt the needles in the back of her brain, like a series of wires had broken and the ends were sticking into her nerves.

Abbie parked near her house and walked down Elmwood Avenue toward her favorite taco spot. The street was dotted with old Victorians, and twenty years ago as part of an urban revitalization project they'd been painted in wild, bold colors: lavender and hunter green, pistachio and lime. Just walking down the street made you feel like you'd entered a fairy tale, though some of the paint was now peeling around the corners and doors. A few of the Victorians had been turned into boardinghouses by owners unable to meet the mortgage payments; one had even become a halfway house for heroin addicts. That was the one with the men smoking on the porch all day long.

It was Abbie's dream to buy one of the big Victorians and bring it back to its glory, refurbishing it painstakingly by hand, putting down the new polyurethane herself, choosing the new and unfashionable wallpaper, scouring church sales and yard sales for the right dining room table. Every time she walked down Elmwood, she would debate what was her current favorite, what she would buy if a few hundred thousand dollars fell into her lap. Right now it was 182, a rambling gray and white beautiful monstrosity with a widow's walk and two tall spires that were topped in black tiles that made them look like pine cones.

She stopped in front of the house, feeling the late afternoon sunshine across her face, and imagined herself two years from now, in spring, painting the porch with old overalls on, waving to her neighbors and complaining about the weather. She felt a little stab of happiness for the first time in weeks.

At Mighty Taco, she ordered a taco salad and a loganberry drink – a local specialty – and sat in one of the booths close to the window that looked out on Elmwood. Something about the plastic monkeys had been bothering her, lurking in the back of her thoughts but refusing to be nailed down. She stared out the window, trying to coax the thought from the back of her brain. She let her eyes unfocus. The edges of the passing cars and the steel-and-glass lawyer's office across the street blurred, and Abbie listened to her own breathing, in and out, in and out.

Without trying to, she realized she'd remembered what had bothered her about the monkeys. The paint – and it was paint, not a dye in the plastic itself – of the eyes and the red collar around the monkeys' necks was worn down, even chipped. These toys were old, heavily used. The killer hadn't gone out and bought a new set to leave behind. Assuming they belonged to the killer, he must have saved them for years. Why?

How many people save their favorite toys, she thought, *and what does it mean if they do? Souvenirs of a happy childhood, or mementos of a howling nightmare, the beginning of his urges to kill? I have to track down the manufacturer,* she thought. *Find out when these things were last produced. Maybe that can give us a maximum age for the suspect. Assuming his parents bought them for him new.*

She was finishing the last bite of the taco salad when her phone rang.

'Kearney.'

'Who were you talking to?'

'Who is this?'

'It's Billy fucking Carney.'

The flesh between her eyebrows creased. Billy sounded wide open.

'I didn't talk to anyone. What happened?'

'I've been getting phone calls. Someone whispering and then laughing this evil little laugh.'

'How many times?'

'Shit, I don't know. Four or five. Always at night. I hung up once and a second later my cell phone rang, same bullshit.'

Abbie told herself to think. Had she mentioned Billy to anyone? No, she hadn't.

'And there's a car I've seen around my house three times since you dropped by. Next time I see it I'm gonna put a brick through its window.'

'Slow down, Billy. I need details. What kind of car?'

'Like you don't know, Ab.'

'Billy, Billy, listen to me. What . . . kind . . . of . . . car?'

'A Taurus. A fucking green Taurus.' .

Abbie grabbed her jacket and slipped into it as she walked, fast, toward her Saab.

'Okay. Tell me where you are. I need to talk to you if you want me to help you.'

'I'm on top of City Hall with a fucking sniper rifle, okay? Aiming at police headquarters. Tell that to the fucks who've been tailing me. Or are they listening in right now?'

Abbie got to her car, slipped into the driver's seat, and started it up.

'Tell me where you are, Billy. You need to talk to me.'

'Why?'

'Because I want to help you, and if there was anyone else who could, you'd have called them already.'

Silence. She could hear traffic in the background. He was out in the open somewhere.

'Tell me now, where—'

'I'm in the Bowl.'

'In the what?'

'The Bowl, the baseball diamonds, Caz Park. Remember? Where I won the state title, Ab. Jesus Christ, doesn't anybody remember anything about my fucking life?'

Abbie began to drive down Elmwood.

'Okay, I'm coming. Just stay there until I come. Don't go *anywhere*, you hear me?'

The line went dead.

THIRTEEN

The Bowl was a sunken circle in the middle of Cazenovia Park, between Seneca and Abbott Roads, where three baseball diamonds faced toward the center, one diamond tucked into each corner. The park itself was a huge, wild tangle of creeks, running trails, secret haunts for Abbott Road kids desperate to escape the eyes of their parents.

When she got to the Bowl, she couldn't see Billy. Plows had piled up mounds of snow and ice, scraped off the streets and dumped on the lip of the circle. And the dusk was coming down fast, sharp shadows stretching out across the snow from the line of trees that ringed the park, the light beginning to turn blue-black.

But once she walked around them, she saw Billy. He was slumped on one of the bleachers, back to her, humped over, his arms folded across his knees and his head lying on his arms.

'Billy,' she called.

No movement. There was no steam from his breath rising above. The air in the Bowl was strangely motionless, the breeze passing above the sunken circle.

'Billy!' she called, snapping back the edge of her jacket and pulling out her Glock. She swept the perimeter of the Bowl. But there was nothing, just an unbroken crust of white snow and shadows coming on fast.

She dropped down the incline into the Bowl and began running. Billy still hadn't moved. When she was ten feet away, he turned his head.

'Christ, Billy,' she said, exhaling a cloud of steam into the cold air.

He nodded but said nothing.

97

Abbie climbed up on the cold plastic bleachers and sat next to him, holstering her gun before he could see it. Billy looked terrible. His hair was greasy and frozen into place. He looked like he'd slept in his jeans and the tan Carhartt jacket he was wearing. His boots were unlaced.

'I still have the trophy,' he said.

'The tro—? Oh.' Her brown eyes softened. 'State championship.'

'Yep. I pitched a three-hitter. That must have been the game that got me all the scholarship offers.'

Abbie frowned sympathetically.

'Oh, yeah, I forgot,' Billy said. 'I didn't get any of those.'

'Bad grades.'

'Yep.' He looked out onto the field, the pitcher's mound a hump under the snow, and nodded.

'Tell me about the phone calls,' she said.

'Just breathing, like I said. In the background, I could hear music playing and once I thought I recognized the song. And then, the last one, a voice said, "Shut your mouth, Carney."'

'Did you say anything?'

'I said, "Tell me who you are and I'll shut yours, permanently."'

He turned to look at her.

'Nice, right?'

It was good to see he had recovered some of his fighting spirit. The Billy on the phone had sounded pretty far gone, a paranoid wreck. Then she saw the bottle of Molson Golden in his hands and realized that he'd been drinking to keep down the jitters.

'I'm going to have someone check your cell phone records. I'm guessing a name didn't come up?'

He shook his head, took a sip from the Molson. Then he turned to her, and his face was ashen.

'Why'd you turn me in, Ab?'

'I didn't turn you in, Billy. This has nothing to do with the feds or the Rez or anything like that.'

'Sure it doesn't.'

'Billy, look at me.'

He stared off at the row of trees, their trunks going from dark green to black as dusk settled over the Bowl.

'*Look* at me, Billy.'

He turned.

'If there are people watching you, it's because of what you told me in the Gaelic Club the other day.'

Billy's forehead creased and his eyes opened wide. He crouched over and his face came close to Abbie's. His breath was sharp with alcohol and Abbie turned away.

'That shit about Jimmy Ryan?'

She nodded. 'Yes. But it's more than just Ryan now. We found another body and it's the same killer.'

'Who?'

'Gerald Decatur.'

'Never heard of him.'

'It's the same killer. Believe me, okay?'

Billy's eyes wobbled. 'It couldn't be,' he said.

Coiled and tense, he began to look around the wide circle, at the mounds of snow enclosing them.

'What else do you know, Billy?'

'What?!' he said, stopping his scan of the horizon long enough to stare at her. 'Like I haven't told you enough already!'

'There's no one else here. I did a circuit around the Bowl before I came down and found you.'

He looked at her, and nodded. 'That's good. That's good. But they have all kinds of surveillance equipment. They can trace you by . . . what are those things called, up in the sky?'

'This isn't about satellites! Or men in trench coats or black heli-copters or whatever else you have in your brain right now.'

'Yes, it is.'

It was growing colder as the sun sank behind the trees. Abbie shifted to look him straight in the eye.

'Whoever killed Jimmy Ryan and whoever is tracking you is prob-ably someone you went to high school with. They grew up right here in the County. They've been to the bar, they've bought you drinks, they know the nickname you got when you were eight. And that's how they're going to get to you, Jimmy. Because you think they're your friends.'

He shook his head and took a long pull on the bottle.

'It's impossible, Ab.'

'If you want them to stop tailing you, tell me what you know about what happened in that back room at the Gaelic Club.'

Billy's head dropped into his lap and he was still for a moment.

'If this really is about them—'

He stopped and stared at Abbie. His eyes looked exhausted, sick.

'About who?' said Abbie.

Billy closed his eyes.

'The Clan.'

'The *Klan*?'

He smiled for the first time, but his eyes looked spooked when he opened them.

'Not the one you're thinking of,' he said quietly.

'You're telling me there's another one?'

'I gotta go, Ab,' he said.

Abbie grabbed his arm. 'Don't make me shoot you, Billy.'

He looked at her bare hand, small against the rough sleeve of his XXL Carhartt, then into her eyes. Then, gently, he pulled her hand away.

The sun had gone down and the shadows were creeping out from the treeline. Billy shivered, and then slid down to the ground, his boots making a loud noise as they broke through the crust of ice.

'Billy?'

He turned to look at her. His face, she thought, had gone from fearful and defiant to haunted.

'I have somewhere I can take you.'

He smiled thinly. 'No, you don't, Ab. There's nowhere you can take me. You should know that.'

'Just get in my car and I'll make sure you're safe.'

He turned and began to walk away. He stuck his hands in the Carhartt jacket and leaned forward as he climbed the incline back to the street.

'What is the Clan, Billy?'

The wind caught his hair and blew it back straight. He didn't turn back.

'Goddamn it all to hell,' Abbie said, pounding the bleacher. The hollow sound echoed dully through the Bowl.

FOURTEEN

Abbie woke in the Saab, parked outside of 124 Dorrance Lane. It was the last registered address of Billy Carney, but he hadn't shown all night. She checked her watch: 8:43 a.m. The last time she'd checked it had been 7:30 a.m. There was a chance Billy could have slipped by her in the past hour, but if so, he was now safely sprawled on his bed, breathing toxic alcohol fumes into his bedroom air.

She tried to stretch in the cramped car. Her back felt like it was made of Legos, put together by a careless child. Her fingers and toes were cold, along with the tip of her nose.

The first thought that came to her was the Clan. Just what was it and what did Billy mean by saying there was no running from it? The likelihood of anyone in the County telling her was next to zero. She needed an authority of some sort, an expert on the County's secret clubs and associations, the ones that had been brought over from the old country and given new blood. And there was only one place for that that was not connected to the neighborhood itself: the Buffalo and Erie County Historical Society.

Abbie started up the Saab, made a left on Abbott, stopped at a Tim Hortons for hot chocolate and a cinnamon roll, and then began the twenty-minute drive to downtown.

The Society was nestled on the edge of Delaware Park, a much nicer one than scraggly Cazenovia, kept well groomed by city taxes and the donations of the old-money families who lived around its edge. It was housed in a big marble building that looked like a Greek temple and backed onto a small lake where birdcalls echoed in summer. Abbie had been there half a dozen times during her school years, for the obligatory class outings. There was the Historical

Society, the Albright-Knox Art Gallery, the fort that gave Fort Erie its name, and that was about it. When they visited the Historical Society, her classmates had snuck out to the lake to smoke or to meet the boys from the other schools scheduled for the same day, but Abbie would wander through its dark, chilly halls looking at each exhibit, even reading the little plaques beneath the Indian handicrafts and the pictures of cholera victims. Something drew her to it. Perhaps, not having a past herself, she was fascinated by the city's rich and largely forgotten history.

Abbie parked in the empty parking lot. A custodian was just opening the door.

'Good morning.'

He nodded, placed a sign that said 'Adults $8, Children $4' next to the door, and pointed toward the desk.

'Do you have some kind of library here, an archives?' Abbie asked.

'That'd be in back. First left.'

'Who's in charge of it?'

'Dr Reinholdt. He's back there, saw him come in.'

'Can you tell me what he looks like?'

The custodian looked at Abbie strangely. 'Ma'am, he's the only one back there. Look for a short, round, miserable old man with glasses. He'll probably be hiding in the book stacks. He doesn't like people too much.'

Abbie nodded, made the first left, and followed a dark, narrow passageway toward the back of the building. On each side of her were pictures carved into the gleaming wood: old white men, beavers chewing on wood, factories pumping smoke, the story of Erie County in pictograms.

When she got to the library, the room was dark. She pushed open the glass doors. There were tall stacks of very old books, sorted onto oak shelves that reached up to the ceiling, with three long tables between them, six chairs tucked under each. It smelled of old parchment and glue.

'Dr Reinholdt?' she said.

The books seemed to absorb the sound of her voice.

'Dr Reinholdt?'

She walked to the wall next to the glass door and found the light switch. She snapped it on.

Something stirred behind the shelves in the far corner.

'Who did that? Martin, you troll, I told you . . .'

Abbie walked toward the voice. When she turned the corner of the shelves, she found a bald man with squarish plastic-rimmed glasses and piercingly intelligent eyes, wearing a slightly dingy short-sleeve dress shirt and suspenders, seated behind a desk.

'Dr Reinholdt?'

He smiled. 'Why, yes.'

'I'm Detective Kearney with Buffalo PD.' She showed him her badge and ID. 'I need to ask you some questions.'

'If it's about the custodian, I haven't killed him yet. Try me again in a month or two.'

'It's not.'

He studied her, his owl eyes blinking awkwardly.

'Sit down, sit down,' he said suddenly, as if he'd just realized she was actually alive and not a mannequin to be ogled.

The only chair in front of the desk was stacked with what looked like old city directories. Reinholdt snorted in irritation and came around the desk, revealing a pair of brown polyester pants that ended two inches above his shiny black shoes, and a pair of argyle socks. He pulled the books off and dropped them to the floor next to the chair. Abbie slid into it.

'I need to know about an organization, possibly a secret one, in South Buffalo. It's called the Clan.'

'The Klan?'

'Not the Ku Klux Klan. Apparently, there's another one. And it has something to do with the Gaelic Club.'

'How interesting,' Reinholdt said, picking up a yellow-paged book that had been open on his desk and turning with a grunt to place it on the floor behind him. 'All I really get back here is high school students wanting me to write their reports on "Daredevils Who Survived the Falls" or some such nonsense. Moon-faced Mongolians.

But a question about the ancient Clan na Gael from a very pretty detective?'

Abbie gave him a businesslike smile and pulled out her notebook.

'The Clan . . . excuse me?'

'Clan na Gael. A fascinating organization.'

'How do you spell that?'

'Clan with a "C." N-a. New word, G-a-e-l. It means "Family of the Gaels."'

'Was it active here in Buffalo? I've never heard of it.'

'Very few have.'

'Can you tell me what it is exactly?'

'Well, the appropriate phrase is "what it *was*." The Clan today is a shadow of its former self. But in its heyday, it was filled with bomb throwers and wild-eyed radicals. Revolutionaries really. And Buffalo was one of their strongholds. Very much like the Ancient Order of Hibernians but . . .'

Abbie gave him a look.

'Sorry. Your Irish surname threw me; a Kearney of the old stock would know. The Ancient Order is a bunch of grizzled old men who get together, wave their shillelaghs – you do know what *those* are, right?'

She nodded. 'My father had one.'

He looked at her curiously, then continued. 'And tell stories about the rebels and the Wren Boys. Never mind, they're not important either. Then the members drink some whiskey, weep about the time they left their poor mothers back on the cow farm, and go home to fall asleep in their La-Z-Boys.'

'I see. And the Clan?'

'Much more . . . hardcore, as they would say now. Back in the late 1800s and early 1900s, they were the true believers, the "action men" as they were known. Irish immigrants who'd come to America to build the railroads or the Erie Canal paid part of their wages to the Clan to buy guns that would be used to kill British soldiers back in their home counties. They smuggled Irish rebels who were on the Black and Tans' list – the Black and Tans were the British terror squads – into America and hid them. And then there was the money. The Irish War of Independence in the 1920s was largely funded by the Clan, out of Buffalo and a few other cities.'

Guns or IRA money, Kearney thought. It might fit.

'Let me get this straight,' Abbie said, leaning forward in her chair. 'The Clan na Gael were running guns to Ireland? How long ago?'

'Well . . .' Dr Reinholdt sat back in his chair and his perfectly round stomach rose into view above the desk. 'That's the question, isn't it?'

He smiled at Abbie. She smiled back.

'If this is an exercise in mind reading, Doctor, it's not working.'

The doctor frowned. 'What I mean to say is that here we shift from the provenance of history to . . . mere rumor.'

'I'll take the rumors,' Abbie said.

The doctor's eyes regarded her, twinkling behind his glasses.

'One moment,' he said, and he stood and disappeared into the library stacks behind him.

Abbie heard him rustling around back there. She turned to look out the window at a pair of ducks swimming across the Society's tiny lake, which for some reason had remained unfrozen. *Could Jimmy Ryan have been running guns into Canada and then on to Ireland?* she wondered. *And using Gerald Decatur to set up the connections across the Peace Bridge?*

Dr Reinholdt reappeared carrying a gray archival box. He opened the hinged lid and stuck his pudgy hand in and pulled out a small sheaf of newspaper articles.

'Here we are,' he said.

He read for a second, then nodded.

'When the twenty-six counties of Ireland won their independence in 1921, the Clan became a supporter of the IRA, who didn't accept the peace treaty. That particular organization I'm sure you're familiar with. For decades, the Irish-American community funneled money to the IRA. They bankrolled the bombs and the bullets that were directed at the British Army in Northern Ireland. They held fundraisers, protest marches for rebels imprisoned in Ulster, and did God knows what else.'

Abbie nodded. Her father had slapped a bumper sticker on the old Nova, '26 + 6 = 1.' The twenty-six counties of the Republic plus the six counties of Northern Ireland equaled one nation. In other words, England out of Ireland. When as a girl she'd gone to retrieve him from the Gaelic Club, she'd see the posters on the wall of pale faces with the words in blood red, 'Free the Belfast 8' or 'Free the Derry 10,' on and on. It had been the background noise of her childhood. She'd never taken it seriously.

Now she leaned her arm on the desk and peered at Reinholdt. 'That went on *here*, in Buffalo?'

'Yes. I mean no.'

She gave him a look. 'Doctor?'

'Not *officially*. No one was ever convicted. But there were, as I said, rumors, Detective.'

'Rumors connected with the Gaelic Club?'

'More than rumors. That's where the men were arrested. Supporting a terrorist organization was the usual charge. I was here for most of the trials. The Clan na Gael had always interested me, so I followed them quite closely. Let's just say that there was considerable evidence to convict, but the juries – always filled with McFaddens and O'Neills and Riordans – always found a technicality on which to release their fair-haired young men back into the arms of a cheering crowd.'

'And this happened as late as the eighties?'

'Yes.'

'Now, Dr Reinholdt. Can you remember whether a man named Jimmy Ryan was ever charged in these cases?'

Dr Reinholdt looked up at the ceiling, whispering the name 'Ryan' through his lips. He sat up straight, then plunged a hand into the gray box. He pulled out several articles, began to read the first one, put it on the desk, and looked at the next one. He did this three times before adjusting his glasses and beginning to read with his lips moving slightly.

'No. There was a Patrick Ryan accused in the last trial, in 1988, but no Jimmy.'

Abbie grimaced. If Jimmy had been part of the smuggling, it

would have given the investigation a motive. Which it so desperately needed.

'But, Detective, you never told me what this was all about. Why would a homicide detective – yes, I caught that on your credentials, despite how quickly you flashed them – be interested in this piece of ancient history?'

Abbie thought about it. With one phone call, Reinholdt could make the connection. Better to have an ally than an enemy.

'Jimmy Ryan was found tortured and murdered in South Buffalo five days ago.'

The smile on Dr Reinholdt's face melted away.

'You don't say?' he said softly.

Abbie watched him. 'Do you think it's possible the murder could – hypothetically, of course – be connected to what we've been talking about?'

His eyes went wide as he thought, then he turned to Abbie.

'It's possible. Yes, indeed, very possible.'

'And who would they want to kill? The British?'

'Of course. Or any informers. They have a long history of those, and a very severe policy in dealing with them.'

Abbie nodded. The thought of an internal betrayal had never occurred to her. Perhaps the killer was eliminating the impure from the ranks of the Clan.

'Thank you, Dr Reinholdt,' she said briskly. 'Now I need to tell you that this conversation is confidential. As much as I've enjoyed our talk . . .'

'Not as much as me, Detective. It's not often . . .' He was obviously going to attempt a compliment, but the effort failed and he looked at her blankly.

'Thank you. But I don't want to hear that you're going around telling your friends about Ryan and the Clan.'

'I have no friends,' he said, spreading his hands wide. 'The position is open.'

Abbie nodded.

'Where are you parked?'

'Out back in the lot.'

'Let me walk you out. There's something I want to show you.'

Reinholdt got up and led the way back not through the glass doors but through an aisle cut through the tall stacks of books behind his desk. She followed. As he neared a green wooden door set into the back wall, he reached for a chain snapped to his belt and produced a bright silver-colored key, which he inserted. He held the door open for her.

'After you, my dear.'

The door opened onto a set of dimly lit stairs that led down. Abbie gave Reinholdt a look and then started down. He followed her through, then closed the door with a bang. She heard him lock it as she felt her way down the darkened stairs. Abbie was wearing her riding boots again, and the heel clicked on the metal stairs.

'Straight ahead,' he said, breathing heavily over her right shoulder.

When they reached the basement floor, Reinholdt hit a switch and hidden ceiling lights glowed yellow. Abbie looked around and knew immediately where she was. *Of course,* she thought, *the dioramas.*

On those high school field trips, the dioramas had been her favorite exhibits. They were exiled to the basement, but they'd always fascinated her and now she saw them again as she and Reinholdt walked slowly along the passageway. Here was the one showing the Seneca Indians who'd lived in Buffalo before the white men came, a young mother with severe cheekbones and a thick black hank of hair falling over her buckskin robe carrying a sleeping baby in some kind of papoose as she sat grinding corn. Here was the frontiersman in a coonskin cap sinking down on one knee as he sighted a bear (painted, awkwardly, on the wall to his left), his rifle gleaming with silver and polished wood.

'You've seen these before?'

'Of course,' Abbie said. 'We came here when I was at Mount Mercy.'

'Ah, if I'd only spied you then from my little perch.'

At the end of the row, Abbie saw a man rearing back, his body caught in furious recoil. She came around the front of the diorama and stopped.

'I remember this one.'

It was the only moment in Buffalo history that had made the city world-famous: the assassination of William McKinley by some kind of crazy anarchist. That diorama, encased behind thick glass, had always horrified Abbie as she stared at it in her tartan skirt, knee-high blue socks, and white blouse. McKinley, his face pale with fright, was shown in the instant before he was shot. The assassin, his neck muscles straining with the tension, had the gun wrapped up in a huge bandage that covered his right arm, which was leveled directly at the president's chest. The gun had not yet gone off.

'The curse of McKinley,' Abbie said.

'Do you really believe that?'

'No. Do you?'

'Of course not. This city has been doomed by geography and its business class. Not by old William McKinley.'

He pointed to a hall to her right. 'This is what I wanted to show you.'

Reinholdt led the way to a hallway where swirls of dust were visible on the hardwood floor. Two metal poles at either side and a thin gold chain spanned the passageway. Reinholdt unhooked it and let it fall. The sound echoed like a fistful of nails thrown to the floor.

Ten steps into the dim hallway and they were standing in front of a black-curtained exhibit.

'We were forced to cover this one up,' Reinholdt said. 'Local sensitivities. But I thought you'd like to see it. More killing, I'm afraid.'

Reinholdt pulled back the curtains and switched on a light. An amber glow lit up three figures, obviously from the nineteenth century. All were soldiers. Two dark-haired men stood in defensive crouches, one on his knee, aiming their rifles at a figure who was approaching from the right.

'The Fenian Raids. Have you heard of them?'

Abbie shook her head no as she walked slowly around to see the face of the other figure, dressed in a mismatched blue uniform, the pants darker than the tight-fitting jacket, the man's shoulders tensed and his rifle held out from his shoulder like a spear.

'Eighteen sixty-six. Some Irish-born veterans of the American Civil War decided that they would attack the only Brits they could find, up in Canada. They called themselves the Irish Republican Army, the IRA – the first use of the term in the world, invented right here in western New York, believe it or not. They marched north from Buffalo to invade Canada and attacked ferociously. Scores died.'

Abbie leaned against the cool glass where it met the wood and looked at the face of the Irish fighter. He had a streak of blood across his right cheek and his lips were curled into a snarl. But it was the eyes that drew your gaze as if they were magnetized; the crystal blue irises drawing in the light from the yellow bulbs deep into their sockets and charging them with some kind of lunatic energy. The man looked as if he were in a trance.

'The locals objected to the depiction of the Fenian man. This hasn't been seen for fifty years.'

'He looks . . . possessed.'

'Yes. I wonder if the artist had some Anglo-Saxon blood.'

'Why did you show this to me, Doctor?'

His yellow teeth caught the light as he smiled. 'If you really are dealing with the remnants of the Clan, if they are still active, they would represent the most fanatical members of an already, let us say, *devoted* organization. They are the holdouts, the Japanese soldier in the caves fifty years after the war is done. This is who you can expect to meet . . .'

He nodded toward the fanatic while keeping his eyes on her.

'The Clan would be very capable of killing whoever had strayed from the true path. In fact, they'd enjoy it. For them, you see, the war really isn't over.'

Abbie turned to look at him. He sat there, toadlike, staring at her. She thanked him quickly and left by the basement door.

FIFTEEN

The air that lay over the snow in Cazenovia Park was so crisp it seemed to have individual layers of cold, like layers of rock in an exposed hillside; it got colder the deeper one dropped. Marty Collins could feel the air get more frigid as the road dipped into a little valley. But his lungs were used to the punishment. He ran this route through the park every day at 1 p.m. before returning home to shower and dress for the second half of his day at the law operation known as Collins & Sons.

He pounded round the curve of the park road, the gray light from the overcast sky barely making it down through the trees. The road echoed to the footsteps of his New Balance sneakers, answered only by crows in the distance. The park was black, empty.

The huge oak with the enormous limbs hanging down – a victim of some forgotten ice storm – marked the end of Mile 3. His lungs were burning, but he wouldn't slow down. This was the only time in his day, besides his solitary breakfast, that he really got to think about where his life was going. And he was thinking about Collins & Sons, specifically that there were no sons anymore. He'd lost Marty Jr. to crystal meth eight years ago that coming February – lost him three years before that, honestly, but the coroner had made it official eight years ago. And Bobby, his youngest, had faded away after his brother's death. Marty suspected he was into something else, not meth, but something slower. Bobby walked around the house like he was haunting it. It might be good to find out what could be causing his pallid skin and his listless behavior, but Marty Collins didn't have the heart to do the research. He'd tried to reach Bobby, taken him on fishing vacations up to East Lake in Canada, tried the man-to-man talks when Bobby stumbled in at 3 a.m., but he wasn't sure the boy had even registered what he was saying. His eyes were usually empty, and when they weren't empty they were hard.

Marty Collins coughed and spit onto the frozen tarmac, then increased his pace. Nothing in the Marine Corps, nothing in the service of the Clan na Gael, nothing in life had prepared him for the loss of his sons. He'd taken up running five years ago to give himself a reason to get up in the morning, and it had saved his life.

He saw a car approach, its headlights on in the gloomy light, weaving across the park road on the higher ground across the creek, maybe a quarter of a mile away. The road was slippery with ice. He moved off onto the border, felt the cobblestone gutter under his feet, and then the softer ground that in summer was covered with grass. The car came closer, and the headlights swept by, blinding him temporarily. Then it was gone, its tires making the sound of hot oil in a skillet on the wet road, and the park returned to shades of black.

Maybe I'll take Bobby out on the runs with me, he said to himself. *We can talk about what he'd like to do, whether he wants to try college again and maybe law school after that.* Marty had built the law firm for his boys. Maybe he'd pushed Marty Jr. too much to follow in his footsteps – he'd always been a terrible student. It came hard to him, English especially. But Marty had pushed him because his father had done the same, and because of his father's toughness on him he'd built a big house on Potters Road and drove a new Cadillac every three years. In Buffalo, in the County, that made him a king.

Marty Jr. had broken under his pressure like a rotten plank of wood. Only Bobby remained. And his wife.

Which meant only Bobby remained. That bitch was back in East Aurora with her sister, waiting for him to call her. She'd have a long wait.

His legs began to cramp, and he smiled at the pain. He'd always had a high threshold for it, his first girlfriends amazed that he could hold a lighter under his overturned palm for ten, fifteen, twenty seconds. You could actually hear the flesh begin to sizzle before the girl would cry out and pull the lighter away. *Why isn't that kind of toughness genetic?* he wondered. *Why wasn't it passed down to my sons as it was to me, allowing me to stand my father's completely random and indiscriminate beatings?*

Mile 4 approaching.

He heard another car come up from behind him and again he moved off the road, his sneakers sending clouds of snow as they struck firmly into the ground. The car came closer and he looked idly over his shoulder to see if he might know the driver. But the headlights never made the turn and suddenly the engine revved higher. Before he could jump aside, the car smashed into him and he felt his right thigh snap like a dry branch and pain unlike anything he'd ever felt arc up through his groin.

He blacked out before he heard the animal sound leave his throat.

Abbie drove slowly down Seneca, feeling worn out. Her brain was muggy, fogged up. What was she even doing out here? Billy Carney was the only one in the County who would talk to her, and he'd disappeared. Or been disappeared. She glanced at herself in the rearview mirror and started at the sight. The flesh beneath her eyes look bruised, her hair was a wild mess, and she looked exhausted, the eyes drained from within. The sinews and joints and the deep muscles ached when she turned her arms or adjusted herself in the driver's seat. She needed a massage in the worst way. It was time to visit the Koreans over on Genesee Street, the hard-handed women with the peasant faces who beat the kinks out of her muscles and put her into a deep, sweet sleep.

Her phone buzzed in her pocket. Abbie grimaced and gingerly pulled out it with two fingertips.

'Kearney,' she said.

'It's Billy.'

She pulled to the side of the road.

'Are you okay? I was out front of your house but you never came back.'

'I know.'

His voice sounded dead.

'You do?' Abbie put the Saab in park and left the car running, concentrating on Billy. 'How did you know I was waiting for you?'

'Listen, I called to tell you that everything is okay. The phone calls have stopped.'

'Okay,' said Abbie. She thought for a moment, then drove slowly along the street, letting cars pass on her left. 'I'm glad to hear that.'

'Yeah, I feel a lot better about things. Must have been drinking too much Scotch.'

Billy hadn't been drinking Scotch at the park. He'd been drinking beer.

'Since when?' she said casually to Billy.

'What?' Billy said.

Abbie saw what she was looking for and double-parked the car.

'When did the calls stop – hold on, I got a civilian flagging me down.'

She got out and walked quickly to a telephone pole with a squat blue box affixed to it at shoulder height. Abbie looked at the old-fashioned police call box. There were a few left in Buffalo, though the mayor had threatened to cut the funding for them the year before. His advisers had told him that some people in Buffalo were now so poor that they couldn't afford cell phones, so the boxes were their last lines of defense against crime. The funding was grudgingly restored.

Just work, Abbie thought as she pulled her keychain out of her pocket. *Don't let the crackheads have stolen the wires for copper.* She found the small silver key, nicked and battered with use; every cop was issued one. She inserted it into the keyhole and opened the heavy door. The phone was black and thick and appeared to have been sitting there undisturbed since World War II, but it looked intact.

She picked up the phone and held it to her ear while she listened to Billy with the other one. A click, a buzzing, and then she heard a 911 operator.

Abbie quickly gave the operator her name and what she needed her to do. Thirty seconds later she was back on with Billy.

'Sorry about that.'

'What are you doing, Ab?' Billy sounded shaky.

'My job. I'm a cop, remember?'

'Okay, okay. Just don't mess around.'

'You were saying the calls had stopped.'

'Yeah. And remember the car I told you about?' Billy seemed boyishly eager now.

'The green one?'

'Yeah, it—'

'What was the make on that again?'

'Uh, it was a Ford, I think. Maybe a Taur— what does it matter?'

It mattered because she was trying to drag out the phone call and give HQ time to run a trace, assuming Billy was on a landline.

'I may want to run it. Don't be so touchy.'

'Listen, I saw the green car and knocked on the window. It was some guy doing surveillance for an insurance company on a neighbor of mine. You know, fake . . .'

There was a pause, and the muffled airless sound you hear when someone is holding their hand over the receiver.

Finally, Billy came back.

'Fake workmen's comp. Classic, right?'

'Which insurance company?'

'What? What the fuck does it matter which—?'

He took a breath.

'Listen, the point is that they weren't after me.'

'That's great news, Billy,' Abbie said. 'Can we meet and talk? I just found out something that I think will make your whole situation a lot clearer.'

'I, uh, I can't make it right now. Got to get ready for this Vegas trip.'

'You're going to Vegas? That's very sudden.'

'No, I had it planned for months.'

The muffled sound again.

'Listen, Ab, I gotta go.'

Abbie, listening to the 911 line, heard only static. They couldn't have traced the line that quickly. She had to keep him on.

'Who's with you, Billy? Why don't you let me speak to them?'

'There's no one here. Why would you say that?'

'Right, there's no one there. But if someone is listening, I want you to tell them something for me. Okay?'

Silence.

'Tell them that if you should disappear, I'm going to find every member of the Clan na Gael in Buffalo – make that in western New York – and I'm going to build an airtight case against them. I'm already halfway there. Are they listening now?'

All she could hear was Billy breathing and the background noise of traffic on Seneca.

'And they're going straight to Attica. Do you know what they call that prison, Billy? The inmates have given it a special name.'

No answer.

'They call it *Africa*. Because the people who run the prison are the Crips and the Bloods from downstate. And not as nice as our Crips and Bloods. Believe me, I've been through there. And I'm going to prepare a welcome for them at Africa. I'm going to spread the word there that the Clan isn't some ancient Celtic bullshit spelled with a "C," it's really the new code name for the Ku Klux Klan.'

'Ab.'

'What they do to middle-aged white guys from Buffalo is not something you'd ever want to see. What they would do to Clan members would be much, much worse.'

Silence again. Then Billy spoke, his voice seeming farther away.

'Ab.'

'Yes, Billy?'

'Go back to Miami.'

The line went dead.

She swept the cell phone up to her ear.

'We have a trace,' the operator said.

'Where?'

'The 200 block of Woodside, between McKinley and South Park.'

'Get Zangara there and any available units. Tell them we're looking for an abduction victim named Billy Carney. Six foot two, 210, sandy brown hair, most likely in the company of other men. Tell them to start knocking on doors and checking backyards.'

SIXTEEN

Abbie jumped in her car and sped toward the Skyway, slowing only briefly for red lights before shooting through. She tried to play out the different scenarios in her head. If someone told Billy the Miami line – wrote it on a piece of paper and held it up for him to read – then he was as dead as Jimmy Ryan. If he'd said it himself, maybe there was a chance.

The wind rocked her car as it crested the top of the Skyway. Eight minutes later she slid to a stop next to the curb on Woodside and got out.

Every third or fourth home on the block was vacant. There were old political posters in some of the windows— 'Vote for O'Neill,' a mayoral candidate from three elections back – and yellowing newspaper in others. Dogs barked from behind rusting fences.

Abbie hustled up the block, looking for anything out of place. She ducked into the first backyard and saw nothing.

'Who's that?' someone yelled. Abbie looked up; a woman in a nightdress was staring at her from an open second-story window.

'Buffalo PD. Do you know Billy Carney?'

The woman slammed the window shut.

She turned and headed back toward the street. Z's black Ford Explorer was just cruising up to the curb. The window slid down and Z turned to look at her from the driver's seat.

'What's up?'

'Billy Carney called me, sounded like he was under duress. We tracked the call here. Take the other end, see if anyone saw a man, mid-thirties, being hustled to a car. I need to find him.'

'Righto,' Z said. The Explorer's engine revved and he moved off toward McKinley.

Turning, Abbie spotted a couple of young boys, clearly brothers, sitting on the steps of a swaybacked porch two houses east of her. They were watching her closely. She walked toward them.

'Hi, guys,' she said, reaching the bottom step and propping her foot on the third one, leaning on her thigh.

They nodded solemnly. The younger one, maybe four years old, was petting a fawn-colored guinea pig. He smiled. The other boy, four or five years older, didn't.

'My name's Detective Kearney and I'm with the Buffalo Police and I really need your help. Have you seen anything strange here in the last thirty minutes or so?'

'Strange how?' the older boy said. He was dressed in a powder-blue down jacket torn at the sleeve, with down feathers sticking out. His face looked like it had built up several layers of dirt and there were streaks of jam around his mouth. The green eyes were mistrustful.

'A group of men, maybe, leaving in a hurry. Strange cars on the street. People you haven't seen before. Anything out of the ordinary.'

'You mean them guys—' the younger boy blurted out. The older one snapped his head left and hissed something under his breath.

'It's okay,' Abbie said. 'No one will get in trouble.'

The younger boy looked at his brother, then dropped his eyes.

'It's okay. You can tell me, really.'

'Nuthin',' he said resentfully.

The older boy turned to look at her, his face deadened, the eyes sharp. Abbie didn't know if it was because her clothes weren't second-hand or because she didn't live on the block or because she was a cop. Such a plentiful buffet of resentments in the County.

'Listen, if you saw something, you need to tell me. I'm trying to help somebody who may be in a lot of trouble.' She looked at the younger boy, caught his eyes just as he was burying his gaze in the guinea pig's fur. 'If that were true, you'd want to help them, wouldn't you?'

His mouth opened and he gave a tiny nod.

The older boy looked away down the street. 'We just came out. We've been watching TV.'

She turned to the younger boy, raised her chin, then looked at the guinea pig. 'He's a cute one. What's his name?'

'Gilbert.'

Abbie nodded and reached out to pet him. Slowly she pushed her fingers forward until she found the little boy's hand resting in the guinea pig's fur. He looked at her quickly and she smiled.

Abbie nodded to reassure him, then mouthed the word 'Where?'

His eyes darted to the back of the older boy's head, then flitted back to hers. They were wide with fear and the boy's desire to help. She felt his index finger rise, sticking out of a hole in his mitten. He laid the finger over hers and held it there for a moment, warm and nervous. Then the boy slowly lifted the finger, his eyes on her all the time, and pointed past her left shoulder.

Abbie squeezed his finger and then dropped her hand to her side.

'Are you sure you didn't see anything?' she said sternly to the older boy. 'I don't want to have to talk to your mom and dad.'

'My mom don't talk to cops. And my dad's in Forest Lawn.'

The cemetery. She nodded, the older boy turning to look at Z knocking on a door. Abbie mouthed 'Thank you' to the little boy and walked away.

'If you hear anything, tell me or my partner.'

The older boy laughed dryly.

She went to the house next door, knocked on the door. It was ridiculous to waste time protecting a five-year-old informant, but in the County he could be branded for life. After waiting for a minute or two, she stepped down the porch stairs and headed across the street.

'I'm going to try this side,' she called to Z. The house the little boy had pointed to was a shabby two-story affair, painted dark green with white trim. As she walked up the driveway, she saw the screen door at the side flapping open. She pulled back the flap on her jacket and hugged the side of the building as she approached.

When she got within a few feet of the doorframe, she saw that the black wooden door was wide open.

Abbie pulled out her gun, pushed the door with her foot, and stuck her head around the doorframe. There was a worn set of stairs directly ahead, and a doormat on the floor that read 'Good Morning Sunshine.' She walked quickly up the steps, pushed a door with her toe and found an empty bathroom. To the other side was the kitchen.

The house gave the feeling of emptiness. She walked through the first floor briskly. In the living room, sparsely furnished with mismatched chairs and a pale green couch, she saw a coffee table with a whiskey bottle and a pack of Marlboro Lights and an ashtray. In the ashtray, a cigarette butt was smoking and a piece of paper gave off a thin wisp of smoke.

'Abbie?'

'In here.'

Z came up the stairs and was standing beside her. Abbie picked up the paper, blew softly on the edge, and pressed it gently between her fingers.

'What is it?'

She held the paper up to the light. A blackened section flaked away and fell to the floor, but a one-inch-square piece was just browned over and not completely burned. Z craned to have a look.

'Marty . . . Collins,' he read.

'Billy told me one of the members of the Clan was named Marty. So this is him. Find out where he lives, will you?'

Z nodded and began to punch some numbers into his cell phone, ducking out the front door for better reception.

Abbie studied the note. It had apparently been written very fast. The strokes got lighter at the end, with the last letters almost unreadable. It was the way you wrote if you had to use one hand. Or if someone was standing nearby who wouldn't have been pleased to see you scratch out a few words.

You had five seconds to write something and you wrote 'Marty Collins,' she thought. *Why didn't you tell me where they were taking you, Billy? I'd rather save you than this Marty Collins. I'd rather save both of you but if I had to choose I'd choose you. Is this note the equivalent of going to your execution with your head held high and in total silence, so your executioners later shake their heads in admiration? Really, you shouldn't have bothered.*

Or did you tell me where to find you and they burned that part of the note? Bad luck. Lousy, no-good, rotten luck, the same you've had for all your life.

The note was half-burned. But Billy didn't smoke. He still had that ex-athlete's thing of trying to look healthy at least.

So he'd had an escort.

Z walked in.

'Martin Collins is a County lawyer who works out of his home.'

'Where?'

'Fifty-four Potters Road. Right on the park.'

She was past him and out the door.

The Saab's engine was revving so loud it sounded like parts were going to come up through the hood. Abbie braked, took a corner onto Abbott, moving the wheel half an inch at the last second, just avoiding a silver-haired woman in a checked coat who was crossing the avenue going south.

'Easy!' Z yelled.

She accelerated. As they came to a red light, she hit the horn and didn't even touch the brakes. Out of her right she saw a cement truck jerking to a stop, its hood popping up and down, and heard the muffled sound of air brakes letting out a huge *SSSHHHOOOOO*.

She came to Shenandoah and made the right, streaked down the small street in five seconds, two-story homes flashing by on both sides, then another right onto Potters. She checked her mirror and hit the accelerator. The park was on her left, the snow lit violet by the afternoon sun. Collins's house was three blocks away.

She swept past a line of parked cars, then suddenly hit the brakes. The car rocked to a stop.

'It's three houses down, Ab.'

'I know. But Billy Carney said he'd been followed by a green Taurus. And look what's sitting out front.'

Z raised his eyebrows. Abbie pointed her chin toward 54 Potters Road, about twenty yards ahead on the right side. Z spotted the green Taurus sitting by the curb, the last in line of parked cars. Smoke was wisping from its tailpipe.

'Got it,' Z said.

Abbie pressed the gas and coasted up to the Taurus. Two heads, white males, in the front seats. She was out before Z had opened his door.

Gun out and pointed down thirty degrees. Watching the driver's head. He saw her coming, a coffee cup rising slowly to his mouth. When it was at his lips, she tapped on the glass with the tip of her gun.

The cop glanced left, his blue eyes aware of the gun. Then he turned to look straight ahead and was lowering the coffee cup to his lap when Abbie pulled the door open. As he turned, she recognized him. She'd seen him downtown coming out of the Chief's office, striding through headquarters looking important. They called him Q. A beat cop, obviously moonlighting for the boys at the Gaelic Club, protecting the secrets of the County.

He looked at her like she smelled bad.

'Where's Collins?' Abbie said.

'You have a warrant, Kearney?'

'Where is he?'

The other man leaned over.

'How's your dad?' he said.

Brown mustache, older.

'He's fine.'

'Tell him I said hi.'

'I will. What's your name?'

The man's face went blank and he sat back in his chair, staring straight ahead.

'Where's Marty Collins? It's urgent.'

Q raised the cup of coffee and both men looked as if they were watching a drive-in movie through the dirty windshield.

Abbie grabbed Q's collar and leaned back, then jerked him headfirst out of the car, the cup teetering back and the hot coffee spilling down his shirt.

'*Hey!* You crazy or something?'

Z had the other guy out by then, pushed up against the car. He leaned in to whisper something Abbie couldn't hear. She had Q spread-eagled on the hood of the car, facing the park.

Abbie leaned in over his shoulder, her lips two inches from Q's ear. 'Where's Collins?'

Q shook his head. He was beefy. Looked like he lifted weights, but his neck was thick with fat.

'I don't know what you're talking about.'

'What were you doing out here? Bird-watching?'

'You know who I am?'

'I know you were the one who was supposed to be watching Marty Collins when the killer cut his face off.'

His head snapped left and one big blue eye swept over her face before he looked back down.

'What are you talking about?'

'Collins is next. It's happening. Soon. Maybe even now. Is he inside?'

Three beats.

'Yeah.'

Abbie called to Z and they hustled the men into the house. The front door was open and Kearney left Q in the front hall as she ran up the wide staircase and checked upstairs. Three bedrooms, two bathrooms, all tidy and empty. She did a second look-through, saw the little door cut into the hallway ceiling, got a chair from the second bedroom and pulled it underneath. She reached up and pulled the handle down.

The attic smelled like mice and Christmas, and it was empty of everything except boxes and spider webs.

Z met her at the foot of the staircase.

'Nothing here. Basement's clean.'

Abbie stared at Q, who was standing by the front door, leaning against the lintel. He stared defiantly back.

'He has to be here. No one's gone in or out.'

'Does he ever leave the house, for any reason?'

'Just to go running, but we follow behind in the car.'

'Did he go running today?'

Q shook his head. 'No, he said he hates the smell of the exhaust when the wind changes.'

'So maybe he went running without you. Check upstairs for his sneakers and whatever he wears when he goes out.'

Q looked at Brown Mustache.

'*Now.*'

The two men moved up the stairs, and Abbie went to the kitchen window. The house backed on the Cazenovia. She could see a triangular flag fluttering in between pale branches. The golf course.

The stairs pounded above her head.

'His running gear is gone, but I swear . . .'

Collins could have gone out the back, cut through the trees and straight onto the golf course.

'When does he usually go running?'

'One o'clock.'

Abbie checked her watch. 'That was three hours ago. You dumbasses have been guarding an empty house for *three hours?*'

'Let's go,' she called to Z.

When Abbie swung out and made the right into the park, she saw the Taurus pull in behind her.

SEVENTEEN

Marty Collins came to, breathing raggedly, his head hanging down on his chest. His eyes swam with tears clotting with the cold, then focused on the New Balance logo on his blue zippered sweatshirt. Past the sweatshirt, the snow was red and pitted. A second later the pain cleaved into his brain and he screamed and screamed.

I must have been knocked into the bushes that lined the side of the creek and caught in their thorns, he thought when he'd run out of breath. *I'm going to die here.* He looked up. The sun was dropping over the branches above; the afternoon was turning to dusk. How had no one found him yet?

'Oh God, have *mercy!*' he yelled, and he saw a pair of crows lift from the top of a nearby tree.

In the silence that followed, a voice answered.

Marty Collins looked around at the gloom around him. There was a figure sitting in the snow eight or ten feet away, its back against a curtain of black brambles. It wore a green-and-black-checked wool coat and a black ski mask, and it was sitting on its haunches, watching Marty.

'What did you say?'

'No merthy.'

The voice was like nothing he'd ever heard. It was like a kid with a speech impediment. Marty Collins had the uncanny feeling that he was speaking to an evil child.

'Help me, please. I was hit by a car and—'

He pushed his chest forward to get clear of the trees, but something was holding him back. He jerked his right shoulder forward, but there was a cord tied to his upper arm and anchored somewhere behind him. He tried taking a step, but the tiny pressure he placed on the broken leg sent a jagged explosion of pain up through his pelvis and gut. It took him minutes to regain the power of speech.

'Just help me,' he moaned. 'Just please go get help.'

The figure said something.

'What—'

'Aythe driving huckar.'

Marty tried to block out the sickening pain to decipher what the thing had said.

'AYTHE drivin huckar.'

'You were driving the car? *You?*'

'Yes.'

Marty Collins stared at the black eyes, and his bowels slowly went cold. A thought slipped through the agony in his brain, disappeared, then returned, more insistent.

'You killed Jimmy Ryan, didn't you?' he said.

The figure just stared.

'Listen, listen. Just get me out of here and you don't have to see me again. I will tell them nothing, do you understand me?'

The man in the ski mask reached behind him and took out a large knife. It flashed silver in the darkness, reflecting the glow of the moonlight and the snow. The man's eyes, black through the slits of the ski mask, regarded him.

'Why didn't you run when Jimmy Ryan was found?'

Whyn't you run-n Himminyryne wuzfound?

It sounded like one long moan but Marty Collins got the sense of it.

'Why should I?!' Marty yelled, his face reddening. 'I've done nothing to be ashamed of.'

The knife sounded along the hard ground like it was scraping flint.

Then the lisping voice again. Was it disguising its true voice? Marty hung his head as he deciphered what the thing had said:

'Each one chooses one. Jimmy chose you.'

Marty Collins swept his head left and right, filled with hatred for that drug-dealing scum Jimmy Ryan. He had never wanted him on the rolls of the Gael. It was a sacred institution, and Jimmy was a useless con artist who was beneath the Clan's history, its illustrious and unfulfilled calling. But the others had outvoted him. They needed Jimmy, they said. They had to have him.

The scraping of the knife on the ground brought him back to the park. He looked up at the killer. If it was who he thought it was, he was as good as dead.

'Is this how you repay us, traitor?' Marty said slowly. Hot indignation temporarily blocked the grinding pain from his leg. 'We *saved* you.'

The figure laughed, a booming laugh that seemed to return from the trees filled with steel.

'You have no idea what we did for you,' Marty sputtered. 'You have *no* idea.'

The figure laughed, and the sound seemed to return from the trees filled with steel.

The figure stood up. It reached up and began to unzip the green-and-black-checked jacket. Marty Collins dipped his head. 'Cut me down from here. *Cut me down, you animal!*'

When Marty looked up again, the jacket was off, and the thing had turned its back to him. Marty heard the sound of a zipper, and the thing began to take the sweatshirt off. The bare right shoulder came into view.

Marty Collins stared despite himself. His eyes widened.

After a few seconds of complete bafflement, he understood. A gasp escaped his lips. He tried to speak but the words were just a grunt of steam into the air.

He'd been wrong. In his mind, the face of the man he'd thought was behind the mask dissolved, replaced by a different and more terrible one, the killer's true face. Marty Collins understood now who the man standing before him was, and he knew that Jimmy Ryan had understood at the end, too. He realized why Jimmy had spilled his guts so quickly, and for a moment he had a flash of empathy for Jimmy that seemed to warm his shivering body. And the feeling was for himself, too, for the mutilated thing he would soon become.

The figure advanced toward him, the black ski mask still on, the knife at his waist. When he reached Marty Collins, the figure breathed for a moment, willing Marty to raise his eyes. When he didn't, the knife point pricked into Marty's chin and lifted it.

The man stared into Marty's eyes as he dropped the knife to his stomach, just below the belly button. Then he whispered something into Marty's ear and gave the blade a hard cutting flick.

Abbie sat in her office, a can of Diet Coke hanging listlessly in her hand. It was 10, and there was no one in the cubicles around her.

Her mind went over and over the events of the night. After leaving Collins's house, followed by his bodyguards, she'd driven up and down the park road three, four, five times. There was no sign of Marty Collins. Then she and Z had gotten out on foot and walked the road in the dying light, looking for footsteps leading away from the path he'd been running. There were only two that were fresh. One had led to the side door of a single-story house on the edge of the park. Inside they'd found the homeowner, Joseph Dumbrowski, forty-six and a plumber, having a beer at his kitchen table. He'd told them his car had broken down on Abbott, so he'd come through the park road and cut over to shorten the trip home. His boots matched the tracks in the snow. And unless he'd carried Collins on his shoulders, there was no way he'd been anything other than alone.

The other track consisted of two pairs of footsteps that led to the old brick custodian's hut looking out over the Bowl. There they'd found two teenagers, one male and one female, with two 52-ounce bottles of malt liquor, curled up for warmth like sleeping kittens. The lock was broken and the teenagers had thrown some files around, smashed a computer screen before settling in for a nap. Runaways. They'd seen nothing. No cars, no runners, no blood, no suspicious ski-masked strangers lurking on the park road. They'd been sent back to their families in the rich suburb of Orchard Park in the back of a squad car, half-blitzed and bitter.

Which meant one of three things. Either Marty Collins had taken a different running route for the first time in years, or he'd made it to the Seneca Street end of the park and disappeared there. Or the killer had caught him on the park road and got him into his car. Which meant he could be anywhere right now.

She listened to her voicemails. Detective Mills from Niagara Falls PD had called to ask her out on another date. She smiled wanly and made a mental note to call him. But no dates yet. Not until she had the killer. *One man at a time,* she thought.

EIGHTEEN

The first call to the Buffalo Fire Department came in at 6:40 a.m. The second thirty seconds later. A brush fire in Cazenovia Park. The squad on Abbott Road, used to the calls for fires raging in one of the abandoned two-family homes that dotted the County, finished their coffee before walking leisurely to their open lockers and slinging on their coats and boots. Five men climbed aboard the gleaming red engine before hitting the siren and heading down Abbott to Cazenovia Park Road. By then they could see the black wisps of smoke rising from the middle of the park. They sighed. They knew the snow was deep and breaking trail to the fire with sixty pounds of equipment would leave them drenched in sweat after just a few minutes.

The first to reach the site was Captain Edward Burns. He followed the creek, followed by three men. He could hear the sound of wood splintering in intense heat before he saw the red flames after a dogleg turn in the creek bed. When he turned and found the fire before him, it was consuming a stand of small oaks surrounding a tall elm tree. At the foot of it stood a thick bramble of black scrub, so tightly interwoven it looked like a mesh of wrought iron. To get hoses directly on the fire, they would have to go through it. But first he had to have a look.

Burns, breathing heavily, powered his legs through the last of the ice-rimed snow and dropped down to a little path that had been stamped into the snow at the entrance to the bramble. He held a large axe in his right hand, and he broke the ice ahead of him as he lurched forward.

'The little fucks have been back here,' he called to the man behind him, Mulcahy. 'Tell Dispatch to call PD and see if they can find any punks walking through the park with matches or a lighter.'

'If I catch 'em' said Mulcahy, out of breath, 'I'll put 'em under the ice myself.' He stopped and began to relay the message while Burns staggered on toward the circle of bushes.

Burns took a deep breath and broke through the last crust of ice and stumbled into the entrance to the bramble. The light disappeared. It was strange. The branches ahead of him were so perfectly laced together they seemed to have been arranged that way. He could hear the crackling of the dry timber ahead of him, but once he was in the dark brush, only tiny shoots of sun lit up the gloomy interior. He took four steps, ducking down to avoid the brambles that came down like a low roof over his head. The sound of his men tramping behind him faded as he entered the bush.

Finally, he saw the white of the snow and the red of flames through the dark branches ahead. He gripped the axe, ready to clear the brush away from the base of the tall trees that could light up and send sparks to the dead oaks that studded the park grounds. His kids played in Cazenovia Park during the summers, and it would be a shame to lose more of its trees. One of the brambles caught at his shoulders and threatened to hold him fast. He jerked forward, a tremor of claustrophobia shooting through him.

'Fucking punks,' he said.

He ducked his head down to avoid one last branch, but his helmet caught it and it snapped with a pistol-like sound. He closed his eyes to avoid the thorns and sharp twigs, then fell to his knees and began to shuffle forward. Finally, head down, drops of icy water falling onto his bare neck, he broke through into the center, exhausted. When he opened his eyes, he saw that the burning trees were actually farther away than he thought, twenty or so yards at least. He was now inside a nest of black branches, around ten feet in diameter. His eyes began to adjust to the gloom.

With a grunt, Burns jerked off the ground and back to his feet. The red he'd seen through the branches wasn't flame. It was the snow itself, turned scarlet with . . . what the fuck was that? Blood. The snow was saturated with it, dark scarlet blood splashed around the interior.

'Jesus, Mary, and Jo—'

Burns snapped the axe into the air frantically, his eyes searching the bramble for something ready to spring at him. His other hand grasped for the radio that had been strapped to his shoulder, but the branches had torn it free and now it dangled somewhere around his knees. He was too petrified to drop his eyes from the woven mesh around him.

He thought of animal sacrifices, the rumors of dog killers and Satan worshippers in the woods at night coming true right in front of his eyes.

Muffled voices answered his call, but the words were blunted by the thick branches. Burns hefted his axe in his hand, feeling he'd been drawn into a trap, and that a knife was poised, waiting to split his scalp.

As he turned slowly to the left, axe heavy in his right hand, out of the corner of his eye he saw the pale thing, and he instantly dashed for the entrance.

'*Mulcahy!*' he screamed. '*MULCAHY, WHERE ARE YOU?*'

The voices grew closer. Burns ran to the passageway and crouched there, hunched on his knees, his hand groping for the radio swinging against his thigh. Finally, with a grunt, he found it and brought it to his lips.

'Dispatch, Dispatch, this is Burns 2-1.'

'Go ah—'

'Get Buffalo PD on the scene. We got some kind of animal sacrifice and blood all . . . all over the ground.'

The sound of crashing came clearly through the passageway. Burns looked up to see the wide eyes of Mulcahy approaching in the gloom. He was crawling on his knees.

'Cap, what is it?'

'It's a – it's a—'

'Take it easy.'

'*Don't tell me to take it fucking easy.* The sickos have been killing dogs in here.'

Mulcahy's eyes tried to peer around him into the center of the brambles.

'Guys, hold on,' he called back. 'We got something for PD.'

He looked directly at Burns.

'Cap, go around me, I'll take a look and then we'll know what to tell the cops when they get here.'

Burns nodded. He wiped his mouth with his hand, then began to squeeze by Mulcahy on the right.

'Don't touch nothin',' he said.

'Believe me, I won't.'

Burns felt the adrenaline drain away as he saw the sunlight grow closer. Finally he was out into the open and he stood up to relieve the cramping in his back and to let the sunlight play on his face.

When he opened his eyes, he saw the other two firefighters looking at him strangely.

'You okay?' said the first one.

'No, I'm not fuckin' okay. The devil freaks've been at work back there. Goddamn delinquents. I'd like to—'

The eyes of the second man shifted off his face to over his right shoulder and Burns heard movement behind him. He turned quickly, the axe bobbing in the air.

Mulcahy emerged from the black brambles, his face ashen. He took a gulp of fresh air and looked around, his eyes unfocused.

'Did you see it?' Burns said.

Mulcahy dropped down his haunches to the snow, then sat back. He brushed a shaking hand through his ginger hair.

'Yeah, I saw it.'

'Can you believe they skinned a dog like that? Evil little—'

'It's not a dog,' Mulcahy said.

Burns dropped the axe to his side.

'What did you say?'

'I said, that's *not* a dog.'

His eyes came up and met Burns's.

'It's a man. They skinned him and hung him in the trees like a fucking anatomy lesson.'

Forty minutes later, Abbie stood outside the bramble patch. A trail to it had by now been beaten down into the snow, and there were things thrown to the ground around her: an empty Pepsi bottle, green and white packaging for a syringe, a coil of black plastic binding. She was waiting, watching the crows circle in the sky.

She called the Missing Persons desk at headquarters to see if there was anything new on Billy Carney; she'd phoned a report in the evening before. The cop who answered said that a detective had gone by the Gaelic Club again that morning but had been met with silence and stone-cold stares. Abbie snapped the phone shut in anger.

Was Billy waiting for her somewhere in the park, waiting patiently in his grave, carved up like Marty Collins? They'd found the victim's wallet and there was no doubt the flayed man was hanging just yards away. They hadn't checked this part of the park because no trail had been broken from the main road after Collins had gone missing. But the killer had obviously outfoxed them. He'd snatched Collins, put him in a car, driven out of the park, taken a right on Seneca, gone a half mile down, right again down some local roads to a street that dead-ended back at the park. The end of that street was fifty yards from where she stood, completely hidden over the small rise in the ground to the east, and offered a shortcut for residents to the basketball courts and the park pool on hot summer days. A gap had been cut into the dead end's fence there, years ago probably, and the chain link curled back to allow bodies through.

It was a perfect setup: the dead-end street occupied by two burned-out cars, a graffitied concrete wall, and the brown shards of Genesee beer bottles that had been whipped against it. A place where no one would see something being dragged out of a trunk or a back seat, a place that had been consigned to invisibility by years of freak parties and sloppy sex, consensual and otherwise.

A man, his green hood pulled almost completely over his face, emerged from the passageway holding something in his hand. He stood up and Abbie saw the blond goatee of Michaels, the crime scene tech.

'You ready for me?' she said.

Michaels nodded. He handed the plastic baggie he'd been holding to Abbie. She took it and saw inside what she knew would be there, had to be there: a brown plastic monkey, its hands held to its sides and the eyes squeezed shut.

'You told us it'd be there. Took a while, but I found it.'

Abbie turned to look at the thing in direct sunlight. Now she had to decipher the exact emotional intent of a mass-produced toy from thirty or forty years ago. Why was the monkey hugging itself? In excitement or despair? Was the monkey afraid, or was it laughing a hearty belly laugh?

'Where?' she said.

'It was . . . inserted into a fold of skin that had been peeled away from the body and left hanging. On his back, near the right shoulder blade.'

The toy appeared to be from the same set as the others. The paint around the left eye was worn away so that you could see the raw white plastic beneath it.

'Okay. Anything else?'

'We found his wallet placed neatly on a nearby tree stump. This might interest you.'

Michaels handed her a business card. It was ivory, heavy stock, with embossed lettering.

It said 'The Buffalo Gaelic Club' across the top in green letters, then in the middle, 'Marty Collins, President' in black.

Abbie shook her head. In her mind, all other possibilities just flew out the window. The killer was targeting members of the Clan na Gael. End of discussion.

'How'd he die?' she said. 'I know we can't say officially until the coroner arrives, but give me your call.'

Michaels shook his head. 'Blood loss or exposure, one of the two. Besides . . . what you'll see in there, there were no other major injuries except a major break to the right femur.'

'Exposure?'

'He was out here for a long time. I found cuts to the palm and deep grooves on the inside of the fingers, with small bits of wood impaled in each of them.'

Abbie looked at the tech.

'He was alive when the killer put him into the trees?'

Michaels nodded. 'Yep. Probably stunned while the perp wove him in, but he struggled and tore at the branches. Didn't do him any good.'

'What else can you tell me?'

Michaels looked down at a plastic-covered notebook that he'd brought out from his hip pocket.

'I'm going to guess the blood – and there's a lot of it – is all his. The killer milked the body for it, spread it around the snow in there evenly, like he was painting a floor.'

'Any similarities to the first two?'

'I just saw pictures on the Niagara Falls case, of course, but it's the same guy. The knife blade looks the same, the cutting patterns. But this time . . . It—'

He broke off and Abbie looked up from her notes.

Michaels's face looked greenish.

'You'll see.'

Abbie nodded. 'Okay, I'm going in. When the coroner shows up, send him through.'

She snapped her notebook shut, put the pen in her inside coat pocket, and pulled her hat lower over her forehead. When she looked up, she found Michaels hadn't moved and his eyes were on her.

He swallowed. 'He's getting better, you know.'

'Yes, Michaels, I know.'

'Fast.'

Abbie nodded.

'Have you ever seen this before?' Michaels said with a frown.

'No.'

'So how's he doing it? It's like he's skipping ahead at warp speed.'

Abbie grimaced. 'I think he's been planning this for a long time.

The killings are scripted. He knows what he's going to do, doesn't waste time. He's following a story of some kind in his head, I don't know. And these little things—'

She held up the monkey.

'Means the motivation goes way back. Childhood even. If you had twenty years to think of how you'd kill someone, you'd probably do it pretty well, too.'

Michaels nodded.

'You'll have the write-up on my desk when I get back?'

'Sure.'

Michaels moved past her and Abbie headed for the tunnel entrance.

She took a breath before she ducked and walked in. A starling chirped as it swung by overhead. The light was more intense, throwing hard interlaced shadows onto the path as she bent slightly and cat-footed her way in. The ground was turning to slush under the boots of so many firemen and cops.

When she reached the circle, she stood up. The red snow had been scooped away and placed in plastic garbage bags to see if the blood all belonged to Collins. The brambles around her had clearly grown together thickly, but at ten feet she could see the green-white ends where a knife had cut through branches. The killer had created a sanctuary, she thought. He wanted to spend time here, alone, with Collins. Even in the dead of winter, he couldn't be certain that a boy chasing a dog or a bird watcher wouldn't stumble on this little obscure piece of the park. So he'd made the cover impenetrable.

Slowly, she turned.

The body was to her left and she felt her left knee give a bit when she saw it. The skin was mottled red and the faintest blue, the transparent blue of a fish gill. Collins was naked and spread-eagled, his hands and feet pinned tightly against the thick brambles, his small penis almost hidden in the nest of reddish-brown pubic hair. Two folds of skin had been cut just below the clavicle, then straight down to the belly button. Collins's body was thin and wiry but his chest wasn't tight with muscle. There was flesh and fat there, and it had been spread open on both sides, pulled back like a suit jacket open to the wind. The white of the rib cage was visible under one thin, near-translucent layer of skin.

The same had been done to the arms, the legs, the face. There the superficial layers of skin had been expertly sliced open and pulled back to each side of the forehead and pinned there so that Collins seemed to have on one of those strange hats that Swedish nuns wore. Strips of flesh hung from the cheeks, now stiffened by cold, and the web of bluish veins were clearly visible, as clear as the highway lines on an old gas station map. The cheek muscles were bunched above the rictus smile, each strip ridged on top of the next. With his flesh peeled away, it looked like a Pygmy or some kind of Amazonian forest dweller was trying to emerge from inside Collins's face, an old Indian bursting forth.

Abbie swallowed, then stepped to the body. She imagined she could hear the little wings of flesh make a tiny threshing noise in the wind, but that was impossible. She did a quick check of the front of the body but could see nothing cut away, no trophies taken. Again, she felt the whisper of a private conversation, just like she had at the church where Jimmy Ryan died. But this message was even more personal.

She stepped back. What was the killer saying?

First a church and now a crude forest re-creation of the Crucifixion. But again something was off. Collins's ankles, the skin split open to display the thick runner's muscles and fat veins, were eight or ten inches apart, not closely bound like every depiction of Christ on the cross that she'd ever seen. The arms weren't straight across, they slanted down at an angle of ten degrees or so. A killer working from an image in his head would have made this right. He had hours, and he was good with his tools. The legs would have been in a straight line and the first thought in a person's mind would be *Christ on the cross.*

But the legs were out at an angle, and the arms were wrong.

The killer is not interested in games of detail, Abbie thought. *He's making* one *point and one point only.* It was like the groove carved just beneath Jimmy Ryan's belly button, saying 'Do you understand? No? How about now?'

Quick, just one impression, she said to herself. *What is this about? What do you see?*

But no single revelation came smashing down on her. She saw only details, heard the starlings fighting in a nearby tree.

Okay, if it's not a crucifixion, why this pose? She went back to the brambles, shone her flashlight into the thicket of shadows. She played it upward slowly and saw among the twisting shapes a few straight lines. She followed the lines to the body and then reached her bare hand in through the tangle. One came out toward Collins's right ankle. She touched it. A thorn raked against her thumb and she drew her hand out fast.

'Damn it,' she hissed. She sucked the blood that welled up from the pad of her thumb and stared at the brambles. Then she pressed her fingers together and slipped the hand in again, bending her wrist to avoid the sharp thorn.

When she touched the straight line, she realized it was nylon cord, taut with Collins's weight. The killer must have brought it with him. She got her flashlight out again and followed the cord from the ankle to a small stout trunk of a tree five yards away.

The killer had stripped Collins of his clothes. Displayed him, was that it? Then he took the first layer of skin off. Then the second. Slowly. It must have taken time and patience to work out here in the dark and the cold.

Had Collins been hiding a secret? Was he pretending to be someone he wasn't? Or was it sexual for his torturer, punishing the nude body while exposing it for everyone to see?

But how did that fit with Jimmy Ryan?

Too damn fancy, Abbie. You're out here in the elements. He drained him of blood, slowly. He didn't cut his dick off.

Why? It seemed low on the ritualistic quotient. He didn't paint messages in the snow or daub the trees with satanic symbols. He slowly, methodically, bled him out and then left him in the wind.

She tried to imagine the scene, the killer nicking a vein with his sharp knife, holding a bowl as the blood spurted into the bowl, making the tinny, urgent sound of a farmer milking his cow. She leaned in for a look, Collins's body shaking above her in a gust of wind, the patches of flesh slapping gently against the face. There were the little dabs of dark gray glue on the inside of Collins's forearm. Bandages.

You bandaged him up to keep him alive longer. You dragged it out as long as possible, didn't you?

Ladling the warm red stuff onto the snow. Would a red steam rise as the warm blood hit the frozen ground? A wave of nausea passed through her, and Abbie closed her eyes.

Come on, Absalom, this is basic stuff. The killer had one overwhelming thing to tell you and you can't feel what it was?

She went closer to the body and examined it. Up high on the shoulder she found a tiny cut mark, almost purple against the translucent skin. She pushed the bramble near his ankles and got an angle on the back of his legs. Nothing. She leaned into it and looked further up. Clean skin. But when she drew back, she found another, deeper cut, just under the belly button.

Cuts at the shoulder and the waist, where the material would have been tightest. So the killer snipped his clothes off, she thought. Cut the waistband and then sliced down the loose fabric. But that wasn't enough. He peeled back the outer layer of skin itself.

Looking at the body, she had a vision of what Collins had suffered.

Stop intellectualizing, Absalom. One impression.

Now.

'Cold,' she said out loud, startling herself.

Cold. He wanted Collins to feel the deepest cold. The body was spread-eagled against the bramble because that gave it the greatest exposure to the wind, wicking away body warmth. He took away his clothes, he bared every inch of his body, even slowly removed the heat-giving blood. It was like he was taking the body down to some absolute zero.

That was what the killer was whispering to Collins. '*This is what cold is.* Feel it? Understand? Now we go lower.'

She shivered. The sun was beginning to dip behind the tallest of the branches above her, sending spiky shadows down onto the mud-colored snow.

*   *   *

As Abbie drove back to headquarters, she went over the Jimmy Ryan case. She was confident in her evaluation of the Collins scene. It was about cold, exposure. But what did that mean for the Ryan killing?

With Jimmy Ryan, the killer had a huge church to do his work. But he'd dragged Ryan down those stone stairs to the small room beneath the floor. Then he stuffed him into the undercroft, still alive probably, and let him strangle himself to death in that tiny, confined space, the rope tied to feet and his neck slowly tightening as he kicked.

What was that about? Isolation?

Did it mean anything that Ryan was hidden away and Collins – though concealed for the time it took to kill him – was left exposed to the world? Again, her mind demurred. It wasn't about contrasts. He wasn't drawing distinctions between the two deaths. He had used each for one phase of the story.

Isolation and cold. A personal story, she thought, but whose? The killer's, or the victim's?

She pulled out her cell phone, dialed information and had them put her through to the Historical Society. When she got Dr Reinholdt on the phone, he seemed to purr with pleasure.

'I've been waiting for your call,' he said.

She could almost picture him, perched on his chair like a perverted Weeble. 'That's good to know, Doctor, but I need some information.'

'Who's dead now?'

'Another member of the Gaelic Club. You'll be hearing it on the news, a Marty Collins.'

'They're dropping fast, Detective.'

'And that's why I need your help, Doctor. We talked about the history of the Clan na Gael, but I doubt someone is hunting them for reasons that go back a hundred years.'

She heard Reinholdt suck his teeth in thought.

'I wouldn't be so sure about that. If you really do have a Clan-killer loose in the County, there are several possibilities, and one of them is what is colloquially known as the Troubles. The state of war that exists between some true believers and the British government.'

'I realize that. But there are indications the killer has a personal motivation.'

'What indic—'

'I can't go into that, Doctor, and I'm sure you'll understand why. What I need to know is what other possibilities exist. Now that the Troubles are over, what has the IRA gotten into? Drug trafficking? Arms? Are there different factions I need to know about, both here and in Ireland? Recent violence involving members?'

Silence on the other end of the line.

'I have a colleague, now retired, at the State Department in Washington who was briefed on these things up until a few years ago. She's a hometown girl, and a fanatic for Seneca Indian relics, which I send her every so often when some idiot brings one in after finding it with their metal detector. I'd be happy to cash in a favor if you'd like.'

'That would be a huge help. I'll call you back this afternoon?'

'I'd rather you come see me.'

'I'm afraid I can't do that. It's an active investigation and it's eating up all my time. I'll make sure to call you, though.'

'I'll be on pins and needles.'

Abbie slipped the phone into her bag and then, unable to control the impulse, wiped her hand on her wool pants. Then she grabbed the wheel and made a sharp left onto Potters Road.

When she pulled up to Collins's house, she took it in this time: squat, heavy-timbered, boasting a broad front porch with a rectangular opening onto the street that looked like a gunner's window in a large pillbox. The lawn was beautifully cut beneath its coating of snow, the bushes healthy and cared for, and the hunter-green paint with mink-white trim was a few years old at the most.

Spotting money in the County was easy. Anything that was brightly turned out – a car with new wheels and a detailed paint job, or a house, or clothes – spoke of income. And Collins's house said it loud and clear.

There were two cars in the driveway – a late-model Grand Cherokee and a brand-new Cadillac. The Taurus was gone. She climbed the wooden steps and rang the doorbell. A deep bass note sounded inside; so far away, it sounded as if it had gone off in a second basement.

She turned as the door opened. Framed in the stainless-steel screen door was Billy Carney.

NINETEEN

Billy had been transformed. His lanky hair was freshly cut into a stylish overhang, he wore a dark wool suit that shaped his ex-athlete's body into a thin V, a crisp white dress shirt with a wing collar and a thin black-and-green-striped tie. His face looked freshly scrubbed and he eyed her through the screen door with a composure that momentarily silenced her.

Billy smiled quickly, looked behind him, murmured something to whoever was just behind the wooden door, and then opened the screen and stepped onto the porch. Abbie's eyes drifted down the length of him, ending up at a pair of new leather oxfords, the swirling whorls of the design subtle in the winter light.

'Jesus, Billy,' she said. 'I thought you were dead.'

'Dead?' he said casually, walking past her. 'What made you think that?'

Billy reached the white porch rail. He scanned Potters Road up and down before turning to face her, leaning the back of his powerful thighs against the rail.

'*You* did, on the phone yesterday. What happened to you?'

He shrugged. Underneath the new clothes, she sensed a new confidence, a willingness to displease.

'What do you mean?'

'What do I mean? You look like Bugs Moran.'

Billy reached inside his suit jacket and pulled out a pack of Marlboro Reds. 'Who's Bugs Moran?'

I wonder when he started smoking, Abbie thought.

'An Irish gangster. You should read a book once in a while.'

'You should have a drink once in a while,' he said. Billy lit the

145

cigarette with a thin gold lighter and breathed in the smoke. 'And relax.'

'You said you were going to Vegas.'

'Change of plans,' he said. 'A new position opened up. Had to stay in town.'

'How nice. A new position with who?'

Billy did the not-important frown.

'A private company.'

'The Clan?'

He leaned away from her, sucking at the cigarette as he appraised her through slit eyelids.

'What's that?'

She gave him a look.

Billy held his hands up. 'Is this an official question?' he said.

'I can make it one.'

He exhaled and looked away down the street.

'I don't think you can, Ab. But let's be friendly. The executive committee of the Gaelic Club.'

She nodded. For a moment, she felt a sudden urge to embrace Billy, for all the disappointments and failures that the new suit and the good shoes and the gold lighter were in payment for.

Then she wanted to slap him.

'I thought you were going to disappear. Instead the Clan bought you out. That's nice for you. But I have a feeling it's going to end the same way.'

'How?'

'With you dead.'

He leaned toward her and looked at her from under his naturally perfect eyebrows.

'Not likely.'

She glanced down as he pulled back to the railing.

'Where'd you get the piece?'

'The what?'

'The gun.' She pointed at his chest. 'There.'

He looked down, then back up, avoiding her eyes.

'If you're going to play in this world, at least learn the basic terminology.'

'It's licensed. Went down to register it yesterday.'

'Some cops from the County put you at the front of the line?'

He smiled.

Abbie sighed, then walked to the rail and leaned against it, facing the house's huge plate glass window. She noticed that heavy drapes had been pulled across it since she'd arrived.

'You sure you want to do this?' she asked.

She watched him in her peripheral vision. Billy looked at his new shoes, then raised his head and nodded.

Abbie sighed and then rose, walked to the door.

'How can we help you, Ab?' said Billy.

She turned. Her face was grave.

'*We?* I'm here to talk to Mrs Collins.'

He met her stare with a steely one of his own.

'She's resting. Can't talk to anyone.'

'We'll just see about that.'

Abbie opened the screen door and rapped hard three times on the door. When it was opened, a beefy, red-faced man with a paunch opened the door. He looked flustered.

'Who's that?'

She pulled out her ID, held it up.

'Detective Kearney. I'm here to talk to Mrs Collins about the murder of her husband.'

'She's resting. Please leave your card and—'

'Who are you?'

'I'm James Collins, her nephew. Now, if you don't mind . . .'

James Collins looked like an accountant who was more comfortable with numbers than actual human beings. He was sweating now, looking like he wanted to slowly close the door and sit quietly in the basement for a while.

'Mr Collins, is the family interested in solving this case?'

Collins looked nervously past her to Billy Carney. Abbie turned and sent him a fast look. Billy nodded.

'Of course we are. But my aunt needs time. She's only just arrived back from a visit to East Aurora and heard the news.'

'If the family wants to find out who murdered and skinned alive your uncle like a deer—'

She heard Billy get up and turned to hold a hand out his way.

'Then she *has* to talk to me. Today.'

The nephew stared at her.

'Please try and understand—'

'I'm paid to solve murder cases, Mr Collins. If you'd rather have the blood of the next victim on your heads, so be it. I understand that certain people are putting pressure on you not to cooperate with me. But if you're relying on Billy Carney here and whatever boy desperadoes you have inside to catch the killer, then let me guarantee you that other people are going to die. Horribly.'

James Collins looked like he wanted to grow wings and fly. As it was, he stroked his tie once.

'Your card,' he repeated.

She snapped open her card case and stuck a card into the frame of the screen door. Then she leaned in and lowered her voice.

'If I find out you or your aunt had information about the killer you didn't share with me, I'm going to make that clear to everyone in Buffalo. Including the next victim's family. Do you understand me, James?'

She turned and headed for the street. Billy was watching her, smoke drifting up around his face.

'Playing rough, Ab?'

Her look was of the stone-breaking variety.

When she walked onto the fourth floor of HQ the next morning, Perelli saw her coming from his corner office. He raised his right hand and the tips of his fingers bent inward twice. She nodded as she came through the door.

'Have a seat.'

Abbie glared at him. A sit-down in Perelli's office was never good.

'Marty Collins. Tell me what you know.'

Abbie felt her skin itch.

'He's dead,' she said.

Perelli studied her. 'No shit. The whole city knows that. In fact, I've just received a call from Grady.' Bill Grady was the chief of police.

Perelli leaned across his desk.

'Who got a call from the mayor.'

Abbie looked up, startled. 'The mayor called him about Collins?'

'No, the mayor called him about the police budget for next year, but at the end he asked what was happening with the Collins investigation. Which was clearly the whole point of the call. And when a mayor mentions a case after talking about the budget, Kearney, the implication is very clear. Do you know what the implication is?'

Abbie thought for a second.

'The County vote.'

'Very good. Maybe you should be chief of police.'

The Irish in Buffalo had always held the advantage in numbers and political power. They'd elected a string of mayors going back to before Abbie was born. All of them had either been born in the County or had claimed it as their spiritual home, suddenly showing up at Bishop Timon football games, communion breakfasts and bingo nights at the Gaelic Club. But with the slow strangling of the city, more whites had left than blacks. As bad as things were in the County, things were worse on the mostly black East Side – the people there had less education, fewer skills. They were nailed to the pavement. They had nowhere to go, so they stayed. And a few of them even voted.

So now the numbers were roughly even. When, three years before, an Italian and an Irish candidate had failed to reach a consensus on who would represent the white neighborhoods, the black candidate, Reginald Theribauld, had snuck in and Buffalo had its first black mayor. It had made *USA Today* and caused a small ripple nationally – a civil rights 'first,' if a minor one. The mayor's seat in Buffalo was no longer a prize to be fought for and won; it was scraps for the desperate.

'What did the Chief tell Theribauld?' Abbie said.

'That there was probably a connection through the Gaelic Club.

That we were tracking it down. I'm sure that failed to calm the mayor's nerves.'

'There is a connection.'

'So I repeat my original question: What do you have?'

'Jimmy Ryan and Marty Collins were member of a semi-secret organization within the Gaelic Club. It's called the Clan na Gael.'

As she began to recite the details of her case, Perelli sank back in his chair and ran his hands through his thinning black hair.

'It's an old organization with roots in the movement to free Ireland from British rule. Back in the day, they took up arms, even went to war.'

'Here?' Perelli asked incredulously.

'Yes, but not for a century or so. They adapted, started providing money and arms to the IRA in Belfast. Even though Ireland is a republic and has been for decades, they believe that Northern Ireland remains . . . unfree. So they're true believers in the cause.'

'And something happened to make someone unhappy with this Clan?'

'It looks that way.'

Perelli nodded. 'What do Collins's family say? Enemies, recent threats?'

Abbie knew this was coming, knew what her answer would mean to Perelli.

'They haven't talked, so far.'

'They haven't talked, so far,' Perelli parroted. 'Tell me you've been over there.'

'Of course I've been over there. And his wife is unable to talk right now.'

Perelli's eyes grew harder. 'The same thing that Jimmy Ryan's family told you.'

'Yes. But I'm working around them.'

Perelli made an explosive sound with his mouth and turned toward the window.

'"Working around them" sounds like code for . . . I don't know, fucking bullshit.'

'I don't speak in code, Chief. You know me better than that.'

'Yes, I do. Listen . . .'

He swung back to face her.

'Maybe we should bring in—'

'Don't even say it.' Abbie instantly found herself on her feet, leaning three feet over Perelli's desk.

'Excuse me?!' Perelli shouted. 'Have you forgotten who the goddamn commanding officer is around here?'

'You are, Chief. But I thought you were about to say—'

'What?'

'That I can't work the County.'

Perelli's gaze dropped to his desk. 'I didn't say that. I said maybe you could use some help.'

'Some help in the form of a nice Irish detective, a local boy, you mean? Are you saying that they won't open up to a woman, is that it?'

'A woman from outside the neighborhood. You know the County as well as I do.'

'No, I know the County *better* than you do. And I know this case better than anyone.'

'What do you want me to do, Abbie?'

'What I want you to do is *back me up,* sir. Call the powers that be over there and tell them if I don't get some cooperation, there's going to be open hunting season on the Irish.'

'You have no idea what you're saying!' Perelli shouted. 'You want me to *threaten* the Irish community of this city with *further* murders of their . . . of their . . . loved ones, if they don't talk to you? Is that what you're saying?'

Abbie stalked away. Perelli slammed a file onto the desk.

'Where are you going?' he roared.

'It's not about me being from outside,' she said quietly.

'What?'

She turned to face him.

'It's . . . not . . . about . . . me being from outside the County.'

Perelli scoffed. 'No? That'll be a first.'

'With all due respect, Chief, you haven't been down there in a while. There's something about these murders that scares the County to death. Even the friends I grew up with are afraid to talk. Not because of who I am, but because of who the killer is.'

Perelli grew still.

'What you're telling me, Detective Kearney, is that the people in the County know who is committing these murders?'

'No,' Abbie said. 'If they knew, the killer would be dead.'

'Exactly. Thank you. Thank you very fucking much. So what?'

'They know and they don't know.'

Perelli threw up his hands. 'I can't . . . what does that mean?'

'Put it this way. If they don't know who he is, they know *why* he is. They know where he came from. It has to do with what the Clan was up to. Something has come back, some old political fight, or some falling-out between the members.'

'I'm giving you seventy-two hours,' Perelli said in a conversation-ending tone.

'Seventy-two hours? You're putting deadlines on my investigation now?'

'The mayor, the chief, and I agree that you've done good work here. You've established a link between the murders. But if the people won't talk to you, you're going to be severely hampered in what you can achieve.'

'That's bullshit. I don't need some Irish boy by my side to comfort the natives. That sends a bad message. They'll go straight to whoever you send with me and I'll be out in the cold.'

'Exactly where you are right now.'

Abbie strode over to Perelli's desk. He watched her approach, his chin shoved down into his striped tie. She laid her fingers on the edge of his desk, like a cool and collected DA with all the facts on her side.

'Chief.'

She waited until he made eye contact.

'This killer has control of his agenda unlike anything I've ever seen before. He's executing a plan and he's not deviating from it. He's already so far ahead of us that we're barely able to understand what he wants. If you put someone fresh on this, he'll finish his plan before we even know what hit us.'

Perelli stared at her with a pained look, as if he had a toothache. Abbie could tell that she'd just become his mother, his wife, another woman he didn't want to listen to.

'Abbie, get something for me to wave in the mayor's face. If you want backup, put some faces on this desk. Suspects. A chain of evidence. Enough with the ghost stories.'

He threw his right hand up in the air and let it slap back on the table, loud.

'Whatever the fuck you want to call it. Get me a living, breathing human being. Got it?'

'Will the killer do, or just anybody?'

Abbie was out the door before Perelli could bite her head off.

TWENTY

Abbie consoled herself with a Super Mighty from the Mighty Taco drive-thru and brought it back to headquarters. Z was at his desk as she sat down.

'Eating healthy, I see.'

'Word of advice. Don't start with me today.'

'What happened?'

'Collins's family clammed up. Wouldn't even let me in the door. They're taking the issue to the United Retard Irish Council, or whoever they expect to solve this thing. Damned voodoo Micks.'

Z shook his head.

'You're going to tell me, "I told you so."'

'Yeah,' he said. 'I am.'

'What do you want me to do? Leave them to sort out their own dead, is that it?'

'Hell no. I'm just as frustrated as you are. I just think you've got to realize who you're dealing with.'

'And who's that?'

'Damned voodoo Micks. They don't change.'

She sat back in her chair, pulled the burrito out of the bag and stared at it.

'You'll never guess who's guarding the widow Collins.'

Z looked up at her.

'Billy Carney.'

'No!' Z seemed genuinely shocked. 'You thought he was dead for sure.'

Abbie took a bite of the burrito and nodded as she chewed. She could feel the nutrients pumping into her bloodstream, calming the rage. She really needed to eat better – and more often.

'He's been reincarnated. As protection.'

Z shook his head. 'Amateur bodyguards. Short life spans.'

Abbie nodded again.

Z got up and pulled on his heavy winter coat.

'I'm off.'

Abbie, lost in thought, nodded.

'Hold on,' she said.

Z turned.

'You're right. We need to go around the County instead of hitting a brick wall there every time.'

Z spread his hands, saying *What have I been telling you?*

'Can you drop by Circuit Court for me? See who Marty Collins represented in the past, say, twenty years. Look for drug dealers, gang members, East Siders who look sketchy. Also, look for any County types he represented, anyone with a connection to the Gaelic Club. Maybe the link between our three victims is through a court case.'

'Should I pack a suitcase?'

'From what I remember in Miami, the court clerk can do a computer search by lawyer.'

'They do that in Miami? How nice. Here the records are probably six feet high and turning yellow.'

Abbie smiled. 'Next time, lunch is on me, goombah.'

Z waved a hand and headed for the glass doors that led to the elevator.

She wiped the corner of her mouth with a napkin, set the burrito to the side, and whipped out her phone.

'Kearney.'

'It's Dr Reinholdt.'

'Yes, Doctor. What were you able to find out?'

'Well, it's a pretty murky picture. There are quite a few possibilities. Are you sure you wouldn't rather discuss this face-to-face?'

She rolled her eyes at Z's empty cubicle.

'I'd love to, but I can't.'

He sighed. 'All right, then. The Clan na Gael is part of the IRA. There are no real distinctions in the context we're discussing. The

IRA laid its arms down in 1998 after the agreement with the British government. Many of its prisoners were released; its guns were turned in; its mission was effectively over. But of course 1921 repeated itself.'

'I'm sorry, Doctor, my knowledge of Irish history isn't quite as sharp as yours. Please elaborate for me.'

'The IRA split, just as it did when Ireland first won its independence in 1921 – without the six counties that now make up Northern Ireland. A faction didn't recognize the agreement; they wanted all or nothing. So the IRA went to war with itself. The same thing happened about a decade ago. So today you have a rogue element – they call themselves the Real IRA, how original – still wearing the ski masks . . .'

Abbie stopped writing.

'Ski masks?'

'They're called balaclavas in Ireland. Very popular with the boys. Lends a certain mystique to the kneecapping.'

'Okay, go on.'

'So the old IRA and the Real IRA are engaged in a low-level war for control. It's resulted in quite a few dead bodies scattered all over the Republic and Northern Ireland.'

Abbie nodded. The idea of revolutionaries or terrorists or whatever you wanted to call them falling out with each other had already occurred to her. It fit the savagery of the crimes. But to reach all the way across the Atlantic and touch the County?

'Are you still there, Detective?'

'I'm here, Doctor. Please go on.'

'There's more. The war with the British is still a live issue for the Real IRA. So they're continuing to run guns into the country and raise money and buy plastic explosives. The whole gamut of terrorist infrastructure, you might say. They've even partnered with outfits like FARC in South America, sending their men over to train the rebels there and getting money and weapons in return.'

'And FARC runs drugs.'

'Oh, they're notorious for it.'

'Is it possible that the Real IRA is trying to open up a drug business in the States? Bringing a supply in through Canada, using their connections from the old fund-raising days?'

'It's possible. Even some of the IRA members who laid down their arms couldn't give up the taste for rebellion. My contact says parts of the organization basically transformed itself into a criminal gang once the peace treaty was signed. Heroin in Belfast, cocaine in Limerick, it's all run through the old revolutionary network.'

'Interesting,' Abbie said. 'They had the transportation networks from gunrunning, they had the contacts in the underworld, and presumably they had money from their hardcore supporters.'

'Yes. I guess it's not easy to become an insurance adjuster after you've been throwing bombs at a police barracks.'

Abbie mm-hmmed and scratched a few final notes.

'Thanks for getting back to me.'

'I have nothing but time over here, Detective.'

Abbie checked her watch and decided a workout was in order. She jumped up, made a beeline for the elevator, and in twenty minutes was at her health club three blocks away. An hour on the treadmill and ten minutes each at three workout stations had her blood pressure percolating in her ears. A hunky guy on the abs cruncher watched her as she did shoulders, not even bothering to glance at the TV behind her. He had good hair and a rich guy's smirk.

A steam shower brought her blood pressure the rest of the way down. On the way out of the club, she turned right and ducked into a Starbucks two storefronts down. She ordered a chai latte and reached into her bag to pay for it, pulling out her orange leather wallet.

Her cell buzzed as she pulled out the money. It was Z. 'At County Clerk,' it said. 'Get here now.'

Abbie walked into the County Clerk's office, a Depression-era dump of a building on Court Street, faced with yellowing limestone. It was cold enough to see her breath inside – she wondered if the city was having trouble paying its bills – so she kept her jacket on as she milled through the lawyers, frustrated citizens, and bond runners who were forming up lines. She checked her phone. No signal.

Damned Z, she said to herself. *Why didn't he tell me* where *in the building he was?*

She ducked her head in three offices before stopping to think. She checked her watch. It was 12:45 p.m. She sighed.

'Ma'am,' she said, flagging down a passing guard, dressed in a dark blue uniform with gold rope trim. 'Where's the cafeteria?'

The woman swiveled and pointed toward a door. 'Two floors down, make your first left, then another.'

Abbie thanked the woman and headed to the stairs. When she pushed open the heavy wooden door two floors down, she made two lefts and smelled macaroni and cheese after the first one. She found Z sitting at the first table to the right in the near-empty cafeteria. He was nursing a coffee and eating a danish while he leafed through a six-inch-high stack of documents.

'Anything interesting?'

He looked up, then motioned with his coffee cup to the seat across from him.

'What'd I tell you about the stacks?'

'You're going to get Cop of the Month. What'd you find?'

Z put down his coffee, placed the document he'd been reading to the left of the stack, and pulled a manila case folder from the top.

'This.'

Abbie flipped open the file and saw a mug shot of a man with burning black eyes and a six-day growth of dark beard.

'Seamus O'Murchu,' Z said, pronouncing the 'ch' as a hard 'k.' 'Or "O-Mur-tchu." How the hell you say it I have no idea. In December 1980, he was caught coming across the Peace Bridge with a nine-millimeter tucked in his waistband.'

Abbie was reading the charge. 'And Marty Collins took the case.'

'Yep. First call this guy makes. Must have had the number in his back pocket.'

'He was traveling on a British passport, resident of Clonmel in Northern Ireland. A record of arrests for intimidation, possession of a handgun . . .'

'And look who was driving the car.'

Abbie flipped ahead a page, then another. She began to read again. 'Jimmy Ryan.'

'None other.'

'Never charged, but he's mentioned here in the arrest report. He said he'd gone up to Niagara Falls to do some gambling at the Indian casino when O'Murchu offered him twenty bucks for a ride back to Buffalo. O'Murchu claimed that he'd been cleaned out playing black-jack and couldn't afford the bus back.'

Abbie looked up. 'Z, that can't be true. They only sell round-trip tickets on those bus coaches that go up there. You need proof that you can make it back to the United States before they let you in. The Canadian government didn't want to be responsible for a bunch of broke gamblers.'

Z took a sip of his coffee and shook his head wonderingly. 'How do you know this shit?'

'I had friends in high sch— never mind, it's not important. What's important is that the guy lied.'

'And I'll bet Jimmy Ryan knew it. Who goes up to Canada and gives a perfect stranger a ride back across a border? The guy could have been carrying heroin or his passport could have scanned for an outstanding warrant. Jimmy's street-smart by this time, he's not going to take that risk for twenty dollars.'

'You're right. You think it was a meet?'

'Of course it was. He went up there to get this guy, and the idiot forgot about the gun he was carrying.'

She sat back in her chair. A bunch of lawyers walked into the cafeteria, arguing loudly about the hockey game the night before.

'This is August 1980. Jimmy's mother said he started hanging out at the Gaelic Club right before he started at National Grid. When was that again?'

Z pulled a notebook out of his lapel pocket.

'Hold on, hold on. I have the interview with his boss here.'

Z licked his thumb and began flicking through pages.

'Nineteen eighty. He was hired in January.'

Abbie nodded. 'So he's been going by the Club by then. He's got a record for minor drug offenses, small-time dealing, and I'm sure everyone there knew that; it's impossible to keep something like that secret in the County. He has connections across the border. Then seven months later, he's caught coming back with an armed IRA militant, who has Marty Collins's number in his back pocket for emergencies. What does that tell you?'

'Jimmy's in the Clan already.'

'And he's their errand boy. Meeting their contacts and escorting them across the border.'

Z swirled his coffee in his cup, his shoulders hunched over. Abbie tapped the edge of the table.

'But for what?' she said. 'A meeting? Were they setting up some kind of new drug route?'

'Could be.'

'It could be, but I'm not convinced. Look at where Jimmy Ryan lived; if there's a house owned by a National Grid route-walker, it's that. He didn't have money for luxuries. His wife said he took out a second mortgage on the house just to pay for Catholic school for the kids. And Collins had money, but not drug distribution money. I want you to get his tax returns, see if they match up with his lifestyle.'

'Done.'

'If they were opening up Buffalo as a drug entryway to the U.S., don't you think they would have lived better? Don't you think Jimmy Ryan, from all we know about him, would have splurged on a fishing boat, or a vacation home up in Crystal Beach? But he didn't have money like that for twenty years. And not to hear one whisper of his drug deals, not one? The County's good at keeping secrets, but not that good.'

'Guns?'

'Same problem. If the Clan was exporting guns through Canada and across the Atlantic, where's the money?'

'Maybe they were doing it for the cause.'

The face of Jimmy Ryan's mother popped into Abbie's mind. The pride in her boy was practically shining out of the woman's face. Had Jimmy been involved in wholesaling cocaine to western New York, would her eyes have been glowing with motherly pride? Would she have accepted his death so easily?

And then there was Billy Carney's transformation from a has-been to a sleek young gangster. She knew Billy; he'd been looking for a role to play ever since he tossed his baseball glove in the back of his closet. Fronting for a drug outfit? It was dirty, unheroic. It didn't scan.

But running guns for the IRA? In the County, that would earn respect. A great deal of respect.

'Let's think about what we know. We know the killer is hunting members of the Clan na Gael. We know the Clan is or was involved in supporting the cause of the IRA. Billy Carney said there were four members; two are dead. The Clan isn't cooperating, and we can assume they're hunting the killer, too. We know that Jimmy Ryan was bringing something across the border and there's an IRA connection. We know Jimmy had a past with drugs. And we know the killings have been very well thought out and highly personal.'

'There's the ski mask.'

'Right. He wears a mask. But we don't know *why.* Is he protecting his identity against cameras and possible eyewitnesses, like any skel who's going to rob a 7-Eleven? Or is he protecting it because people in the County would know him in a minute?'

'He could just be cold. My fucking pipes froze last night.'

'He's not just cold, Z.'

'My head is starting to hurt, which means it's time to stop thinking. What else?'

'The monkeys.'

'Dead end. I checked with the manufacturer like you asked. Production started in 1968. They made millions of 'em. If you throw a stick on Genesee Street, you're going to hit three people who played with them as a kid.'

'But it gives us a glimpse into motive. It's personal. More than that, it feels—'

Z winced. He hated when she used that word in a professional context.

'It *feels biographical,*' she said, leaning in. 'The murders involve the killer's past in some way. Those toys were worn down with use. Someone loved them. Let's put it this way: it could date the origin of the motive.'

Z hunched over and stared angrily into Abbie's face.

'That's where you drive me crazy. If the toys are personal, they date the whatever the fuck you called it – the origin – to when? When's the latest someone plays with things like Monkey in a Barrel? When they were eight, nine? Are you telling me that Jimmy Ryan did something to this wacko when they were in grammar school and now, twenty years later, he's come back for revenge?'

Z leaned back and spread his arms in supplication.

'Ab, come *on*.'

Abbie folded her arms and leaned back against the backrest of the chair. Her mind was spinning.

'It's a black box. We can't know what any of it means until we have a leak from inside the County. We *have* to get someone to talk.'

'Right. Sure. I've been up and down South Park and Seneca talking to all the young business executives and Internet millionaires that drink dry martinis in the bars there. And they're stumped. I know when someone's holding back and this ain't it. They're in the same position we are. Spectators. The Clan or whoever is running the show has this wrapped up tighter than a Catholic girl's panties.'

Abbie made a face.

'Sorry. Tighter than, uh . . .'

'Forget about it, Z. I can feel a bad Jewish reference coming on. Who's the person most likely to talk? Who's most desperate right now?'

Z tapped his fingers on the table, looked past his shoulder. He looked like a contemplative walrus, thought Abbie. Finally, his eyes switched back to hers.

'The two remaining members.'

'Exactly. They know they've got a bull's-eye burning through the back of their shirts right now. And, if the Clan isn't using them for bait – which I find unthinkable, knowing how the County feels about all things Irish – then they must have the two of them locked down somewhere, with no access except for the absolutely trusted. We need to go back to the bars and find out who's gone missing from work unexpectedly. Whose house has a car parked in front of it day and night? Who's canceled their bowling night out with the boys?'

'That's good.'

'But it's not good enough. Let's face it, Z, we're not even playing at the killer's level right now. And you know how much I like that.'

'You look tired, Ab.'

'You keep saying that.'

'You keep making me say that. Go home and get some rest.'

'I will.'

'No, you won't. You're going to go find Patty Ryan.'

Abbie smiled.

'Now, how'd you know that?'

'Because she knows something you don't. And we all know that's one thing you can't stand.'

TWENTY-ONE

When Abbie rang the doorbell at Jimmy Ryan's house, it was his mother who answered.

'Abbie! You've come for the photo.'

Abbie hadn't expected the old woman, but she smiled. 'Well, yes.'

'Come in, come in.'

Abbie stepped through the door onto the semi-shag carpet.

'I found it yesterday,' she whispered. 'God knows what Patty was thinking – it was taken out of its frame and hidden away beneath the Waterford clock on their bedroom mantel. A strange place for a photo, don'tcha think?'

Abbie tilted her head and made a face. 'With all that's happened . . .'

'Sure, her mind's in a thousand places. The paint stuck to the bottom of the clock as I lifted it. I hope she doesn't notice.'

That's odd, Abbie thought.

'Wait here.' Mrs Ryan's smile faltered and a look of spreading horror came over her face as she turned away. 'Now let me think where I put it.'

Jesus Christ, thought Abbie. *Please remember where you put it.*

With one palm on her forehead as if she were a magician guessing a card, Mrs Ryan weaved her way toward the kitchen.

There was the clatter of drawers opening and cupboards being searched. Abbie sighed and studied the mantel. All the pictures were there except the one of the three men. If Mrs Ryan did find it, she hoped someone could recognize the back of the third man's head. There was no doubt Jimmy Ryan and Marty Collins were the other two.

Mrs Ryan bustled back into the living room, her face beaming.

'We're just like a pair of spies, aren't we, Abbie, like what's his name – James Bond.'

Her face was close to Abbie's now, and it had the terrible, friendly intensity that old Irish people sometimes had – the bursting blue eyes and the lips pulled back over the big shiny teeth, as if they were preparing to take a hungry little nip at your nose.

She slid the picture away from her chest and placed it in Abbie's outstretched palm.

'You'll make sure to take care of this?'

'Don't worry, Mrs Ryan. It's safe with me.'

Abbie smiled. And again she marveled at how calm this woman was, with her son dead and in the ground just a week ago. *And she hasn't even asked me how the investigation is going*, Abbie thought.

Abbie said her goodbyes and turned to leave.

'When this is all over, you come to my house for tea,' the old woman said, pronouncing it *tay*.

'I'd be happy to,' Abbie said, feeling a little ashamed of how she'd tricked the old woman into finding the picture, while at the same time her brain tingled with giddiness at having it in her hot little hand.

She turned and pushed the screen door open and stepped onto the porch. When she heard the wooden door close with a rush of air, she looked greedily down at the photo.

'Damn it all—'

It was the wrong picture.

Abbie smacked the photo against her palm and stamped on the porch, turning to stare at the door. A tiny burst of water from a puddle there sprayed against her pant leg as she looked to see if Mrs Ryan was watching her from behind the curtains.

Had the old woman switched it or had it been hiding under the clock for months or years? *That crafty little bitch*, she thought. *That scheming old . . .*

Abbie sighed and stepped down to the first porch step. She looked down at the picture again. It had clearly been taken the same day as the other one, but now the third man was different. He was taller and wearing a green polo shirt and his hair was chestnut brown and slicked back.

Her eyes darted to the man's face and she almost tumbled down onto the concrete path. Her vision slurred and her mind seemed to swerve and dip like a Tilt-a-Whirl.

Abbie dashed for her car at a dead run.

Sean MacCullahy took a modest sip from the pint of foamy Molson Golden and settled back in the stout wooden chair. He felt the beer slip down his throat. It was a harmless little drop, a tiny sting from the tail of a monster that had consumed nearly half his life. Having the taste was like nodding to a murderous old friend, now locked in shackles, begging through thick iron bars to talk shite about the old days. Sean had one beer and one beer only every time he came to the Gaelic Club, just to say he could. The whole crowd knew he'd beaten the drink, especially the ones who'd taken the Pledge – the Irish Church's oath, whereby young men and women swore never to touch alcohol. Even they would nod at him with a gleam in their eye, though they couldn't know the first thing of what he'd been through. But he'd nod back to them, peaceable now within himself.

Good man, Sean, they were saying with their eyes. *Show the fecker who won.*

Won? Drink had nearly ruined his life. Not nearly, it *had*. He'd been a black-browed terror to his wife, Colleen, whom he'd buried twelve years ago after exhausting her faith in the power of God. He'd barely known his two girls and one boy except as targets for his late-night rants on the subject of their mother's whoredom and their probably being the offspring of some guinea trashman (the coloring on Margaret, his oldest, had always seemed suspiciously dark to him, her cheeks dusky even in the deepest winter).

He'd made a *hames* of his marriage, as they said back in Cork.

And yet he'd had a sterling career as a cop, retired now twenty years. Proved what you could do with a hickory nightstick and a mean disposition. And in his fourth day off the job he'd sworn off the drink. It made him wonder if it was alcohol that had cursed him, or the streets of Buffalo. After he'd left them, he'd never felt the urge to lose himself in a bottle.

But he'd survived it. His second girl, Colleen like her mother, was even talking to him now, over the phone. Who knew, he might get to see his grandkids one day.

He let his eyes drift across the crowd and settle on John Kearney, sitting across from him now, his old partner in the First Ward.

'Did you see the car he pulled up in?' John said.

Sean looked over to see where John had indicated with the nod of his head and the gaze of his steely blue eyes. Ah, Patrick Carduzzi. Half-Italian and half-Irish, but he preened around the Club like the son of Saint Patrick. The fool.

'Was it a big Cadillac?' Sean said.

'Course,' John Kearney said, and they laughed. 'You can take the guinea out of a person, but . . .'

Sean caught John's slitted eye and they both cackled. How right he was. On St Patrick's Day, the man practically painted himself green. Just awful.

Through the crowd, Sean saw a strange black-haired woman approach. A look of incomprehension spread across his face. What was she doing in the Gaelic Club? His eyes narrowed before he realized that, of course, it was Absalom Kearney. She'd brought him here today. He was losing his mind, too.

He liked Absalom. Hardworking, a good daughter to John. She had no choice about who she was, after all – she'd been taken from her natural surroundings like an orphaned kitten – and Sean accepted that. Hot-tempered when roused to it, but wasn't he the same way himself?

He took another drink, and nodded at Tom Murphy, the embezzler.

Sean remembered the day John told her he was adopting an orphaned child, the absolute shock of it. 'Y'are *not!*' he'd blurted out, but John had gone silent and grim and his eyes were like coals from the bottom of turf pit. John would never discuss it afterward. For him, it was some kind of holy obligation. What else could possess an Irishman in 1982 to adopt a gypsy-looking child and give it his own name?

John had looked exhausted, worn down to a shadow, that day that he carried Absalom home. In one arm he'd carried the toddler, wrapped up in a dirty green blanket. The other hand held an old Bible with a cordovan cover and a photograph album with a faded green cover, taken from the mother's things. *It's more than a Bible you'll need,* thought Sean at the time.

But he'd never asked why John had done it. It was none of his business.

'Gentlemen,' Abbie said as she placed a cup of coffee on the table in front of him, the cup making a tinkling noise against the saucer. She did the same for her father, tea with milk. John never drank coffee. How well Sean knew that, after twenty years of buying the man a Red Rose tea every morning without a cent in payment.

'Good girl, Abbie,' Sean said, giving her a bright smile. John nodded curtly and ignored the tea. Sean, a touch embarrassed, smiled up at Abbie, who for some reason was looking rather intently at him.

At a loss for something to say, he nodded toward the crowd at the bar.

'Don't bother with us, now. Go find yourself a young man.'

The girl laughed, richly, deep in her throat.

'Thanks, Mr MacCullahy. But the youngest man here just had both his hips replaced.'

He smiled.

'Have everything you need?' She leaned over and smiled, staring him directly in the eye.

'Fine, fine,' he said, again a little confused.

The girl was trying to be her father's daughter. She'd always tried.

Sean rearranged the coffee so it wouldn't spill if someone bumped the table, then looked up to see Absalom talking to a tall man in an Irish rugby shirt, with his back turned to the table. She was, Sean noticed, tapping her breast absently as she talked. He watched her hand flutter for a second, a long-buried erotic urge pushing at his bowels.

She looked over at him. He stared back, trying to decipher the look in her eyes.

'Oh, Jaysus, I forgot,' he said suddenly, looking at John.

Sean reached into his lapel pocket and casually pulled out a photo.

'I found this picture in my drawer in the workshop. Couldn't remember where it was taken. You and Marty Collins, God rest his soul.'

He slid the picture across to John Kearney, who was pulling his gold-rimmed reading glasses out of the LensCrafters pouch he carried in his front shirt pocket.

'Marty?' he said, an edge of concern in his tenor voice.

He picked up the photo shakily and studied it.

'And that other one. Jimmy Ryan. Looks like it was taken out at the lake.'

''Twas,' John said, and his eyes grew big behind the powerful lenses.

'Did I take it?' Sean said, looking away. 'I can't remember now.' He'd always been an able liar. Came with being a drunk.

'No, you weren't there. I . . .'

John's cheek, webbed with blue veins, suddenly began twitching.

'Sean?'

'Yes?'

'Where'd you say you found this photo?'

'In my workshop, back at the house. In my old fishing box.'

John's eyes were dangerously aflame.

'Then you're a born liar. What the hell is this?'

He threw the photo face-up on the table, then clouted it hard with his open hand. The slap rang in the air like a bell clap, and the buzz of conversation dimmed, faces at the bar turning to look. John's entire face was red now and his pale lips were set in a straight line, like a petulant boy.

'Where you goin'?' Sean said. 'Sit down—'

'Where'd you get that picture?' Yelling now.

'John, calm down and have your tea.'

But John Kearney pushed his seat away and stumbled back. Then he turned toward the door and was lost in the crowd.

A few seconds later, Abbie slid into the chair.

'I tried my best, Absalom.'

'I know you did.'

Sean looked down at the photo, studied the three men. He sighed; he was sure he hadn't been there. And he couldn't understand why it was so important to know who took it.

'Couldn't you just ask him yourself?' he said finally.

He regretted it instantly, for the sharp jab of pain that came into her bright blue eyes.

TWENTY-TWO

Abbie spent the rest of the afternoon trawling the bars of the County for information on missing men in their fifties or sixties. She started in the bars of South Park, dank, dark rooms even in the middle of the day, lit only by the yellow lights over the pool tables and the red and white glow of the cigarette machines, with shadowy figures moving beneath stark cones of light. There was usually someone holding their face with a busted paw, victim of a fistfight, or muted sounds of couples battling in the alleyway behind. Abbie didn't bother to ask about the blood and the noise. Maybe the County was beginning to work on her, finally, as everyone predicted it would. She ignored the wounded and asked each bartender about regulars who'd gone missing.

The answers she got drove her mood down further. There were about three dozen men gone in South Buffalo. There was a crane operator who'd lost his job and disappeared last week, leaving his German shepherd to starve to death. There was a fireman who'd never got back on the plane from the Vegas 'training convention,' which was really a whoring and gambling spree paid for by dollar bills placed in buckets of men going door to door in their metal hats. He hadn't been heard from since. Maybe he'd stayed in Vegas because he liked the novel sight of the sun in January. His neighbors had rung his wife's doorbell to see if there was anything they could do, but the woman had told them to fuck off, he was no good anyway and she was moving to North Carolina. There were barbers, insurance agents, Costco managers, and a whole squad of unemployed that had gone less dramatically, slipping away in a swirl of rumor and unpaid bills. And none of them had left a forwarding address.

By the end of the night, the soles of her shoes were sticky with rancid beer, and her hair smelled of cigarette smoke. Maybe Billy Carney had been right with his talk about the Rez. An invisible war was under way that she was powerless even to interrupt, a war of attrition.

When she came home, she was about to put her key into the lock when she noticed something by the hallway light. Something stuck under her door. It was white, the corner of a piece of paper. She dropped down and studied it. The paper was blank, but there was clearly more of it under the door. Abbie took the corner and began to pull.

As it came out, she saw writing in green – but it wasn't a note. It was the packaging for a 50cc syringe, made by Hamilton.

Abbie stood up quickly and stuck the key in the lock. Turning the door handle, she burst into the room. And she knew from the quality of silence that her father was already gone.

Billy Carney was watching the Buffalo Sabres lose again on TV. A can of Molson Export sat on the coffee table next to his cell phone and the Sig Sauer. The volume was turned down low. It was the third period and the Sabres were down by one against the Maple Leafs. Billy watched the figures of the players sway and dash, willing someone to put the puck in the net.

When he heard the noise, it sounded like it was coming from the side of the house toward the Riordans. He scooped up the Sig and slid to the wall in two steps, reaching over to kill the light switch, all in one herky-jerk motion. His eardrums seemed to throb as he listened in the dark, the plasma TV glowing as Rick Jeanneret called the play-by-play. Billy found he was calm.

The sound had come from the bathroom. A scraping noise. He slid his back along the wall until he came to the hallway. Suddenly, he turned back and looked at the TV screen, then bent over double and padded over to the coffee table. He hit the power button and the picture died. The quiet of the house surged into the room.

You think you're hunting me, you coward? Billy thought. *You got it backward. I've been waiting for you.*

The Sig felt snug in his hand as he padded quickly to the wall and threw his back against it. Billy's heart was pumping painfully. He felt the edge of the wall and made the turn slowly into the hallway, the tube socks on his feet – Bishop Timon green and gold stripes around his calves – masking the sound of his movement.

Billy ducked his head and peered into the gloom of the hallway bathroom. The moonlight was coming through the window and the porcelain sink was glowing. As he edged further along the wall, he could see the shower curtain was stretched taut. Hadn't he left it pulled back to the wall when he showered that morning? He tried to think back but couldn't remember.

I hope you're in there. I'm going to put one through your eye socket and watch you die.

The sweat on his chest felt cold. He was afraid, sure, but . . .

Billy's face tensed and then he strode into the bathroom, ripping the curtain back. It was empty.

He breathed out with a 'Haaa,' and the gun smacked down on his thigh. His body seemed made of rubber.

Then he noticed the window. The bottom of the chintz curtain was rippling in a silent breeze.

The window that had been shut for three months against the winter cold.

The Sig came up, shaking. The moisture in his mouth disappeared and his tongue felt as dry as a lizard's. Billy backed out of the bathroom, his spine a column of ice. He looked wildly up and down the hallway.

Nothing.

Then he heard it again. The scraping. It was coming from the bedroom this time.

Billy turned. The white trim around the open door seemed to glow in the gloom.

He ran to it, sliding the last few feet on the polished floor. When he hit the doorjamb, he slid down to his knees, then brought the Sig up and around, rotating it fast toward where he'd heard the sound. He hugged the doorjamb as he brought his right eye around to follow the gun.

The scraping stopped.

Billy whipped his head around the doorframe. Curtain blowing again, but nobody there.

He heard footsteps crunching in the snow.

Billy took a deep breath. *I'll call it in,* he thought. *No need to be a cowboy,* he thought. *I'll get Mick over here, and Tommy—*

BOOOOMMMM. BOOOOOMMMM.

Someone was banging on his front door.

The sound seemed to send concussion waves back to where Billy was crouched on the floor. Something was trying to knock the door down. Knock the fucking *house* down.

He got up, his eyes painfully wide, and brought the Sig up. The door was directly in front of him along the glossy length of hallway. He could see it shiver as another blow hit it.

The lock rattled.

He got up and began walking toward the door.

BOOOOOMMMM.

He brought the Sig up and the right corner of his eyelid began to tic.

Suddenly the green glass in the door window exploded inward. The Sig waved wildly as Billy stopped at the entrance to the living room. He could see the snow in his front yard through the hole and feel the thin current of cold air streaming into the room.

A black-gloved hand came snaking in.

The hand began to search for the lock, tapping against the wood like a blind man.

Billy hissed in a sliver of breath and felt the ridges on the Sig trigger tighten against his index finger. He took aim at the center of the door and he visualized the hole that would be blasted there and the scream of the fag—

Before he could complete the thought, the door shot open. A blast deafened him and his vision went white. He coughed hoarsely and was reaching for his eyes when something slammed into his thorax and pile-drove him back to the floor. It landed on top of him and drove the air out of his lungs. The butt of the Sig bounced hard against the floor, and the gun went skittering away.

Gasping for air, Billy struggled wildly but he was pinned to the floor by the animal strength of the thing pressing down on him. He felt the hot muzzle of a gun pressed to his forehead. He opened his eyes and saw the white ceiling. Directly above him, a gaping hole had been blasted in the plaster and dust was drifting down.

He shook his head wildly, trying to get the dust out of his eyes. Finally they cleared enough to see Abbie Kearney sitting on his chest. Her eyes were hard and not quite sane.

She moved the gun from the middle of his forehead and jammed it into his open mouth.

I'm going to die, he thought.

'Where . . . is . . . my . . . goddamn . . . father,' Ab said. But it wasn't her voice. It was the moan of a crazy person who hears nothing and sees only darkness.

'He'th okay, he'th okay.'

The gun barrel twisted. He could feel the muzzle rotate on his tongue, the circle hot.

'Show him to me, Billy. Or you die.'

'He'th thafe, Ab.' The gun pinned his tongue to the floor of his mouth. The pain was making his eyes water and the tears leaked down toward his sideburns. He bucked against her thin form but she ground her thighs and butt into his stomach and he found he couldn't lift her off. Her thighs were like tensed steel springs.

His ears still ringing, Billy took a breath. Then he stopped bucking and relaxed his body. A gentle look came into his eyes and he slowly reached up with his hands. When the palms touched the cold outer layer of Abbie's black down jacket, he pressed her shoulders gently.

'Okay, Ab, okay.'

Her eyes seemed to swivel and then focus, like an old-fashioned film camera changing lenses. Slowly she took the gun from his mouth. Billy felt his tongue unclench painfully. He looked at Ab's eyes, the bruised flesh around the eyes. *My God, what's happening to her?*

'He's at Mercy Hospital,' he said. 'Room 1014. He passed out. He's under sedation.'

The look in Abbie's eyes changed from madness to terrified worry.

'How do you know this?' she whispered.

'We had a guy watching your house when you were out. He was in the hallway. He heard the thump of your dad hitting the floor.'

Abbie rested her palm on his chest and the weight of it startled him, as if she were about to collapse on top of him.

'My father was in the Clan,' she said in a dazed voice.

Billy nodded. 'For years.'

'Who's the other one, Billy?'

He took a breath. 'I don't know.'

The look came back into her eyes.

'Ab, I do not fucking know.'

She raised her knees off his chest and began to stand, her butt high in the air.

Billy took a breath. 'Jesus, you had me sc—'

She grabbed his shirt and pulled him up, his shoulders seeming to levitate off the floor. Her strength startled him.

'Ab, what were you—'

With a grunt, she pivoted sideways, slammed her hip into his crotch, and threw him over the couch.

Billy crashed through the coffee table and felt the glass cut deeply through his right forearm.

'*Ab!*'

She was going to kill him.

He stood up as she came racing around the couch. Her hands came slamming against his cheek and the two of them careened toward the living room windows. At the last minute, he swung her around and pinned her with a cry against the window.

'Ab, listen to me!' he shouted.

She opened her mouth to speak and then swiveled her neck and tried to bite his hand with her teeth.

He pushed his forearm into her neck, pinning her knees with his legs. His crotch was pressed against her stomach.

'Okay, I'll tell you – if you'll *calm the fuck down.*'

She began to breathe fast, then her eyes came back and locked on his. They were almost sane now and he breathed out.

'Okay?'

She nodded.

He dropped his arm away from her. He winced, the pain of his gashed arm coming to him sharply. It felt like there was a shard in there still cutting him from inside.

'You're a fucking sick one, you know that? I ought to tie you up.'

She looked at him, the mascara smeared around her eyes.

'Who is he?'

'Fuck you. Shoot me.'

She dropped the gun to her side.

'Who, Billy?'

Billy took a deep breath. 'His name's Joe Kane,' he said. 'We just found this out. Nobody knew except one source who finally gave up the name. He used to be a cop. He disappeared four days ago.'

'Is he dead?'

'We don't know.'

TWENTY-THREE

She called the hospital and spoke to a Dr Singh. Her father was indeed under sedation. No diagnosis yet. He told her they would know more in the morning. It wasn't a stroke, that they did know. And she could see him tomorrow at the earliest.

When the phone call ended, her body seemed to droop. This was the third fainting spell in the last six months. But at least he was safe.

She put her cell phone on the frame of the shattered table. Then she looked over at Billy.

'He's doing okay.'

Billy nodded.

A hank of disheveled hair hung over his forehead. The dish towel wrapped around his right arm was beginning to leak through. A drop of blood spattered silently on his dirty carpet.

She tilted her head and looked at it, then up at his face. Her brows arched.

'Even?' she asked.

Billy looked up. 'Even?' he said.

'Yeah. Even?'

'What the fuck do you mean, *"even"*?'

'For junior prom. Are we even now?'

Billy threw up his hands and collapsed back into his chair.

'I was half a second from blowing your head off. *Half . . . a . . . second.*'

'And I was half a second from doing the same to you. Like I said, even.'

He looked at her eyes and wondered how he could even consider forgiving her. The madness in her eyes was gone and it had been

178

replaced not by remorse but by a bruised sadness. He stared into their depths, his anger draining away. He brushed the rest of the plaster dust off his clothes and looked Abbie up and down for the first time that night. She turned toward him, hitched her leg up on the couch cushion, rested her elbow on her knee and her chin on her palm, and looked at him levelly.

His eyes drifted down the length of her, seeing her for the first time not as a thin and intense schoolgirl from Mount Mercy, but as an electric thing. The memory of her body pressing down on his, its sinews and muscles, was still imprinted on his mind, and a thin pall of heat seemed to cover his stomach and crotch where she had ground into him. His eyes came back up, noticed the silky material of the shirt straining at the button between her two upturned breasts, and his eyes continued up the torquing flute of her neck, the curve of her lips – had she applied *lipstick* before coming to nearly kill him, or did she do it while she was on the phone? – the full cheeks and the blue eyes, now calm with the power of her body.

They watched each other for a moment, and the sound seemed to vanish out of the room and all he could hear was her breathing, not his.

'You put your gun in my mouth,' he said.

She smiled, a wicked look in her eyes. Arching her back, she stood up slowly and walked over to him. He noticed for the first time that her thighs had filled out since Mount Mercy days and the skin was mimicked by the thin gray wool of her slacks so that she appeared naked. His eyes got no higher than her thin red belt as she stood in front of him.

She placed her hands on top of his as they gripped the arms of the leather chair. And she slowly bent down.

'I do believe,' she said, 'I can make that up to you.'

As he led her to the bedroom, Abbie felt the last tendril of blackness leave her mind. She didn't remember much of the past twenty minutes. But now her eyes and mind were aligned and tracking in slow motion. She could hear the tap of her footsteps on the oak floor, hear the hum of the refrigerator, the wind in the eaves of the house next door. She reached up and touched Billy's sweater, on his back between the shoulder blades. Her jacket lay on the floor behind her.

The grief that had shot through her on hearing her father was sick had left her body aching for comfort. Billy was here, and he was lovely and warm. And she didn't question it at all.

When they got in the room, it was dark and the white sheets on the bed glowed lavender in the moonlight. She knew he was going to be aggressive, to reclaim something she had snatched away for a moment, and she was happy as he turned and reached to her right breast and mashed it with his big hand, tweaking the edge of pain as he pinched her hard nipple. She groaned and pushed her body against his, curling her hand around the back of his neck. Her middle finger reached far enough to feel his jugular and the blood raced beneath her fingertip and she bit the flesh next to it.

It was like she'd pressed a button inside him, and he bit her lip as he pulled her down onto the bed. She began to surrender to him now.

He was rough with her, in the beginning. Instead of unbuttoning her blouse, he put the edge of his right hand at the neck and ripped downward, the buttons disappearing into the dark and making tiny sounds as they hit the floor. He grabbed her by the neck and threw her against the bed and he covered her with his body as if she had caught fire and he wanted to put out the flames.

She let him. She let him pull her hair back and bite the flesh of her neck. She let him sink down, leaving tiny bites along the muscles of her stomach as she pushed her fingers through his beautiful hair. She let him because she wanted it, too.

When Abbie opened her eyes, Billy was on his stomach, asleep. She propped herself on one elbow and looked at his body, the wide shoulders and the small indentations of his spine leading down to his naked ass. How fun it would be to slap it and wake him for another turn. But that was in the future. That was for Sunday mornings, in another future, one of many possible futures. Not now.

Her father was in the hospital and the killer was still loose.

Abbie felt lighter than she had in years. She leaned over and pressed her breasts against the warm surface of his back, laying her cheek on his and feeling the light ruffle of his breath on her nose. Her arms reached around his ribs and she gave him a quick, strong hug.

'Goodbye, Billy,' she said.

Twenty minutes later she was dressed and heading north toward home. She phoned the hospital and made sure there was a cop at her father's door. They assured her there was, and another at the entrance to the ER.

Abbie revisited the events of the night, beginning with the moment she'd awakened – that's all she could compare it to – sitting on Billy's chest with her gun in his mouth and his hands softly squeezing her shoulders. That gentleness had saved them from something ugly, she thought. It had called her back.

She made an inventory of all the night's surprises. She inventoried his physical attributes, smiled, and counted herself satisfied. He'd asked her about the shooting-the-ceiling trick and she said from her Victorian-house obsession, she'd recognized the house as a prewar model that would have plaster ceilings.

'What if it wasn't plaster?'

Then I would have shot you in the foot, she said.

'What if you'd missed?'

I wouldn't have.

He told her what she was suspected was true: when he called her after disappearing two days ago, during the traced call, there *had* been another man in the room, some bruiser named Sheehan. He'd been armed and listening in on their conversation. The threat she'd made about the Clan and Attica Prison might have saved Billy's life. Instead of killing him, they'd offered him a job in exchange for his silence.

So he'd forgiven her for the madness more easily than he might have otherwise.

As she drove, a new thought crept into Abbie's mind, pushing in against the rush of memories, unwelcome. A frown replaced the lazy smile on her lips. Abbie tapped the steering wheel three times and her eyes went left. She pulled into an all-night 7-Eleven on South Park, swung into a parking space. She gave the two guys loitering by the door a don't-you-dare-touch-my-car look and headed for the pay phone at the corner of the store. She didn't want to use her own phone.

'Nine-one-one. What is your emergency?'

'I heard a shot fired on Dorrance Lane.'

'What number?'

'One twenty-four, it sounded like.'

'How many shots?'

'One.'

'How long ago?'

'Forty minutes.'

'Hold on, ma'am.'

The low tone of being put on hold filled the earpiece. Abbie turned to check on the skels by the door. They were inert.

'Ma'am, we had another call and checked that out.'

'You checked it out? What does that mean?'

'It means we knocked on the door.'

Abbie was silent.

'And it looks like we spoke to the owner. It's been checked out, ma'am.'

Her mind was racing.

'And everything's okay?'

Billy and she had been loud, but not loud enough not to hear a nightstick banging on the front door.

'What did I just say? Ma'am, can I get your name?'

Abbie hung up quickly. She stared at the phone while the fluorescent lights buzzed above her head.

Back in her car, she called Z.

'Jesus, Ab, normal people are sleeping.'

'I know who the third man is. It was an ex-cop named Joseph Kane.'

'Kane?!'

She could tell that he was fully awake now.

'Did you know him?'

'Yeah, I knew him. How'd you find out?'

'I slept with Billy Carney, how do you think I found out?'

'Very funny,' he said uncertainly. Then: 'Kane. I'll be god-damned.'

'What do you know about him?'

'Enough to never want to run into him with the lights out. Meet me in front of the house.'

When she pulled up twenty minutes later in Williamsville, the sleepy suburb where Z lived, he was waiting in front of his house, breathing out great puffs of steam. He trundled into the passenger seat of her car and sat down heavily.

'Where we going?' she said.

'Eden. Kane moved there after he got out of Attica. I printed out a Google map.'

Abbie gunned the engine and the front wheels spun and then gripped the wet pavement. The car fishtailed and shot down the street. She crossed over Transit, blowing through red lights without even slowing down. In eight minutes, she swept up the on-ramp to 90, heading south.

Z grabbed the handle on the ceiling until the Saab straightened out on the empty highway, banks of dirty snow shooting past on either side, then turned to her.

'So you think Kane is next on the list?'

'The Clan thinks so. They're looking for him.'

Z rubbed his eyes and then his hand moved up to his forehead.

'What do you know about him?' Abbie said.

'I walked the beat with him downtown. And the guy was like nothing I'd ever seen.'

Cops usually meant one thing when they said that.

'He was dirty?'

'Hell, he was filthy. He played football in college, a strong safety at Oswego State. Blew out his knee as a junior or he might have had a shot at the pros. He came back to Buffalo with a limp and a pissed-off attitude. The world had cheated him out of millions, so he was going to take it back bit by bit.'

'He doesn't sound like a candidate for the Clan na Gael. Was he into Irish nationalism and all the rest?'

'Ohhhh yeah. You'd get into his squad car and he'd have all kinds of rebel music playing on the radio, klackety-klack, the landlord killed my father, then some hillbilly fiddles.'

'They're not hillbilly.'

'What?'

'Hillbillies got their music from the Irish, not the other way around.'

'Same difference. His father was from the old country, and he had it bad. His family back there were a bunch of bomb-throwing radicals. And when they took football away from Kane, that's what he turned to.'

'Billy said he got caught and did time.'

'Yeah, he shot a drug dealer on the East Side who he said pulled a gun on him. He was stupid. The prints on the gun were his, not the suspect's, and they found half a kilo of coke stashed up inside the wheel well of his Impala. He'd been shaking the guy down for years and the first time he doesn't have the money, he shoots him.'

'So he lost his badge?'

'Yeah.'

'And got sent away, I'm guessing. Where?'

'Attica.'

Abbie saw the towering walls of the state prison in her mind.

'Let me ask you this. Was he put into protection there?'

'How would they do that? You know that place. It's fucking medieval.'

'True,' she said. 'They don't have separate protection cells. Anyone taken out of general population for their own good goes into solitary. So he did time in the hole.'

She tapped her fingers on the wheel.

'You ever been to Attica, Z?'

'Nope. And I don't want to.'

'It was built in the thirties, the same look and feel as Sing Sing or Alcatraz. Made completely out of stone. The cells are tiny.'

'Okay.'

'What does the undercroft at St Teresa's, where Jimmy Ryan was found, remind you of?'

'I don't know, a really shitty place to die?'

'It's tiny and it's made of stone, just like cells at Attica.'

Z turned his head to watch the guardrails fly by.

'What if Kane's angry about getting sent away?' Abbie said.

'So why isn't he murdering *cops* then?'

'Maybe he thought the Clan could protect him. You know the Gaelic Club is practically a retirement home for Irish cops. And there's one other thing.'

'What?'

'Attica's got an old steam-heating system that's never been updated. The prisoners are always filing rights-violation suits on it. In winter, it's cold as hell.'

Z turned to look at her.

'Marty Collins,' he said.

Abbie nodded.

'What if the killer is writing his autobiography in corpses?'

TWENTY-FOUR

Eden was one of the tiny farming towns that ringed Buffalo on three sides. It took twenty minutes to get there. Abbie kept her window down to keep awake. When she started to smell horse manure, she knew they were close.

She jumped off the highway and nudged Z. He checked his service gun and stuck it back in the shoulder holster. Then he grunted, reached down for the Slammer near his ankle, popped the cylinder, spun it and stuck it back in the leather case.

The clock on her dashboard read 2:14 a.m. The streets of Eden were cloaked in mist, the fields of tall corn and wheat visible behind the small, widely spaced houses. The town center was two blocks long. A blue neon sign advertising pizza burned in the fog.

'What is he doing living out here?' Z said.

'Getting away from it all,' said Abbie. 'Anyone who isn't from around here will get reported real quick. Maybe it's a kind of security system all by itself.'

'Right here,' Z said, looking at his map.

She made the turn.

'Ahead on the right.'

Abbie killed the lights and crept toward the house.

'Goddamn it,' she said, gunning the engine.

When they pulled up to the house, they saw three cars, one jack-knifed on the front lawn. The place was lit up from within, sending broad yellow beams into the foggy fields. Through the white-framed windows, Abbie saw men moving within, stepping slowly and studying the interiors of the rooms as they went.

The front door had been kicked in or battered in, and the glass in

186

the front window was missing a jagged section. Two men were conferring by the front door.

They looked up as Abbie slanted the Saab to a stop.

'O'Halloran,' she said through gritted teeth.

Abbie got out and headed straight for the homicide detective, who was looking over a paper with a short, grim-faced cop in a trooper-style hat.

'What the hell are you doing here?' she said as she charged up.

'Investigating a case. You?'

O'Halloran handed the paper to the other man.

'You mean *my* case.'

O'Halloran glared at her, then nodded apologetically to the other cop. The trooper stared at Abbie and walked away.

'Are you trying to embarrass me, Kearney? I got a confidential tip and I decided to follow it through. Got that?'

'Bullshit,' Abbie said, the breath blowing white. 'Why didn't you call me?'

'Do you know the meaning of "confidential"? I didn't want the news broadcast over half the state. Your cases seem to get out of control.'

'Where's Kane?'

'Who gave you that name?'

'*My* confidential source. Where is he?'

O'Halloran stepped down the stairs. The grass was covered with dew and was silver-green in the light. He walked to the middle of the lawn and Abbie followed him. When they were out of earshot of the men coming through the front door, O'Halloran turned.

'He's gone.'

'Gone where?'

'No idea. He didn't leave a note giving me his vacation plans.'

Abbie looked back at the house, studying the kicked-in door. She looked around. The neighbors' houses were dark, weather vanes turning silently on the roofs.

'I'll bet there hasn't been this much excitement in this town in years.'

O'Halloran didn't follow her eyes.

'What's your point?'

'Why aren't the neighbors out here asking what's going on with their good friend Joseph Kane? Asking if there's anything they can do to help? In most farm towns, you'd have half the population over here.'

'Maybe Kane wasn't too friendly.'

'Maybe someone told them to keep themselves inside.'

O'Halloran smiled. 'Go ahead and bang on some doors, Kearney. Knock yourself out.'

'Who's your snitch?'

O'Halloran paused.

'I'm going to humor you. Last night, in a bar on South Park called the Golden Nugget, an addict told me Kane had shaken him down years ago, before he got shitcanned from the Department. When the skel threatened to go to Internal Affairs, Kane bragged that he belonged to a secret society that protected him from prosecution. Total immunity. No one from it went to jail, because they were serving a higher cause and the hierarchy reached all the way up. Okay, Kearney? Now get off my fucking back.'

'So you decided to rush on over here in the middle of the night and roust him?'

'Exactly.'

'I see two possibilities here. Either you're running some kind of parallel investigation for the Clan and its friends in the County, hoping to get the killer and do God knows what to him before I can catch him. Or you approve of the little murder spree Kane's on and warned him I was coming, then stormed in here to cover your tracks, to make it look like we're on the same team.'

O'Halloran's eyes were gray and yellow in the glow of the interior lights, but he said nothing.

'I'm going to check Kane's phone records. If he got a warning call from inside the County, I'm going to have you up on so many charges you'll have to use both hands to count them.'

'You know what? Your father's name only goes so far, Kearney. Don't try my patience.'

'This is a warning, O'Halloran. There won't be a second one.'

O'Halloran smiled. 'You talk to me again like that, I'll turn that pretty little mouth of yours ugly.'

Abbie stepped toward him, her hand curling into a fist. Suddenly an arm slid across her midsection. Z stepped in between her and O'Halloran and began to push her back gently.

'Come on, Ab.'

O'Halloran was still smiling at her. She could actually picture cracking his teeth with the butt of her flashlight.

'Stay out of my case, O'Halloran.'

Z pulled her toward the Saab.

'I want all of them, Z,' she spit out. 'The killer, the people protecting him, and O'Halloran's crew.'

'We'll get them. Just calm down.'

O'Halloran left five minutes later, squealing away with two civilian cars filled with pasty-faced white men glimpsed in flashes of headlights. Abbie and Z were already searching the ex-cop's house. They stayed for three hours, just the two of them. But it had been picked clean. The computer was gone and the table on which she guessed it sat had been sprayed with furniture polish so you couldn't even see the outlines in dust. There were fresh garbage bags in the cans out back, and in the can under the kitchen sink. Some of Kane's clothes were still there, but it was hard to tell if what he'd taken was for warm or cold weather. The fridge still had food, although the milk had turned. The past-use date was two days before.

The neighbors reported that Kane had arrived four years ago, said he was a former Buffalo cop who'd had enough of the city, too dirty and chaotic, said he wanted country views. He'd kept to himself, shopped in town for food and gone to Buffalo to buy anything bigger. He didn't have a girlfriend or relatives, at least any who came to visit him, he watched an occasional Sabres or Bills game in one of Eden's two bars, and he favored the BBQ restaurant in town. They had two mantras. 'He kept to himself.' And: 'He worked all the time, we hardly saw him.'

Worked for who? Nobody knew. Did he have regular visitors at the house? Not that anyone could remember. Friends in town? Nothing came to mind.

'It's like the County,' said Abbie. 'But with overalls.'

When she and Z got on the highway at 6:30 a.m., she checked her mirrors every few miles. But there was no one there, just miles of gray asphalt and whipping curtains of snow squalls covering up the tracks she had made through the snow. Again she could hear the burring sound of snow crystals on the road.

Her neck tingled. She had the feeling of being watched over; maybe not physically followed, but *watched over*. Someone knew where'd she been and where she was going even before she did.

TWENTY-FIVE

Abbie drove straight to Mercy Hospital. She was met in the ICU waiting room by Dr Singh, tall, impossibly thin, with rimless glasses, careworn eyes, and silver hair, which contrasted with his bronze-colored skin. He shook her hand before sitting in the plastic chair next to her. From the way he sighed as he sat down, she knew the news wasn't good.

'Your father hasn't regained consciousness. He responds to physical stimuli, knee tappings and so forth, but he hasn't woken up. I don't want to shock his system in any way, so I'm taking a wait-and-see attitude at the moment.'

'I thought you said he's going to be okay!' she nearly shouted.

'I still believe that.'

'What do you think it is?'

'There's a bruise to the right temple. He may have suffered a concussion when he fell. The brain could have bounced around, doing itself some injury, but there's no sign of cerebral hemorrhage or bleeding. His eyes look good. But I need to run some more tests before I can go further with that diagnosis.'

'I want to see him.'

'Of course,' he said, taking off his glasses and pinching the bridge of his nose in exhaustion. 'Come with me.'

Her father looked tiny in the bed, the skin drawn tight over his face, his bare arms laid straight down on the white sheet that covered him, violet-colored depressions where his veins used to be. She took his right hand and found it terrifyingly cold.

Abbie watched her father's chest rise and fall, the deep lines of his face. She could hear the occasional PA announcement and a bell ringing insistently in another ward, but the hospital was peaceful. She checked her cell phone and called Z, asking for news of Kane. Nothing. He hadn't been seen or heard from. She was starting to think he was dead, his body just waiting to be found.

She slipped the phone into her bag and looked up suddenly. Her father's hand had tightened on hers. His eyelids fluttered.

'Dad?' she said, standing.

He seemed to be emerging from a dream, trying to catch hold as it slipped away. His pupils contracted and the cobalt-blue eyes turned to her.

'It's you, then, my darling?'

Abbie smiled, her eyebrows arching wistfully. *He must be dreaming about his dead sister,* she thought.

'Dad, it's me, Absalom.'

'I know who it is,' he said in a clear voice. 'Aren't you my darling girl?'

'I . . . I—'

She was going to make a joke about checking which drugs they were giving him, and stockpiling boxes of it, but his words were too unexpected. She took a deep breath and narrowed her eyes at him. The bones of his fingers pressed on her palm. He studied her, his old charmer's smile curling the corner of one lip.

'You're feeling better,' she said. 'You gave me a scare.'

'It all went black. I was—'

'No need,' she said.

He nodded and his eyes traveled over her face. She felt suddenly self-conscious; she couldn't remember him looking at her like that since she was a teenager.

'How goes the manhunt? Have you found your man?' He peered at her intently.

'No, not yet. I had a few questions for you, actually.'

His laughter echoed off the walls, and then suddenly he had a coughing fit. Abbie jumped up and poured the paper cup on the tray next to the bed half full of water. She held the cup to his lips and he drank slowly, the lips dry and chapped.

He settled back on the pillow.

'Water!' he cried. 'I thought you would have brought your father some Jameson's, at least.'

'Next time,' she said.

He nodded. 'Now tell me this. Was it you who put Sean MacCullahy up to showing me that photo?'

Abbie smiled. 'Well, *I* couldn't ask you. You would have clammed up.'

'Indeed, indeed.'

His eyes twinkled mischievously.

'You're a smart girl, Absalom. I would never have thought of putting that little scene together. Very nice. And you *almost* had me.'

'Dad, the picture—'

Something passed through his face – a tremor of fear, perhaps, but he quickly regained his composure.

'Soon I'll tell you everything you need to know about that picture.'

She wanted to know now but you couldn't rush John Kearney.

'Do you know when I realized you were going to be a detective, just like your old man?'

Abbie sighed and sat back down. She shook her head no.

'The Easter egg hunt.'

Abbie smiled. 'You always loved that time of year.'

'My mother loved Easter,' he said, a trace of hoarseness in his voice, turning to the window that looked out over Abbott Road. After a moment, he turned back. 'Do you remember the year I'm thinking of?'

'Of course. You told everyone that the egg had a hundred-dollar bill on it. You're lucky the whole County didn't show up.'

'I gave everyone a slip of paper with one clue, Abbie.' His eyes studied hers. 'What was it?'

'Is this a test?'

He frowned, to say *Of course it's a test.*

'I remember, Dad.'

'Everyone opened the paper and they ran to the mailbox on the front of the house, like a flock of geese who'd heard a gun go off. I looked down and there was only one kid still sitting there, as if she was meditating. You.'

'The clue was a trick.'

'Of course it was a trick. But you didn't fall for it. You were studying my face, and your lips were whispering something. What was it?'

'I was thinking about what was written on the paper: "Look in the place / where the man in blue / puts the thing / he hides from you."'

His eyes lit up. 'Not bad, eh?'

'Corny.'

'Everyone else screamed, "The mailman!" and went running for the mailbox. But not you.'

She shook her head. 'Not me.'

'Because I'd written "*hides* from you." The mailman doesn't hide the mail, he delivers it. And our postman, Mr Croakley, was a drunk who couldn't make it through the day without a sip of his juice.'

'I saw him lift a bottle of brandy out of the milk box one day when I was coming home from school. And that's where the egg was.'

Abbie smiled, trying to hold back tears.

'Dad, the picture.'

He closed his eyes and shook his head gently.

'Come here, my girl.'

She stood up and went to his side, tears in her eyes.

'Dad—'

'Shhh.'

He reached up and stroked her hair, which she'd forgotten to pull back in a ponytail.

'Black as Cromwell's heart, that's what they used to say about your hair.'

She nodded. 'I know. I heard it enough.'

'But not me. I always thought it was handsome.'

She gave him an accusing look. 'You mean "pretty." And I never heard you say that.'

'You've forgotten! Of course I did.'

'Maybe in the shower you whispered it.'

He laughed. 'I knew that Easter that you'd join the Department. I could see it in your eyes, standing there with the egg and the hundred-dollar bill.'

Abbie took a deep breath and let it out.

'I wanted you to see me, Daddy.'

'I did. Course I did. And I knew that you'd be as good as I was. Because you saw what lay behind things. And that frightened me to death.'

'Why?'

'I made a mistake, Abbie.'

The look – fear, guilt? – came to his eyes and stayed put. He shook his head and looked away from her.

'What mistake, Daddy? Tell me. Why is someone hunting the Clan?'

From over her shoulder, she heard the door open and felt a rush of disinfectant-smelling air spill into the room. She didn't take her eyes from her father's, but he only smiled.

'Mr Kearney!' a voice said.

Abbie turned to see a thick-bodied nurse with curly dirty-blonde hair spilling over her white uniform.

'You're awake.'

'Shouldn't he be?' Abbie said.

The nurse looked at her. 'It's time for his shot.'

Abbie watched the nurse as she walked to John Kearney's side and began to pull open a syringe from its paper casing. She took the clear bottle and held it up at eye level, then dropped it to her waist and placed the needle tip on the rubber lid.

Abbie walked around the foot of the bed and came close to her father from the other side.

'Dad—' she said, softly.

Her father nodded. He was still smiling, but the energy had drained from his face.

'Soon, Abbie. Tomorrow we'll talk all about it.'

Abbie watched the nurse give him the shot, and waited until his eyes fluttered shut again.

When she left the hospital, clouds were beginning to cover the sun.

Sleep was impossible. Driving always helped her think, so she got in the car. She replayed every word of the conversation in her head as she drove, first through the County, up Abbott and down McKinley and over to South Park. She found she couldn't focus on the case, only on her father's words. Was it the drugs doing the talking? He hadn't been that sweet to her since . . . Well, since forever.

Well, if it was the drugs, she didn't care. She remembered every word he said.

She decided to drive to the Lucky Clover motel in Niagara Falls, where it had all begun. Maybe visiting the scene would spark something in her, help her assemble the jumble of puzzle pieces in her head.

Clouds fully obscured the sun as she drove over the Peace Bridge and into Niagara Falls. She drove to the Lucky Clover's parking lot and turned off the engine. Her angle gave her a clear view of the action. The Clover was busy today, mostly with transients and prostitutes. She watched the alkies stumble out of their rooms and the businessmen johns hurrying out of their company cars for a quick session before going home to dinner and the kids. When they left, the whores hung by the open doors of the rooms and gossiped awhile before collecting their things and heading back toward Niagara Falls Boulevard.

She needed to eat something. A headache was gathering at the base of her neck, sending exploratory waves of blackness behind her eyes.

Was Kane the killer or the next victim? Was the Clan out to kill him or to protect him? If he was the killer, could they really mean to cover for him, to keep him out of her grasp and let the murders of two of their own people go? What could he possibly have on the County Irish to hold that kind of power?

Or had Kane already been taken care of, marched out of his house, taken to a farmer's field, shot in the back of the head and buried? Nobody would think twice about a gunshot out in Eden. Hunting was a way of life out there. Like the mountain man who scavenged the roadkill, people didn't involve the authorities unless it was absolutely necessary. If he was in a fresh grave in some cornfield, she'd never know about it.

She began to nod off in the parking lot, feeling spacy. The mist from the Falls was running down the Saab's sloping hood in thick streams.

Abbie woke up, freezing, curled in the front seat of the Saab. She could hear water. She was still in the parking lot, but the motel was lifeless now, the doors closed and the only light coming from the office.

Everything was dank and gray. A freezing rain was lashing down from a sky roiling with black-edged clouds. It was a storm coming in from over the lake, and from the looks of it the rain was going to get a lot worse.

Abbie turned the key and the Saab revved up. Cold air blasted out of the heater vents, and her portable police radio, charging in the cigarette lighter, switched on. Several big yawns creaked her jaw open and she shivered in the cold.

The hoped-for epiphany hadn't come. The pieces of the case were still unconnected in her mind. No flash of insight. She turned the heater to full hot and thought of calling Z.

The dispatchers were sending out calls on her portable radio. Her mind tuned in, but it was all chatter: kids stealing beer from a 7-Eleven, a domestic off of McKinley. She checked her cell phone – no messages from Z or anyone else.

She decided to get something to eat.

Abbie was reaching to turn on the car radio when she heard the dispatcher's voice rise an octave.

'Unit 6, Unit 6, report of an EDP on the Peace Bridge, American side, facing north. Car parked in the right lane.'

Abbie's hand paused on the radio knob, then dropped back to her lap.

A voice answered the call: 'Dispatch, this is Unit 6. ETA is twelve minutes. Got anyone else?'

'That's a negative.'

'All right, then. Unit 6 responding.'

Abbie's brow creased. An emotionally disturbed person on the bridge? It wasn't known for suicides, like the Golden Gate in San

Francisco. In fact, she'd never heard of anyone jumping off the Peace Bridge. Especially in the middle of winter.

Abbie shifted into drive and eased the Saab out of the parking lot. She'd take the back streets back to the U.S., to avoid the casino traffic. She looked for the signs to the bridge.

Something veered into her thoughts. The killer crossed the bridge to murder George Decatur in the motel. Jimmy Ryan came over it to escort an IRA man back to America. Marty Collins took the case.

The bridge was part of every single killing, if only in a small way. It was the thing that linked them together.

Abbie saw a sign saying 'Peace Bridge – U.S.A.' and merged into a three-lane street, traffic moving fast. The turbo kicked in and the opposing traffic on her left whipped by in blurs of color.

Abbie saw the arc of the Peace Bridge approaching ahead, black against a gray-black sky. An arrowhead of bright yellow crash barrels flashed through the windshield of a slow-moving Impala ahead of her.

'Unit 6, status?' the dispatcher called on the radio. 'EDP no longer in sight. May have jumped.'

No one jumps from the bridge into that freezing river, Abbie thought. *Not willingly.*

Abbie jerked the wheel right, accelerating as she went, blew past the Impala and got back in the left lane. She shot into the bridge lane and the road inclined up. Traffic was bunched at the entrance ramp, with a gap to the left next to the collision barrels.

Abbie slammed on the gas. The Saab slid on the freezing road and began to fishtail. The collision barrels flared up in her side window at ten feet and closing, and she swore, then punched the gas hard. Her wheels sent a terrifying thump up through the floor of the car as they passed over the warning bumps. The car groaned as it came out of the skid and jumped a curb, then shot up the ramp, the bridge's superstructure looming in the twilight.

The traffic was thicker here and she began weaving through cars, hitting 60 mph, laying on the horn furiously. Ahead were the bridge tollbooths, with red lights winking as cars waited to pay their way into the U.S.A. Abbie touched the brake and rolled her window down, then punched the gas and barreled toward a lane with a red X blinking above it. As she swept through, she had the image of the toll collector's pale white face on her right.

A startled Canadian cop, standing just in front of the custom official's booth, turned, his hand reaching toward his gun.

'Buffalo PD,' Abbie shouted, slowing to flash her ID. He nodded and waved her on up the incline. She shot past the customs booth and pressed the accelerator.

The rain whipped down in sheets and Abbie heard thunder rolling in from the American side. As she gunned the engine, all that was visible ahead was the flick of an occasional brake light. The river to her right was high and thrashing against the boulders in the river. All she could see ahead was steel-gray darkness and the occasional flash of light along a black strut.

Traffic on the bridge was backed up near the crest of the bridge. Abbie skidded to a stop behind the last car and pushed open the driver's-side door. A gust of wind exploded into the car. As Abbie put her foot down, rivulets of water pouring down from the crest splashed up her ankle. She stood up and the wind bucked against her. She slammed the door shut, immediately turned her back to the wind, unzipped the hood of her jacket from its compartment around her neck, and pulled it free. The wind tore at it and a drumming noise filled her ears, but she finally managed to yank it over her head and cinch the cords tight.

Brake lights bobbed in the darkness as the rain lashed across her eyes. Abbie angled toward the railing on her left. She groped in the blackness until she found the top bar of the railing and swung herself over. For a horrible moment, she thought she'd misjudged and this wasn't the inner railing but the outer one, and she was going to plunge into the dark water that roared beneath her, but her shoes smacked against a metal grill. There was a narrow pedestrian path ahead of her, sectioned off from the traffic lanes on her left. Abbie straightened up, turned to lean into the howling wind, and began to climb. The bridge hummed through the hood as the metal cables seemed to vibrate to the gathering storm.

She ran, but the slick metal grill almost caused her to go face down on the walkway. She pulled out her gun and held it tight against her right thigh and hurried ahead, trying not to slip.

The sound was deafening and ahead was blackness with a line of red brake lights on her left. Abbie couldn't even see where the bridge ended and the sky began. The rain speckled her vision the few times she lifted her head up to check her progress. But the incline was slowly leveling out.

Suddenly she saw a figure moving away from her on the walkway, dark, bent, and moving fast toward the American side.

Abbie pointed her gun and shouted, 'Buffalo Police!' but the wind tore the words away.

The figure seemed to merge into the blackness and disappear. Then suddenly she caught its outline against the lights of Buffalo. Abbie dropped to one knee to frame the outline against the glow and saw that it was a man, head down.

'Stop and put your hands up! Police!'

The figure turned, reached into its pocket, and pulled out a black object.

Abbie yelled, *'Stop right there or I'll shoot!'*

A blaze of light shot from the figure's midsection, then flicked up. She could see a bright yellow coat with three bands of white reflector paint. The flashlight was pointed at the figure's bright yellow jacket and the logo 'Buffalo Fire Department.' Under the yellow helmet and visor tilted down against the wind, she saw the bottom half of a male face, stubbled with dark hair.

Abbie blew out a breath in relief, stood and holstered her gun. She waved the fireman closer.

'Could be . . . ,' the fireman yelled. He was holding on to the rim of his helmet, trying to stop it from blowing off. The wind was whipping by so hard she could hear only some of what he was shouting.

'Could be what?'

He said something that sounded like *'Sue-thide.'*

'You see it?'

He nodded.

'How long ago?'

His words were mangled by the shrieking wind. He tried again but Abbie only shouted, *'What?'* and cupped her hands over her ears to show she couldn't hear.

The man nodded and held up ten fingers.

Abbie nodded back. A gust of wind bucked her up against the outer railing and she caught a glimpse of white surf forty feet below.

She pushed herself closer to the fireman and shouted, 'Did he leave ID?'

The fire helmet shook back and forth and the man's lips turned down at the corners.

Abbie nodded and began to move past him. The fireman grabbed her arm as she passed. He yelled something but the wind was shrieking up the roadway and its pitch rose with his voice.

'What?' she yelled.

'. . . *help orrr* . . .'

'What?'

The storm seemed to be roaring into a hurricane. She was able to catch only part of what the fireman was shouting.

'Someone helped him over the railing?'

The fireman nodded.

Abbie gave him a thumbs-up to show she understood, then pointed up at the top of the span. He nodded and turned into the blackness ahead of her.

The gale blew up through the metal grate walkway and it felt like the wind was trying to lift her off the bridge and send her spinning into the Niagara. Abbie switched the gun to her left hand and grabbed the railing with her right. The lights of Buffalo bobbed ahead of her to the south, the rain whipping across her vision at a thirty-degree angle.

A branch of lightning flashed in the black sky. And suddenly Abbie saw it.

A white shape appeared and then vanished ten feet below her. A white shape like a face.

Abbie backed up against the outside railing, pointing her gun down. How could someone be *below* her? The face had gleamed for a split-second blue-white flash of lightning, then disappeared into the blackness.

The rain pounded against the plastic hood as she crept forward, gun still trained downward.

A lightning flash illuminated the scene below for a half second and she saw the face ten feet below her, not looking up. This time it was moving away from her. Her heart fluttered in fear.

'Stop!' she shouted, but the lightning flashed away and the man was gone. She remembered that the Peace Bridge had work platforms below the roadway. But the platforms didn't go all the way to shore; they reached only across the middle span and led nowhere. So if he was down there, he was trapped, unless he could climb back on the main roadway and somehow sneak past her.

Abbie bent over the railing and looked wildly left and right into sheets of rain for a ladder. She could smell the river churning beneath her.

Underneath she saw the black outlines of the bridge superstructure. Then she heard something moaning in the wind.

A white face swept past, ten feet below, moving away from her again. The face was turned toward her. But the man was walking *backward.*

'Buffalo Police!' she cried, sticking her gun through the railing to try and get an angle.

Flash, the man turning – slowly, almost as if in a dream, and retracing his steps. Abbie's gun dipped to follow him, but again he was swallowed up in darkness.

Abbie desperately tried to clear her eyes of the streaming water, but everything was blurred.

'Buffalo PD,' she shouted again, but the wind whipped her voice to shreds. Could the perp even hear her down there? The rain was drumming so loudly on the steel bridge she could barely hear herself.

She pulled her radio out of her pocket.

'Dispatch, five-ten.'

Come on, come ON.

'Five-ten, go ahead.'

'I have a Caucasian male on the underside of the Peace Bridge. Will not respond to orders. I need units here with ropes and a stretcher.'

'Roger that. Where on the bridge?'

'Midway. Request expedited.'

'Roger.'

The dispatcher began to call more units as Abbie stood and began to feel her way forward. The top railing was round and thick and she could feel paint flake away under her hand. She slid it forward. If she was right, the perp was directly beneath her now.

Her fingers brushed something on the rail and she snatched her hand back. *Jesus Christ,* she thought, *is that what I think it is?*

Abbie's fingers tapped along the railing, rain bouncing three inches off her exposed wrist, which was already beginning to freeze. She took a step and reached further along. *Where was it? Did I pass it?* All of a sudden her hand touched something rough.

She found the thick rope looped three times around the railing.

A face flashed in her mind. A pale white face.

Her mind dropped into a Tilt-a-Whirl spin.

Abbie lurched over the railing and cried out 'DAAAAAAD!' staring into the white-speckled darkness of the roaring Niagara, surging past like a locomotive.

Black water rushing by. The bridge shaking in the wind.

Then the man moved lazily into view.

Not pacing. Swinging.

'DAAAADDDDD!' she cried, and reached over for the rope. It was thick and fibers came off in her hand as she clawed it. But the body on the other end of the rope was too heavy. She could barely lift it a couple of inches before the weight and the wind snatched it away.

The spray whipped her face. She felt her mind slipping, tilting into the black.

Abbie peered into the darkness, praying, her lips moving as water pelted her face. Then lightning streaked once more across the sky.

She saw a body on a bucking rope.

It was white, naked. Finally, she remembered her flashlight and pulled it out of the jacket pocket. The rope popped and moaned in the wind as she clicked it on and then turned the beam downward.

The body was mangled. *It doesn't look right,* Abbie thought.

'DAD, CAN YOU HEAR ME?' She leaned farther out and saw the outline of the huge gray concrete base that supported the bridge.

He must have slammed into it, breaking his bones. I have to get him up or he's going to be smashed to a pulp.

But as she watched, she realized the body was swinging free, missing the edges of the concrete base by a few feet. Why did the body appear so mangled and broken?

She made out a tiny thin line of black around its neck. The same line along the top of the shoulder just above the arm. And the left. And then she saw something that turned her stomach.

She swiveled and slammed her back against the railing, sliding down. She collapsed, relief and horror surging through her. *Thank you, thank you, Lord.*

Down below, the body swung freely through the pelting rain. It had to be Joe Kane. And his head was facing the wrong way.

TWENTY-SIX

Perelli walked into the meeting and slammed down a four-inch stack of files.

He coughed.

Abbie sat in a chair in a corner. Her eyes were circled with black. She felt if someone touched her, she would tip over into some kind of bottomless dream. The room was filled with men: O'Halloran, Alexander, Z, Perelli, plus some others, men she assumed were from the mayor's office, standing awkwardly in the corners. The edges of the faces around her were blurred. She needed caffeine or sleep.

'Okay, let's get this started.'

He looked over to Abbie, who didn't lift her head.

'Detective Kearney, you want to tell us how you knew to look for the latest victim on the Peace Bridge? Do you have information you want to share with this department? Or its goddamn chief?'

Abbie looked over at Z. They hadn't had a chance to talk. He didn't meet her eyes.

'It wasn't information. It was a hunch.'

'That was a hell of a hunch. Please elaborate. And I want you to leave nothing out. Nothing, understood?'

Abbie's head felt heavy. She felt she was drugged, even though she had barely closed her eyes the night before. What was the densest matter on earth? Some kind of metal, she thought. The name fled her brain.

'Abbie?'

She looked up. Perelli was staring at her, his anger masked by what appeared to be fear.

'Yes?'

'It's your meeting.'

She glanced around at the faces. They turned away, all except for Z, who nodded and gave her a go-get-'em smile. She must look like hell.

'What do you want to know?'

'Let's start with Joe Kane.'

Abbie felt a wavelet of nausea lap at the base of her skull. The other two hadn't bothered her as much, but what happened to Kane . . .

'Do you need a moment?'

'He was . . .'

'Yes?'

'He was cut up and put back together again. Backwards. The head was sawed off, then sewn back onto the neck just above the collarbone with sailing thread, the kind of thing you repair a sail with. We found a store at the marina had been broken into. That's probably where he got it.'

The room was still.

'The arms, the same thing. Cut off and rotated 180 degrees. And the legs. The tongue was cut out and not found with the body. Cane's penis was cut off and inserted into his anus. The monkey was found inserted above the severed right arm before it was reattached to the body.'

She'd stood by the coroner as he did the examination. What bothered her was how the body looked. A Frankenstein job, she thought, but didn't Dr Frankenstein want to create a human being? Wasn't it a noble experiment gone wrong? She couldn't remember, but she thought so.

This killer wanted only to destroy. The reversed feet pressing against the stainless-steel table made the stiff body stick up, as if it were shoving its shorn genitals into the air. At first, the Latino mortuary assistant hadn't known whether to lay the body on its back. He'd looked at her, confused. She'd told him to proceed the way the body was.

'My working theory for the last few days is that the killer has been telling us his life story. More importantly, he's been telling the victims, showing them how he lived at certain points in his life. Obviously he feels they are responsible. So he is forcing them to relive his pain and anguish.

'Jimmy Ryan was forced into a very confined space. Marty Collins was made to feel as cold as humanly possible. And now Joe Kane . . .

'The killer feels violated in some way. Reversing the head and the limbs . . . it's like a distress signal. Something terrible was done to this man – and not just physically. Or not *primarily* physically. He feels his humanity was violated. And then what he did with the genitals. I'm guessing he was raped.'

'That sounds like prison.'

'A lot of it sounds like prison. Confinement, exposure, possibly sexual abuse.'

O'Halloran cut in. 'Okay. But how did you know to look on the Peace Bridge?'

'Like I said. It was a hunch. It began with the information about Jimmy Ryan's earlier arrest. He was caught on the Peace Bridge.'

'Yeah. And?'

'He wasn't found with guns or drugs. The Clan wasn't exporting either of those. I should have made the connection.'

It wasn't entirely true. The light that had gone on in her head had to do with Mrs Ryan's face days after her son had been killed. It was a special calm, the calm of a martyr's mother. If Jimmy had been bringing in dope or AK-47s, even if they somehow benefitted the IRA, the woman's face would have been lined with shame and grief. She knew the County too well. Mrs Ryan's behavior was all wrong for a drug mule's or a gunrunner's mother. It was right for something else.

Her eyes had been shining. As if her son's death had finally revealed some meaning to her. The truth of her son's wayward life.

The phone call to Reinholdt twenty minutes ago had confirmed her thinking. It fit now.

'What connection?'

'The Clan weren't exporters. Just the opposite.'

Perelli sighed and looked up at the ceiling.

'Why are you fucking with me, Abbie?'

She looked at him.

'They were importers. We had it backward.'

'Importers of *what?*'

'Isn't it clear? People.'

'People!' Perelli barked. O'Halloran, sitting next to him, quietly wiped some spittle from his face.

'I should have caught it when Reinholdt told me originally. For a hundred years, the Clan was a full-service support organization for the IRA. They supplied money, political support, votes for pro-IRA candidates in the U.S. But that was happening all over the Northeast. Buffalo was nothing special. There was only one thing the Buffalo branch could do better than any other, because of where the city is geographically.'

'And what's that?'

'Make Irish rebels disappear.'

Perelli rubbed his eyes.

'When the Italian mob had someone that was bringing them too much attention in America, what did they do?' Abbie said.

Perelli frowned. He hated questions about the Italian mob.

'They got rid of them.'

'How?'

'Shipped them back to Italy.'

'Exactly. Well, the IRA had the same problem. They had members who'd done things in Northern Ireland that made them marked men, hunted by the British cops and special forces. If they walked out onto a street in Belfast, they'd be spotted in a minute. If they hid, informants could always turn them in. And if they were caught, they could be worked on and turned into informers themselves. So they were sent to America.'

'Through Canada is what you're saying.'

'Yes, through Canada. The direct route was too suspicious and heavily watched. They had to bring them over a border. And in Mexico, a pale Irishman would be as easy to spot as . . . as . . .'

Her brain refused to go any further.

'As a polar bear in Africa,' Z piped up.

'Thank you. So they brought them through Canada. That's probably why Jimmy Ryan was brought in. He'd taken drugs across before, he had the connections, maybe he knew a guard or two at the bridge who would look the other way for a cut. Gerald Decatur, as well. They worked the border together. That's why none of the Clan members were flashing money, like they would have with drugs or guns. They weren't bringing in money. And that's probably why the Gaelic Club tried to keep it a secret. The people they brought in may still be living here.'

'Here?'

'Here in the country. How many stayed in Buffalo? Who knows? My father is the last member of the Clan left, and he's not talking. But the whole Irish community had an interest in keeping quiet what they did.'

'So we think the killer is . . . an IRA guy?' O'Halloran said, his brow creased with thought.

'That's my guess. He was brought across the bridge into the hands of the Clan and then . . . something went wrong. Maybe Kane and the others didn't find him the job he wanted. Maybe he hated America. Maybe he never wanted to leave Northern Ireland. And he started killing the men who brought him over.'

'A lot of fucking maybes,' O'Halloran mumbled.

'You have a better theory?'

O'Halloran said nothing, just stared at her, then dropped his gaze to her chest. She looked away in disgust and turned to Perelli

'So long story short, that's why I went to the bridge. I heard on the radio about a possible suicide. I saw something that looked like a man up there. It fit. It was the next chapter in the story the killer is telling.'

'Do we know what happened to these killers after the Clan brought them across?' Perelli asked wearily.

'We can only guess, but an Irish accent in the County would barely be noticed. Plenty of the old folk still have brogues, and there are enough cousins and nephews coming to visit them from Dublin or wherever so that the accent doesn't stand out. Jobs could be found, fake IDs. Once they were here, they could disappear. There were lots of ways. The Clan sponsored Gaelic lessons. Who were the teachers? The IRA is full of Gaelic speakers – it's part of their program of getting rid of British influence. Or if they played the accordion, they could become a visiting musician. Nobody asks questions in the County. It was perfect.'

Perelli stared past her.

'And these men were, what?'

'Freedom fighters or terrorists, depending on how you look at it. But they were the ones the British wanted the most, the ones too hot to ship down to the South and to try and hide in Dublin.'

'So what you're trying to tell me,' said Perelli, standing up and leaning his hands on the conference table, which protested with a low groan, 'is that the IRA shipped its most notorious killers here to Buffalo, gave them false identities and just . . . let 'em loose?'

He stared openmouthed at Abbie with a sickened look on his face.

Abbie nodded.

Silence.

'Fuckin' Micks,' said O'Halloran, but the joke died.

'Most of the rebels, I'm going to guess, weren't killers at heart. They were men who believe in a cause. Once they were removed from their environment, they went straight. They're probably spread out from New York to San Francisco now.'

'Except for one.'

Abbie nodded. She wanted to sleep, to forget the night before. But now the killer had slipped past her again. He was further away than ever before.

'One of them wasn't doing it for Ireland. That was just a convenient excuse for him. He was killing *because he liked killing*.'

Perelli's head was in his hands. He nodded. 'Okay. So we know his background, which helps a little. But what exactly are we looking for?'

Abbie slumped back in her chair. The killer's face was a blank to her, a buzzing void, cloaked by black electricity.

'He's about five foot nine, give or take an inch either way, judging by the Lucky Clover tape. He's right-handed. He likes to wear a black ski mask. He may have a strange way of speaking, with a trace of an Irish brogue. He may try to disguise this. He most likely did prison time. And we need to contact the British authorities in Ireland to get the mortuary records of every IRA-related killing in the past thirty years.'

'Why?'

'Because from what I saw, he's not new to this. He knows how to cut up a body.'

The room went silent. Finally, Perelli looked up as if he was surprised the detectives were still there.

'You heard her,' he barked. 'Find me a list of those fucks the Clan brought to my city. And find it fast.'

TWENTY-SEVEN

When Abbie stepped outside, she found a snow squall swirling around the building, whipping snow horizontally across her face. As she began to walk, following the direction of the snow, she felt the wind press a cold hand between her shoulder blades, even through her thick down coat. It seemed to be urging her forward.

She turned the building's corner and the wind swooped around with her, blowing her hair past her cheeks with a fresh gust of power. Her boots crunched on two or three inches of freshly fallen snow, heavy with moisture, the kind of stuff you prayed for as a kid, as it was perfect for making snowballs. Abbie saw the Saab – covered by a fresh blanket of snow – through a curtain of blowing white flakes and reached a gloved hand into her pocket, taking out the keys. She was about to hit the unlock button when suddenly she froze stock-still.

The monkey face drawn on the hood of her car wasn't an exact replica of the toys found at the murder scenes, but it was close enough.

She walked hurriedly to the Saab. The lines of the monkey face, already filling with snow, had obviously been carved with a finger. They would have been wearing gloves, though; no need to get the techs out here. Underneath the foot-high face, which she could see had a pronounced frown and two slit eyes, she saw an arrow sign pointing to her driver's-side wheel.

Abbie spun around. The streets around her were abandoned except for a few shadowy figures clutching the lapels of their coats around their necks and leaning into the stiff wind. None of them took any particular interest in her. Just office workers trying to get home before the storm shut down the roads.

She reached under her jacket and felt the butt of the Glock, then edged toward the driver side of the Saab. Nobody crouching there. She reached into the wheel well and felt around. The note was taped to the metal body just above the wheel. She ripped it out, then hurriedly hit the unlock button, slid into the Saab's driver's seat, turned the key in the ignition, and waited for the heater to blow hot.

When the air in the car had nudged above arctic levels, she opened the note. Three lines written in block letters using a black ballpoint pen.

IF YOU WANT TO KNOW THE TRUTH ABOUT JOE KANE, WALK ONTO THE LAKE AT DAWN TOMORROW FROM THE SMALL BOAT HARBOR. WALK DIRECTLY NORTH, TOWARD THE HUT WITH THE RED ROOF. COME ALONE.

Abbie listened to the blast of the heater as she thought. Why the lake? It was frozen now straight across to the Canadian shore. It was safe to walk across, but the only people out there this time of year were the ice fishermen, who spent hours in their huts or tents waiting for the northern pike to bite. Abbie thought they went out there just to get away from their wives and to drink beer.

The more she thought about it, the better a spot it was. There was no way to bring backup or to approach without being seen. Anyone walking out there would be as exposed as a black bug on sugar. The only way off the ice quickly was snowmobile. Impossible to set a trap, unless she got the whole Department involved. And the person who wrote the note knew she wasn't about to do that.

She wasn't even going to tell Z, she decided. Because he would tell her not to go.

John Kearney lay in his hospital bed, watching *Judge Judy*. The words did not go together. He couldn't tell who was accused of what, though he'd taken an immediate dislike to the man on the left, who was leaning aggressively over the lectern at the good judge. He was big, Spanish and his face was shaped like a pineapple.

John seemed to be looking out at the world from behind a fogged screen. He could see things but not touch them. He could hear but not speak. As weak as a baby sparrow. That's what his mother said to him, all those years ago, up in the hatefully cold house on the top of the stone hill in West Clare. When he broke something, or he rode the horse so hard it would stand in the barn shaking, its flanks coated with sweat.

'John,' she said, smiling, 'enjoy your strength now. It won't be with you forever.'

Always smiling, his mother. And what did she have to smile about? A drunk for a husband, a terror for an only surviving child, her daughter dead in the ground after getting TB from the cow's milk.

The nurse looked at him now as he moaned loudly.

Siobhan, his sister, struggling in the bed, burning through the sheets back in Clare. And the knock on the door the night before she passed. Every time someone was about to die in the small towns of Ireland, it was believed and more than believed, it was *known,* that just when their spirit had decided to leave the body but hadn't yet gone, four knocks would be heard. And the night before Siobhan died, his mother had been sitting by her bedside in that stone house, he in his bed in the corner, not asleep but watching.

The four sharp raps on the door, so sharp you felt the knucklebone.

How his mother had *screamed.* He tried to close his eyes but they wouldn't obey.

John had known the minute he heard her cry that he would leave Ireland. The country had killed his sister, but it wouldn't kill him.

The nurse turned and looked at him with a concerned face. Jaysus, had he screamed just now? Ever since the Alzheimer's had started, the far past had been more concrete to him than the passing moment. It was as if he was falling back, falling back to what would never leave him, and that was Clare and hunger and boyhood.

His mother had known death was coming for her daughter. She'd known she was going to lose quiet, dutiful Siobhan, the one she confided to and leaned on when her husband and son lacerated her heart with drink or fighting in the town. Her only solace. Why had God not taken him instead?

He'd been waiting for the knock for weeks now, on Abbie's door or this one. He knew the name of the man who was coming. So John Kearney had one last mission to perform for the Clan, to wipe out its only great mistake.

And then his account with the old country would be paid in full. Ireland had given him nothing. He hadn't joined the Clan for Ireland. He'd joined because he'd broken his father's heart by leaving Clare.

His father had been a strong Republican. Though the words were never spoken, John knew his father had helped the cause as much as a poor farmer could. When John would come home from hunting rabbits, a cold dusk in the sky, strange men would be collapsed in his cot, his mother whispering, 'You'll sleep in your sister's bed tonight.' The TB bed. Him staring at the men, their muddy boots hidden behind the stove, the air rank with sweat and fear, the men gone in the morning before he got up. He knew they were IRA fugitives. And then he found the guns in the stone fence, while looking for foxes with his best friend Pádraig down the road. First they'd looked at the foot of the haystacks to see if any had made their homes there, then by the crooked tree that they'd thrown stones at for target practice, then in the fence that bordered their property. And there they found the black gleaming guns, two pistols wrapped in heavy oilcloth. The kind of pistol, he later learned, that you couldn't buy in the Republic, issued only by the British Army in Ulster. And so taken from dead men.

And he felt, not heard, his father behind him, come charging out of the house. Pádraig running away without a word, his brown hair waving in the wind as he dashed for home, away from the beating that was sure to come. And when John turned, his father's face purple with fear and rage.

Ah, Dad, are you waiting for me? It won't be long now.

The nurse turned from the table.

'Okay, okay,' she said. 'I'm giving you something.'

Had he said something?

She came closer to him. But it wasn't a nurse. She was wearing scrubs, but her face was familiar. Wasn't this James Byrne's girl,

Rosemary? He'd known her as a child. He didn't know she was a nurse now; the last he'd heard she'd been working downstate at some prison. Good Lord, the thought of a girl going into that pit of hell. Had she moved back home? No, he would have heard.

'I won't talk, Rosemary,' he said, but he knew he'd let out another moan from the look of pity on her face.

A bee sting in his arm. The bees in Clare died in the wintertime. Darkness, darkness.

TWENTY-EIGHT

Abbie parked the Saab in the lot of the Small Boat Harbor and walked past the bait and snacks hut, its windows shuttered for the winter, onto the weathered wooden dock. The ice lay below it, the lake frozen right to the shore. Abbie walked to the end of the dock, reached for the wooden pole driven deep into the lake's bed, and stepped off onto the ice. The General Mills silo was to her left, the highway behind her, and the expanse of the lake, frozen and silent, straight ahead.

The light was just murk, everything a hostile shade of blue. Even the ice looked pale blue and fluorescent, as if it were one of those long bulbs dying out and giving off its last rays. Abbie shivered as she walked due north, her feet crunching on the ice. These winter mornings unnerved her somehow. Everything was blue and black and gray, like the world was encased in ice and silence every morning until the sun could warm up the earth enough to coax a bit of life and color out of it. Now, with the sun just a slit of pale fire on the horizon, the cold was winning. It was pressing down on everything; it was making her lungs ache with the effort of walking.

She glanced up ahead and to her right. She could see a group of ice-fishing huts, bare specks, a shade darker than the ice. The person who'd written the note was probably out on the ice already. Most of these huts were for weekend fishermen – only the craziest ones took a vacation from work and stayed out here for days on end. And they'd be sleeping off the Molsons from the night before.

The ice was as solid as city pavement, but with ridges and small breaks in it cut by the wind. There was a dusting of flourlike snow on top that she kicked up as she walked. The huts were growing larger, but she saw no figures, no signs of life. She left her Glock on her hip.

At thirty yards away, she spotted the red roof and adjusted her path toward it. The hut itself was just unpainted plywood nailed together, not one of the prefab things you could buy and set up. No windows. There was a black Ski-Doo snowmobile next to it. The hut lay past two yellow-painted fishing cabins that sat ten feet apart from each other; she'd have to walk through the gap to reach the rendezvous.

The morning was still and the sound of traffic was fading away more with every yard she walked. They would hear her coming.

She stopped a short distance from the gap between the yellow huts, watching for any movement.

'Hello?' she called.

Her voice echoed out across the ice.

She looked over her shoulder. No one at the Small Boat Harbor; she could just see the Saab in the parking lot, all alone. She turned back.

'Hello?'

She thought she heard a footstep crunching the snow.

'Is anyone there?'

Suddenly a curtain of snow came rushing toward her. Abbie raised her hand to her face but the wave of snow crystals rushed up from the ice, stinging her face and filling her lungs. She gasped and whipped around, turning her back to the wind. The wind seemed to inhale suddenly, tearing at the clothes on her body, and then the gust was past her. The crystals dropped back to the ice and lay there innocently, sparkling in the morning sun.

Abbie turned. Beyond the yellow hut, a man was standing, unmoving. He had to have been hiding behind one of the huts, then stepped out when the snow cloud swept by. He wore a red ski mask, pulled tight against the skin, a dark blue boiler suit and brown snow boots. And he was watching her.

Abbie tried to slow her breathing. Was this the figure from the video? This one looked thicker in the chest somehow.

The man tapped his hip.

'Put the gun on the ice.' The voice was deep and somehow familiar. White male, Abbie thought. Forty or forty-five at least.

'That's not going to happen,' she said.

Steam leaked out of the mask's mouth hole.

'Then I jump on my Ski-Doo and you never catch the psycho.'
The man seemed to be trying to control his voice. No expletives, no
rise and fall in the voice.

Abbie took a step toward him.

'Turn around,' she said. 'And raise your arms up.'

The figure raised his arms, then twirled slowly. The pockets of the
boiler suit were flat against his body. If he had a gun, it was inside
the suit. If he went for it, she could get to him before he could reach
the pistol. It was worth the risk.

Abbie unholstered her Glock, bent over, watching the man all the
time, and laid it on the snow.

'You wanted to tell me something,' she said, standing up. 'I'm ready
to listen.'

The man stared at her.

'How do you know the men of the Clan?' he said accusingly.

The sun was coming up on the lake rim. The man was outlined
sharper against the light now.

Abbie raised her hand to shield her eyes. The man hadn't moved;
he seemed rooted to the ice. 'I followed the dead bodies,' she called
out. 'I didn't know who they were until I found them.'

Smoke out of the mouth hole. The man's head barely moved. 'Who
else is being hunted?'

'Aren't you here to tell me that?'

'I'm asking you.'

That voice. Where did she know it from?

Abbie slitted her eyes against the sunlight.

'The fourth man is next. Is that you? Is that why you're here meeting
with me?'

Snow kicked up around the man's feet and his legs disappeared in
white. His torso seemed to float in the air. Abbie blinked rapidly;
crystals were blowing into her eyes. Each time one hit, her vision
warped and her eyes began to tear up.

The man began to reach for something in his right pocket.

'Stop!' Abbie cried, ducking toward the Glock.

The man pulled out a silver key that twinkled in the sun's rays.

'I have to show you something,' he said in the same dead voice. 'Bring the gun if you want.'

He turned and began to walk toward the red-roofed hut. Abbie turned and scanned the ice behind her. No one approaching from behind. The cars on the 90 were like fast-moving toys, the sounds of their engines barely reaching her.

The man disappeared behind the hut. She hesitated.

'Come on,' his voice seemed far away now, blocked by the hut. She edged to the right and finally caught a glimpse of him. She could see the profile of the red mask, bent down as he fiddled with the lock.

Abbie picked up the Glock and began to walk between the yellow huts.

She heard the lock jitter. The man cursed and she heard the door groan, as if the man was pulling at the lock and rocking the door in its hinges. *Does he have the wrong key?*

Her feet crunched on the snow, sending a shiver up her leg. She edged toward the yellow hut on the right, trying to keep the man in sight.

Why doesn't the key fit? Abbie thought. More of the red ski mask came into view with every step. Now she could see his head and the left shoulder.

The jingling had stopped. The man wasn't looking at the lock anymore. He was looking at Abbie.

And then she began to fall.

Her scream was choked by black water. She'd gone through the ice and she was in the lake, the water so cold it first felt like burning oil. Her gun went spinning away and the breath was kicked out of her lungs as Abbie thrashed and reached for the rectangle of pale light five feet above her head, but already the current was pulling her into blackness. She kicked upward desperately.

Her mind screamed. The water in her throat was burning, burning. She jerked her body and felt the nails of her hand scrape against the underside of the ice. She clawed at it but there was no hold there, only smooth ridges that her hands slipped across in terror. It was the nightmare of the tumble off the Skyway, the nightmare she'd envisioned a hundred times. She was going to die.

A hand appeared, descending down from the rectangle of light. A white hand. It gestured lazily, closing and then opening and then closing again. *Come*, it was saying. *Come.*

Her body seemed to be shutting down. Her legs were going dead and the feeling in her face and arms was fading. *Kick, Abbie,* she cried to herself. *Kick or you will be unconscious in one minute.*

She didn't so much kick as spasm her whole body. The last bubbles of oxygen in her lungs seemed to expire as she thrust upward and reached for the ghostly hand.

Oh, God, let me die but let me die above the ice. I can't take being entombed in this blackness.

The hand came closer and she thought she saw the red mask rippling above it. Finally, the hand dipped down and caught hers and began to pull her upward. She closed her eyes and pushed toward the rectangle.

The hand pulled her up and she broke the surface of the water. She gasped a lungful of air and screamed it back out.

The man was squatting at the edge of the rectangle cut into the ice. He didn't pull her out. Instead, he took his right hand and rested it on top of her hair, streaming with water.

Abbie heard her gasping voice in her ears. She couldn't make words.

The man looked at her, through the holes in the mask. 'Shut up, you stupid cunt,' he said calmly.

Abbie reached up and grasped at the edge of the ice. Her hand was frozen into a claw.

'Gettttt—' No more words could get past her chattering teeth. The man looked over, then slowly reached down and pushed her hand off the ice. She thrashed helplessly in the water.

He stared down at her. The eyes were crisp blue in the red eyeholes. 'Listen to me.'

Abbie stared at the mask in terror.

'Who's next?' he said.

'Whaaaaa—'

The hand pushed Abbie's head down into the dark lake, and water flooded into her open mouth. Her vision filled with blackness and the water burned her eyes.

She came back up with a high-pitched gasp.

'You mother—'

The man answered, his voice almost a moan.

'*Who . . . is . . . next?*'

Abbie could only stare wildly and shake her head. The current was pulling at her body and her feet floated up under the ice, her toes bumping against the underside. She fought to stay vertical but the strength was draining from her body and being filled with a leaden blankness.

'Who?' the man said calmly.

Abbie gripped the edge of the ice and lay back. Her hand reached for the boiler suit, but in almost comical slow motion. She wanted to pull him in with her. She would pull him down into the inky depths and they would die together.

The man batted her hand away, then leaned over the hole, steam flowing past the mask.

'If you don't get off this case,' he said, enunciating each word, 'they'll never find your body.'

With that, he stood up. Abbie's eyes grew wide and she grunted, '*Noooo.*' But the man turned and began to disappear over the lip of the ice. The top of the red mask was the last thing to vanish.

All she could see now was the gray sky. Her hearing was growing sensitive, and she heard, or thought she heard, the traffic from the 90 like a steady electric hum. Her body below her waist was disappearing. She couldn't feel her legs, just an area of frigid nothingness where they should have been.

Abbie took a ragged gasp of air and reached toward the ice with her shaking hands, reached past the clean-cut edge. *If I don't get out on the first try, I'll float all the way to Canada under the ice,* she thought as her mind began to dim. Her body wanted that. Her body wanted to sleep.

Her hands rested on the burning ice. She bobbed once, twice, then with a hoarse scream she pushed her palms flat and launched out of the water. She got her torso out up to the waist, water splashing down onto the powdery snow, and her cheek sank down to the ice. She was facing north, looking out on the vast expense of ice lit by the rising sun.

The man was nowhere to be seen.

TWENTY-NINE

Two hours later, Abbie was in the Saab, the air from the heaters just starting to reach her bones. She stared at the lake ice, turning golden in the morning sun.

She'd managed to crawl out of the ice hole, her clothes freezing on her in the open air until it felt like she was wearing a suit of stiff leather. The crawl to the hut had taken her fifteen agonizing minutes. If it had been ten feet farther away, she wouldn't have made it. But she'd got to the plywood structure, found the small window that looked away from shore and broken it with her elbow, then crawled through the opening and collapsed into the hut, which smelled of musk oil and the peculiar yeasty tang of Genesee Cream Ale. There was a blanket there, a smelly old army blanket, but to her it was the loveliest thing she'd ever felt on her skin. She'd taken off all her clothes and wrapped herself in it, sitting on a stool that served the fisherman when he was crouched over his hole on the ice.

After an hour, her body temperature had returned to normal; her clothes were sodden instead of icy. She'd squeezed herself painfully back into them and walked back off the ice.

He was out there last night, she thought, *when it was snowing. He cut a long hole in the ice between the yellow huts and lay a piece of cardboard over it, or something flat. He pegged it down at the corners. He let the snow cover the trap and then led me to it.*

The man didn't move like the killer in the motel video. And he'd asked her things the killer should know. He was probably Clan, wanting to know if his name was on the list. But hadn't Billy said there were only four Clan members? Jimmy Ryan, Marty Collins, Joe Kane, and

224

her father. Three dead and one in the hospital. All accounted for. So who was the man on the ice?

A shiver knocked her teeth together in the tight space of the Saab.

After thirty minutes, Abbie started the car, headed south on the 90 and drove home. After standing under a hot shower for twenty minutes, she put on fresh clothes and headed back to the Saab. She drove to the Buffalo Gun Center on Harlem Road and replaced her Glock 19 – now at the bottom of Lake Erie – with the same model. Then she drove to headquarters.

Once there, she said nothing to the men around her. *Maybe one of them was holding my head underwater three hours ago,* she thought.

I didn't meet the killer, she thought. *I met my competition.*

Abbie and the other detectives divided up the work of searching for the list of assassins. The working theory was that some Clan member must have kept a tally brought across the border. The only chance of finding a list lay with the three victims: Ryan, Collins, and Kane. Perelli had ordered them to check homes, offices, work lockers, everything.

Abbie had chosen Collins's home. Lawyers were record keepers, she thought. Collins gave her the best chance.

When she arrived at the house on Potters Road, the door opened an inch to her knock and a pale young face appeared in the gap.

'Yeah?' he said.

'Buffalo PD.'

If it was possible for a face that pale to go paler, it did.

'Yeah?'

'I have a warrant to search the house.'

She held it up. The whole Buffalo judicial system – beat cops, judges, prosecutors – had snapped into line. The city was terrified now. O'Halloran had been ordered to stop pursuing the killer on his own and fall in behind Abbie, and to share all information, at the price of his badge if he didn't. She could have hauled the mayor down for questioning if she'd wanted to.

The young man's blue eyes went unfocused.

'I . . . I, um, the house is a mess.'

'Open the door.'

'Can you come back in ten . . .'

Abbie pushed the door open with her foot, slamming it into the man's chin. He went stumbling backward, and she stepped into the dimly lit foyer with the ascending stair ahead of her and a small desk with sympathy flowers sitting on it.

The young man was standing in a flannel shirt and jeans, barefoot, rubbing his chin and looking at her from beneath an overhang of greasy mouse-colored hair. With hatred.

'Who are you?'

'Bobby Collins.'

'Bobby, I'm here to search the house. Don't get in my way. Are you alone?'

'Yeah. Can I . . .'

'Yes?'

'Can I get a break if I tell you where the stuff is?'

Abbie stared at him for three seconds before she understood.

'It's your lucky day. The warrant's not for drugs. I need to look at your father's papers.'

A shock of relief spread across the face, followed by the tightening of his mouth.

'Why didn't you say so?' Bobby said truculently. 'You can't just barge in . . .'

'Just stay out of my way, Bobby.'

Abbie turned left into an old-fashioned parlor. She got immediately a sense of thick wood furniture gleaming in the shadows. When the Irish made it in the world, they bought furniture by the gross ton. At least it wasn't covered in plastic.

'Where's your father's office?'

'What office?'

She turned and walked up to Bobby.

'This visit is about to turn from a murder investigation into a drug sting. Let me ask you a question, Bobby: where's your bedroom?'

Bobby stared at her from underneath his greasy bangs, his close-set eyes filled with impotent anger.

226

'The office is that way,' Bobby said, pointing through the parlor toward the back of the house.

It was surprisingly modern. A bare black Ikea-style desk with no drawers, a steel-gray Dell notebook placed on top, metal shelving to the left with folders backed either in blue, red, or yellow, each color occupying two shelves. To the right a small plasma TV hung on the wall, and underneath it was a small couch covered in nubby blue fabric. Marty Collins had been an orderly man. From what she'd learned, the rest of his life was a mess, so perhaps the neatness here was a dam against the rising tide of chaos.

Orderly men like lists, she thought.

She began with the desk. Beside the chair was a rolling set of three drawers. In the top one she found office supplies, envelopes embossed with 'Collins & Sons' in raised green lettering, and a datebook for 2011. She flipped through it. His last appointment had been three days before, a meeting with a Mrs Kleinhan. 'Estate' was penciled in next to it. The other two drawers were filled with case folders, mostly civil, a few drunk-driving charges and an assault, but no names she recognized. The full range of County life: house purchases, wills, divorce petitions, property liens. Marty Collins had been the protector of every significant family in the County that had the money to guard its interests with a two-hundred-dollar-an-hour lawyer. Abbie guessed that his current workload was represented by the drawer files, while older cases went up on the metal shelves.

She went to the doorway and called Bobby's name.

'Yeah?'

'I need to talk to you.'

He came padding down the stairway. He looked sick. Abbie had heard the toilet upstairs flush three times in the last twenty minutes. Bobby had no doubt been disposing of his secret stashes.

'Did your father have a place where he kept special things? His will, family pictures, jewelry, anything like that?'

Bobby leaned on the stair banister. 'How would I know?'

'How would you know? Do you work, Bobby?'

'Here and there.'

'I'll take that as a no. If I had a son who was a shiftless drug addict, with no job and no prospects, I'd sure as hell find a place to keep things away from him.'

Bobby's face was as blank as the wall behind him.

'A safe maybe?'

His eyes betrayed him. They glanced to the left.

'Where is it?'

He sighed. 'In the living room, behind the ugly picture.'

The ugly picture was a family portrait. Abbie glanced at it. Happier times – both sons alive. Bobby even looked presentable in a corduroy blazer and a striped tie jammed all the way up to his neck.

'The combination.'

'How would—'

She turned to look at him.

'It's 5-29-17,' he said. 'JFK's birthday. He used to use my birthday, but he was a spiteful fuck. I'm not the bad guy here, you know.' Bobby turned and headed back to the stairs.

The safe popped open. Abbie reached inside and pulled out a will, two gold watches, a Navy medal of some sort, and an old Bible. She glanced at the other items, turned them over, and pulled the medal out of its presentation books. No marks, no lists of any kind.

She pulled the Bible open.

It was a King James and it smelled of candle wax. Probably an heirloom from the old country, pressed into the hands of a departing ancestor by a parish priest. She flipped hurriedly through the pages. There were no notations in the front. There was a half-completed family genealogy that seemed to end with Marty's father. The pages were clean, a few with their corners turned back. She straightened one of the corners and checked the passages. The story of Job, one in Revelations. But no pen marks. She turned it to the light. No indentations along the lines or under individual letters.

She paged through the back, looking for pen marks or pages with the corners bent back. Nothing. As she flipped to the last pages, she found three lined pages with the heading 'Favorite Passages.' On the first page, in black ink, someone had made a list of citations. At the head of the list were the letters 'PPFO.'

The length of the numbers varied. The first read, '12-4, 8-6, 32-2, 14-9.' Space. Then '2-4, 8-8, 27-1, 19-12, 12-18.' A second column listed a similar set of numbers. There were fourteen sets in all.

Abbie looked at the first set of numbers and flipped back to page 12. It was part of the preface to the translation, and her index finger slid down to the fourth line. Her lips moved as she mumbled: 'Matters of such weight and consequence are to be speeded with maturity: for in a business of movement a man feareth not.'

'In a business of *movement*,' she said to herself.

If this was a simple page-and-line code, it would require three numbers: page, line, and the position of the letter in the line. There were only two numbers in each series. There was something missing.

Abbie checked the next reference. The line read: 'Everlasting remembrance. The judgment of Aristotle is worthy and well known: "If Timotheus had not been, we had not had . . ."'

She snapped the book closed and hurried out of the office, pulling out her cell phone as she headed toward the front door. Once outside, she punched in a number and hurried toward the Saab.

'Dr Reinholdt. So nice to hear your voice, too. I have something for you. Can I drop it off in five minutes?'

THIRTY

After leaving the Bible with Dr Reinholdt, she raced over to Mercy
Hospital. Her father had been moved to a private room that had
opened up on the third floor. There was a cop sitting by his door,
working on a crossword puzzle.

'Are you alone?' she asked him.

'Yes.'

'Put the book down, okay?'

He nodded and slid the book of puzzles under his seat.

Her father's face looked thinner. She stayed by his bedside, holding
his hand. The flesh felt papery. A few times she saw his pupils jerk
behind his eyelids. *What are you dreaming of, Dad?* she thought. *Who's
chasing you now?*

Her phone rang.

'It's Billy. Listen, I need to talk to you.'

She hadn't spoken to him since the night at his house. She felt a
rush of longing for him.

'Don't turn on the charm, Billy, it's really not necessary.'

He sighed. 'Sorry, Ab. Come over when you can. Listen . . .'

'Yes?'

'The other night. Did you try and get in my windows before coming
through the front door?'

'Your windows? Why would I do that?'

'So that's a no?'

'That's a no.'

Silence from the other end.

'Is everything okay?'

'Yeah. Just get here when you can, okay?' He hung up.

She wanted to go to Billy, but the thought that she might never see her father again kept her at the bedside. Finally, twenty minutes later, she kissed her father's sunken cheek, checked that the cop was watching the hallway, then dashed for the elevator.

As she strode through the parking lot, her cell rang again. She recognized the number: Reinholdt.

'Detective?' His voice sounded fluty with excitement.

'You've cracked it.'

'Half a day in the Buffalo Public Library. I was afraid that the code didn't refer to the Bible, and I was right.'

'What is it?'

'Why was there no other book in the safe, Detective?'

Abbie rolled her eyes.

'I don't have time for parlor tricks, Doctor.'

'It's a simple question.'

Abbie stopped and rubbed her forehead. She thought hard.

'I have no idea.'

'Because Marty Collins carried the text in his head. He surprised me. Come by and I'll explain.'

She jumped in the car. Billy or Reinholdt? She was approaching Cazenovia Park Road. Right meant Reinholdt, straight ahead meant Billy.

Billy had a gun. And she had to have the list. She made a quick right, punched the gas and felt the Swedish turbo kick in.

She found Dr Reinholdt at the furthest table in the Historical Society library, sitting in the middle seat. In front of him was a single sheet of paper. He was sitting up as straight as his round body would allow. He looked like a governor waiting to sign an execution order.

Abbie pushed the doors open and the smell of books washed over her.

'Doctor, I don't have a lot—' she said, hurrying toward him.

'I have everything ready for you.' His voice was calm again.

She walked quickly to the table and came around to where he was sitting. Reinholdt nodded as she moved behind him, tilting her head to read the document, but it was turned over to its blank side.

'A brief synopsis,' he said.

'Doctor, with all due respect—'

Reinholdt continued as if she hadn't spoken.

'At first, I thought like you that there was a number missing. And there is – but it isn't the last number, it's the *first*. Do you understand?'

'No.'

'The page number is missing. The document the code derives from is so short that it doesn't require page numbers. The two numbers are actually the line and the letter position within the line.'

Abbie straightened up, intrigued despite herself.

'A poem?'

'Excellent. My first instinct as well. And if it was a poem, who would have written it?'

'Yeats?'

'Bravo. The cliché Irish poet, I've always found him rather unbearable with his mooniness and pathetic love affairs. I tried all the classics, "Sailing to Byzantium," "Easter, 1916," the obvious choice. It's about the uprising that began the Irish revolution.'

'I know what it's about. Doctor, please, what did you find?'

'I found out it wasn't Yeats.'

'Then who was it?'

'*PPFO*. How obvious could it be?'

'Not very, apparently.'

'P . . . P . . . F . . . O. What is the founding document of the Irish revolutionary movement?'

She felt the urge to cold-cock him with her Glock and abscond with the document.

'I have no idea.'

'The speech given by Pádraig Pearse over the grave of O'Donovan Rossa in 1915. The original call to arms. Everything in recent Irish history flows from it. Popularly known as Pádraig Pearse's Funeral Oration. PPFO.'

Abbie nodded, hurrying him along.

'Pádraig Pearse, a schoolteacher and fanatic – and gay as the queen of spades, like a number of the early leaders – called forth the valiant men of Ireland to rid the nation of the oppressors. His speech became the . . . the Declaration of Independence for the rebels.'

Reinholdt looked over his shoulder, his eyes gleaming back at her.

'Any member of the Clan na Gael worth his salt would know it by heart. Don't you see? It was a sort of security device – no need to keep the document around for prying eyes to stumble on. And it's just one page.'

He turned, picked up the yellowing sheet and turned it over. She saw the heading, 'Pádraig Pearse's Oration at the Grave of Donovan O'Rossa (1915).'

'There are many different printings, of course, and each one changes the line breaks. I nearly lost my mind searching for one that would give us Christian names. I found a copy of the original downtown, and of course, that was the one Collins had in his head. I—'

'Doctor, I'm sorry to do this.'

Abbie reached around for the yellow sheet, snapped it off the table, and began to run for the door.

Her last glimpse of the doctor was of his forlorn shape slumped at the table.

Abbie raced to the parking lot and fumbled for the keys. When she was inside, she jammed the gear into drive and fishtailed toward the exit. On to Delaware. Through downtown, edging through red lights and then slamming the accelerator. Right on Tupper Street and onto the Skyway.

Abbie came off the Tifft ramp and barely made the turn without slamming the passenger door into the concrete abutment. She raced down Tifft toward the County, pushing the car faster and nearly taking a teenager crossing McKinley out at the knees.

'The fuck—' he yelled at her, but she was gone before the rest of the words could reach her. She turned left on Abbott, her back wheels sending up sprays of water, then whipped the wheel left on Dorrance Lane.

She saw the lights from two blocks away, the neon blue and red flashing off the second stories of the wooden homes. There'd been no chatter on the police radio.

Must be a fire, she thought.

But there was no ribbon of smoke in the air.

When she got closer, she saw two police units. They were in front of Billy's house. A cold hand gripped the bottom of her stomach.

No, it can't be.

Abbie raced up to the house and angled the Saab into the curb, slamming the brakes to a stop. She was out the car before the headlights dimmed, and ducked under the yellow police tape.

Just let him be alive. Please, that's all I ask.

A cop saw her coming and stepped out of the doorway. She was inside the living room, and there was Billy on the floor. But the face wasn't Billy's anymore. It was a bad Halloween mask.

O'Halloran was kneeling beside the body, checking his pockets.

She heard someone scream as if their body were being torn apart. O'Halloran turned, his face mottled with shock.

'Kearney, what the f—'

The floor loomed up at her, the rug Billy had bled on after she threw him over the couch. But now there was a lot more blood on it than she'd remembered, soaked deep and crimson.

She remembered nothing after that.

THIRTY-ONE

When Abbie came to, she felt light, as if she would float away. She was sitting in her cubicle at headquarters. Z was holding a cold cloth to her forehead and talking to someone on his phone.

'You know there's no way that can happen . . . ,' he said quietly.

The lights were sending stinging rays into her eyes. She felt her eyelids flutter. Involuntary response.

Suddenly, bile rose in her throat, along with the memory.

'Billy.' She reached for Z's arm.

With an infinite weariness, Z slipped the phone into his shirt pocket and grabbed her shoulders. His eyes came parallel with hers. Sad walrus eyes, red-veined. And something fearful in them.

'Don't think about that now. You shouldn't have seen that.'

'Is he dead? Just tell me.'

Z pulled his chair around the foot of the cubicle wall and sat heavily across from her. He took her hands in his.

'He's dead, Ab. Looks like he was number four.'

A wave of nausea rippled through her stomach. *No, not Billy. It should have been me.* She was the reason Billy was dead. Whatever he was going to tell her had cost him his life.

'I should have gone to him first, Z. Why didn't I go to him first?'

'Ab, there's nothing you could have done.'

'I could have saved him.'

Z dropped his head.

'What did you say?' Abbie said.

He looked up. 'Huh?'

'You said he was the fourth.'

Z nodded.

'The fourth? There's no way. Billy . . .'

His face came to her with the name. The smiling, gentle face of Billy Carney.

'Billy wasn't part of the Clan,' she gasped out.

Z shook his head. 'They found a toy. In his mouth.'

'That can't be right. Billy's an innocent bystander. He was going to tell me something and the County killed him.'

'Are you up to taking a walk?'

'I think . . . I think so.'

'Okay, hon. Come on then.'

'Where are we going?'

'Conference room. Perelli wants to talk.'

He lumbered heavily beside her. Her feet seemed as if they were moving a thousand feet below her, boats creeping along as she watched from a high-flying plane.

She saw Perelli and O'Halloran waiting in the conference room. *I don't want to hear the details,* she thought. *What does it even matter?*

Perelli saw her and his expression changed. He nodded to O'Halloran. When she entered, Perelli took her elbow and guided her to one of the black vinyl-backed chairs.

'How're you feeling?'

'Not good.' Z answered for her.

She lowered herself shakily into the chair. O'Halloran moved to the other side of the table.

'This won't take long. Things are moving fast. I want to talk to you about Billy Carney.'

Poor Billy. My beautiful boy.

'He called you today?'

'Yes,' she said, barely audibly.

'What time?'

'Around thirty minutes before I came . . .'

She saw the living room again, Billy looking as though he'd dropped from ten stories, his face a welter of blood.

'Kearney, can you hear me? What did you two talk about?'

'He knew something about the case. Something new.'

'Did he say that?'

'No. He was going to tell me, but . . .'

The tears seemed to sweep up from nowhere. She pressed her cupped hand over her mouth. Her eyes crinkled at the edges to prevent a flood of tears.

She saw Perelli watching her, his eyes dry.

'Are you okay?'

'No, I'm not okay.'

He paused, then went on.

'You had reason to believe he was going to tell you about the Clan case?'

'Yes. He also . . .'

'Yeah?' O'Halloran said.

'He asked me if I'd opened his windows the other night.'

'The other night?' O'Halloran again.

'Yes. I went to talk to him about my father.'

'Uh-huh.' Perelli now. 'And what's this about the window?'

She looked at him.

'I don't know. Someone must have been messing with him. I came in through the front door.'

He leaned toward her. 'Listen, Abbie. You've been under a lot of stress lately. I know this case has been personal for you, with your father involved and all.'

They're all personal, she meant to say. *But this one was more. Why deny it?* She said nothing.

'I want to make this easy for you. We found a toy monkey jammed into Billy's mouth.'

She closed her eyes but not before a single tear slid out.

'It can't be. It doesn't fit.'

'It fits.'

'How?'

Perelli gestured with his hand to O'Halloran. O'Halloran stared at her while he reached inside his Donegal tweed jacket and pulled out an evidence bag.

Inside she saw the monkey. His arms reached straight up above his head, like he was being held up. She took the bag and turned it to scatter the glare from the overhead fluorescents.

'This one . . .'

'Yeah?' Perelli said.

She heard the door close. She turned to see Z was walking away toward his desk.

She turned back to the monkey. Something was different about it.

'It looks newer.'

'Oh, I think it's the same idea.'

O'Halloran reached into his pocket again. Another evidence bag. Like a magician with the many-colored scarves. She watched his eyes as he pulled it out and laid it on the table.

It was a slug.

'We dug this out of the ceiling in Billy's living room,' Perelli said.

'Just below where he was found,' O'Halloran said.

Perelli looked at her. 'Any ideas?'

She felt as if she were stepping over a cliff in darkness.

'It's mine.'

'We know,' O'Halloran said.

She felt Perelli's hand on her shoulder.

'How'd it get there?'

His voice was all wrong. He should have been furious. She'd discharged a gun and not reported it, a breach of Department rules. She looked up at him.

His eyes were soft, softer than she'd ever seen him. And it hit her.

'I'm not the killer,' she said. 'Call Dr Reinholdt at the Historical Society. I was with him until just before the murder.'

'All you needed was ten seconds for Billy Carney to open the door and you to fire a warning shot into the ceiling, then slash his throat. Why'd you use a knife instead of your gun?'

Abbie only stared at him.

Perelli shrugged. 'You get back in your car and circle back. Two minutes total. I drove it myself. Tell me how I'm wrong.'

She wanted him to blow up, to pound the desk. Or tell her to stop talking nonsense. But instead he was treating her like some kind of invalid.

'I didn't kill Billy Carney,' she said.

O'Halloran's eyes were as hard as stone.

'You killed all of 'em,' he said.

'What did you say?'

Perelli took something out of his shirt pocket, a small black piece of plastic.

'We found this in the bedroom. It's a common listening device. Works on radio waves. Distance of two hundred yards. Someone was listening to Billy's conversations.'

He turned it over in his hands, studying its components. Then he looked at her.

'Did you hear him talking to his friends at the Club? Telling them he knew who did Ryan and the rest? Is that what made you kill him?'

'*Why would I kill those men? Why?*'

'Goes back to when your father got you, I think. Is that it? He pulled you away from your real family and you hated them for it. Or was there more? Was there any kind of . . . abuse, Abbie, that all the boys were involved in? If that's it, I can understand.'

She stood and pushed the chair away, looking at the two men wildly.

'Are you out of your minds?'

'Sit down, Kearney,' Perelli said quietly, turning the chair toward her.

'*Chief.*'

He frowned sympathetically and nodded at the chair. 'Sit down.'

The black waves were coming. They were lapping at the back of her brain.

'What about the blood?'

'What—'

'The techs sent out all the blood samples from Cazenovia Park. There was only one partial match, from a swab taken from one of the branches that Collins was tied to. He ran it against all the files of the investigators who worked the scene, to eliminate them.'

Perelli leaned over.

'You came up a match. There wasn't enough to do a full DNA run, but he's got enough for a 95 percent maternal match. Good enough for me.'

'I . . . I cut myself.'

'Stop bullshitting me, Abbie. You cut yourself *after* the samples were taken. You saw Michaels walk out. He had the swabs with him. That was the last time he visited the scene.'

How could her—

'Someone put my blood there.'

'Okay, O.J.,' O'Halloran said.

Perelli shot him a look. Then he leaned down until his face was eye level with hers.

She didn't want to look at him.

'The scene was sealed off immediately after the body was discovered. No one came in and out.'

'Then it was a cop, Chief. You *know* O'Halloran was running a parallel investigation. They'd prepared this ahead of time for the next crime scene. Why can't you see that?'

Perelli's eyes were eighteen inches from hers, magnified by his steel-rimmed glasses. The warm sympathy had drained away. He looked at her like he would a noxious bug on a slide.

She could not speak.

'You're insane, Abbie. You don't even know it. You tell me what happened and I'll personally escort you to EC Med for a psych evaluation. They have real nice facilities there – you know that, you've escorted prisoners there yourself. It's a hospital, not a prison. You belong in a hospital right now, Abbie. Until we can get this figured out.'

'Stop calling me Abbie.'

Something flitted in the back of her mind. She started in her chair. 'What is it?'

She shook her head violently. *It can't be,* she thought. Something was squeezing her brain. Her lips twisted violently. Out of the corner of her eyes, she saw O'Halloran's eyes widen.

'What is it, Abbie?'

'I couldn't have done those things,' she whispered.

'You're right.'

'I'm right?!' she shouted.

'You've heard of split personality disorder. I think that's what we're looking at, don't you? It *wasn't* you, Abbie, it was someone else inside you.'

'How can you say I killed those people? I wasn't even there.'

'We checked your whereabouts for all four cases. You were unaccounted for, as far as we can tell. We've rebuilt your last two weeks. There's room for the murders.'

O'Halloran leapt up from his chair, his teeth gritted and his blue eyes ablaze.

'You killed them, you fucking cunt. You thought you were smarter than all of us, with your Ivy League bullshit. But we got you.'

'You framed me is what you mean.'

O'Halloran's fist had smashed across her face before she even saw it coming. Her head whipped sideways and pale stars exploded inside her head.

When she opened her eyes, Perelli was shoving O'Halloran back in his chair.

'Sit down. *Sit the fuck down*. What did I tell you, O'Halloran?'

The Irish cop was snorting with hatred, staring her down. His eyes never moved off Abbie's.

'I knew Jimmy Ryan. She's probably got his eyelids in her god-damn pocket, Chief.'

'I don't give a fuck. Sit down and stay down.'

Perelli turned to her.

'Tell me about Jimmy Ryan,' he said.

'I was first detective on scene,' she said. Her voice sounded suddenly robotic to her.

'You mean St Teresa's? The church you grew up going to? People tell me you knew that place like you were raised in it.'

'I didn't—'

'How did you find out about the Clan? Your father was part of it.

Did you hear him talking on the phone one night? Were you playing amateur detective in high school? Just tell me, Ab.'

'Chief, I'm not—'

The sound of his hand on the table was like a pistol shot.

'*Tell* me!'

Abbie shook her head.

'I have one more thing to show you. I wasn't going to – the DA asked me not to – but I'm going to do it as a courtesy to a fellow cop.'

His eyes loomed larger as he leaned in.

'Then you *will* talk to me. Or you're going to a cell in the holding center, mixed in with general population, where no cop should ever be. And I'm going to personally hang your badge around your neck as you walk in.'

He went to the cabinet in the corner. Abbie's eyes followed him.

Perelli opened a drawer and pulled out a book. She couldn't see the cover.

This had all been planned out, she thought. But was Perelli part of it too? It was essential to know that. Who else was part of the frame?

O'Halloran was smiling at her now. She wanted to say something smart, but she didn't feel smart.

Perelli came back, holding a book in his hand. But it wasn't a book. It was a picture album with a faded green cover. Abbie stared at the album as Perelli dropped it to the table.

'Where did you get that?'

'We found it in your basement, along with an old Bible. Do you know who they belong to?'

'My father.' He'd had it forever, adding pictures to it as the years went by.

The room seemed to grow dark. She felt claustrophobic, brightly colored spots appearing in the corners of her vision and shimmering there. She felt the black wave washing closer and closer to her eyes.

Perelli opened the photo album's cover, standing over her as he flipped through the heavy pages. As if they were relatives looking at loved ones, long gone now.

Pool party. Fantasy Island. High school graduation. The last picture
– her and her father in Niagara Falls. Smiling their lies.

'That's it,' she said, her voice choked.

'No, it's not.'

He turned the two blank pages. Then she saw it, stuck under the
inside flap of the jacket cover. The corner of a faded photo, the old
kind from the eighties that had no white borders. Perelli's thick fingers
reached under and plucked it out.

With a cold shock, she remembered it. Remembered not the picture
but the moment. She'd been around two years old. Her and her mother
in the cold place off of Main Street. One of their many homes, always
cold, always dirty. Hunger in her eyes.

She couldn't look at her own face in the picture. Abbie's gaze fell
to her hands. And in the right one, what was that, pushed up toward
the camera to show how much she liked the gift?

A toy monkey, as clear as day.

THIRTY-TWO

Perelli had been as good as his word. She was taken to the holding center.

'Name?'

'Absalom Kearney.'

The female cop looked up, her face scouring Abbie's for a full few seconds.

'Middle name?'

'Margaret.'

'Let's get your fingerprints.'

No special privileges. They had to segregate by sex, so she was thrown in with the female drug dealers and the gang members and the whores and skels, and they parted like the Red Sea for her, and she'd found her way to the corner. Ninety-five percent black, with one lonely Latino girl nursing a cut above her eye. The blood dripping to the floor in splashes. She felt she could hear the blood hit the floor, like a raindrop in a puddle, but that was impossible. Wasn't it?

The place was dark, and it stank of gin and vomit and unwashed clothes. The walls were slab concrete. She pressed her back into the corner.

Oh, Absalom, what have you done? What brought you back here to Buffalo? You should have stayed away stayed away stayed away.

At 2 a.m., the screeching began to die down. The meth freaks came off the tops of their high and huddled together for warmth. The cage grew cold. Abbie waited, hunched in the corner, seeing the skels fall asleep one by one, feeling like a gargoyle watching over a doomed city.

At 9 a.m., she was brought before a judge and charged with the murder of Billy Carney. The other charges would follow. Bail set at $1 million. She watched the entire scene as if she were looking at a TV. Even her 'Not guilty' seemed to come from the mouth of an actor.

The sound of metal scraping metal. Abbie's head snapped up. Something told her it was near dark.

'Kearney, Absalom.' The cop at the door had a long chain of keys hanging in his hand. He was looking at her with a face made blank by effort.

Her limbs were frozen stiff. She unfolded painfully from her crouch and began picking her way through the curled-up bodies on the floor.

'You've been bailed.'

'By who?'

'Zangara, the stupid fuck.'

'You put up your house,' was the first thing she said to him.

He was silent, all the gregariousness drained away.

He nodded.

'Linda's going to kill you.'

'Linda,' he said, 'is the one who made me do it.'

She looked over at him. 'Do you believe me, Z?'

Z, her fort, her friend. He turned away, looked out his side window as they drove down Delaware. They'd taken the back way out of the holding center. Z had managed to keep her away from the cameras that were no doubt stationed out front.

'I told you to get help.'

'Help for stress, Z, not for being a serial killer.'

She couldn't see his face, but she heard the sigh.

'Yes, I believe you.'

'Thank you anyway.'

He made a left.

'Where are we going?' she said.

'You tell me. We can't go to your place, unless you want to walk into a media circus.'

'Take me to the Reverend.'

Z nodded.

If he'll have me, she thought. *Where else is there to go?*

'Z, I need one more favor.'

He looked straight ahead.

'I need the list of IRA fugitives, the one I found in Marty Collins's Bible.'

Z sighed. 'It's in Perelli's office. He's not handing out copies right now. They want to control the investigation.'

'You have to get it for me. The killer is on that list. I need to find him.'

Z turned to look at her.

'I can't lose my badge, Ab. I can't do that to my family.'

'I won't let that happen.'

She tried to think.

'Don't call or text me, don't come by the Reverend's. Just leave the names in the third booth at Mighty Taco, the one near the window. Tape it under the table. I'll pick it up in an hour.'

Z nodded.

He pulled up to 278 Hertel and she opened the door as he slid to a stop.

'Ab.'

She turned and leaned in the car window.

'Yes?'

'How'd the killer know about the monkeys?'

Her fingers curled in her palm.

'I wish I knew.'

John Kearney watched the door open and saw the nurse come in. She was new. Rosemary was gone. This one was tall and red-haired, with wide hips, and he didn't recognize her.

The new nurse was young. She walked toward him with her left arm held tightly by her side, the hand hidden.

Sure, you don't have to hide it from me, he thought. *I'm a corpse laid out. I can do nothing to ye. She must feel guilty. How much are they paying her? Or have they told her the old story, and is she doing it for the Gaelic boys?*

The nurse approached, tapped the tube full of clear liquid that led down to his arm.

'How are we this morning, Mr Kearney?'

The surface of his face lay calm and impassive, like a lead blanket over his mind, which never seemed to sleep.

I'm fine. How do I look?

'Just a shot for the pain.'

Nothing can touch the pain, he told her with his eyes, and she looked away. John Kearney thought of Abbie, and something burned in his heart.

The nurse injected the milky liquid into the tube as he watched. When the plunger was fully depressed, she took it out. She looked at him like you would a wax statue, her eyes avid to see the living dead man.

As John Kearney watched her go, something caught his attention. She'd done something different from Rosemary. The routine – the small bit of chat, the syringe, the milky substance into the tube – was all the same. But there was something missing.

What was it? His mind couldn't latch onto details like it used to. It glided over things, unable to fasten on their edges, their meaning. There was a detail here that mattered.

Think, John.

The little wheel. The white plastic wheel. She'd forgotten to turn it. The little wheel that let the new liquid flow into his arm.

He watched as the tube began to run dry, droplets of clear liquid left along its side like raindrops.

One last chance, he thought. Lord, please. *I won't waste it. My business is almost done.*

He felt a tiny prick of feeling in his right hand.

Abbie slid into the booth at Mighty Taco. She'd bought a salad and a loganberry, though she wasn't hungry. She watched the other diners around her, but there were no whisperings or sudden turns of the head. She wore a blue and red hat with a 'Buffalo Talking Proud!' decal sewed onto the brim that she'd found in the Reverend's emergency bin for abused and destitute girls. Apparently, it disguised her well enough so that no one put her together with the photo running on *Eyewitness News*.

She took a bite of the salad, holding the fork in her right hand. With her left, she slowly felt under the table. After finding a wad of old gum, her fingers touched a wad of paper. Abbie carefully tore it away from the table, the long strands of tape finally releasing it into her hand.

Her fingers brushed something else as she pulled the paper toward her and stuffed it into her pocket.

Abbie took a sip of loganberry, laid a fork lengthwise on the pale yellow tabletop. She looked around at the other diners. She took another long sip from the straw and set the drink back down.

Then she reached her hand underneath the table, felt the Slammer suspended in a web of heavy tape, and pulled it free.

At 2 p.m. sharp, Maggie Tooley left the nurse's lounge where *The Price Is Right* was winding up. She was going to tell her boyfriend Pat that she didn't want this job anymore, she didn't care what they would pay her. The old man in the bed was starting to freak her out. The eyes seemed to follow her wherever she went in the room, even though they never moved. And they were all liquid and shiny, like a cow's eyes.

What was in the syringe that she gave him every four hours? She could guess. It was something that kept him alive but trapped in his own body. It was wrong. But the money was good, and Conor needed winter boots. He needed a lot more than that, including a father, but mostly right now he needed winter boots.

She walked down the hall, dodging the janitor, the patients pushing their own intravenous stands with the wheels on the bottom, and the duty nurses. Those bitches, both of them local girls, looked right through her as they went on their rounds. They'd been warned off of her, but the least they could do was say hello.

The cop must be on a break, she thought. She knocked on the door, then caught herself. *What's he gonna do, say 'Come in'? Maggie, get your brain clear.*

She opened the door. 'Mr Kear—'

Pat was going to murder her. The blanket was thrown to the floor, and the bed was empty.

Abbie opened the list of IRA killers and spread it out on the car seat. Then she laid the funeral oration of Pádraig Pearse next to it. Her eyes wandered across the second document.

Is this what it's all about? she thought. *The thing that started everything? It has seemed right, before we turn away from this place in which we have laid the mortal remains of O'Donovan Rossa, that one among us should, in the name of all, speak the praise of that valiant man and endeavor to formulate the thought and the hope that are in us as we stand around his grave.*

Jesus Christ, the Micks and their obsession with death. She was sick of it. Her eyes drifted down the page.

I propose to you, then, that here by the grave of this unrepentant Fenian we renew our baptismal vows; that here by the grave of this unconquered and unconquerable man, we ask of God, each one for himself, such unshakable purpose, such high and gallant courage, such unbreakable strength of soul as belonged to O'Donovan Rossa.

For a moment, she thought of her father. The words seemed to fit his hardness. 'Unbreakable strength.' She felt she was getting a glimpse of the part of his life that had been always turned away from her.

Finally, the end:

They think that they have foreseen everything, think that they have provided against everything; but the fools, the fools, the fools! – they have left us our Fenian dead, and while Ireland holds these graves, Ireland unfree shall never be at peace.

The cry – *the fools, the fools, the fools!* – seemed to ring in her ears. Was she one of them? Another outsider blind to the patterns?

Concentrate, Absalom. What we need is a name.

She turned her eyes to the list of coded names. The first column would have his Irish name, and the second his American one, his cover name given to him by the Clan. She began translating the first cover name.

She picked up her cell phone.

'Z. Everything you got on a William Preston. Look for anyone in his fifties or sixties who applied for everything at once: Social Security card, driver's license.'

Z told her he'd call back within the hour.

THIRTY-THREE

'Mills.'

'It's Kearney.'

She'd had an idea. If she was being framed, who was to say the killer wasn't a Buffalo cop? There were too many coincidences: the blood swab, the monkey face traced on the Saab minutes before she left police headquarters. While she waited for Z to call back, she would run down one hunch with the cops in Niagara Falls.

'Hey.'

She could tell by his voice he didn't know she'd been arrested, and that he still wanted that date she'd been putting off. Either that, or he was an incredible actor.

'How's the Outlaws thing?' she said, hoping to keep things casual.

'It's demented is what it is. The more I know about these people, the less I want to know. The Warlocks lead didn't pan out. They swore up and down they had a peace treaty with the Outlaws and had no reason to kill their officers. So we think it's an internal split, a power struggle, but the fucker killed everyone standing, right?'

'Right, but—'

'So we go back to the Outlaws headquarters and this time go over it like King Tut's tomb and what do we find in the basement?'

'I don't—'

'A fucking *pit*. They held one of their members in a little hole in the ground with a rebar screen over the top. Must have been for punishment. We found old chicken wing bones and Pepsi bottles down there. Maybe the fucker gets out and he decided to give them some of their own. I can't blame him. Gunned down the whole leadership, and the two newbies who pulled up on their bikes at the end.'

She heard a creaking sound and the end of a yawn.

'Christ, I've barely slept going through that shithole.' Mills sighed. 'But you have your own problems. What can I do for you?'

'You said you ran the plates of every car caught on closed circuit near the Lucky Clover. I need to know if you came up with a Buffalo plate.'

'They were almost all Buffalo plates. Casino traffic.'

'But anything from Buffalo PD?'

Silence.

'Buffalo PD? What would they have been doing trailing Decatur?'

'Can you just check?'

'It's a good thing you're hot, Kearney. When we both catch our killers, how about that dinner?'

'I've had the casino buffet, thanks.'

He laughed and hung up.

Z called back with the details on William Preston. He was fifty-two and employed by Temp Solutions at 1899 Oak Street. Abbie revved up the Saab and was in front of the nondescript seafoam-gray building ten minutes later. She walked through the doors praying no one would recognize her. A receptionist with brown mousy hair and a simpering expression watched her approach the front counter.

'We're not accepting applications.'

'That's nice, but it's not what I'm here for. I'm looking for William Preston.'

'Bill? But he's not here anymore.'

'Where'd he go?'

'He just didn't show—'

A thought visibly dawned on the receptionist's face.

'Hold on, I better let Mr Alexander answer that.'

Abbie nodded. As the receptionist pushed back her chair and turned toward the back of the offices, Abbie spotted a tall blonde woman two desks behind the reception area. She had a bouffant hairdo with black roots and her eyes were shadowed with light blue eye shadow. Those eyes were now following her, the corner of the woman's tongue visible over the frosted pink of her lipstick. It wasn't a friendly look.

Abbie turned quickly and walked to a display that showed multicultural young people working at a variety of jobs but smiling emphatically under the slogan 'A WORLD of Talent.'

'Like I said, we're really not taking any applications. We're full up.' The receptionist had returned.

Abbie nodded. 'I heard you the first time, thanks.'

'Can I help you?' A thickset black man in a tan long-sleeve dress shirt and a brown-and-cobalt-blue-striped tie appeared from behind the receptionist. He was squat and wore a perfectly straight mustache; he looked more like a drill sergeant than an office manager.

'I'm looking for Mr Preston.'

'He doesn't work here anymore.'

'Do you know what happened to him?'

'I got a call on Monday. He said . . . he said that he was taking his family and moving to Atlanta.'

'Did he say why?'

'Yes, he did. It made me wonder if he was really going to Atlanta or if he was headed to some kind of mental institution.'

Abbie looked at him quizzically.

'Why's that?'

'Because,' the man said, his gaze studying her clothes before jumping to her face, 'he said he was leaving for a very unusual reason: there was a demon on the loose. Exact thing he said to me. And that he wasn't going to be around when it knocked on his door four times. What the hell's he mean by that?'

'I have no idea. Did he leave a forwarding address or number?'

'No, he didn't. I went by his house to drop off his last check and the house was dark. I looked in the window and everything was gone, except for a kid's bike and an empty Samsonite. Looks like they left in a real big hurry. I kept the check.'

Abbie laid her card on the counter. 'If you get a forwarding address, will you let me know?'

The man nodded. Abbie's gaze shot past him. The tall blonde

woman was gone from her desk. Was she off somewhere, quietly calling the police? Abbie's eyes must have betrayed her concern, because the man turned, following her gaze, then swiveled back around.

'Everything o—?'

The front door slammed back against the wall and Abbie was halfway to her car.

As Abbie drove back, Mills called her back. No cop cars on their list from the Lucky Clover. As soon as she hung up, the phone buzzed again.

'Kearney.'

'It's Reverend Zebediah. I just got a call for you.'

'From who?'

'He said he was your father.'

'My fa—? My father's in the hospital, unconscious. Are you sure, Reverend?'

'Now, how would I be sure, Absalom? The man said he was your father.'

'He didn't remember my number?'

'No. Apparently not.'

His voice sounded strained. The tension must be getting to him, too.

'What did he say?'

'I have no idea if he's in his right mind, but what he told me was, "Reverend Zebediah, tell Absalom to come to where the black rabbits run." "Where the black rabbits run" is what he said.'

Abbie nearly plowed into a car crossing in front of her. She realized she'd blown through a red light. A furious blast from a car horn grew distant in her ears as she considered what she'd just heard.

'Absalom?'

'Yes?'

'Are you okay?'

'Don't know, Reverend,' Abbie said as she spun the Saab into a U-turn.

THIRTY-FOUR

The taxi pulled into the parking lot of the Tifft Nature Preserve and parked in front of the little caretaker's hut. It was the only vehicle in the tiny gravel lot. John Kearney got out and stared at the preserve.

The taxi driver was yelling something.

'What's that?'

'Twelve eighty,' the man said. He was fat and a thick growth of black hair crawled up from his open shirt to his neck and up his cheeks.

'What d'ye mean, twelve eighty?' John said. Was this guinea trying to steal from him?

'The fare!' the man said angrily. 'For driving you here.'

'From where?'

The man looked away, then his gaze swung back to John angrily, as if he wanted to kick his teeth in.

'From the hospital, and your house.'

'*What* hosp—'

And then it was there, clicked back in place, the memory of the hospital and the tubes and the nurses who weren't real nurses.

He let the insult slide away into nothingness. He was past all that now.

'Never mind, never mind. Take this.'

He pulled a twenty out of his wallet and handed it to the man and began to walk toward the arched entrance to the preserve. He heard the driver yelling. John wanted no change, had no use for it, but he didn't turn to tell the driver this. His mind was clearer than it had been in days, the sedatives having almost completely worn off. He'd had to wait until the cop sitting by his door had gone for a bathroom break, but he'd made it out of the hospital with his clothes and one other thing now stuffed in the pocket of his good cardigan. He guessed the cops had been looking for someone trying to break into the hospital, not out.

The taxi pulled away, kicking up bits of gravel, and zoomed off. John looked up. The sun, glowing orange and red, was setting over the lake, and its beams as they bounced off the water were split by the struts of the Skyway. As he watched, a Canadian goose broke from the reeds and banked away from the lake, heading south.

He had to keep his mind clear for the next part, keep the Alzheimer's away, push it back like you would a flood of water under the door, push it back until he was done.

The sheets of paper he'd taken from the nursing desk fluttered in his hand, the long sloping lines of his handwriting covering three pages. He carefully folded them once and then once again. He tucked the sheets in the pocket of the dress shirt, and began to walk.

He stepped over an ice-rimed puddle. He didn't have his winter coat. They'd snatched him away, the Gaelic boys, before he could grab it. Who was it that had struck him with the small billy club in Abbie's house? He'd never seen the face before. 'For your own good' were the last words he'd heard.

How he'd loved this little preserve. There was nothing like it back in Clare, the ground back there too hard and rocky to spout these enormous stands of grass. Who cared if the plants sucked on poisoned water from the steel plants? Everyone said that Ireland was so unspoiled. It was unspoiled because it was poor, because it had been kept poor. Here the grass fed on the chemicals of his great adopted city, and they grew to the size of giants.

John crossed the parking lot and walked underneath the little wooden archway that led to the trails. The sunlight was instantly swallowed up by the tall grass. He didn't need it anyway. He knew where he was going.

He listened for a car. There was only quiet and the bass horn of a tugboat on the lake, but that meant nothing. He'd learned to respect his enemy. Too late to do the others any good, but so be it.

The reeds made a sawing noise as they rubbed against each other in the wind, the noise of a Chinese fan clicking shut when a gust drove them together. The winter had taken all the moisture out of the reeds. He reached out and grabbed a stalk as he went by. It crackled as he bent and broke it.

There was another sound behind the sound of the reeds. He stopped to listen, his lips turned down into a hard frown. It had been a rustling noise, but it was gone now. He turned and hurried ahead.

At the first fork in the path, he hesitated, then turned right. An arrow-shaped wooden signpost had been hammered into the ground, its words lost in the dusky light.

The path was descending slightly. He tried to move his feet faster, but his knees pained him. Suddenly, he was falling, the ground rising up terrifyingly fast. He didn't have the strength to cushion his fall, and his hand landed on something sharp as he hit the ground. He lay there a moment, expecting a blow to the back of the head, but nothing. He rose himself up on hands and knees and the reeds whispered above him as he panted. He'd tripped over a root; the palm of his right hand was bleeding. It felt as if a layer of skin had been torn away. But he had to keep going. Surely the killer was here now. He was the last of the Clan. He would be followed, but he no longer cared.

John Kearney stood awkwardly, bent over at the waist. He hurried along the path, turning left at the next fork in the pathway. His breath came faster and his knees began to ache. The reeds were reaching above his head, forming a canopy above which the weak sun only penetrated here and there. He felt the wind sweep in from the lake along the tunnel, turning the reeds to their pale side and setting his teeth to chattering.

Finally, he reached the little opening and saw the wooden bench. He staggered toward it, out of breath, and reached for the metal arm. Here it was, cold to his touch. He'd forgotten the scraped palm and it burned on the freezing metal. His breath came in ragged bursts of steam.

I'm ready now, he thought after a few seconds, raising his eyes to the entrance. *I'm ready for you. The last offering I'll make to Ireland is your bloody corpse.*

There was no sound of traffic. The reeds thrashed against each other as if a small cyclone had set down yards away.

He pulled out the sheets, and looked around for a rock.

Must hurry now. Faster, John. For the love of God.

He groped under the seat and found a heavy round stone. He brought it up and laid it on back of the bottom sheet, turned over to avoid being soiled by the stone's underside. He let the pages go and they fluttered in the wind, but the rock pinned them to the wood.

He saw flashes of his own handwriting as the paper flailed wildly. He didn't need to see the words to know the first line, because it had stayed in his memory: 'I, John Kearney, proud member of the Clan na Gael, am responsible for the murders of Jimmy Ryan, Marty Collins, and Joseph Kane.'

The wind dropped away.

John Kearney looked up.

A figure stood at the entrance to the clearing. It wore a black ski mask and by its side was a long, shining knife.

John Kearney stood, holding on to the metal arm before letting it go to face the killer full on. His arm came up and a trembling finger pointed at the mask.

'Do y'not think I know who you are?'

The figure stepped forward, ice crackling under its foot. The wind rose.

John's hand sought the deep pocket of his cardigan. He jerked on something as the figure advanced. Finally, he pulled it free. His old service revolver.

'Take off that goddamned mask,' he cried, the wind making the words gutter in his mouth.

The figure made a strange noise.

'What's that?' John roared in the gale. The wind took the long silver bands of his hair and whipped them around his head.

The figure reached up and grasped the top of the hat. Then it slowly pulled it off and held the mask down by its thigh, flapping there in the strong breeze.

John Kearney trembled from the shock of it. 'Jesus, Mary, and—' He stepped back and stumbled on a stone, falling backward.

The figure moved quickly toward him, the knife coming up, and John Kearney cried out as he brought up his trembling gun.

And what he cried out was: 'Forgive me.'

A Mr Tom Mariani, thirty-four, was in an Oldsmobile Cutlass heading south on Tifft Street, on his way to his twelve-hour shift at the gas station that sat at the corner of Tifft and South Park Avenue. He later reported hearing a single shot, then two more, in quick succession. And then silence.

THIRTY-FIVE

The Skyway was wreathed in mist and the Saab cut a tunnel through it as Abbie pushed it to eighty-five. When the fog broke, Abbie caught quick glimpses of the preserve down on her left. The wind was pushing the reeds almost flat to the ground.

The Saab nearly skidded as she came flying off the exit ramp and the left back wheel slammed into the concrete curb. Abbie felt the muffler rake over some stones, but she gunned the engine and the Saab slid back onto the road. She covered the hundred yards to the parking lot in four seconds. When she pulled in, the lot was empty.

Abbie bolted out of the car and ran for the reeds. She swung under the wooden gateway and along the first steps of the path. As she ran, the feeling of being watched grew so strong that she reached for the Slammer in her pocket and glanced at the dark gaps in the grass as she flew past. At the first fork, she turned left, running flat-out now. It opened into the still orange lake, rimed with ice. Nobody there. Only the sounds of the wind and a soft patter, like someone else running.

'Dad!' she shouted. 'Dad, where are you?'

Abbie turned around and ran back down the path, the cold starting to bruise her lungs. At the fork, she turned left and went running downhill. The grass swayed across the path, driven by the wind, sometimes lashing across her forehead and temporarily blinding her.

'DAA-ADDDD!' she shouted.

When she came to the clearing, she pulled up. There on the bench was her father, his back to her, slumped over slightly to the left.

He's resting, she said to herself. *He walked too fast and now he's resting.* But then she saw the blood on his shirt.

260

Silently, she ran to him, her right hand holding the gun close to her thigh. When she got to the bench, she fell to her knees to look at his face, her hand resting on the small of his back. John Kearney's brilliant blue eyes stared out, devoid of life.

'*Dad?!*' Abbie cried. Her hand gripped his jacket and she pulled his face to her chest. 'Dad, wake up, it's Absalom.'

Only the sound of the wind. She'd seen the knife wound as she'd come close to him, and now she could feel the warmth of his flesh being wicked away, draining away like blood. She looked down and saw the gun lying on the ground. His old service piece.

Abbie let go of her father, her forehead sank to the ground, and she sobbed. Her hand dropped to the dirt and clawed the earth and her mouth tasted dirt, but she couldn't rise or speak, the waves of grief coming like convulsions.

Finally, she stood up and spun around.

'You animal!' she screamed at the soughing reeds.

She pulled up the Slammer and blasted a round into the swaying reeds. Nothing. Tears streamed down her face. She turned in a fast circle, blasting away at the tall grass and the black spaces between.

Nothing.

Abbie sat on the bench, leaning her head onto her father's back. It was cold, the rough wool of his cardigan brushing against her cheek. She didn't want to look at him again, at the face with the eyes wide and the mouth palsied and crooked, the single tear through his shirt, and beneath it, the V-neck T-shirt that she'd bought him, saturated with blood.

Oh, Dad, she thought. *Come back to me.*

The wind blew his silver hair as if he were drifting underwater. She reached over his shoulder and laid her hand on his cheek. He'd never allowed her to touch him like that. She traced the line of his jaw with her hands as tears swelled in her eyes.

Sirens. She stood and looked above the tall grass and saw two police cars climbing the slope of the Skyway half a mile away, the silhouettes dark against bulging black storm clouds, the blue lights flashing like sparks.

Abbie closed her eyes.

She was crying not only because the body was warm and she'd just missed saving him, but because she'd believed for a sickening moment when the Reverend had called her that *he* had been the killer, her own father, and the summons to the reeds had been an invitation to her own death. She cried because the secrets of her childhood were wicking away to the cold air.

Why did he do it, Dad?

Her hand touched a piece of paper next to her father's body, the corner flapping in the wind. Abbie reached around and found the letter pinned underneath a large rock. She rolled it off and pulled the pages toward her. As the sound of the sirens zeroed in like the buzz of an approaching wasp, she read the first line.

The sirens grew louder. She looked up and saw the two cars at the Skyway's peak. She reached around her father and hugged him a final time.

She held the sheets in her right hand as she began to run.

Back in her car, Abbie drove two miles before pulling over. Her hand was still gripping the letter. She dropped the crumpled pages to the passenger seat and gently smoothed them out. Two sheets.

I, John Kearney, proud member in good standing of the Clan na Gael, am responsible for the murders of Jimmy Ryan, Marty Collins, and Joseph Kane.

There is no refuge in Ireland for the enemies of the Crown. In decades past, our freedom fighters would be sent to Botany Bay in Australia aboard the prison ships, reeking and foul. We in the Clan na Gael would not allow that any longer. Two soldiers had been caught in 1977 while trying to enter San Francisco Harbor on a fishing boat and were sent back to Long Kesh Prison. We vowed that would never be allowed to happen again. In 1978, the other members and I offered the IRA leadership our services. Any member in good standing who needed a fresh start away from Northern Ireland, we stood ready to help.

Marty Collins handled the legal aspects – he got new driver's licenses, Social Security cards, and the rest. Joe Kane raised the money. We never asked where it came from and never cared. Jimmy Ryan set up the first few transfers across the border, but he was, sad to say, a disappointment in this because of his gambling and his carelessness. To make sure things went smoothly, I began traveling to the Canadian side of the Falls in 1980 along with him.

How the IRA got the men to Canada was never any of my business – I assumed by freighter or with false identities on commercial planes. But it was understood that their ID would never stand the test at the American border, whose agents were always on the lookout for our boys. We had to find another way to bring them in.

I would go to the casinos in the Canadian Falls and play there for a few hours. The soldier would be brought into the casino or we would meet in a hotel room paid for in cash. I would tell the men what was going to happen and what they needed to do. I also asked them if they were claustrophobic. A few of them were, and those we had to give a great deal of whiskey – and in one case a handful of sleeping pills bought at a local pharmacy for a man who'd taken the Pledge – so that they could make the trip. For there was only one way across the border, and that was in the trunk of my car.

We would drive to a parking lot or out into the country north of Fort Erie, and I would put the soldiers in the trunk. I would then drive to the border, show my license – in those days, you didn't need a passport – along with my ID as a Buffalo police officer. I was never stopped.

Once I had the men in Buffalo, Jimmy Ryan found places for them to live and work, while Marty Collins got their paperwork together. We had friends in the County who would speed up the process, though I won't name names. Everything was done as if these men were returning heroes from a foreign war, which indeed they were.

We brought 14 men across. Though they'd often emerged from the bowels of a British prison, or from the freezing cells at Long Kesh, we never had a single problem with any of them. We were proud to *welcome them to our shores and give them the freedom the British had denied the Irish people for centuries.*

Until 1982. I will never forgive the IRA for what happened then. Unknown to us, they sent us not a soldier but a degenerate, a stain upon the banner, a murdering blackguard. We were told his name was Fergus MacBrennan from Derry. MacBrennan, a name my father always mentioned when telling me of the chiefs of Corca Achlann. A fine name for an Irish rebel, we thought.

It was only the first lie.

Abbie flipped the page, but there was nothing else. She looked around the Saab to make sure she hadn't misplaced a sheet of paper. The killer must have taken the final page with him. She wiped away a tear and pulled out the list of IRA assassins from the inside pocket of her coat. 'Fergus, Fergus,' she whispered. She began to work the codes. The grief for her father had been laid aside so that she could see the killer's face before she killed him.

On the third try, she cried out.

'*F,* here it is.'

But the second letter was *I.* She went through the progression just to be sure. *Finlay. Goddamned Finlay, not Fergus.*

Her finger traced the next name, then her eyes darted to the funeral oration. Slowly she worked through the codes. Three names starting with *S,* one with *J,* two *M*'s, three *N*'s, three *P*'s, one *W.*

After ten minutes, she'd gone through the entire list. She slammed the steering wheel. No other name even starting with *F.*

How could Fergus not be here? Was my whole theory wrong from the beginning – is there another layer of this that I haven't seen into?

She shivered and started the engine. It wasn't only the missing name that confused her, the thought that she might not be able to find him now that his work was done. Another detail had blazed out at her the moment she read it: the year her father had brought the killer across.

1982. The same year he'd adopted her.

*   *   *

The four members of the Clan na Gael were all dead. Billy was dead. Numbness crept across her insides. Her face felt like a heavy rubber mask welded to the bones of her skull.

The list of assassins was all she had. Surely one of them knew who Fergus MacBrennan from Derry was.

Her hand shook as she coded out the next name on the list of fourteen killers. Sorcha O Bruic was the Irish name. When she did the American cover, she stared at it in shock.

She called Z.

When he answered, she said calmly, 'It wasn't me. I didn't kill my father.'

There was a silence that sounded like a hand was being held over the phone. Three seconds later, Z came back on the line.

'I know it wasn't you. Are you okay?'

'I'm going to be going away after this.'

'After what?'

'After I blow his head off.'

'Come in, Ab. That's the only way.'

'So the killer can walk free? He murdered my father, Z.'

The sound of Z's voice changed, echoed now, as if he'd stepped into a small, enclosed space.

'Listen to me. The County is in an uproar. I know you didn't kill your father, but they don't. There's practically a shoot-to-kill order on you now, and I'm not just talking about cops. Do you hear what I'm saying?'

The people who would have cared are gone now, she wanted to say.

'I have a name for you.'

'No! Come in.'

'I have a name, Z. The only way to find the killer is if one of the other assassins knows his M.O. Just help me to get this animal and I'll do whatever you want.'

Z blew out a breath.

She gave him the name.

'Dolores? A *woman*?'

'Yeah, a woman.'

Silence and what sounded like teeth grinding. Finally, Z blew out a breath.

'I'll call you back in ten. But, Ab, this is the last one. Then you come in.'

She hung up.

THIRTY-SIX

The Saab shot west, came down Seneca Street, then made a right on the park road. The trees were skeletal, black branches dripping with wet snow. Her tires sizzled on the wet tarmac as she sped through the winding road at 75 mph.

The address was in the County. Dolores Riordan, originally from Derry, female assassin of the IRA. Now she was married to a fireman, with three kids, two boys and a girl, all grammar-school age. She lived at 46 Spaulding, off South Park. Z had done well.

I'll have a target on my back as soon as I get out of the car, she told herself as she turned on Abbott Road into the County. *They'll think I was the experiment that failed, the monster from the East Side who came back to the County just to murder her father and his corrupt old cronies. The name Absalom Kearney will be spit out like poison for generations to come.*

She came up on Spaulding fast, skidded as she put the Saab into a right turn. The house was six down on the left. She eased down on the brake as she pulled up. Another cape, shingled front, painted a light blue. A black Dodge pickup truck with dried mud sprayed up on the side was parked in the driveway. The street was empty except for two lank-haired teenagers walking toward her, eight or nine houses away.

Abbie pulled out the Slammer and opened the driver's-side door. She got out slowly, eyes scanning the street. No curtains parting at the windows yet, no curious neighbors asking who the woman at Dolores's house was. That wouldn't last very long. She approached the house with the gun down by her side.

Suddenly the picture window shattered and exploded outward. A splinter of glass nicked Abbie's cheek and she whipped her head back and fell to the ground. Instinct drove her behind the Dodge truck; she crawled toward the rear wheel as two more shots sparked off the concrete driveway. When she got to the back tire, she reached up to her cheek. Her finger came away with a heavy drop of blood coating the skin.

Abbie crawled along the side of the Dodge, her left hand touching the truck's cold metal. A gun boomed and the rear tire inches from her foot blew out with a loud bang. The echo of the gun's report drummed in her ears.

The IRA trains them well, she thought. *That was close.*

Abbie ducked up and peeked through the Dodge's passenger window. There was a figure next to the blown-out window, the shape of a head tilted in from the frame.

'Dolores!' Abbie shouted. 'I just want to talk.'

Two fast shots and she felt the whisper of a bullet past her temple. The truck lurched sideways and pressed against her side. Dolores had shot out the front right tire with the second bullet.

'Put down your gun and just talk to me,' Abbie called out.

She felt along the ground beside her. There was a half-deflated football lying in the small strip of yard next to the chain link fence that separated the Riordans' property from their neighbors', but nothing else.

Dolores Riordan shouted out something, but Abbie couldn't understand a word. Thick, brambled words that rang a distant bell in Abbie's memory.

Gaelic, the damned woman was speaking Gaelic.

'I'm not IRA, Dolores,' Abbie called out, cupping her right hand around her mouth. 'Do you hear me? *I'm not IRA.*'

The next bullet whined above her head before exploding into a maple tree on the street with the sound of an axe slamming into a block of ice.

Abbie looked at the bricks bordering the concrete drive. She bent down and felt along the line. At the same time, she turned to eye the door, estimating distances.

The first two bricks were firm. The third one gave a little as she rocked it back and forth.

With a jerk of her shoulder, she brought the brick up. Abbie felt the rough edge of the brick and began to count. *One one thousand. Two one thousand. Three one thousand.* On four, she took a deep breath and hefted the brick toward the front door, gasping as it left her hand. The brick crashed into the screen door, and the sound of falling glass was swept away by the boom of a gun. But by then Abbie was sprinting toward the side door.

She threw her back to the shingled siding, the Slammer down by her side, and quickly jogged to the corner of the house, then turned the corner into the backyard. There was a patio back here, and she found the glass door that should lead into the kitchen from the back. It was unlocked. *Sloppy, Dolores. The killer would have slit your throat by now.* Quietly Abbie pulled the door and crept inside.

Abbie eased into the kitchen, the Slammer leveled in front of her.

A plate of sugar cookies was cooling on the kitchen counter. The fridge's motor kicked on as Abbie searched the shadows for Dolores. Quietly, she slipped across the linoleum floor and placed her back to the doorframe leading into the living area. She heard breathing and slowly brought her head around to see into the next room.

Hallway, a leather couch and loveseat, a green carpet that seemed too expensive for the house. And there was Dolores Riordan positioned beside the front door. She was a petite brunette woman dressed in a red-and-white-checked apron and dark jeans, her back arched as she held the gun in her left hand, aiming out through the blown-out picture window. As Abbie watched, Dolores leaned her head out to get a better look at the Dodge.

Beyond her, Abbie saw neighbors on the sidewalk in front of the house, uncertain of what was happening, their pale faces staring, mouths opening and closing.

Abbie brought the Slammer up and centered the sight on Dolores's pretty brown hair.

'Hold it right there.'

The woman froze.

She spoke. Gaelic again, the thick sounds coming from deep in her throat.

Abbie shook her head slowly as she kept her gun trained on Dolores Riordan's head.

'I told you, I'm not IRA. I'm Absalom Kearney from the Buffalo Police and I'm not going to hurt you. Put the gun down.'

The woman's head sank a couple of inches, as if Dolores were listening intently.

'I came to get a name from you. The name of the man who killed my father.'

Dolores Riordan breathed deeply.

'Don't do—'

Dolores swiveled her hip back and the gun barrel came up. Abbie flicked the tip of the Slammer left and fired.

Dolores Riordan hit the doorframe and went down. Abbie covered the distance to her in three steps and banged her gun on Dolores's wrist, knocking the pistol out of the assassin's hand. It went spinning away and Abbie crouched over Dolores's face, her eyes wild.

The bullet had caught Dolores in the shoulder. Blood welled up through her white blouse and began to peek through the checked fabric of the apron. The woman was breathing with a faint rasp. Abbie leaned down, the Slammer next to Dolores's left temple.

'Who is Fergus MacBrennan?'

Dolores Riordan gurgled something and shook her head sharply.

Abbie took Dolores's hair in her right hand and banged her head sharply on the floor.

'I'm guessing the IRA gave you all cover names when you worked for them. Operational names. One of them was a Fergus. What was his real name?'

She said nothing. The eyes were black, strangely depthless. Was she in shock, or just preparing herself to die?

'He killed my father, Dolores. Do you want to bleed to death or do you want to see your kids again?'

Suddenly Dolores coughed and red drops sprayed out from her lips, a few landing on her pale cheek. Her eyes went wide with fear.

'I must have nicked your lung. Sorry about that. But it's filling up with blood now, which means you're going to die faster than I thought. Come *on*, Dolores.'

The woman tried to say something.

'What was that?'

Dolores gasped for breath.

'We called him Houdini.'

Her voice was strangely light when she spoke English. Even musical.

'Why?' As she spoke, Abbie pressed her left hand on the woman's shoulder wound to slow the bleeding.

'Because . . . made people disappear. A magician. Loved to cut up the bodies. When we needed someone gone, an informer or such, we'd bring them to Fergus in his basement in Derry.'

Abbie heard voices now, yelling Dolores's name. Soon the neighbors with the guns would take the lead. Abbie reached over and pushed the front door shut with a terrific bang.

'What was his given name?'

'They didn't tell us.'

'But you know it,' said Abbie.

Dolores's mouth opened like a fish flopping on the shore, and she sucked in a whistling breath.

'Go fuck yourself, you dirty bitch.'

Abbie took the pressure off the wound. Blood gushed up through the apron fabric and Dolores's eyes went wide.

'I feel—'

'Don't get smart with me, Dolores. Fergus was from Derry. You're from Derry, or somewhere close. I hear it in your accent. Too many nights in the Gaelic Club for me to miss that.'

Eyes staring.

'You knew him growing up, didn't you? Before the IRA gave him a new name?'

The lips bloodless in a grimace. Then a nod.

'And you saw him once he came over? You even know his new identity here in America, don't you?'

'Dolores, are you okay?' A deep male voice from outside.

Abbie looked down.

'Last chance.'

'Dolores, is she in there with you?'

Dolores Riordan nodded.

'We thought,' she whispered.

'You thought what?'

'Thought he was cured.'

Two sharp blows on the front door, which shook in its hinges.

'He wasn't cured. He's killing again. *What's his American name?'*

Dolores Riordan's eyelids fluttered up and the black eyes were growing distant, looking straight through Abbie.

'O'Halloran,' she whispered. 'Dennis O'Halloran.'

THIRTY-SEVEN

The three-quarters moon was ruffled by dark gray clouds. The weather reports on the car radio warned of another squall.

Abbie made the call from her cell phone. She had to call information to get the number. Once the operator had it, Abbie told her to make the connection.

The phone rang three times.

'Gaelic Club.'

Fiddle music and the babble of voices behind it.

'I've seen that bitch everyone's looking for.' In her best County voice.

The sound of voices was closed off on the other end, like the speaker had cupped his hand over the phone.

'Who is this?'

'Can't tell you. I don't want to be part of a lynchin'.'

'Where is she?'

'Down by the lakeshore, past the Small Boat Harbor. At the foot of the grain silos.'

A pause.

'I'll tell him.'

She hit the red button and the call cut off.

Enormous slate-colored rocks littered the shore. Silvery flecks in the boulders gleamed in the moonlight. Abbie felt the sandy surface of one craggy rock as she leaned to take a look at the Skyway, the lake frozen and silent behind her. A city dump truck – yellow against the gray – passed along the elevated highway, as small as a child's toy, probably on its way out to pick up a load of salt to do the roads. A small red compact car was going the other way. Their headlights crossed like lances and then they were past.

The whole city was laid out in front of her, downtown to her left, the lights of the auditorium and the sandstone slabs and long chestnut-brown windows of the *Buffalo News* building. Tifft and the approach to the County was straight in front of her. To the right, the massed shapes of the old steel mills and their enormous slag heaps. Behind her, the frozen lake; a man walking across would be visible from half a mile. Only the looming presence of the old General Mills grain silo behind her blocked a perfect view of the ice, as it threw a hard-edged shadow over everything around her. But no one was going to walk over from Canada to kill her tonight.

I've had enough surprises, she thought. *Enough and more than enough.*

For a moment, she considered calling Z and laying out the whole case against O'Halloran, getting him to talk to Perelli, allowing the justice system to work. O'Halloran's past as a killer in Northern Ireland would work against him. He had probably been the one who had opened those windows in Billy Carney's house, trying to find out what Billy was going to tell her. Had he heard the call where Billy talked about the new information he needed to give her? It was the only way it made sense.

She remembered O'Halloran's face when she'd walked into Billy's house, the bulging eyes. It wasn't fury over Billy's fresh corpse, it was the thrill of the murder slowly ebbing away.

O'Halloran had access to the County machinery. He could have gone to the EC Med Center and gotten a vial of her blood – most cops she knew kept a supply on hand there in case they got into a firefight and needed a transfusion. He could have brought it to the little bramble patch where Marty Collins had been hung and dabbed a bit on the branches, or slipped a swab into the tech's samples from the scene. Not hard to do. He was working the night the monkey face had appeared on the Saab hood; he could have left the note in her wheel well and gone back upstairs. And he fit the description of the man who'd nearly drowned her under the ice the next morning.

As an Irish cop in good standing, he was hooked into the news-wire and the County machine. He had eyes everywhere through the neighborhood. A thousand little informants feeding tips to the killer himself. O'Halloran must have loved it, sitting fat and pretty at the center of the web, able to track her every move.

But why kill her father and the other Clan members who'd brought him to America? Her father had probably gotten him a job with the police department. They'd risked their careers to get him across safely. Maybe he just liked killing, and he wanted to extinguish his past so that he'd never go behind bars again. Wiping out the last people in Buffalo who knew his real identity.

Abbie blew out a breath into the blue-black night air. *O'Halloran wants to erase his past, and I want to find mine. How ironic. What I wouldn't give for a history like his – to know my roots back five generations, to have fought for the place I loved. And here he is snuffing out the little lights that trace him back to Ireland, the ungrateful bastard.*

To her left, a few small boats sat in the harbor, frozen in, the windows dark. Maybe the owners had forgotten to pay their fees and the marina's managers had left the hulls to snap and break in the ice, as examples to everyone. The place stank of dry seaweed.

She checked the Slammer and found the extra bullets Z had taped to the side, now loose in her coat pocket. She pulled them out and tucked them deep into her pants pocket. If she had to duck between the boulders, she didn't want them falling out.

The wind shifted and Abbie heard a tiny whine buzzing in the air. She looked up in the sky and scanned the horizon. Helicopter? It couldn't be. There was nothing up there except blackness and scudding clouds.

The wind shifted and the sound disappeared.

Abbie raised her head over the edge of the boulder and checked the Skyway again. Three sets of headlights were heading south from the city. She watched the first one pass the Tifft exit, two hundred yards away, then the second.

The third slowed and came down the ramp, hesitated, then nosed into the harbor entrance. Abbie watched it, eyes even with the rock edge. It looked like a Department car. The headlights lit up the rutted snow in the road, then gray boulders, and finally the steel bar across the entrance. Abbie had parked along the service road half a mile away, then walked back in until the silos were behind her.

The car stopped and the lights cut out.

Abbie heard the tinny sound again. It sounded like a small motorcycle. She scanned Tifft and the service road running perpendicular to it, but nothing was moving.

As the car rolled up to the barrier, she trained her gun on the dark outline of the driver.

A click. The car door opened and a figure emerged and stood behind the door, looking toward the lake. The door slammed and the figure came walking toward the guard's booth thirty yards away. It stepped around the barrier and was twenty yards away. Fifteen. Still too dark to see the face.

Abbie stood and pointed the gun at the figure's chest.

'Stop right there,' she shouted.

The figure stopped, its hands in its pockets.

'Hands *up.*'

The figure hesitated.

'Ab?'

Something stabbed at Abbie's heart.

'Z, is that you?'

The sound of footsteps on gravel as he came forward.

'Yeah, it's me.'

Abbie pointed the gun at Z's head, outlined against the sky.

'*Stop.* What are you doing here, Z?'

'I got a call from O'Halloran. Said you'd been spotted out here. Looked like you might be suicidal, going to jump down the silo.'

The sound of the motor again, getting louder and then disappearing, whipped away by the wind.

Abbie stood absolutely still, listening. Then her eyes snapped back to Z.

'Z, do not move,' she said, raising the gun.

Abbie could see his face now, gray-black in the gloom.

'Are you pointing your fucking gun at me?'

'I don't know what's going on, Z. O'Halloran is the killer. I'm bringing him here.'

'O'Halloran?'

'Yes.'

Z came closer.

'How could he—'

'Do . . . not . . . move,' Abbie said. She stood her full height and stepped slowly around the boulder, the gun level with her shoulder.

Z's voice was louder. 'I put up my house for you, where my *kids* live, and you have the fucking audacity . . .'

'Just let me get this figured out.'

'You think I'm selling you out, Ab?'

'Z, don't come any closer.'

'I came here—'

An enormous BOOM erupted from over her right shoulder. Z grunted and went down.

Abbie whipped her gun hand around and caught a flash from the foot of the silos. The top of the boulder exploded behind her and she felt shards cut into the back of her neck.

She threw herself to the ground.

Goddamn it, that wasn't a motorcycle engine. It was a snowmobile. He came across the ice and got behind you. Now he has you framed against the lights of the Skyway.

Abbie reversed on the gravel and began to crawl toward Z. She could hear him moaning ten feet away.

'I got him in the chest.' She recognized O'Halloran's voice, excited now. 'Leave him there. I'll finish him off after I do you.'

Abbie pointed her gun and blasted off three shots toward the voice, then pulled herself through the freezing gravel. She heard Z's ragged breathing. She reached out and felt the shoulders of his thick wool coat in her hand. He was gasping now with panic.

BOOM. The whine of a bullet snipped the air over her right ear.

'Hold on, Z,' she whispered. 'Hold on.'

O'Halloran's voice rang out. 'Crafty bitch,' he said. He was closer now. Abbie looked wildly over her shoulder. All she could see was the gleam of the rock edges. Then a shadow. She blasted off another shot and with a grunt pulled at Z's wool coat, dragging him toward the car bumper. She felt the seams begin to rip.

Damn it, Z, why couldn't you have lost some weight? We're both going to die out here.

A figure rose behind a rock. Abbie threw herself right, rolled, hearing the gravel explode where she'd just been.

The figure disappeared. Abbie ran to Z, grabbed him, gave a desperate heave and, gasping for breath, dragged him the last few feet behind the car.

She saw Z's lips moving, but no sound came out. She bent down to his ear and whispered.

'Z, I'm sorry.'

'Junior,' he whispered. His son.

Abbie nodded. 'I'm going to get you home to him. Hold on.'

She fumbled in her pocket for her phone.

A gun blast, and a *thunk* into the side of the car, which rocked slightly on its wheels.

'By the way, Billy Carney asked about you.' The voice was closer now. He was moving right, to come around Z's car from the driver's side and finish her off.

Hurry, Absalom, hurry.

'He begged me not to hurt you.'

If she called 911, O'Halloran would find and kill her. If she didn't, Z would bleed out. She felt Z's pulse. Weak and fading. Her heart surged with fear for him. Z's face looked bloodless in the moonlight.

'I sliced his eyeball in half just for asking.'

The crunch of a footstep.

She punched 911 on the keypad and hit the speaker button, thumbing the volume all the way up.

Then she ducked down and crawled to the car's front bumper and lay the phone behind the front wheel. She pushed the green button and scurried back.

In the breathless pause, she silently pushed three bullets into the Slammer's rotating chamber.

Ringing. Abbie peeked above the hood, peering at the gray-black rocks.

'Nine-one-one, what is your—'

A shape in the blackness. She squeezed off three fast shots and heard a shout of pain.

'Was that shots fired?' the 911 operator's voice rose with concern.

Abbie ran forward and scooped up the phone.

'I have an officer down at the foot of the old General Mills silo,' she said crisply into the phone. 'I need an ambulance to the Tifft Street exit. Officer Zangara is bleeding out. Get them moving *now*.'

The operator blurted out the beginning of a question, but Abbie thumbed the red button. She ran back to Z and crouched over him, whipping her jacket off her shoulders and placing it over Z's chest. She pressed down hard on the wound.

'Ambulance on the way.'

The pain on Z's face was terrible to see.

'Get him?'

'Think so. Hold on.'

A rattling sound came from behind a boulder striped with white. Abbie approached, the Slammer leveled at the edge. Her steps were careful as she crept up on the boulder. When she was two feet away, she eased the gun up and angled it over the top.

O'Halloran lay with his gun resting on his blue boiler suit. Blood was pumping up from under his palm as his eyes stared madly. Abbie reached over, pulled his service revolver out of his right hand, and tossed it behind her.

'Can you hear me?'

O'Halloran's eyes grew wide and shifted to her face.

'How did you know about the monkeys?'

The corner of his lip jerked down spastically.

'Hel . . . helped bring you home, you cunt. Don't you remember Un . . . Un . . . Uncle Dennis?' A laugh escaped his lips. 'Doesn't matter, you're fucked now.'

'Why, O'Halloran? Tell me why you killed them.'

Something in his eyes flared, and a confused look came over his face. He mumbled something.

'What was that?'

Abbie shook his shoulder and his eyelids flicked in pain. They fluttered once and began to close.

She reached over and whipped her hand across his face.

'You will NOT die before you answer my question. Why did you kill my father?'

The eyes wandered and then came back to Abbie's face.

'Do you hear me? O'Halloran?'

A long sigh escaped his lips. His eyes closed, and the right eyelid twitched.

A siren came cutting across the wind. Abbie looked up and saw an ambulance headed straight up Tifft toward her.

The ambulance swerved through traffic as the EMT radio blared from the front. Behind them, Abbie saw the red lights of the second emergency vehicle, carrying O'Halloran. He had died without saying another word.

Z lay on a white cot spotted with blood. A female EMT was finishing up taping the IV to his arm, but his skin still looked corpselike in the harsh interior light of the ambulance.

The EMT looked at the heart monitor, holding the inside of Z's wrist. She barked a few numbers to the driver, who relayed them on the radio. The ambulance rocketed over a pothole and Abbie reached for the ceiling to steady herself.

The EMT watched the monitor, then nodded to Abbie, turned, snapped open a drawer, took out a syringe in its packaging and began to strip it open.

'Better talk now before I get this in him,' she said.

Abbie slipped closer to Z, kneeling on the rubber floor.

'You okay?'

He nodded. Abbie laid her hand across his forehead. He was colder than he should have been.

'Two minutes to a fat disability check,' she said.

He smiled, then muttered something. Abbie bent down to hear.

'Thought you shot me, you dumb bitch,' he said.

Abbie smiled. 'If I shot you, you'd be dead, dummy.'

His eyes remained on hers, crinkled with pain. Abbie bent closer to him.

'I know, Z, I know. I'm sorry I didn't trust you. It was like everyone was out to get me. You know how it is.'

He nodded. Then he turned his head and whispered something to her.

'What?'

She put her ear down closer.

'We are the County.'

THIRTY-EIGHT

Abbie lay on her couch staring at the ceiling while the voice of Boy George filled her living room, 'The Crying Game.' A song from 1990-something, but it sounded very eighties with its sweeping synthesizers. And, of course, Boy George's hauntingly sad voice. 'And then before / you know where you are / you're saying goodbye.' A last moan from him and the song ended.

Abbie blinked twice, then hit Replay on the remote. The CD player clicked softly and the song began again.

The tenth time in a row? The twelfth? She felt like she was inside the song's rich melancholy and she didn't want to leave.

Wouldn't it amuse them if you went and lost your mind? she thought. *Wouldn't it just be the talk of Abbott Road? Absalom Kearney, hero cop, found jabbering away on Elmwood Avenue, listening obsessively to washed-up eighties sensations until she died of dehydration. They'd laugh about it at the Gaelic Club, and they'd say that the bitch had been crazy all along, and hadn't Dennis O'Halloran, God rest his soul, been right to try and finish her off?*

It had been eight days since that night on the shore, beneath the grain silo. Eight days in which she'd been cleared of murder, gotten her badge back, along with a commendation. Days in which she'd ducked the photographers of the *Buffalo News* and spent most of her time holed up in her apartment. Z's wife Linda had dropped off two enormous pans of lasagna, and her neighbors had knocked at her door several times, softly calling out her name. Detective Mills from Niagara Falls had left two messages, joking about the casino buffet and the date she'd promised him, but his voice sounded, well, concerned.

282

She didn't want to talk to anyone. She didn't know what to say. Or to feel.

The music washed over her again and she listened the whole way through, then clicked the remote control. She was getting hungry; nothing but outright starvation, however, would get her off the couch right now.

Something was jabbing at the back of the mind, a thought wanting to be heard, as though far away someone was yelling at the top of their voice but not loudly enough to make the words clear.

It's over, she said to the voice. *Leave me alone to fall apart in peace.*

Finally, after two more replays of 'The Crying Game,' she sighed and went to the kitchen to make tea. She got out the Red Rose tea bags and then opened the dish cabinet, managing to avoid looking at her father's teacup, which had been moved to the back corner. She took down a green enamel mug and placed a tea bag into it as the kettle began to whistle.

Was it something Mills had said? Something in the blur of the last day that had stuck in her mind. What had he said? It was about that Outlaws case he was working. It was looking more and more like an inside job, a deadly political duel within the Outlaws themselves.

She hoped he solved the case, but it meant nothing to her.

But that wasn't it. Not quite.

The tea kettle let out a shrill whistle and then clicked off, the sound of the water bubbling seeming to fill up her small kitchen. Abbie detached the large cylinder from its base and poured the steaming water into her mug. The water slowly turned a rich, swirling brown. She took out the tea bag, stirred in sugar and cold milk, and slowly walked to the table to sit.

The cage in the bottom of the gang's hangout. That was it. It had lodged in her thoughts like a branch in a flooded river. But after the flood had rushed away, it lay there still, bare and unconnected to anything else. So the Outlaws were barbarians. What about it? Everyone knew that. And they'd kept a prisoner in their basement. Their women were half slaves anyway, traded and exchanged like baseball cards. There was nothing new here. Horror was everywhere.

O'Halloran was brought across the Peace Bridge the same year she'd been adopted.

She'd found out about the monkeys. O'Halloran had remembered the toy she carried when he'd picked her up at the City Mission with her father. John Kearney had probably scooped the picture up at the City Mission along with her things, and O'Halloran must have looked at it, his fat thumb running across the photograph, noticing the little toy. To implicate her, he'd bought a new set of monkeys and worked on them a bit, made them look old and worse for wear, then he'd dropped one at each scene. It was impressive, in a way. They'd even found a brand-new, unscuffed stash of the toys in O'Halloran's glove compartment.

Her questions had been answered. O'Halloran was the killer; he'd murdered Billy to stop him from telling her what he knew; it had been O'Halloran out on the ice in the red ski mask. She'd been to see Z twice in the hospital and he was getting released in two days; she was planning on visiting Billy's grave whenever she could get out the front door; and she'd been reinstated at Buffalo PD.

The world had repaired itself as much as possible. So why was her mind so unsettled? As much as she felt her father's absence as a cold hole blowing through her chest, it was more than that sorrow. Something else was needling her.

O'Halloran had substituted one thing for another. New toy monkeys for old ones.

She closed her eyes. Boy George was singing, 'One day soon / I'm gonna tell the moon / about the crying game.' She had to get the *Best of Culture Club* CD. She wanted to hear more of that voice . . .

The thought was back. She saw a face, or half of one, a face lit by lightning. She closed her eyes and slowly rubbed her temples with both index fingers.

No, Absalom. Let it go.

She couldn't.

Abbie picked up her cell phone and dialed Mills's number. She'd heard the warmth in his messages, and she'd liked it. But she hadn't yet called him back.

'It's Kearney,' she said when he answered.

'Hey,' he said dully. Then his voice perked up. 'Oh, *hey*. Kearney, how the hell are you? Everything okay? I mean . . .'

'I'm not really sure. Zangara is getting better.'

'What about you?'

'I'm . . . I don't know. It's going to take time.'

'I know. I'm not going to say "If there's anything I can do," because you already know that.'

'Yes, I do. Thank you.'

Pause. 'So you're obviously calling me up to make that date . . .'

She smiled.

'The buffet is on tonight,' he continued. 'And we get five dollars in chips if we go before ten. Is that an irresistible deal or what?'

Say yes, she thought. *Put on that green dress you like and go up and meet the man and forget about all of the things you've seen. Let it go.*

'You're on. But I need a favor first.'

'Shoot.'

'Can you check if you have an unsolved murder from 1982, probably late April, early May.'

Mills sighed. 'Jesus Christ, Kearney. Do you ever take a day off?'

'Apparently not.'

'We have all the open cases collated in a file. It's on my laptop. Hold on.'

He put down the phone.

Say no, she thought. *Say that 1982 was a perfect year for closed cases at the Niagara Falls PD. Say you'll meet me at the casino doors and we'll dance to the corny music.*

'You there?'

'Yes,' she said faintly.

'Joseph Padarski, thirty-two.'

Silence.

Then she said, 'Tell me he wasn't a biker.'

'Um, yeah, he was. Why?'

Abbie closed her eyes. 'An Outlaw, right?'

'Yep. I'm looking at his picture. Nasty dude. Wanna guess his weight?'

'Last question. The basement of the Outlaws house. Was it heated?'

Mills's voice sounded dead. 'They don't heat any basements up here, Kearney. Too damn expensive.'

Silence.

'Kearney? What is this all about?'

THIRTY-NINE

As she drove to the East Side, the snow came down in sheets. A nasty night, a night to stay in and read a good book. The only stores open were the liquor stores, which never closed, and a few corner delicatessens selling the last of their bread and milk before the storm covered the city.

She parked the Saab in front of the Reverend's building and got out.

That little girl, Rashida, was sitting on the stoop in her braids and an oversize jacket.

'Hi, Detective Kearney.'

'Hi, Rashida. Is the Reverend around?'

'Yeah. I saw him inside with that smelly man from down the block.'

'Thanks.'

She entered the hallway, lit by a single bulb hanging from a dark wire. She rang the Reverend's bell. The sound of voices from inside. Men's voices. The door opened and the Reverend looked at her in surprise.

'Absalom! You're back already?'

'Can I talk to you?'

She stood there, willing herself to leave before it was too late.

'Let me finish up here. I'm about to get this young man into a city program, just what he needs. Will you stay out here while I say a prayer with him?'

She nodded.

He looked at her closely, then pursed his lips and shut the door.

Three minutes later, a young man with a shaved head, dressed in an army fatigue jacket and jeans, his eyes wide with excitement, came out, nodded once to himself, and shut the door with a bang.

'Evenin',' he said.

'Good luck,' she said.

'Don't need luck,' he said. 'I've got the Lord with me now.'

The door opened again. Abbie slipped by the Reverend.

'Glad you came by.' The Reverend swept around her, head down, lost in his thoughts, and sat in his desk chair. 'I wanted to ask you about giving a talk to some fifth-graders over at Jefferson Elementary. I'm running out of role models to bring 'em over there, and if I brought the famous Absalom Kearney, they'd be floating on air.'

She looked at him.

'I need to talk to you about something, Reverend.'

His eyes were liquid in the low light of the desk lamp. His bald pate caught some of the amber glow from behind.

'Sure. Sit, sit.'

She sat on the hard wooden chair and looked at him. She felt she barely had the energy to move her lips.

'How did my father have your number?'

He seemed to be frozen in mid-gesture, looking at her, frown lines deep on his forehead.

'What now?' he said, his body very still. 'How'd your father—'

'He called you up and told me to meet him at Tifft. You passed on the message. How did he have your number?'

The Reverend shook his head. 'He must have looked me up. I'm in—'

'I checked his cell phone records; the bill arrived yesterday. He didn't. He dialed your number directly.'

'Maybe he had it written—'

He realized the mistake then, and he smiled.

'He had it because you knew each other. Your phone number hasn't changed in thirty years, I'll bet.'

'The Lord kept me where I was needed.'

'Your phone number hasn't changed, has it?'

'No, Absalom, it hasn't.'

'Who did he trade O'Halloran for?'

His gaze left her eyes and fell to the armchair. He seemed to be on the verge of speaking, and then he stopped and looked at her.

'Absalom, what are you talking—'

She shook her head. *I will not cry,* she told herself.

'No,' she said. 'You tell me now. A biker was killed in Niagara Falls in 1982, the same year I was adopted by my father. The same year that O'Halloran was brought across the border. I think O'Halloran killed that biker, and the Clan traded someone to get him back. Who did my father trade O'Halloran for?'

The Reverend's eyes were deep, flickering with the amber light.

'Why, you.'

Abbie shook her head again.

'Who did he give the Outlaws? Who did *you* give?'

The Reverend exhaled loudly. He began to knit one hand into the other, the powerful hands kneading the flesh over and over.

'You could never understand, Absalom, as bad as you want to. You'll never understand it.'

'The name, Reverend.'

He dropped his hands, rubbing the lines of his forehead, before looking up at her. She had never seem him so depleted, so old looking.

'His name was Michael.'

'Michael who?'

'Michael Minton. Your brother.'

Her eyes closed and she rocked forward once in the chair. She felt if she didn't move, she would explode.

'Michael. Like the archangel Michael. My mother opened the Bible for that name, too, like she did for mine?'

He nodded. 'I didn't know her then. But she came to me for help with Michael, when he was starting down his path.'

'My brother. My only brother.' Her voice was shaking.

He studied his hands.

'By the time you were born, you wouldn't have wanted to know Michael. He was twelve years older than you and headed to hell by the fast road—'

'He was only fourteen years old when you sent him away? *Fourteen?*' Her hand was pressed to her mouth.

289

She stared at the Reverend, waiting for his objection, but instead he looked pleadingly at her.

'Do you know how beautiful a child you were, Absalom? How *bright*, even at two years old? I told your mother I'd never met a child with such intelligence in her eyes. Never in my life.'

'What happened to my brother?'

'You had more promise at two years old than most of those City Mission kids have at twenty-five. I said so then and I was right. I wanted one child to have a chance. Can you understand that?'

He stood up and turned his back to her, staring at the books on the shelf as he spoke. It was as if he were searching for one that would explain everything.

'When Michael was about fourteen, things started happening in the neighborhood. First we started finding cats left in alleyways. Without their heads. I recall about four of them.'

He turned to look at her.

'They'd been tortured. Their fur burned off by a cigarette lighter while they were alive.'

Abbie's eyes narrowed. 'And you traced them to Michael?'

'The cats turned up dead near where he stayed.'

'That's it? No one ever saw him abusing the cats?'

'No, Absalom. But there was more. The fires.'

'What fires?'

'We had an arsonist loose around here in '81, '82. Abandoned buildings mostly, plenty of them to use as kindling wood. But some occupied ones, too. The person would put some old newspapers and cardboard boxes and some lighter fluid in the basement and light 'em up. Two of the places where Michael had been staying were burnt out.'

'You have no proof he did it. And, yes, fire-starting and torture of small animals are two early traits shared by serial killers. You knew that, didn't you?'

'I learned that.'

'But they could also be the signs of abuse. Disturbed children do the same things. He wasn't a serial killer at fourteen, Reverend.'

'Maybe not. But then there were the robberies.'

'What robberies?'

'Bad ones, push-in robberies, you know. His victims were terrified, Absalom.'

He turned.

'They said the young man had this look in his eyes.'

'A look in his eyes. Because he wore a ski mask, didn't he?'

'How did you know that?'

Abbie said nothing, only closed her eyes.

'They told me about how he was almost disappointed to find their little stashes of money,' the Reverend continued, 'or a bit of jewelry. Something told them that he'd come there to kill, to hurt them, and robbing was just an excuse. And his voice sounded like your brother's.'

Abbie shot out of her chair. 'This neighborhood has more ex-cons that you can throw a stick at, arsonists, robbers. Half the men on this block probably have a record. But you pinned it all on Michael.'

'I had to protect my community.'

'And what if it *was* him? He was desperate for money, his mother was a heroin addict. He was lonely and neglected. These are the signs of a boy crying out for help, not a psychotic killer.'

'When he left, the robberies stopped. They *stopped*, Absalom.'

'Even if he did everything you say, it wasn't too late to save him. Only a tiny percentage of kids with those traits go on to kill, Reverend. It wasn't too late.'

The Reverend turned away, back to his books.

'But you sold him to the Outlaws in exchange for some IRA assassin.'

The Reverend said nothing.

'Why did they Outlaws want a teenager? What were they going to do with him?'

'I don't know that.'

'You *tell* me, Reverend. Why—'

'I do *not* know that. Your father told me there needed to be an exchange. If I gave him someone for the Outlaws, he would take you and give you a good home. The best schools. You ended up at Harvard,

Absalom. Do you know what that meant to the people at the City Mission? One of their own at Harvard?'

Abbie stared ahead. Her face felt as if it had been jabbed with a powerful anesthetic. The only thing she felt were tears welling in her eyes.

'And so my father adopted me?'

'That's right. To save you.'

'To save me?!' she shouted. 'Don't . . . you . . . dare.'

'Your mother was dying. *I* couldn't take you in. No one could, no one that I trusted to see to your upbringing. I went to the foster homes that would take you in, Absalom. They were . . .' He covered his face with his hands. 'They were *not right* for you!'

'You knew all along, didn't you?' Abbie said.

'Knew what, my child?'

'You knew it was my brother killing all those men from the County. He was hunting them down. And you told no one.'

The Reverend nodded.

'Why?'

'I'd done enough to him.'

'And maybe, just maybe, you thought they deserved to die?'

He looked at her, his eyes colder.

'Four white men die and the city is turned upside down. We've had that many casualties here every six *months* for as long as I've been here.'

'It's no excuse,' Abbie whispered.

He turned and slapped his palm against the desk.

'Did you come here to judge me, Absalom? I got you out so that you could make something of yourself.'

She looked up at him. 'The police in Niagara Falls found a dungeon in the Outlaws' basement, weeks before the killings started.'

The Reverend turned quickly toward her.

'*What?* What dungeon?'

'The dungeon you sent him to, Reverend.'

'The robberies stopped, Abbie.'

'You sold him off and you sold me off.'

The Reverend shook his head slowly.

The room seemed to lift and swirl about her. She knew now. She closed her eyes and buried her face in her hands.

'Where is he?'

'Where is wh—'

'*Michael.*'

'I don't know.'

'Don't lie to me. Not anymore.'

'I haven't seen him in almost thirty years. In fact, I think I may be next on his list. But I won't run. I will never run.'

'Back in the day, at the time of the fires, where did he live?'

The Reverend shook his head. 'In an abandoned SRO hotel on Main. Sometimes he'd sleep rough there when your mother kicked him out. He was lost to us. You must understand that.'

'Where on Main?'

'Corner of Hertel.'

She turned to leave.

'Absalom.'

She wouldn't turn.

'Absalom, he'll kill you before he goes to prison.'

FORTY

Main Street was dead quiet as she walked past office buildings and the old apartment towers, wooden boards in the windows and For Sale signs ripped and fluttering gently in the wind. Downtown Buffalo was practically deserted, a few office workers who'd stayed late walking with their chins jammed into their jackets. A club on her right opened its doors and a drunken frat boy wearing nothing but a UB T-shirt and jeans, feet bare, was flung out by a bouncer, who checked that the man was breathing, face-down on the sidewalk, before turning and strolling back to the doorway.

The trolley bell sounded from blocks away. Above her, the street-lamps buzzed as she walked, hands in pockets. She felt as if she'd stepped back into another decade. She headed west until she saw the street sign for Hertel Avenue.

The building was dark, no lights visible in its six or seven stories, the top of it indistinguishable from the night sky. The cotton-swab-shaped streetlight in front of it had been vandalized, the plastic shell with a jagged hole at its center. She smelled urine and, for some reason, mildewed bread.

Abbie pushed hard on the front door, made of heavy steel. It relented with a rusty groan before jamming against something inside. There was just enough room for Abbie to squeeze by. Once inside, she clicked on her flashlight. The beam danced over the floor of the building. Plastic detergent jugs, old diaper boxes, so old the lettering and color had been leached away. Snow was falling inside the building, small columns of it circling down from holes in the roof. The quiet was deep. It seemed like she was disturbing a place that hadn't been entered for years.

Her flashlight swept over boxes of rotting cardboard. An orange plastic corsage with fake baby's breath, still in its box. A black patent leather shoe. She wondered if the front of the building had held a wedding store or a tuxedo rental place.

Something shifted above her. Abbie froze.

'Michael?'

A movement, shuffling. A rat? Could rats climb inside the walls to the other stories? She'd heard stories of rats swimming across the river to get to Buffalo when Niagara Falls had become too deserted to support them. If they could do that, they could climb beams.

She swept the walls and saw wigs, naked mannequins, and an old poster on the wall. 'Make Your Special Day Extra-Special,' it read, above a picture of a bride in a seventies-style wedding dress and tiara. 'Rothman's Bridal' was printed at the bottom of the sign in capital letters.

Twenty feet ahead, something rustled beneath the garbage. The beam of her flashlight played over the mounds of cardboard and junk. The crest of one mound shifted.

'Michael, is that you?' she called.

Laughter from the far recesses.

'Michael, is that you?' someone called back, the voice high and mocking.

Her Glock made a snicking sound as it came out of the leather holster. She straightened her arms out behind the gun and flashlight, held together, and walked slowly toward the voice, glancing now and again at her footing in the piles of trash. Behind the studs of a now-vanished wall, she saw a pile of clothes heaped in a corner. Watching where she placed her feet, she moved closer. Her gun came up.

She called his name again. A rag was brushed aside and suddenly there was a human face atop the mound of clothes. White, gaunt, a woman. The eyes were yellow-green beneath a swath of greasy gray hair and they regarded her calmly.

'Where's Michael?' Abbie said.

The woman only smiled brightly.

'Can you hear me? I'm looking for a man in his early forties. Have you seen anyone like that here?'

But the woman only stared at Abbie. Then she reached a hand deep into the coats that topped the pile and, a second later, produced a half-eaten chicken leg. She took a bite, her yellow-brown teeth feeling for the meat. Then she began to chew slowly. Her eyes fogged over.

Doesn't even know I'm here, thought Abbie.

Something thumped to the ground behind her. Abbie swiveled, her heart beating fast.

It was a paper bag, wrapped with a yellow string. Tied to one end of the string, now swinging lazily from the impact, slowly losing velocity, was something small that glinted in the gleam of her flashlight.

She turned and began walking toward the bag. As she got closer, she saw that the thing on the end of the string was a toy monkey.

Abbie stared at it, then pulled back her jacket flap and holstered the Glock.

She looked up.

'Michael, come talk to me.'

Nothing, just snow drifting down and moonlight on black struts. She walked to the bag, nearly tripping on a rusty pipe jutting up from the garbage. *If I fall,* she thought, *I'll sink into the mess and never get out.*

She spread her hands out away from her body and picked her way carefully toward the bag. The monkey had stopped swinging. She reached down, pulled the string, and the top of the bag eased open. She looked inside.

She took out a bib. A green pelican on a white background. She didn't remember it. She brought it to her nose. It smelled faintly of pears.

She heard footsteps, the rusting stairs groaning out a rising note as the person stepped off them. She didn't look up. It was him. He was coming to her.

The flashlight lit up the inside of the bag. Next was a photo of a young woman in a cheap black frame, the picture slightly out of focus, as snapshots from the seventies always seemed to be. Abbie lifted it out. Her mother was dressed in a paisley dress, her hair up, wearing some Aztec-looking earrings with cheap green stones. *You looked happy,*

Mom, Abbie thought. *Were you a little bit high or just glad to be with someone who wanted a picture of you? Was the man behind the camera my dad?*

Abbie tried to pick out the features that resembled her own, searched for her face in the blurry snapshot. Then she carefully returned the framed picture to the bag.

Inside was one last item: a paper. The last page of her father's confession.

Michael had killed her father, not O'Halloran. O'Halloran had only done Billy Carney, afraid he'd found out the truth about his IRA past. The rest of the killing had been done by her brother: Gerald Decatur, lured to the same room at the Lucky Clover motel where the swap for Michael had been made decades ago. And Jimmy Ryan and Marty Collins and Joe Kane and her father. After Michael had turned on the Outlaws and settled his score with them, he'd come home to avenge himself on the Clan.

She sensed the figure twenty feet away, then saw his right shoulder outlined in a window fronting on Main Street.

The figure made a sound. Abbie shivered, then looked up, playing the words over in her mind until she could make sense of them.

'I have a place,' it had said.

She looked up. It was the man from the videotape at the Lucky Clover, dressed in a green-and-black-checked jacket, dark jeans, and the black ski mask, the dark eyes pinning her to the ground. He was very still.

You're the reason I came back to Buffalo, she thought. *Somehow I must have known about you, though it seems impossible.*

'They cut out half your tongue, didn't they, Michael? The Outlaws? So that you couldn't tell anyone who you were?'

She didn't want to put her flashlight on him. She was afraid of what she'd see.

His eyes were just visible through the round holes. But she couldn't read the expression.

'Michael, I'm your sister. Do you . . . remember me?'

The head was still. Traffic noises.

Then a small nod, up and down.

She felt a rush of warmth in her chest. *Don't cry, Absalom. He wants you to be strong, to be the answer he's been searching for.*

'I've waited so long, Michael. I didn't even know you existed. You know that, right? Please tell me you knew that.'

'Youf horgot me.'

How many hours did he practice to be able to speak this well, down in the hole? How many years learning to talk again?

Abbie shook her head back and forth.

'I didn't forget you, no, not that. I never remembered you. That's different. I was too young. Please believe me.'

She saw his fist compress, the knuckles growing pale. He said nothing, but his shoulders slumped.

The figure slowly shook its head. In its right hand she saw a knife, its blade dull in the weak light.

He was too damaged to go into the world. He would kill again. But she could find him a place where he wouldn't suffer as he had suffered in that pit . . .

'I can't let you go, you know that.'

'Yeth, you can. We can go 'gether. I have a place.'

A place? Was their reunion part of his plan?

'Michael, why did you kill those men?'

'WHY?' It was a scream of rage and disbelief. She saw the cords in his neck stiffen and the knife turned in his hand. *'For uth. For what they did.'*

So he'd killed to bring them back together. This was the ending he'd wanted; the two of them together again. He thought he could be normal.

'Michael? Michael, please listen carefully to me. I can't let you go.'

His body stiffened and she thought she heard a breath escape his lips.

'But you won't go to prison, you'll go to a hospital. And I'll visit you every day, I promise you that.'

She stepped toward him, carefully placing her feet in the uneven trash so as not to fall and startle him.

'Michael, can you take off your mask? I want to see you.'

Do you look like me?

The blade turned in the dim light.

'Let me see your face,' she said. 'Please? I'm your sister.' It was all she could think to say.

He reached up and violently pulled off the hat in one motion, as an angry child would. His hair sprang up unevenly, matted down on the right, uncut now for months.

Michael Minton had a long face, a thin nose like her own, and darting, wide-set eyes beneath a wrinkled forehead. He looked, she thought, like some kind of backwoodsmen from frontier days, and younger than his forty-three years. Abbie stared at a face in which pieces of her own were present but distorted in a squint of fear and hatred. Michael's mouth was working, the lips pressed together.

It was like someone who was angry had smashed her face and put it together again – maliciously.

The Outlaws had branded the number '1' above his left eye, the pink flesh as wide as a finger and uneven. One for one percenters, it meant in biker language, the one percenters who rejected authority. But what it really meant was that Michael was their property. The ridged tissue looked painful even now.

Even if she wanted to let him go, where would he run to with that mark on his face?

Her eyes shifted and met his, childlike and defiant. He looked away and down.

'Michael, will you come with me?'

He shook his head.

'I'll protect you. Nobody will *ever* hurt you like that again. Believe me, Michael, please.'

Michael's eyes met hers and terror flashed through her. *What is he seeing in my face? What he would have looked like if I'd been the one taken, and not him?*

He will kill me, she thought. *I've destroyed his dream and he knows it now.*

Michael mumbled something.

'What was that?'

'Came back furroo—'

I came back for you.

'Michael, listen to me. I know you came back for me. And I'm so thankful you did. We're going to be together now, just like it should have been. You're not going back in the hole.'

She shouldn't have mentioned it. He stepped backward.

And then a dark space seemed to open under her feet, like it had on the lake. In that instant, she knew what he would do.

Snowflakes cut across the beam of light as she saw him staring at her, the eyes wide and fearful. Suddenly the knife flashed at his waist and appeared to rotate at her through the blackness, coming at her face, the thick blade blinking light and dark as it turned. She cried out, falling backward, desperately ducking away. The flashlight in her hand bounced off the ground and snapped off.

She heard him gasp.

'Michael!'

Everything was black except the stars in the missing roof. Abbie got to her knees, scrabbling in the rubble for the flashlight. *The bulb is burst,* she thought to herself, *it's no use.* She turned and, in the dim moonlight, saw Michael splayed backward on a pile of rubble, his eyes open wide, and blood seeping down under the collar of his jacket.

'Oh, no, please no.' Abbie scrambled up and moved toward her brother, nearly losing her balance on a rotten beam of wood. She clambered past it and touched his leg gently, then moved up toward his face.

He had cut his own throat. *Deep, oh, too deep,* she thought as she looked once and then snapped her gaze away, toward his eyes. Abbie reached for his left hand, the one without the knife, and clasped it in her own.

'Michael, can you hear me?'

His eyes were wide, unseeing, and his head shook slowly back and forth slightly. His lips opened and closed but nothing came out.

She leaned over, aligning her eyes with his, so that he would see her. A wedge of hair that had come loose from the rubber band holding her ponytail brushed against his right cheek. 'I'm here,' Abbie whispered, then said it again.

His calloused hand closed on hers, powerfully, and she winced, but his gaze was focused on something above her left shoulder.

'Don't go,' she said. 'Not yet, do you hear me?'

A sudden whistle of air came through his lips, and then a spasm seemed to start at his knees and move up his body, rattling the boards underneath him. Abbie gripped his hand harder and pulled it quickly to her chest, whispering his name twice. He blinked, and then his eyes locked on hers and she smiled warmly, mouthing his name one more time. Michael gasped, as if he'd been holding his breath on a long dive, and then his hand relaxed in hers.

Once his breathing stopped, all Abbie could hear was the traffic from the side streets off Main.

She slowly traced the scar on his forehead and the tears came fast.

FORTY-ONE

The spray from the Falls felt cold on Abbie's skin. She and Mills walked along the rim of the crater, talking over the sound of the pounding water and nodding to the passing tourists. A busload of Amish had apparently pulled in. They smiled in their homemade denim clothes.

It was true. Canada was so friendly. She watched the water tumble over the Falls and felt the earth under her feet vibrate ever so slightly.

'Now, what does this date include?' Abbie said, nodding to an Amish man with a beard.

'I told you,' Mills said, guiding her away from the railing. 'It's called the Total Canuck. A leisurely walk along the promenade here, a trip on the *Maid of the Mist,* dinner at the Skylon Tower – the food sucks, but the view? Knock the eyes out of your head.'

Abbie smiled.

'A carriage ride and then home to my—'

She laughed. 'What happened to the Indian casino buffet?'

'The buffet? That's *after* you meet my mother. You don't get the buffet just like that.'

He took her hand. It was easier now to have him touch her.

Mills had turned out to be the ideal boyfriend for the last six months. He'd dealt with people in shock before. He'd done three years in the Canadian Coast Guard, he told her, pulling fishermen out of the freezing Baffin Bay north of the Arctic Circle, cutting their survival suits off with a diving knife, which was made easier as they'd usually lost weight in the sea, thrashing around for hours and burning off fat. In the rescue boat, as their teeth chattered together, he remembered their eyes, blank and searching at the same time. It was like the last few hours had emptied their eyes out, and they needed to be refilled with something other than scenes of ice and water.

For the first three months, he'd said, Abbie had that same desolate look.

The first time they'd gone out, two months after she'd found Michael, Abbie had felt she was in a trance. They'd simply sat in Tim Hortons – his idea – and sipped hot chocolate. Mills told her later it was like sitting next to a hospital bed with a person who is heavily sedated and wants only to know that you are there, that you're physically present. But you cannot touch her, because every part of her skin has been torn up or burned.

She hadn't wanted to talk about Michael. Four months later, she still didn't want to.

But he'd gotten the facts, she knew. He'd been pulled into the case once they'd made the connection between Michael Minton's killings and the Outlaws massacre. He knew that the Billy Carney murder had been pinned on O'Halloran, pretty conclusively. There was the supply of toy monkeys they'd found in his glove compartment, the stupid bastard. O'Halloran's cell phone had pinged off a tower two blocks from Carney's house twenty minutes before the murder, when O'Halloran was supposed to have been home thirty miles away. And on a second sweep by techs, his DNA was found on a windowsill; he'd most likely come through the window to cut Carney's throat. The motive was simple prevention: Carney had called around the County asking about the Clan, and O'Halloran knew that soon enough the trail would lead back to him. The cop had placed the listening device in Carney's house and knew that he was about to reveal his suspicions to Abbie. O'Halloran could have been sent back to England to face justice. Carney had to die.

The ironic thing was O'Halloran had probably believed that Abbie really was the killer, that she'd returned to Buffalo for revenge. He hadn't been trying to frame her; he'd been trying to convict her. He didn't want to kill her, because snuffing out an active-duty Buffalo cop was too much of a risk for a man living under an assumed name. So he'd waited. And then he'd seen a way. He'd set up her meeting with Z by the grain silos, and tried to kill them both. Maybe he was going to say she shot Z and then he shot Abbie to save himself.

The Outlaws slaughter had been closed, too, and the killings officially attributed to Michael Minton, along with the murders of Jimmy Ryan, Marty Collins, Joe Kane, and John Kearney. A Buffalo fireman had reported his jacket and helmet missing the day Kane was found – Michael had stolen them and disguised himself on the Peace Bridge, even fooling Abbie as he made his escape. And it was Michael's blood, not Abbie's, at the Marty Collins crime scene; because they were brother and sister, the genetic profile was 95 percent identical, a maternal match. Three more toy monkeys had been found tucked in an old coffee can in the abandoned building on Main; Michael had apparently scooped them up when John Kearney had arrested him, remembrances of his little sister to take along with him to hell.

And when he'd returned for revenge, he'd placed the toys as mementos of the crime committed against him – and as messages to his little sister, the detective. Reaching out even as he killed the men who'd separated them forever.

The rest of the details were still filtering in, Abbie knew. Dolores, the IRA killer living in Buffalo, had survived her wounds and was in the process of being deported back to Ireland. It was clear from John Kearney's letter that he'd gone to the rendezvous in the nature preserve expecting to meet O'Halloran and kill him. But her father had missed his target. His service revolver was missing three rounds, none of which had struck home. He was an old and feeble man, and his aim was off.

Niagara Falls PD had sketched out most of Michael's last twenty-nine years through bits and pieces of Outlaw club gossip and the evidence found in the dungeon. Mills had told her about the interviews he'd done with the surviving Outlaws. Now that all the officers of the club were dead, Mills had told the other members they would face charges on the kidnapping of Michael unless they cooperated. And so parts of the story had spilled out.

For the first two years in Canada, Michael had been forced to live in the pit. During the autopsy, his back was found to be crisscrossed with torture marks. The weals were pink and thick, made by amateurs with spoons carved into brands and heated over a fire. There was a skull, the blazing guns of the Outlaws' insignia, but also a big cock and balls burned into the flesh and maybe a dozen cigarette marks and the circle of the old-fashioned car lighters. Mills believed that a couple of the Outlaws were probably gay and had visited Michael for late-night rape sessions when he was brought to them as a teenager. There were other theories out there but he wasn't buying them. He suspected that was the intention all along. The Outlaws just wanted a bitch boy. Abbie, sadly, believed he was right.

After two years, Michael had stopped fighting back and they let him out of the pit. Then they put him to work, doing the Outlaws' dirty work. For example, cutting up bodies of Chinese illegals the gang had smuggled into Canada in shipping containers and who'd suffocated or died of thirst on the way over. Michael dismembered them and the Outlaws had buried them in the woods north of Fort Erie. Niagara Falls PD hadn't been aware that the motorcycle gang had been into human trafficking.

After a few years, the Outlaws found that Michael had an appetite for violence as strong as, if not stronger than, their own. By the late eighties, Michael Minton had become the gang's enforcer.

'Hungry yet?' Mills said, taking Abbie's arm as they walked toward the Horseshoe Falls.

Abbie shook her head.

She still couldn't get the autopsy pictures out of her mind. She even imagined that she'd felt the scars through his jacket. When they'd found her in that abandoned building on Main Street, she'd been holding Michael, hugging his bloody body to hers. 'I thought he was going to kill me,' she kept saying. A trick of the light, probably, the knife blade flashing as Michael brought it up to his throat and cut it. Made it look like it was coming at her.

By his body they found the bag and the last page of John Kearney's letter:

Fergus, the man you know as Dennis O'Halloran, was brought to Canada by the IRA. He was drinking in a Fort Erie bar when he started a fight, purely for an excuse to kill a man, I think. But the man he chose was an Outlaw. And Fergus killed him. The Outlaws beat him half to death and were going to finish him off when he told them who he was and how much he was worth to people across the border. They locked him away and we sent Jimmy Ryan to negotiate a price. They would not talk to a cop.

They didn't want money. They had all the money they wanted from the drug trade. What they wanted was a man in exchange for the one who'd been killed. And they specified a young man, a teenager – they said they wanted someone to sell coke in the high schools. We had no reason to doubt them. We knew they'd find somebody regardless.

I went to the Reverend Zebediah, who I'd known from my years working the East Side. I explained the situation. I told him I was willing to save one if he gave me another. There were young men in downtown Buffalo that terrified their own kind, and I asked for one of them to trade with the Outlaws. For his life we would get two back – O'Halloran and any child the Reverend named.

I didn't know then the kind of monster O'Halloran was. And all I could think was, how could I let a soldier of Ireland die at the hands of some bikers, after he'd served his country? If I arrested the Outlaws for kidnapping, O'Halloran would be deported back to England. The escape route to America would be closed forever. There was no other way.

The Reverend chose Michael Minton, and I agreed to adopt his baby sister, Absalom. I arrested Michael that night. But instead of bringing him to the precinct on Delavan, I took him to where he was staying and let him collect a few things. I handcuffed him and transported him across the border in my trunk. We made the exchange in a motel room called the Lucky Clover.

I learned later that the Outlaws used him in ways I couldn't predict. It made my stomach turn. We heard rumors of the marks they'd made on his flesh, and cutting off half his tongue. I would have sent no human being to that fate. But by the time the stories reached us in Buffalo – of a man kept in a cage – it was too late to do anything about it.

The Clan began getting reports on what had become of Michael.
How he'd taken to his work, which was killing. A few of us feared he
would come back to Buffalo. But we closed our eyes and saw to the
needs of the living.

Now I must speak to my daughter. Absalom, I cannot say I loved you
as a father should have. You reminded me too much of how you'd come
to the County, and the hateful things it took to bring you there. But I
watched over you. I would come into your room on many nights and
watch you sleep, silent all of those years because of the many secrets I
kept. It was wrong, but I loved you in my own way. Please believe me.
It's the God's honest truth.

Now O'Halloran has returned to killing and you are in danger from
him, and from the police.

If I don't manage to stop this man who should never have lived, he
will take my life, but I am not anxious about that. Absalom, I give it
gladly for yours as any father should. I'm sorry I didn't do better.

John Kearney.

The sun was setting. They stood by the railing and watched the
seagulls wheel in front of the tumbling water. Abbie felt Mills's hand
cover hers.

He followed her eyes toward the brink of the Falls.

'Closer look?' he said, walking to a nearby two-eyed telescope on
a stand bolted to the promenade. Abbie followed.

Mills slipped two quarters into the coin slot and she stepped onto the
little railing at the base of the telescope and fixed her eyes to the holes.
She adjusted the focus and turned the thing slightly to the left. Mills
followed the line out and saw that she was looking at downtown Buffalo,
a misty shadow of buildings on the horizon, obscured by the spray.

She stepped back from the telescope and looked at Mills.

'I almost let him go,' she said.

'Michael?' he asked.

She nodded. 'I wanted to.'

Mills nodded slowly. 'Ab, he was your brother. That's perfectly
natural.'

She turned to gaze at the Falls. 'Everyone thinks he came back for revenge. But I think he killed those men for me. For *us*. So we could be a family again.'

'You tried to save him. But he was too far gone.'

Abbie held her hand over her eyes and looked at the city skyline in the distance. Her new house was back there, the small Victorian on Elmwood Avenue, badly in need of repair, that she'd bought with the money her father had left her in his will. When the contractors were done putting in the new bathroom, expanding the kitchen, and fixing the leaky slate-shingled roof, she was going to get to work making it her own. She'd already found a Shaker dining table that she loved and had her eyes on a whimsical sky-blue dresser for the bedroom, $250 in the antiques store near Chippewa. She'd already decided she would paint the exterior a bright kelly green with Richmond bisque trim. It would be a silent tribute to John Kearney and an acknowledgment of her old neighborhood, a splash of County color in the midst of Buffalo's bohemian section. She would move in on September 1, just as the neighborhood kids began walking down her block to the Catholic school catty-corner from her. She would sip her homemade hot chocolate and watch them parade by in their tartan uniforms from her kitchen window, and she would be home at last. She would be happy.

Abbie took Mills's hand and they began walking toward the roar of the falling water.